SPARK

OF

ASH

SPARK
OF
ASH

MOLLY E. LEE

Entangled Publishing, LLC
10940 S Parker Road
Suite 327
Parker, CO 80134
rights@entangledpublishing.com

Entangled Teen is an imprint of Entangled Publishing, LLC.

Visit our website at www.entangledpublishing.com.

Edited by Heather Howland
Cover design and illustrations by
Elizabeth Turner Stokes
Interior design by Toni Kerr

ISBN 978-1-64937-173-7
Ebook ISBN 978-1-64937-230-7

Manufactured in the United States of America

First Edition May 2022

10 9 8 7 6 5 4 3 2 1

an imprint of Entangled Publishing LLC

ALSO BY MOLLY E. LEE

To Daren. My night sky. My ever-churning ocean.
My everything.

PROLOGUE

DRAVEN

Harley giggles as I lean over her on the bed, laying a line of kisses down her neck.

"Am I forgiven yet?" I say against her smooth skin.

"I don't know," she says, her words strained as I work my way back up to her jawline. She tilts her head to give me better access. "Are you done trying to push me away for my own good?"

"I'll never stop believing you deserve better." The words tangle in my throat, and I pull back just enough to study the flecks of gold in her green eyes. "You should be mated to someone who isn't a walking time bomb, leashed to a life of servitude."

"That's not fair," she argues, and it isn't for the first time. We've had three blissful weeks working for Delta, the leader of Conilis who took me and Harley in after we left Rainier's realm and taught us how to farm, while also enjoying some much-needed quality time together that doesn't involve demons trying to kill us. "You don't get to make that decision for me."

I kiss the corner of her mouth, the line of her jaw, and down to her collarbone. "I know," I say between kisses. "As much as I don't think I'm worthy of you—"

Her fingers slide around to my neck, gripping me tightly. "You're killing me with that," she groans.

I laugh as I work my way back up to her mouth. "You're my mate for a reason," I finish, and that certainty fills me with more hope than I've ever felt before. She's fully accepted the bond now, so there is no going back. "And I'll spend the rest of my life making it up to you."

"There is nothing to make up for," she says. "But," she continues, grinning. "Since I love the way you apologize, I don't know if I can ever *truly* forgive you."

I steady myself on one arm, freeing my other to trail my fingers over her bare arms. Chill bumps erupt under my touch, and everything in me narrows to the absolute gift I've been given. As a siphon, I never thought I'd be able to touch anyone again without draining them, but Harley is immune to my powers.

"Then I'll never stop," I promise.

I slant my mouth over hers, and her grip on my neck tightens as she kisses me back. I take everything she gives and give her everything back in return. I can't stop wondering how in the hell I got so lucky to be mated to this incredible, fiery girl.

The Antichrist and the divine Judge who was sent to kill her. Who would have thought?

"I love you," I whisper between kisses.

"I love you," she says, grazing her teeth over my bottom lip. "Do you have to go?"

A twinge of guilt twists in my chest. I've returned to Earth a few times in the last three weeks, all in an effort to help Ryder, my twin and fellow Judge, adjust to his new world. He's doing surprisingly well, but I can't stop the climbing anxiety when we go too long between visits. "Maybe I—"

"No." She sighs. "I can't be selfish. Ryder needs you."

Relief that she understands floods me, but I let a low growl rumble in my chest anyway. "Don't say his name while we're like this."

She bursts out laughing. "Okay, jealous and primal one."

There's that smart mouth that I love. I kiss her until she's breathless again, then reluctantly draw away. "Tell me to stay, and I will."

"No," she groans, gently sliding off the bed. Fuck, she looks amazing standing there like that, hair all mussed from my fingers tunneling through it, her lips swollen from my kisses. "You need to go. We're safe here. We have all the time in the world together now. I just have to get over my fear that the Seven will activate you the minute you set foot there."

The terror in her eyes has me rushing off the bed and smoothing my hand along her jawline, forcing her to look up at me. "I've told you," I say, trying to sound as reassuring as possible. "The odds of that are so slim, you shouldn't let it worry you."

I understand her worries, but I've done a good job of convincing myself that there is nothing to them. The Seven don't even know where I am, and sometimes they go months before requesting a status update. They probably think I'm still following Harley around, studying her to see if she truly is the Antichrist.

Spoiler alert: she absolutely is, but they don't need to know that.

She visibly swallows, forcing out a nod. "I can't help it, Draven. These past weeks have been the most amazing of my life. I can't help but feel—"

"Like you're waiting for the rug to be ripped out from under you?"

"Yeah," she says. "Exactly like that."

It's been three perfect weeks.

And now forever stretches out ahead of us.

But forever has never been in the cards for me.

I hate the dread in my gut threatening to rob me of this joy. I've never been lucky. These moments with Harley feel like stolen pieces of time that someone will demand payment for soon. I stifle a cringe at the thoughts and shove them down inside me until I can't feel their sting anymore.

Harley needs me to be strong, so that's what I'm going to be.

"Nothing could keep me from you," I say, brushing another kiss over her lips. "I'll always find you, remember?"

"I remember," she says and settles her head against my chest.

I hold her there, longer than necessary but shorter than I like. The sooner I get to Chicago, the quicker I can get back to her.

After I reluctantly release her, we both hurry through what has become our morning routine—eating a quick breakfast and getting ready for work. I almost feel guilty for keeping her up half the night, especially when she has to work the fields this morning solo, but the relaxed, blissful look she wears is enough to chase that guilt away.

I pause outside the doorway of the little home Delta has graciously loaned us in exchange for our work in her community and kiss Harley again, dragging it out as long as possible before I have to call on the strength of my power to pull away from her.

"Tell Ryder I say hello," she says, putting distance between us. If she hadn't, I don't know if I'd have been able to leave.

With one last grin, she heads toward the main road that will lead to her section of Delta's crops.

"I'll see you soon," I murmur as she disappears down the road.

· · ·

An hour later, Ryder glares at me as he swings the door open and waves his hand for me to come inside. "You know, you've really got to start showing up with food."

"I've fully stocked this place," I argue as he shuts the door behind me. "And you have a phone now. DoorDash is a thing." I glance around the apartment that used to be mine, the little dive I secured when I was tasked with watching Harley. That seems like years ago instead of months.

Ryder heads to the living room, sinking down onto the couch. "I know," he says, his tone a little less sharp.

I settle myself in the armchair across from him. "How are you adjusting to the food here?"

"I'm in love with it," he admits. "Humans have come a long

way. The things they do with cheese?" He groans, shaking his head. "Amazing."

I laugh, and he does, too. I live for moments like this with him. Moments where he feels more like the twin I used to know instead of the madness-stricken Judge who was tortured for too long in the Ather.

Anger simmers beneath my skin.

If I could kill Marid again, I fucking would.

"How's your murderous little antichrist?" he asks.

I cock a brow at him. "Great," I say. "She says hello."

Ryder gives me a wave.

I huff out another laugh. "Any word from the Seven?"

"Esther met with me last week. She wants to fold me back in slowly."

"Did you tell her about…everything?" I hate the uncertainty in me. Esther has always been my ally among the Seven, but letting her in on the fact that we're trying to get Ryder back into the Seven's sights so he can spy for us? Not exactly a show of trust.

"No," he says. "I still think telling her everything would be a bad call. I kept it basic. Not outright lying but…" He sighs. "I left you and your antichrist out of it. And the need for me to play spy. It'll be easy once Esther gets me in. They'll be too shocked to think I'm anything other than the Judge they always knew," he says. "Since I was supposed to be dead and all."

I swallow hard, grief and guilt twisting me up. "But you're not. You're here; you're safe. You're indulging in modern-day cheeses. Life is good, yeah?"

Ryder's turquoise eyes—their color the only difference between the two of us—go distant for a moment, and I know to remain quiet. He's prone to slipping into that aimless look more often than I'd like, but I can't blame him. He spent an *eternity* in Marid's realm. It's a marvel he survived at all, let alone has the ability to make jokes or smile or laugh.

One day at a time. I'll support him while he heals the

traumas of his past. Once again, I feel split down the center. Half of me wants to stay here with him for as long as it takes to help him feel whole again. The other half is already yanking on my soul, begging me to return to my mate.

I nod at the TV when he blinks a few times, coming back to the present. "You catching up?"

"Streaming is one of my favorite things about this modern world," he says but shrugs. "Still, it was easier when the Seven did the divine download on me. I hate the slow pace I'm absorbing things now, but I'm okay, Draven. You don't need to keep checking on me."

"I'm not checking on you," I argue.

Ryder shakes his head, his black hair identical to mine, but his brushes his shoulders where I keep mine short. "Really? Because you've been dropping by so much it's like you think I'm going to light up the town or something." He glances down at his fingers. Lightning crackles over his smooth golden skin, then radiates in his eyes.

The charge in the room brushes over my skin, raising the hairs on the back of my neck.

"But I wouldn't say no to a solid mission," he says, reeling in his lightning. "My powers are begging for release."

I shudder at the idea of not using my powers for so long. They build, and with the amount my brother and I have? It's dangerous to not use them. Puts us on edge, making us a threat to anyone who might be unfortunate enough to trigger us.

"You need some help?" I ask. "I can't power share with you, but I can siphon some, if you need it." I hate that I can't help my brother the way anyone else can. Can't connect our powers and take the edge off. Being a siphon is a curse.

"Yeah, I'll pass on that," he says, rolling his eyes. "Feeling you drain the power from me is about as fun as a walk through snake-infested waters." An icy glaze covers his eyes before he blinks it away. "Offense meant."

I shake my head. "Your call," I say. "Just don't let it go too long. I can ask Cassiel to take you out to help work some of them off, if you want."

"I have the Death Striker's number," he says. "If it gets bad enough that I want to hang out with him?" He winces. "I'll just run back to the Ather and fight with your little antichrist. She's always good for a brawl."

I grit my teeth, ignoring his attempt to rile me. "You hate Cassiel that much?" Ryder wants nothing to do with the Ather; he'd told me that much when I asked him to stay with Harley and me. And I totally understood his need to escape the tortures from his past, but Cassiel's company is a *way* better option than diving headfirst back into Plainville.

"Oh, don't go all bleeding heart on me," he says. "He despises me just as much."

I pinch the bridge of my nose, a sharp headache forming out of nowhere behind my eyes. "He would do it," I say. "To help you."

"No, he wouldn't," Ryder argues. "He'd do it because you asked him to. He's nothing if not loyal."

I sigh. "Cassiel has saved my life more times than I can count." I leave out the fact that he'd become more of a brother to me than my own twin. "And I'm trying here, Ryder. I want us to…" I lose the words as that sharp pain mounts, followed by a tangy taste on my tongue.

My heart races, and I bolt from the chair.

"To be brothers again?" Ryder asks, looking up at me like I've grown another head. He rises to stand before me. "What's up?"

The breath in my lungs stalls, panic lashing through my veins.

A sweeping sting of searing white light blots out my vision. *No.*

I stumble through the apartment, desperate to find the door, but white covers *everything*.

A buzzing roars in my head so loud I can barely hear Ryder as he yells my name.

No. Fuck. Please no.

My fingers find the door handle, and I shove my way outside before a ruthless fire burns right through the center of me.

I drop to my knees, not even feeling them crack against the sidewalk.

Harley.

I reach toward our bond.

Try and wrap my mental fingers around the connection between us.

I'm Draven.

I'm Draven.

I'm—

My ears pop.

The pain disappears.

I can see again.

I scan the area as I rise to my feet.

"Get the seer," a voice I recognize commands inside my head, offering a mental image to go along with it. The seer is no more than nine years old, blond, with ivory skin and blue eyes. The voice gives me an address, and I turn right on the sidewalk.

"Draven!" Someone calls from behind me, and I spare a glance over my shoulder.

Ryder. A fellow Judge. A brother.

"Where are you going?" he calls, jogging to keep up with my determined pace.

"Mission."

He halts in his tracks, falling behind.

I leave him.

He's not part of my mission.

Get the girl.

Get the girl.

Get the girl.

I pound on the door of her residence, and a man opens it. "Draven, what are you doing here?" he asks like we know each other.

I've never seen him before in my life.

I search the recesses of my mind, finding nothing but a foggy wasteland.

I shrug, drawing on the familiarity, using the bits of what the divine file in my mind offers me—just little pieces of intel to complete the mission. "I need to get…" I swallow, something stinging my chest as I search for the name of the seer. "*Ray*." There it is. "I need to get Ray somewhere safe."

The girl in question bounds up behind the man.

"Draven!" She reaches out her tiny fist, and I stare at it blankly before returning focus to the man.

"Where's Harley? Is she all right?" he asks, frantic, and the little girl drops her fist, worry coloring her eyes.

I nod, even though I have no clue who he's talking about.

"We have to go," I say, sending my shadows toward her in an attempt to carry her.

She bats them away, heading toward the sidewalk. "I'll walk."

Works for me. I take up position by her side—

"Draven!" the man yells, rushing behind me.

A crack of energy blazes to my left as another figure materializes, stopping the man in his tracks.

Power radiates from the being with silver eyes and ink-colored wings. He seems familiar, something itching the back of my brain.

We worked together once, I think.

I shift my stance, drawing my power and wrapping it around me and the girl.

No time to puzzle it out.

Have to get the seer to Aphian.

"Draven," the creature calls, his voice like ice. "Where are you taking Ray?"

"Home," I say, then slip into the shadows.

CHAPTER ONE

HARLEY

"It's Ray," Cassiel says. "They...they took her. I didn't know. I didn't know until it was too late."

My body trembles, my mind fracturing as all the calm chips off of me like chunks of ice. The powers in my blood rise, swarming me so fast it hurts. "*Who?*"

"The Seven." He says more, but I can't hear him over the ringing in my head.

I *left*. I stayed here. Peaceful, content. Not a *hint* of a threat from me, the Antichrist, against Earth. I took myself off the chessboard, and they...

They *dare* to take her? How did they even know she was there? Have they been watching this whole time?

The rage I keep bottled, the anger I thought dormant—it explodes.

And the entire area around me bursts into flames.

Nothing stops the waves of fire pouring out of me.

Nothing stops the flames from licking up the stalks of crops in my little section of the farm, scorching everything in their path.

Shit. No. Delta and her people need this food. *Get it together, Harley*.

I clench my eyes shut, drawing my power back as fast as I possibly can. My breath comes in great gasps as I lock down my power, hating the sight of the ash all around me but not fully capable of caring.

Cassiel's great wings flap, blowing the hair back from my face as he lands. I want to apologize, but I can't. I don't have the words.

All I have is rage and hate.

The Seven...they took her. I thought not accepting my role as Rainier's daughter would help keep them from looking too close at me—at what and who I loved—and they just proved me the fuck wrong.

They'll regret it.

I reach into my pocket, pulling out the ring Rainier gave me before I left.

My ring. A band of silver holds up a stone of purest black, the shape of both a diamond and a hexagon combined. The sharp points glisten as if it's winking at me.

Cassiel tracks my movements as I poise the ring above my right-hand middle finger.

One heartbeat, then two, and I slip it on, knowing the decision I'm making and not caring.

I am accepting my birthright.

And unlocking Rainier from his prison in the process.

But that's a problem for future me.

My powers ignite, the well shifting to an infinite, endless pit. Suddenly, I'm not so tired or scared. For a few precious moments, there is only power pulsing and healing and ebbing in every crevice of my soul.

If the Seven want a fight? Then Rainier and I will sure as hell give them one.

I arch a brow at Cassiel. "Who?" I say again, grinding out the word. "Who, exactly, took her?" I need specifics so I can kill the right person. Slowly.

Anger and panic shape his features. "Draven."

Power and adrenaline braid together in my blood, making my skin feel too tight for my body. I suck in a sharp breath, guilt clinging to my chest at the ashes we stand in.

Draven took Ray.

The Seven have them both.

And I totally just burned down a quarter of Conilis's crops.

Shit, shit, shit.

I glance at the ring on my right-hand middle finger, the ebony stone flickering with power.

"Cassiel," I say, my voice hoarse from my rage. I look up, locking onto his eyes. "Are you with me?"

"Without question." His hair, as black as his wings, falls messily over his forehead as he dips his head, approaching me with caution. I try and loosen the tension in my muscles, but there is no point. Fight or flight runs rampant through my body, and right now I want to do both.

"Harley—" Cassiel goes rigid. "*Shit*." His wings expand to their full length. "Do you trust me?"

"I *hate* when people ask me that."

He groans, raising his hands toward me. "Just, don't go nuclear for five seconds," he says, then a loud crack splits the air, a bolt of pewter-colored lightning striking down the middle of him. He vanishes, and I cover my eyes from the blinding light.

I barely blink away the impressions on my eyes before the ground trembles at my feet.

"Ah," a masculine voice says. "What a mess you've made, child."

I glare at the creature before me, at his condescending tone. He's tall and broad-shouldered, his muscled body covered in robes of pearl and ivory, his silky blond hair hanging past his shoulders in perfectly smooth strands. Enormous wings stretch behind him, the feathers cream and chiffon, but their tips are stained with red. His eyes are arctic blue as he looks down his nose at me.

Some inner instinct tells me he isn't of the Ather.

"Who are you?" I grind out the words. And why did Cassiel disappear right before he arrived?

He arches an eyebrow at me, folding his pale arms behind his back as he walks barefoot through the ashes. "Such a waste," he says, kicking at the soot on his feet. "Delta will feel this loss when trying to keep her people fed, but I suppose the Antichrist doesn't care for others, do you?"

My blood boils. "Who. Are. You?"

And how the hell does he know who and what I am?

He stops his circling. Flames dance over my fingers, unhindered and hungry. The power rolling off this creature is enough to coat my tongue with a bitter, citrusy taste, and I flick my fingers, my earth powers latching onto the ground beneath his feet in case I need to bury him.

The creature eyes my dark flames, the silver flecks in them glimmering, and then he glances at the ground beneath him before looking back to me. "I wouldn't do that if I were you."

I narrow my gaze, my flames pulsing wider over my hands.

"Not if you want your sister to live," he adds, and I go still at his words. He smirks, a cruel, dark smile. "I plucked your location from Draven's mind."

Ice shoots through my veins.

He's one of the Seven.

"Though his mind is a stubborn thing. I could only glean so much before I pushed too hard…" He purses his lips. "I'm afraid he's a blank slate now when it comes to you."

Rage rises in me like I've never known. I want to light him up. I want to beat and claw and *tear* at him. My entire body shakes with the effort of holding back my powers.

"Why did you take them?" I ask, my tone coated in fire.

"I had such aspirations for you," he says. "When I took you from your mother, placed you in that home on Earth…" He sighs, shaking his head. "I made a mistake. I thought you would be weakened by the darkness."

My stomach plummets at his words, angry tears lining my eyes. "What did you do to my mother?"

"I'm here to correct my mistake," he says, totally ignoring me. "I'm nothing if not adaptable."

I flick my fingers, pointing my right hand at him. "You need to let Ray and Draven go," I say, my voice low and deadly serious.

"Or what?"

"I'll burn you to the ground. Each and every last one of the Seven—"

His laughter cuts across my words.

Oh, hell no. I take a step toward him.

"She'll die," he says, narrowing his eyes on me. "Ray will suffer endlessly before her death if you don't do what I say. And I'll make Draven deliver the torture."

An axe lodges itself in my chest with the threat, stopping my advance.

He smiles again, tipping his chin. "Good girl. If you do what I say, then Ray will be treated as an honored guest of the Seven. She'll be fed, clothed, trained in her seer powers—"

"What do you want?" He's shackling me with an invisible bond, using the one thing in the world I care about most to get me to yield.

I'm going to fucking kill him.

"I wanted everything from you once," he says, and I glare up at him as he steps into my personal space. "You were going to be my unmatched weapon. Things have changed, though, and I have a better use for you. I want the Seven Scrolls," he says. "Only you or your damned father can retrieve them, but if you gather them and *willingly* give them to me, I can wield them."

Rainier mentioned the Seven Scrolls when he wanted me to partner with him to kill the Seven. He said they were a failsafe weapon designed by the Creator—his sister—to use against the Seven if they ever abused their great power.

"Why would you want a weapon designed to kill you?"

He laughs again, and I curl my hands into fists. "There is so much you don't know. It's pathetic. Bring me the scrolls," he says before I can protest, "and I'll let your sister and Draven live. If you don't? I'll make good on my promise. She will suffer at the hands of the one you love."

"And if I give them to you?" I grind out.

"I will release Ray back to you."

I see the lie in his eyes. "And Draven?"

"He is a Judge. A divine soldier who answers to *me*. You were foolish to think you could hide him here. He's never belonged to you."

Dread sweeps over me. I know who he is now. And the situation is way worse—and far deadlier—than I thought.

"Aphian." I say the name Draven mentioned before in his horror stories about training with the Seven. This is the one who hates him for what he is, for the powers he's absorbed as a siphon. "You're Aphian."

The most powerful of the Seven.

CHAPTER TWO

HARLEY

He bows, a smug sort of look on his face. "*One* of Seven. Don't test me."

I clench my teeth, biting back the words I want to say. I leash my powers, which are begging to char his bones and bury him here in Delta's field. I bet he'd make stellar fertilizer.

"You have three weeks," he says, spinning on his bare feet, his robes billowing behind him as he stretches his wings. "Don't fail me. Ray's life depends on it."

A burst of white light wobbles the air before him, and he disappears.

I let loose a roar, the ground where he just stood shooting upward in columns, making it rain dirt and ash.

Someone grabs my shoulders from behind, whirling me around. I reach my fist back, ready to burn and raze and—

"Harley," Cassiel says, his tone imploring.

I blow out a breath, sinking to my knees.

Cassiel follows me to the ground. "I felt his presence a second before he arrived," he says. "I couldn't let him see me. He can't know I'm your ally. He'd put me in the Divine Sleep or worse, and then what help would I be to you?"

My heart pounds against my chest, my fingers aching to draw blood. "What are the chances I can save them both if I ignore his threats and have you take me to the Seven's location right this second?"

"Zero," he answers honestly. "Aphian activated Draven, Harley. I don't know how he knew he was there or if it was coincidence, but Draven looked right at me and didn't recognize me."

My eyes widen, and a rage that matches mine shines in his. "They can do that?"

"They can, but it's rare. Usually, they awaken us from the Divine Sleep, mentally download us with what we need, and leave the rest of our memories be."

I curl my lip. "Aphian said he only got some information from him before he pushed too hard. That Draven is a blank slate now."

"If Aphian tampered with his memories *that* much..." He shakes his head. "He's been planning it for a while. It's not something the Seven do lightly, and it takes a hell of a lot of power to accomplish it."

My stomach churns. How can anyone be okay with violating another's mind like that?

I stand up, Cassiel following as the newly unleashed powers inside me fight against the chains I've wrapped around them until I can barely breathe.

The people I love are in danger.

Once again.

Because of what I am.

Cassiel hisses at something he sees in my eyes, and he steps forward, gently clutching my shoulder. "We will get them back," he vows. "I am with you. But we have to be smart. You heard Aphian. Ray suffers if we go against him. Even if you and I combine our powers, we can't stand against all of the Seven alone."

I clench my eyes shut, hating the angry tears biting them. I hold them back, reaching internally. The mating bond is still there, but where it's usually a blazing chain of white-hot light, the metal links are now coated in a layer of ice.

Because the Seven turned my mate into a ghost.

Took my little sister.

"They have to suffer," I say, opening my eyes. "Especially Aphian."

Cassiel nods. "And in order to be strong enough for that—"

"We need the Seven Scrolls," I finish for him. "Not because Aphian wants them, but because I'm going to use them to destroy them all."

I refused Rainier's request because I wanted to stay off the Seven's radar.

Wanted Ray to grow up on Earth and live her life without fear of monsters hunting her because of me.

Wanted to live here with Draven, stealing the time we deserved.

I can still taste his kiss from this morning. How can so much change in the span of a few hours?

I shake off the urge to fall into a pitiful puddle and instead race from the razed field. I find Delta easily enough, rapidly explain my situation to her, and pair it with an apology, vowing to make up for the damaged crops.

She tells me to go, and I turn to Cassiel.

"Can you get me to Rainier's?" I ask. "Fast?"

His obsidian wings stretch to their full length, and he moves so quickly I barely register it. One second, I'm on the solid ground; the next, we're catapulting through the air and successfully leaving my stomach behind. I have to dig up my breath from the pit of my stomach before I can breathe again, and when I draw in air, it's cold and crackling with energy.

"Close your eyes," he says.

I immediately obey. Ice coats every inch of my body, and a blazing bright light shines behind my closed lids. We're falling like two lead weights dropped from the sky—

We jerk to a halt.

Cassiel sets me on my feet.

"Whoa," I gasp. "What the heck—"

I'm instantly tackled by a massive wolf.

I wrap my arms around the hellhound's neck. "Missed you too, Wrath." I lean into his support, so glad to have the massive midnight-black hound back in my arms. I saved him from the

Machis Pits—the same intense fighting ring where we found Ryder, Draven's twin. He's missing half an ear, has razor-sharp teeth, and is far more intelligent than even some humans I've met on Earth—and he's all mine.

I follow Cassiel into Rainier's castle and up the winding stairs, wondering if my biological father felt his powers restore when I put on the birthright ring he gave me a few weeks ago.

"Daughter." Rainier's voice is deep, rough, and this side of astonished when we enter the room. He's clad in his signature black suit, his hair slicked back, and those red eyes of his are wide as they take me in.

"What's up, Firestarter?" Wallace—my previous Ather guide and new BFF—bounds across the grand dining room in Rainier's castle. Her long black locks are adorned with a new set of gold rings and amethyst gems that set off her deep brown skin, and her full lips are painted ruby red. I return her embrace, but her eyes hop from mine to Cassiel's, and she huffs. "Shit," she says as she releases me. "You didn't just make your father go all glowy for fun, did you?"

Rainier moves away from the crackling hearth, his confident gait eating up the distance between us in a few strides.

"Glowy?" I ask as Rainier looks at me questioningly before reaching for my hand. He doesn't take it until I nod. He grips my right hand, grinning as he spies the ring on my middle finger.

"Yeah, it was a real show," Wallace says, cocking a brow at me. "One second we're chatting about how to stimulate the economy in some of the less fortunate realms, and the next he drops his whiskey and starts—"

"Burning," he says. "My powers restored when you accepted your birthright, Harley."

"Burning? You glowed *cherry*-red," Wallace argues. "Like, *all* over."

Rainier closes his eyes like he's searching for patience.

I wish I could laugh. Wish I could join in with Wallace's teasing, but there isn't a spot inside of me that feels the humor.

"What happened?" Rainier asks when his eyes are on mine.

I glance at Cassiel, who grunts and crosses the room, grabbing a glass and filling it half-full with amber liquid. He sets the crystal decanter down on the bar a bit harder than necessary, then drops into one of the twelve chairs at Rainier's favorite dining table.

"Help yourself," Rainier says, glaring at the angel of death. But my heart aches for Cassiel. His broad shoulders dip low beneath his white shirt, the whorls of black ink decorating his olive skin visible beneath it. He's radiating pain over the fear of losing his best friend so much I can practically feel it.

Rainier releases my hand, then reaches up to cup my cheek. "Tell me," he says, his voice lowering between us. Sincerity rings out from his red eyes, and while I want to tear away from him, tell him to stop acting like the father I never had—we don't know each other well enough for this—I'm just…broken.

"They took Ray," I blurt out, and the words unleash the grief and anger I've barely held back. Tears stream down my face, and Rainier guides me to the closest chair. I sink into it, my lap instantly filled with giant hellhound head. I run my fingers through his fur, using his support to get a fucking grip.

Wallace drops into the chair next to Cassiel. "When you say *they*…"

Cassiel slides a crystal glass across the table, and I catch it with my free hand. I inhale the contents in one gulp, using the sweet burn of the liquor to quell the tears.

"The Seven. Thanks, Wrath," I say when he licks my face, then glance at Rainier's raised brow. Probably because he called the hound by a different name. "Lazarus is a mouthful. He's always been Wrath to me. Sorry."

Rainier takes a breath, his hand curling into a fist. "They forced your hand."

Wrath settles at my feet, sighing heavily like he hasn't breathed in the weeks I've been gone. I understand the feeling, and I give him extra pets as I try and sort out my mind.

"Excuse me, sir," a familiar voice interrupts us, and I go stiff in my chair at the sight of the Overlord. He's just as he was weeks ago when he trapped me and Ryder on his desolate island. An ethereal creature whose smokelike cloak and hood hide most of his features—except his eyes, those crushing blue eyes that always make chills erupt on my skin.

I know he's Rainier's go-to guy, a way to learn about what's happening in the Ather while he's been trapped here in his realm, but after the Overlord drugged me with indigo smoke and flew me to a magical island designed to test my worthiness or imprison me there forever, I'm not his biggest fan.

"Reports are in from the elemental lands," he says, eyeing me before refocusing on Rainier. "They're seeking aid again, despite how many times I've insisted that the curse on your realm doesn't allow you to send any."

"I'll send it," Rainier says, and the Overlord tilts his head. "When Harley decides to break the curse."

I shift my right hand beneath the table, not showing off the birthright ring I've clearly and totally accepted. Why is he hiding the fact?

"I'll report back," the Overlord says, then pauses in the doorway. "Do you and your guests need anything?" He looks to me, the cloak over his head shadowing his face. "The princess enjoys the lavender cookies, correct?"

How did he know what Ather treats I'd grown to love over the last few weeks?

The Overlord shrugs, eyeing my confused expression. "You were on my island," he says. "It whispered things to me about your preferences. I'm here to serve my king and his daughter—"

"We're fine," Rainier cuts him off. "Thank you, but this is a private meeting."

The Overlord bows at the waist, ushering out of the room without another word.

"Why didn't you tell him?" I ask Rainier. "I've accepted my birthright and the powers that come along with it."

Not to mention unleashing my biological father's powers in the process.

An alertness shifts under my skin at the mention of his powers, some kind of inner recognition I can't explain. The well of power inside me seems to rise up in his presence, almost like two flames merging together to create an even bigger fire.

Apprehension hits me again. What *will* he do with his newly restored gifts?

"I will, in time," he answers, which doesn't actually answer my question. "Right now, we have much more pressing matters."

"Right," Wallace says, returning to our earlier conversation. "Why are we still here?" Her power crackles over her skin, and her warm brown eyes shift to indigo in a blink. "Let's leap," she says, referring to her teleportation power—what she calls *leaping*. "Take them back from the bastards."

My heart swells a fraction at her instant support. Especially since she hated me when we first met. We've come a long way.

"The wards chaining you to your realm are gone, right?" Wallace asks Rainier when we're all silent.

"Yes," Rainier finally answers, seeming to come back from somewhere deep in his mind. "I felt them crumble the minute my powers were restored."

"Let's roll, then," Wallace says, then nudges Cassiel. "You have to know where the Seven are holed up, right, Death Boy?"

Cassiel doesn't even bother to growl at her, he's that lost in his mind. "I do," he says.

Wallace shoots me a concerned glance.

I have nothing to offer her.

I can't look much better.

She shoves out of her seat, gaping at each of us. "Can someone please explain why we're sitting here while those assholes have Ray? We should be—"

"Aphian activated Draven," I say, and another wave of pain crashes over me. Memories of the past three weeks flash behind my eyes—laughing and teasing, kisses and passionate nights.

Gone.

In a blink.

And when I do see him again? He won't even recognize me. His mate. He won't remember how we laughed when I accidentally picked weeds instead of fruit, thinking the beautiful buds were useful, the first time we were in Delta's fields. He won't remember the time I burned our first home-cooked meal in Conilis or the way he ate it anyway, just to make me feel better.

Fear grips me. What if he *never* gets those memories back?

"They made him take her," I say, bitterness sharp on my tongue. "And now they have them both, Wallace. Don't you think all I want to do is race over there and burn them all to the ground?"

Her shoulders drop. "Then let's fucking *do* it, girl."

"Aphian found me in Conilis," I say. "He knew I'd come for them. He threatened to have Draven torture Ray to death if I don't do what he wants. I want nothing more than to slice my flames through him, but…"

"You can't," Rainier finishes for me. "You'd be signing Ray and Draven's death certificates."

Wallace sits back down. She snatches the decanter from Cassiel, pouring herself a drink. "The Seven obviously targeted the two people you love most to keep you in check."

"How do they know?" I ask. "Ray, I understand, but Draven? How can they possibly know how much he means to me?" Being mates isn't something we advertised. Even Draven had initially kept it from me under the guise of my own protection.

Because he was terrified this would happen.

I hate that he was right.

Rainier considers. "Could Ryder have told the Seven—"

"Ryder wouldn't do that," Wallace cuts him off, and his glare widens on her.

"I agree with Wallace," I say, sighing. "Ryder is our ally now. He wouldn't sell us out. He's prepared to be a spy for us.

It doesn't make sense."

"Then someone," Rainier says. "Someone who knows you, Harley. Betrayed you."

I swallow hard. "There is a very short list of people who *know* me." I think about Kai—my ex–best friend and total traitor—about how he'd been one of those people, or so I'd thought. His death still stings the center of my chest, even if he was never real to me in the first place.

"It doesn't matter who it is," I say, shoving those emotions down. "I'll handle them eventually."

Rainier frowns. "What did Aphian ask you to do?"

"He wants the Seven Scrolls," I say. "I have three weeks to bring them to him."

"Holy shit," Wallace says. "And then what?"

"He says he'll release Ray to me, but it's a lie—I saw it in his eyes. He has no intention of ever letting her go. Not when I'll do whatever he asks to keep her safe."

Rainier rakes a hand through his hair, dislodging the perfectly slicked back strands. If anything, it makes him look even more dangerous. "He wants you to collect the scrolls for him and then bestow them as a gift so he can wield their power."

"I won't be doing either of those things," I snap.

Rainier's lips shape a feral sort of smile, flames flickering in his eyes. "No, you won't."

CHAPTER THREE

HARLEY

"I'm guessing you have a plan, then?" Wallace asks after taking a drink. She wipes some stray drops off her lips. "Aren't the scrolls like a no-fail weapon against the Seven, Rainy?"

Rainier's jaw flexes, and I feel a flicker of laughter creeping up from the dredges of my soul. Under different circumstances, I would've loved to know how the past three weeks have gone for these two, my ever-chipper and snarky BFF who'd stayed behind to more or less babysit my moody and slightly cranky father, but as it is, I have revenge to plot.

Rainier nods, blowing out a breath and draining the contents of his glass. "They are the only things powerful enough to combat the power of the Seven."

"I remember," I say, folding my arms over my chest. The ice in my mating bond feels like it's seeping under my skin, chilling the natural fire inside me. "But I didn't pay much attention when you spoke about them," I admit. "There was a lot going on."

Like finding out the king of the Ather is my real father.

And being attacked by The Twelve.

Almost dying…you know, Monday stuff.

"Are they all on Earth?" I ask.

Rainier shakes his head. "There are three scattered here among the Ather."

Oh. Well, that makes things easier. We could have those by the end of the day, grab the rest from Earth in the morning, and storm the Seven's stronghold by tomorrow night. I start to push out of my chair. "Why didn't you say so before?"

"There was a lot going on," he mimics me, and I swear he smiles—like not smirks or tauntingly grins but *smiles*.

"Fair. So, do you know where they all are?"

"No," he says flatly.

I smack the table. "Why can nothing *ever* be easy?" I grit my teeth, forcing air into my lungs. Wrath moves at my feet, sitting up to lay his head back in my lap. It's like his instincts let him know when I'm about to explode into a ball of fire and singe everyone around me. I pet him, stroking his coarse fur to calm down. "Okay," I say when I don't feel like turning everything to ash. "You said three were here?"

"Yes," Rainier says. "I know where *those* are. My sister, delight that she is, cast two of them to the darkest parts of the Ather, knowing no one would ever willingly venture there and anyone unworthy of the scrolls would perish. Those two realms are what the legends of Hell are made of, but they're so much worse than any written history."

I swallow hard. Of *course* that's where we have to go. "Perfect. Tell me exactly where," I say. "Better yet, make me a map. I'll go get them. You do whatever it is you do and figure out where the rest of the scrolls are."

"Consider it done."

I drop back into my seat. "So…what about your powers?" I ask, fingering my birthright ring.

Rainier glances down at his palms, and dark flames identical to mine engulf his fingers. "I'm restored," he says, extinguishing the flames. "Thanks to you."

"But that's not all you can do," I say. "You're the entity the Devil legends were made from—what else did I just give you back?" I ask, hating that I probably should've asked these questions *before* I put on the ring and set off a chain of events I'll never be able to control. But, you know, Aphian kidnapping my sister didn't exactly lead to rational thinking on my end.

"The list of my powers is lengthy," Rainier says, not cocky

but simply confident.

"Enlighten me."

He slides his hands into the pockets of his immaculate black suit. "Reality manipulation, possession, demon summoning, mind manipulation, telekinesis—"

I hold up my hand to stop him. "If you have that much power, fuck the scrolls," I say. "Let's go. There is no way the Seven are more powerful than you."

He cocks a brow at me. "While I'm always a fan of flattery, even my extensive powers are no match for all of them. When my sister—"

"The Creator," I interject. I still can't believe my aunt is the freaking *Creator*.

"Yes," he says. "She ensured it would be so. Her Seven were created as a counterbalance to the power I possess." He shrugs. "I can try. I can go in there and start a fight, but if they band together against me? I will fall."

I swallow hard, my hopes deflating in an instant. If the Seven are strong enough to stop Rainier *with* his powers, *I* have zero chance on my own.

The scrolls it is.

"She's obsessed with balance," he continues. "But, when she instilled so much power to the Seven, I convinced her to help *me* create a failsafe in case they were ever corrupted. She complied because she truly never thought her precious Seven were capable of malicious intent and that the countermeasures would never be needed. She ensured the scrolls and the magic embedded in the incantation she inscribed upon them would grant me enough power to stop the Seven—if the need arose."

"Can I help retrieve the scrolls?" Cassiel asks, his wings ruffling behind him as he straightens in his chair.

"Only Harley or myself can *physically* take the scrolls," Rainier says. "And we must be prepared for a fight. Just because no other beings but you and I can wield them doesn't mean those around the scrolls don't benefit from them. And they will not be keen on letting them go."

He pushes away from the table and heads toward a giant wooden chest in the corner of the room. He throws it open, and I furrow my brow as he tosses things out of the chest over his shoulder. A few blankets, books, and pieces of jewelry fly behind him, landing in a mess on the floor.

"Here it is," he says, holding up an ancient-looking canvas satchel. It's a weathered hunter green with rich brown leather straps and brass buckles. "My lucky pack." He sets it on the table before me, the smell of dust and suede hitting my nose.

I'm not sure which question to ask first—how this dusty bag is going to help us steal scrolls from pissed-off creatures, or what, exactly, it is. "What makes it lucky?" I decide on as I reach for it.

Something both heavy and amused crosses his features as he looks down at the satchel. "It's your mother's," he says, voice thick. "When she came here, she would hardly part with that bag. The day she took it off was the day she started trusting me."

Emotion clogs my throat, and despite the rising questions about my biological mother swarming my soul, I dodge them like tiny bullets. Learning more about her is going to hurt like hell, and right now I need to be as strong as possible.

I clear my throat, peeking inside the bag. There are plenty of pockets, and the material is sturdy, but it's empty. "Um," I say. "Shouldn't there be a bunch of tubes for scrolls in here?"

"The scrolls are already contained within objects my sister chose to magically protect them," he answers.

"What are the objects?" I ask.

"I'm not sure," he says. "She chose them without my knowledge, and she made sure to spell the scrolls with who knows how many traps and tests. She didn't want to make it easy for me or anyone else who may try to use the power within them."

I purse my lips. When I first learned I was the Antichrist, I hit up Google for anything and everything I could find. There was a mention of the scrolls, but I didn't think much about it at the time. "I read something that said they were just rolled-up pieces of paper with a wax seal."

Rainier sighs. "I told you that not every translation of legends is accurate." He motions to himself. "Case in point, my name is Rainier, not Devil."

"Does that bother you?" Wallace asks. "When people call you Devil?"

He cuts her a look sharp as glass, then points at her. "Mark my words, Wallace, if you start calling me—"

"Oh, don't get your tail in a twist, *Devil*," Wallace cuts him off, because clearly she has a death wish.

I gape at her. Then at Rainier, who has some kind of unflinching control as he merely cracks his neck and looks directly at me. "I do not have a tail."

I groan. "I don't care if you have seven heads and seven horns and all that Biblical stuff. Explain more about the scrolls."

"She magically shielded the scrolls so they could only be retrieved by me or any heirs who bear my imprint," he says. "It will be hard. And they may be mere parchment, but the words on the pages are written by the hand of the Creator, and when all seven are brought together, those words are the most powerful weapon in the universe," he says. "And she just… threw them across the Ather and Earth." He almost looks like he's about to laugh at that notion. And in reality, it's hard to resist the bubbling hysteria rising in my throat. Because we're talking about unchecked power and the Creator and scrolls that are *millennia* old.

How is this my life?

I push back from the table, Wrath sticking close to my hip. I scoop up Rainier's bag, slipping the thick leather strap over my head and across my chest. "I'm going to need that map now."

CHAPTER FOUR

HARLEY

"I should come with you," Rainier says, but I can see the wheels turning in his eyes. With me working one area of the Ather and him hunting for the others, we're saving time.

"I'll go with her," Cassiel says, crossing the room to stand on my other side.

"I'll go topside," Wallace says. "Connect with Ryder. See if I can get any more information for us."

Rainier grabs a piece of parchment from the chest in the corner, quickly scribbling across it. He hands the paper to Cassiel. The angel of death examines the makeshift map, then nods as he pockets it. I don't even waste time being offended— Cassiel knows the Ather much better than I do, so he definitely should navigate.

Someday, in the future, I'll have to remedy that. Especially if accepting this ring has made me second in line for the Ather's throne, but I'm *so* not worrying about that right now.

"If you let anything happen to her, Angel of Death," Rainier says, his voice coated in power and promise, "I will ensure *your* death is never-ending. I'll kill you and bring you back so many times you won't be able to—"

"Hey," I say, drawing Rainier's gaze. "You don't have the right to make those threats. Cassiel is my friend. You are…"

Rainier shifts back an inch, almost an imperceptible move as I struggle for a word to call him.

"Overprotective," I settle on. Because it's not like I can call him *Dad*. The only kind of father I've ever truly known was an abusive asshole. Nathan was closer to a father for me, but I never let him in all the way to actually fill the role. And Rainier? I don't know *who* he'll end up being in my life.

And with my life constantly getting fucked? It doesn't really matter right now.

"You know I can handle myself," I tack on.

"No one knows that better than me. I'm your *father*." He says the word with such emphasis that *I* flinch. "That means you have more power than you likely know how to manage. And now that you've accepted your birthright ring? It will only continue unlocking the powers inside you. You think the dark flame and control over the earth are all you inherited from me?" He shakes his head. "There is no telling which powers will manifest inside you now. So, you'll need someone you can trust—someone we can *both* trust—to bring you back from the brink if you start to slip."

He eyes Cassiel. "I won't take back my threat. He needs to understand what he's signing up for. Because two of those realms are the stuff of nightmares, and either one of you could lose yourselves in there if you don't trust each other."

I glance up to Cassiel, eyes wary. "Are you sure you want to do this?"

He dips his head, his wings unfolding to their full length. "Draven is like my brother," he says. "You are his mate. I go where you go."

My heart swells in my chest, my lungs finally loosening with the relief of a plan of action. If I have a task, that means I can execute it.

"Aphian gave me a three-week deadline," I say. "I want to work faster than that. What exactly do we need to do with them once we have all seven?"

"You and I will have to work together to translate the incantation," Rainier answers.

"I got a D- in my French class," I groan. "So, not sure how much help I'll be in the translating department."

"You are my daughter," he says, a muscle in his jaw ticking.

"You will be able to read it. And once we do, it will grant me ultimate power."

Fuck. Really?

Do I want that?

"And I'll use it to eliminate the Seven," he finishes.

That, I can get behind. The Seven are abusers in their own right—forcing Judges like Draven and Ryder, or divine warriors like Cassiel, into the Divine Sleep whenever they feel like it. Or burning out their memories. Forcing them to kill on command. Stealing from peaceful realms like Conilis and using their resources to create weapons.

They have to be stopped.

I know that.

But fully unleashing Rainier? I was already worried I'd done that, and apparently there's an even higher level of power he can unleash. I've only known him a few weeks—who is to say he's *not* really the Devil? What will stop him if he decides to keep going after he eliminates the Seven? Keep using the scrolls' powers to take over the world?

Deal with that later my brain begs me, so I shove the anxiety down. Way down, right next to all my other worries and grief over every single thing that has happened since I turned eighteen.

Future me has a lot of shit to sort out.

"We'll meet you both back here in three days?" I ask finally.

Rainier and Wallace both nod.

"If it takes you longer than that," Rainier says, "we will go to Earth in search of the remaining scrolls."

"Okay," I say. "If that happens, leave word with Kazuki. You can find him at The Bridge in Chicago. He's a friend."

Rainier snorts, and I'm so surprised by the sound that I raise my brows. "The warlock. A *friend*, you say. Only a daughter of mine would keep such company." He looks at the angel of death, the leaper, and the hellhound.

"Wrath," I say, kneeling to hug him. "I'll be back soon. When we go to Earth? I'm taking you with me, deal?"

He grunts, nudging his massive head against my shoulder as I squeeze him. As much as I'd love his help on this journey, I'm not about to take him into the depths of hell with me.

I rise to my feet, turning to face Wallace. "Stay safe," I say, then hug her.

She hugs me back. "You know me," she says, and I flash her a look to say that isn't comforting. She waves me off.

I turn to Rainier, wondering how the hell to say goodbye to him. I can't hug him like Wallace, we're not there yet, but we've just declared war together—

"Stay sharp, daughter," he says, stepping away from me before bowing at the waist. Then he turns on his heels and he's out the door so fast you'd think I caught fire.

"He does that," Wallace says, then glances up at Cassiel. "Bring me back a present, Death Boy."

Cassiel grunts, ignoring her as she strides past us, Wrath hurrying behind her as they follow Rainier.

When Cassiel and I make our way out of Rainier's castle, I turn to him. "You ready for this?"

His wings stretch, the strength in them evident in their mass, the thousands of onyx feathers linking against one another like some sort of supernatural armor. "More than." But he frowns as he looks at me.

"What?" I ask, arching a brow.

"I'm trying to figure out how to do this," he says, reaching for me only to draw his arms back again.

"Do what?"

"Fly with you."

"Don't you have like a thousand years' practice? Why is this an issue? You flew me here just fine—"

"That was an emergency." He walks around me in a circle, muttering something to himself, eyeing me, then his back, before folding his arms over his chest. "I can't put you on my back," he says. "And if I carry you like a football, I run the risk of dropping you."

I gape at him. "What the hell, Cassiel? Just pick me up, and let's go. What's the problem?"

Cassiel groans but awkwardly hefts me up like I'm a piece of unwanted luggage. "Draven will rip my wings out if he catches me holding you like this."

"Ohmigod, seriously? You're his *brother*. And we're about to go to war together. I highly doubt Draven will care if your forearms touch my back—"

"You underestimate Draven's temper," he grumbles.

"Fair enough," I say, shifting in his arms and glancing at the ground. Damn, this is high up. Why does he have to be so tall? "But I've got your back, okay? Or your wings. Whatever. I won't let Draven kill you just because you're helping me with this mission. Deal?"

"Deal," he says, but he still keeps me as far away from him as possible as he launches us into the air.

CHAPTER FIVE

HARLEY

"Have you been here before?" I whisper as Cassiel sets me down on my feet after our quick flight. My boots crunch against the desolate wasteland that looks like a combination of dry black earth and slimy tar.

"No," he says just as quietly. "The souls I've carried have never needed to come this far."

I note the gleam in his silver eyes as he scans the area. They look like a polished blade winking in the moonlight. A shiver races down my spine, and I have to remind myself that he's on my side. He has this aura about him, one that is as cold as ice and as deep as an endless well. The powers I can sense are sharp, deadly, and drenched in years of death and blood.

I certainly wouldn't want him coming to collect *my* soul.

Trees stretch up from the dark earth, their branches bare and twisted and gray. All of them jut at awkward angles, some tangling with one another while others stand in solidarity with the sage sky behind them. It's lit by two overlapping moons the color of moss, casting the bleak area in sickly shades of green and gray.

A crack sounds in the distance, and Cassiel shoves me toward the nearest tree, crowding me against its wide trunk. The thing reeks of sulfur, making my eyes water.

I crane my neck around the trunk, keeping my breathing even as I follow his hunter's gaze. Through the bramble of trees, I can see things skittering between the branches.

Big things.

Things with elongated limbs and tails and horns while

others look downright human, their clothes shredded and hanging from their frail bodies.

I slide back around, pressing my back to the trunk as I look up at Cassiel. "Who brings *them*, then?" I whisper.

"Some of those creatures are born of this realm, a combination of millennia of evolution and whatever powers this place. Others are the souls of the unrest—the ones even beings like me can't contain. They slip through the cracks in the Ather, drawn here to where there is no authority to answer to or rules to abide."

I swallow hard, adrenaline crackling through my veins. Rainier said this was one of the places the Hell legends stemmed from, and now that we're here? I totally get it. My skin feels gritty, my blood chilled, fear clawing at me despite not seeing a clear threat yet.

"So, this is a smash-and-grab job," I whisper.

"Let's try stealth first," he suggests. "There is no leader here, no authority, but the strongest creatures *will* be drawn to wherever the scroll is and likely linger around it."

"Great," I say, trying not to full-on whine. Urgency makes my muscles twitchy. I want to get the scrolls as fast as possible so I can eviscerate the Seven and get my sister back. And Draven. "Will killing the Seven give Draven his mind back?" I ask, my thoughts scattered between priorities.

Cassiel scans the trees in the distance before answering. "I'm not sure," he admits. "No one has ever succeeded against the Seven before, not that many have tried."

"Have they ever done that to you?"

His eyes meet mine, then look away quickly. "They've put me in the Divine Sleep many times, but my abilities allow me certain...privileges."

I raise my brows when he meets my eyes again.

"I can manipulate the Dreamscape," he says. "Being an angel of death has many perks, but that one is my favorite. I can see people's nightmares and dreams before I take their soul.

How they behaved during life is directly linked to what I show them in death. That power also allows me to travel between minds during the Divine Sleep."

He sighs, a muscle tensing in his neck. "There are instances when Draven and I have been locked in Divine Sleep for decades at a time. But after some incredibly tedious exploring, I was able to reach his Dreamscape. We spent those years in sleep keeping the other from going insane." He laughs. "He's still sour about losing to me in chess over a hundred times."

Humor prickles my aching heart, and I reach for Cassiel's arm braced against the tree. I squeeze it in a silent thanks for all he's done for Draven.

"So, no," he continues. "They've never stolen my memories outright. My mind is a tangled web of many lifetimes; it would take too much of their time and power. But Draven? They've kept him in sleep longer than they've allowed him to live. It's easier to steal from his mind. And getting that back? I think it will have more to do with his own strength than anything to do with the Seven's."

I blow out a breath. How can the Creator, my *aunt*, let a group of beings continue doing what they've done to people like Draven and Cassiel? A weight presses down on my chest as terrible images fill my mind—Draven wandering around aimless and empty, Ray being subjected to the Seven's agenda.

I clench my eyes shut.

Aphian won't harm her. He knows I'll never do what he wants if he does.

I repeat the words four more times before I open my eyes again.

Cassiel quietly draws out the map Rainier gave him and studies it, forcing me to focus on the present. There are a million things I can imagine happening to the two people I love most in the world, a million scenarios created to crush me, weaken me, destroy me. That's what they want. Too bad for the Seven—they're only pushing me deeper into my power. Forging me into something they've always feared.

A threat.

A true threat to them for the first time in existence.

I'm going to unleash the ultimate power in the form of my biological father—the damn *Devil*. Let's see how well they'll cope with *him* on my side.

I glance down at Rainier's lucky pack resting against my hip and lock onto that anger, my thirst for revenge a lifeline to keep me from washing out into a sea of despair.

"There is a fortress," Cassiel says, folding the map and returning it to the pocket of his black pants. His white T-shirt is stark against his dark wings, which extend through slits in the back.

I shake out my muscles, focusing inward, finding my dark flames and earth power crackling in my blood with a thousand times more potency than before. My birthright ring has knocked down each and every struggle my powers ever had. And Rainier said there would be more surfacing—who *knew* how many more, with all the powers he has.

Bring them on.

All of them, any of them. Anything that will give me an advantage and help me save my sister.

"High chance of death," I say. "Creepy castle. Sounds right up my alley."

Cassiel's thick black eyebrows twitch, and I swear he almost laughs, but he shakes his head instead.

"What?" I ask.

"It's no wonder you're mated to him," he says.

My heart swells. The bond between Draven and me is frosted with ice, but I can still feel him there. And that's all I need.

"Stay close," Cassiel says.

I give him a firm nod. This isn't a pissing contest about who is stronger. We're a team. And I'm more than happy for him to lead so I can watch both our backs.

Cassiel draws his wings in tight as I walk behind him, my footsteps mimicking his as he steps on every soft piece of ground he can find. He's so quiet it's like smoke gliding along glass, and I try like hell to channel that kind of softness as we make our way across the unstable terrain.

The gray trees grow thick and tight as we move forward. I thought Marid's—the Greater Demon who possessed Ray and tried to kill me—realm of snakes and swampland was bad, but this?

This is *so* much worse.

Screams ring out in the distance, followed by the sharp sounds of flesh ripping apart. Creatures tearing into other beasts with teeth and claws. Bile climbs up my throat as the scents of sulfur and blood mix in the acrid air, threatening to choke the life out of me. I focus on Cassiel's wings, trying to give myself a solid point to cling to when the entire place seems designed to keep my eyes and mind scattering.

Each of his feathers are as long as my forearm and look paper-thin, but the amount of them linked over one another gives his wings a sense of iron strength. There are too many to count, thousands upon thousands of inky feathers laced over what I imagine is a fuckton of muscle. How else can he so easily fly? Especially when carrying others, too? It's a comfort to look at them as we weave through the treacherous forest, a soothing kind of support, like having a bright flashlight when plunged in darkness.

And then I almost laugh, because only I'd find comfort in an angel of death's company. I've never met another like him, but I imagine with their duty of carting souls across the Ather, they share the same sense of detachment. Unlike the Judges I've met—Draven and Ryder and Kai—who seem almost human in their efforts to guard and protect those who can't fight against the supernatural forces around them. Well, except for Kai. Who ended up being an evil piece of shit.

My life has changed so drastically in such a little time,

and yet it feels more natural to me than anything ever has before. Even as we walk into what I know will be one hell of a challenge, my feet move more steadily than they ever did when walking to class or work.

This is who you are, a voice whispers in the back of my mind, and I relish the surge of completeness I feel with the words. I'm my powers and then some.

And I'll use every ounce of them to get my sister and my mate back, starting with whatever monster this realm throws our way.

CHAPTER SIX

HARLEY

Cassiel slows our pace when the trees clear to reveal a fucking *fortress*, just like he said.

It looks like a giant, twisted tree house. One carved and fashioned from the same gnarled trees and slimy black earth we stand among. It's almost as if the thing grew itself. Every angle of the place is off, leaning way too left or way too right. And it's massive, with hundreds of tiers hanging off smaller sections of wood and mud that don't look physically possible, but there they are. Thick black fluid seeps from the seams and creases, almost like the place is weeping.

A creature no bigger than a Pomeranian with spines for hair and bright yellow eyes skitters across one of the jutting branches of the fortress. A loud crack snaps, the branch springing to life as it curls around the creature. The thing yelps, then falls silent as the branch rolls itself inward.

Ice shivers over my skin.

"Well, that was the creepiest thing I've ever seen," Cassiel says.

A twisted laugh escapes me that I quickly cover. "You're an angel of death," I whisper. "And *that's* the creepiest?"

"The fortress just *ate* that thing."

He has a point.

"Do we knock?" I ask.

His eyes flare at me. "The fortress just ate a creature, and you want to *knock*?"

"Well, what's your grand plan?"

He smirks. "Fly," he says, but it sounds a whole lot like *duh*.

I resist the urge to flip him off, instead waving my arm in a *let's get on with it then* gesture. He plants me with a warning look like I need to be careful how I silently mouth off to an angel of death, but I roll my eyes at him.

He reaches for me, steadying me a little easier this time with one arm beneath my knees before propelling us into the sky. I've never been afraid of heights, but watching as we clear the graphite trees and fly over the *creepy-eats-things-fortress* definitely isn't giving me warm-and-fuzzy vibes.

Cassiel banks, his body tensing slightly as he cranes us left, circling above the fortress's high tree towers. His eyes glow as he scans the area below us. I follow suit and point when I see an opening.

He instantly dives, his speed so intense I want to punch him. I try to make myself as small as possible as he shoots for the tiny opening like a missile. Strips of bark and thin branches break off as we dive through, tiny crumbling sounds echoing behind the beat of his wings.

Cassiel lands, setting me on my feet as we find ourselves in a hallway of sorts, the walls made of tightly braided branches and that weeping tar-like goop. The air is thick and hot, and the space is lit by glowing sage lights that tangle in the branches sporadically. I stick close to Cassiel as we notice an opening down the hall. It's at an awkward angle, too, almost like an opened doorway but slanted too far to the right.

Our steps are mirrored and silent as we walk toward it, and we look at each other in a form of silent communication we haven't perfected yet.

I miss Draven's ability to speak in my mind and for him to read mine in return.

I miss him in general, but I shove that feeling way down, intent on finding this scroll and getting the hell out of the creepy McMansion ASAP.

"The scroll should be on this level—more in the center, though—"

A creaking sound stops us dead in our tracks.

Cassiel's wings curl around me as if he can cloak us.

The creaking noise sounds metallic, almost like a rusty wheel turning on an old bicycle.

My heart thuds against my chest as I try to control my breathing. The sound grows louder, coming from the opening not five feet away.

My onyx flames dance beneath my palms, the earth in my blood reaching out to the fortress that feels alive and fights my power's influence.

A child with long black hair plastered to its face rides a tricycle out of the doorway, screeching to a halt before us.

"Ohmigod," I whisper, ice trickling into my veins.

I back into Cassiel's chest, but he doesn't budge an inch.

The child cackles, twisting its head too far to the left, its greasy hair spilling away from a pale green face. Two eyes as black as night focus on us, and a slash of red for a mouth grins.

Not a child. Nope. Definitely not a child.

This thing is more than a regular demon—it's fear and malice rolled into one infinitely creepy package.

"You came to play with me," the creature says in a voice that is both young and old and makes spiders tap-dance on my skin.

Oh, fuck this.

Flames spring to life, coating my fingers.

"Oh, *pretty*." The creature wags a bone-like finger at me. "Does the flame make flesh curl back?" It snaps its fingers, the sound amplified like it's playing over loudspeakers, and surges of the black tar seep from the branches around us, splattering along the floor, smoke rising from the spots it hits. "Cause *this* does," it says, grinning.

We jolt away from the acidic goop. "We're here for the scroll," I say, aiming my flames at the creature. "Leave us alone and you can live."

Cassiel gapes at me, and I shrug. I don't know the rules yet—kill or be killed? That I can get behind, but so far this thing hasn't made a move toward us—

Its cackle is sharp as it throws its head back and laughs. It points to the walls, then slicks its finger through the black goop bleeding from them. The bone sizzles from the acid, half of it disintegrating before it crumbles to the floor.

And the thing doesn't. Even. Flinch.

"You'll die here," it says. "I bet your insides are pretty, too," it continues as it raises its hands, the black goop now pouring from the walls in thick waves.

Panic climbs up my throat.

"It has no soul for me to sing to," Cassiel whispers, his chest rising and falling too fast against my spine.

The creature reclaims the handles on the tricycle. Its feet are bare, the yellow toenails long as claws on each foot as it pushes against the pedals.

We back away as it advances toward us down the hall, faster than the little bike should be able to go. Its mouth widens, a gurgling sound rippling from somewhere deep within.

Like it's hungry.

For *us*.

"I take it back," Cassiel breathes. "*That's* the creepiest thing I've ever seen."

I bark out a harsh laugh, my heart hammering so hard against my chest it hurts. I gather the flames in my hands, shaping daggers and sending them soaring for the creature—

The floor beneath our feet shifts, dissolving into grains of sand as we plummet through the darkness so fast I don't even have time to scream.

CHAPTER SEVEN

DRAVEN

"You know," the little girl—*Ray*—says from the corner of her room in the Seven's residence. "You're being a real jerk." She folds her arms over her chest, glaring at me. She sits cross-legged on her oversize bed, the food on the end table next to it untouched.

She hasn't eaten anything since I brought her here yesterday, and for some reason, that bugs the fuck out of me.

It shouldn't.

She's just a mission.

But Aphian gave me specific instructions to keep her comfortable, and I highly doubt starving herself falls into those terms.

I curl my hands into fists, my shadows coiling between my fingers and up my wrists. "Eat your breakfast," I order from where I stand guard at her door.

She tips her chin up, and the fierce look sets off a domino effect inside me—some internal trigger I can't place. Like a marble pinging through a metal chamber. I blink a few times, racking my brain for why my stomach is suddenly twinging with recognition.

Ray hops off the bed, crossing the large room with careful steps. She looks up at me, studying. "I'm not afraid of you."

Her words punch a brick wall in my mind—

A white-hot pain zaps up my spine, and I cringe against it.

I breathe deeply until it subsides, then glare down at the little girl. "You *should* be."

She doesn't budge an inch. "You would *never* hurt me, Draven."

I curl my lip at the way she says my name with such familiarity. Just like she did at her house. The man acted like he knew me, too—

Nails on a chalkboard screech in my head, and I hiss against the pain.

"Tell me how to help you," she begs.

I shake my head back and forth until the sound stops. "Eat."

She jumps a little at my tone. The fear is quickly swallowed by anger, though, and she glares at me again before stomping toward the mahogany table next to her bed. She eyes the plate of fruit, cheeses, and bread, then glances back to me.

"Is it poisoned?" she asks, deadpan.

I roll my eyes. "Look at your room," I say and swing my arm out to encompass it. "Would you be in here if Aphian wanted you dead?"

The place is one of Aphian's private suites in the Seven's residence, outfitted with every luxury imaginable. Lush carpets, a king-size bed piled high with cashmere blankets and silk pillows, a desk topped with sacred tomes only privileged guests are allowed to touch, and an en suite bathroom with a tub big enough to fit six people. Not to mention the floor-to-ceiling windows overlooking the turquoise ocean below.

Her eyebrows raise, something like victory flashing in her blue eyes. "*Aphian*," she tests out the name. "Is that who's controlling you?"

I scowl at her. "No one is controlling me."

She snorts, rolling her eyes as she plucks a strawberry from the plate. "Yeah, okay," she says, popping the fruit in her mouth.

"Watch your tone," I say in a lethally quiet voice.

"You watch yours," she fires back. "You're not the Draven I know, so I don't have to be nice to you." She swallows the strawberry, grabbing another while grumbling, "*Winter Soldier jerk*."

"You—" The door opens behind me, knocking me in the back. I hurry to step aside, folding my arms behind me and keeping my spine straight as Aphian enters the room.

Ray drops the fruit, turning to face him as he approaches her.

I watch, silent, as he towers over her, his white robes spilling along the thick carpet. His long blond hair is tied at the back in a braid. The white feathers of his wings are tipped in crimson, but he keeps them tucked in tight as he surveys the girl.

"Young Ray," he says. "Did you sleep well?"

"No," she says. "Being kidnapped doesn't really help good sleeping habits."

Aphian chuckles, but it's brief and quickly cut off. "This is your new home. You'll adjust." He lingers, studying her face for a few more moments before whirling around and striding toward the door. "Bring her," he commands.

My muscles clench with the divine order. I move before thinking, hurrying toward Ray and reaching for her with my shadows.

She smacks a tendril away. "I'll walk."

I draw the shadows back as she moves to follow Aphian down the hallway. I stay close behind her in case she has any wild ideas about running away. It would be futile. The Seven's residence is a labyrinth of marble hallways, tens of thousands of antechambers, and hundreds of council rooms. Not to mention the Judges' tunnels beneath the ground. There are also training rooms, weapons caches, and over a dozen restaurants housed within the grand walls. Without knowing which way to go, a person can get lost for days.

Ray is silent as we follow Aphian, her eyes only betraying her curiosity when we pass the giant works of art in gilded gold frames along the walls. The pieces are from every year in history, and there are even more scattered throughout the residence.

Aphian finally makes a sharp right, and I straighten my posture to the nth degree as I note him leading us into the Seven's main council room. It's the largest and most powerful room in the Seven's residence, big enough to house or contain all manner of creatures, including an entire community of giants, if the need arose.

Golden lights illuminate the starkly white room, the eternal golden flames practically dancing atop the empty marble throne in the epicenter of a great dais. Three additional thrones sit on either side of it, each one occupied by a different member of the Seven.

My eyes automatically fly to the farthest on the left, landing on Esther. Her hazel eyes are strained and full of concern as they lock on mine, and something nags at the back of my mind. Her dark brown hair spills in curls over her tawny shoulders, the white gown she wears sleeveless and showing off her pewter wings, which are only half spread behind her.

Aphian points to the center of the room, the marble floor inlaid with a golden compass. I usher Ray toward the center of the compass as Aphian takes his throne in the middle of the dais.

"You called us here, Aphian," Thaddeus says from his position directly to the right of Aphian. He extends an alabaster arm, sweeping it toward where Ray and I stand. "Please, explain."

"Yes, please do," Ray says, staring up at the Seven like they're no more than a group of children, when in truth *she's* the child. Where does she get the nerve—

"You all know the situation," Aphian says, his voice booming in the wide room. "The prophecy of the End Times. The very events I've been trying to stop for centuries." His blue eyes fall on me. "Why I've always tasked one of our strongest—albeit most feared—soldiers to eliminate any being who is suspected to be the Antichrist."

A collective hiss goes through the room, and flashes of too many deaths to count flicker behind my eyes. My fingers feel sticky with their blood, but I resist the urge to wipe them on my pants.

"This again?" Bartholomew says, brown wings ruffling

behind him as he shifts atop his throne. The white flecks dotting the feathers are the same tone as his skin and shimmer in the light. "I thought you handled this situation eighteen years ago when you ripped that babe from its mother and gave it to that vile human. You assured us it would turn the creature to our side, and if not, the Judge would take care of it. Are you saying you failed?"

"Careful," Aphian warns.

"Forgive me," Bartholomew hurries to say. "We are all in a state of unrest."

I don't fault him. I've been on the receiving end of Aphian's great power more than once for a punishment. It's not to be taken lightly.

"I understand," Aphian says even though he looks anything but understanding. He nods to me. "After years of ordering this Judge to eliminate any possible threats of the Antichrist surfacing, I realized the error in my ways. I tried another tactic in an attempt to change the course of the End Times. Sadly, my plans didn't fall into place like I predicted," he admits. "But the memories I've pulled from the Judge's mind are irrefutable. She is the Antichrist we've always feared. She's even set Rainier free from the chains we bound him in centuries ago."

What does he mean? What memories? What evidence?

My brow pinches, and Ray looks up at me in an *I told you so* look.

"Rainier is free?" Hillel asks, his gray dapple wings tensing. His long, straight nose crinkles as he looks to Aphian. "Have you doubled the wards? We should awaken more Judges to triple our guards. He could be on his way right—"

"He's not," Aphian says. "Not with the leverage I have against the Antichrist." He glances at Ray.

"How *does* this one come into play?" Hillel asks as his light brown eyes cast a concerned look toward Ray.

Aphian grins, the smile like a slash from a blade. "This

young one is a seer."

"A seer? Truly?" Judah asks, his grin slick as silk in his wide, tan face, and his wings like the sunset. "There hasn't been one in centuries."

"Quite," Aphian says, and there is a flicker of pride in his eyes. "She will be useful to us with her gifts alone, but she's also the one the Antichrist loves most."

"The Antichrist *loves* this one?" Judah asks. "How?"

"I made it so," Aphian says, more than pleased with himself. "I positioned her in the Antichrist's path. She loves her above all others." His eyes land on me, some hate simmering there I can't understand. "She is our insurance that the Antichrist doesn't interfere with our plans." I can see something else behind his eyes—he's keeping something from the others, but why?

"Where are we with the weapons?" Bartholomew asks.

"We're almost done," Aphian answers. "We've amassed enough, though the loss of The Twelve is a blow to our efforts."

Esther hisses from her throne on the left. The Twelve are dead? And Aphian was working with them before? What would he need—

"Problem, Esther?" Hillel draws out the question, not bothering to look at her. Instead, he examines his nails, which are filed to points at the end.

"You all know my feelings about working with The Twelve," she says. "I've never hidden it."

Aphian groans. "And you know we're all tired of hearing it," he says. "If the Creator hadn't endowed you to us, then I would dispose of your opinions in the way they deserve." He cuts a glare to her. "Painfully."

She arches a brow at him, a cruel smirk twisting her lips. "But the Creator *did* send me here, Aphian," she says. "I would be careful how you tread around *me*."

"Don't threaten me in my own throne room—"

"Is it just *yours* now? Are we your subjects?"

Tension winds through the seven of them, enough to make my chest tighten.

"Enough," Thaddeus says, defusing the rising fight. "Aphian, what is the next step?"

Aphian takes a breath, casting a glance my way. "The Antichrist has risen in her power. Beyond Rainier, she is the only one who has ever posed us—and this world—a threat. We all know the legends, but we're also more than versed on the Antichrist's capabilities. I had hoped to win her to our side, but from what I learned from our Judge's past, there will be no swaying her without leverage." He points to Ray. "She will do whatever we ask as long as we hold her here."

Ray glares at him but remains silent.

"Won't she come for her?" Esther asks, her eyes softening as they fall on Ray.

"I've taken measures to ensure she doesn't," he answers, "but if she chooses to defy me, we'll eliminate her and be done with it."

"What if she gets the scrolls?" Esther pushes.

Aphian grins. "Then she'll be doing exactly what I want her to do. Now, we move into the next phase of our plans. The weapons we amassed need to be tested. And soon. The world is changing. It's been changing for some time, and the Creator has made no move to step in. We have to read this as a sign that we—the Creator's trusted council—are to be the change the world needs."

"You mean to use these weapons on innocent people?" Efrain's golden eyes blaze as he glances from Ray to Esther and back again. He's remained silent until now, his hands gripping his throne, the gold arm cuffs he wears glistening over his dark brown skin.

"I mean to first test them against those creatures that have escaped the Ather and lived among us like they're equals," Aphian says. "Then, I have other well-deserving targets in mind."

"And once you're satisfied these weapons do what you want them to do?" Esther seethes.

"Then we move to the next step," Aphian says. "We show ourselves to the world, take place as the great power we are, and reshape it in our image."

Esther shakes her head, Efrain wearing an equal look of disgust.

"The world has been left unchecked for too long," he continues. "More and more, the humans turn on one another. Wars and violence and diseases that cannot be stopped. The time has come to cast it anew, and now that we have what the Antichrist most desires, she'll play her part in our plan whether she likes it or not."

"And what if Rainier gets ahold of the scrolls?" Efrain asks. "What if it's *him* who comes instead of her?"

"Do you not have ears?" Aphian snaps. "Holding the Antichrist's sister is all we need to ensure I…*we* get the scrolls first." He takes a breath. "Besides, we trapped him once," he continues. A chill hangs in the air, the temperature in the room dropping a few degrees. "We can do it again. He'll be no match for our collective power. I do not fear him."

Esther snorts, and Aphian threatens her with a look.

"He will be no match for our weapons, either." Aphian turns to me. "In the meantime, Judge," he says, lacing his tone with the authoritative command I can't ignore, "you will train the seer. Draw out her powers, then harness them. Whatever it takes. I want her accelerated."

Ray gasps at my side, but I dip my head.

Aphian rises, and he strolls out of the room without a second glance. Thaddeus, Bartholomew, Judah, and Hillel all follow him.

Efrain and Esther linger, standing near their thrones and whispering to each other. Efrain's butterscotch wings curl around Esther in an attempt to shield their conversation. She notices us still standing there, and pity colors her eyes.

"Go," she says, and the command in her voice releases me from the at-attention stance I've held this entire meeting.

I coil my shadows around Ray's hand, urging her to keep up.

"Esther," I hear Efrain say as we reach the doorway.

"They've damned us," Esther responds. "They've damned us all."

CHAPTER EIGHT

HARLEY

My stomach lurches up to make friends with my throat as gravity sucks us through the pitch black.

Cassiel grabs my wrist, yanking me to him so hard I yelp. He beats his wings, and it takes him a few tries before he's able to stabilize us. He hauls me upward, and I get a better grip as we both look down.

"Oh, fucking hell," I groan.

Spears the color of seafoam jut upward from the base of the floor, their sharp tips looking a shit-ton like fangs ready to chew us to bits.

"Must suck to not be able to fly," Cassiel says.

I whip my face up to look at him. "Did you just make a joke, Death Striker?"

"Don't get used to it."

He glances around, and I do the same. There is only one exit point beyond climbing back up to the surface. It's to our right, just past the sea of spikes, and carved right into the twisted tree house. A faint light pulses like a beacon for us to follow.

"Let's get the scroll as fast as possible," I say. "I'm not dying in this tree house."

"Your song isn't even faint in my ears," he says, tilting us so we head toward the opening. "You're safe for now."

The wariness in his eyes as he sets me down on the thankfully solid floor begs to differ. "You've heard my song?" I ask.

He visibly swallows. "When you were poisoned by Marid's serpent."

"What did it sound like?"

He scowls at me. The hallway is so cramped we can barely walk side by side, and the ceiling of tangled branches hangs so low Cassiel has to dip his head. The floor is made of planks of mismatched wood, but for now, I'm just grateful it doesn't disintegrate and that it's mercifully creeptastic-demon-child free.

"What?" I ask. "Is that an off-limits question?"

He considers for a moment, then smooths out his expression. "It's an incredibly personal thing for an angel of death," he says. "But, to be fair, not many are given the chance to ask."

I nod, my eyes adjusting to the low light. The walls are dripping with the black goop, and my insides curl up like dried flowers.

"Why is it so personal?" I ask, more to keep my mind off the terror climbing up my throat. I don't know what it is about this place, but it seems…*intelligent*. As if my worst fears are nothing but guitar strings it plucks for fun.

"It's something only we can hear," he says. "The Death Song acts as a gateway into the being's soul. Tells us everything we need to know."

I stop, blinking at him. He glances over his shoulder. "What did mine tell you?" Did it tell him I'm the horror the world fears? The darkness to snuff out the light? Because after what the Seven did? I *feel* like that more than ever before.

"I'll tell you the next time I hear it," he teases.

I shudder. "Let's hope that's a long time from now and, you know, not in the next five minutes—"

The floor shakes beneath our feet, silencing my words. Cassiel grabs me like he thinks we're about to fall again, but the floor is solid. It's just…*rolling*.

The planks rise and fall in ever-growing waves and, on a particularly large swell, send us smacking against the floor.

We scramble to our feet, and something cuts through the air—

Cassiel jerks me down, and an axe lodges itself in the wood just above my head.

"Thanks," I gasp, eyeing the axe, then look the opposite direction. "What the hell?"

A treelike creature is crouched down, lumbering through the hallway, another axe poised in its bark-covered hands. Holes make up terrifyingly empty eyes and a mouth, and it raises its massive, stump-like foot before slamming it into the planks. They ripple angrily again, jolting Cassiel and me as we hurry to our feet.

I grab Cassiel's arm and hustle down the hallway. "That is *so* the evil version of Groot."

"What the hell is a groot?" Cassiel asks as we skid around a sharp, slightly slanted corner and propel down an even longer hallway.

"Remind me to explain when we're not being chased by a demonic tree trying to chop our heads off. Down!" I shout, and we both drop to our knees. My hair rustles in the wind before a *thunk* hits the wall next to us. Another axe sinks into the wall immediately, and I smack my palms against the rippling planks.

The tree demon lumbers around the corner, its pace slow and clunky but no less intimidating. It flicks its branch-like limbs, and an axe grows out of each hand.

"You're not hiding a sword in your wings, are you?" I ask, breathless. Cassiel scowls at me, and I shrug. "Worth asking." I grab a fistful of his shirt, jerking him out of the way of a flying axe before it can find a home in his neck. I scan the area, seeing another turn just a few feet ahead of us. "Come on!" I race toward the corner, turning only to skid to a halt.

"Dead end," Cassiel says.

I pound on the wall of branches before us, looking for a weak spot. I even try to shift the wood with my earth powers, but it's not responding to me, as if this type of nature isn't made to be wielded. When nothing gives, I release a breath. "Okay, new plan."

"There was a plan before?"

I glare up at him. "You run that way, distract him, and I'll attack him from behind."

"*You* run, and *I'll* attack him," he counters.

The floor ripples again, and I fling my hands against the wall to keep from falling. "Seriously—"

The branches creating the dead end twist and crack, parting like a curtain.

"You didn't go splat," the demon-child creature says, stepping through the gash in the wall. It cackles before launching at us, sharp, bony fingers outstretched. "Play with me."

"*Shit*," I gasp as the thing slams into me. My back smacks against the floor, the hit so hard my vision wobbles for a few seconds.

"Pretty, pretty princess," the creature drawls. It hops on my chest, crouching over me as I try and connect my brain to my limbs again. It gouges that bony finger into my right arm, dragging it down my flesh, wrenching a scream from my lips.

Cassiel reaches for the creature, but an axe flies right past his outstretched arms. He draws them back, then leaps over us to stand between me and the evil Groot that is barreling right for us.

"Ohhh." The demon child curls its horrid red mouth, eyeing my blood on its bones. A black tongue darts out to lick its fingers clean, and my entire body turns to jelly at the sight. Too many demons in Chicago tried to take a bite out of me in the hopes of unlocking the gates between there and here. At least in the Ather, I'm not a Key that lets things out. "You taste like freedom," it says, darting its other hand toward my chest—

I shift beneath it, the stun from the hit finally wearing off enough for me to *move*. I propel my hips and swing my legs to the left, knocking the creature off-balance and sending it crashing against the nearest wall.

A growl trembles in the air between us, but I'm on my feet in a blink, my hands engulfed with my dark flames. The creature slaps its skeletal hands against the floor, screeching as it runs for me on all fours.

"More!" it screams. "I want more. I want it all!"

It launches into the air, springing high above my head.

"Oh, hell no," I say, swirling my hands until four razor-sharp blades of flame fill the space between me and the demon. It can't stop its momentum as it flies straight through my weapons of fire—

Splatters of hot, sticky, rancid liquid hit my skin as it lands in pieces on the floor around me. I swallow back the bile climbing up my throat, wipe my face free of the sickly green blood, and whirl around.

The *clomp clomp* of the tree demon's steps draws closer, but there is no sign of Cassiel. I scan the area, hoping like hell he didn't get knocked out and thrown over the edge at the end of the hallway and to the spikes below.

I bolt out of the hallway, my boots slipping in the blood from the demon child as I race on a burst of energy past the tree creature. Its rough bark scrapes against my bare arms as I squeeze past it, and the viscous fluid from the walls smears my skin. I push past the small gap, lifting my knees as high as possible so I don't fall from the constantly moving planks.

The thing screeches, the sound like a chainsaw splitting wood, and it pierces my eardrums like a hot needle. I groan against the pain, sparing a glance over my shoulder. The thing turns to follow me, another axe growing from its limb.

Dread fills my chest when I keep running, dodging an axe as the thing gains ground on me. Where the hell is Cassiel?

I reach the opening we came in from, skidding to a halt so fast I nearly slip over and fall into the pit of spikes far below. I spin around, bracing myself. The thing is so close I can smell the sulfur-and-rotten-wood scent of its breath.

I raise my fiery fists but hesitate. If I light this thing up, it will no doubt set the entire tree house on fire. Its huge size is enough to spread it so fast we may not have a chance to grab the scroll—the whole reason we're here in the first place.

Dropping to my knees, I dodge another axe swing. The planks ripple again, sending me crashing to my ass. I scramble, trying to back away from the tree's raised axe as it brings it crashing down—

A thunderous snap cracks the air, and the axe clatters by my feet. The creature shakes violently before dissolving into a pile of ash that dusts Cassiel's black boots.

"Took you long enough," I grumble, taking his extended hand as he hauls me to my feet.

"The thing has a massive hit," he says, releasing me. "Sent me crashing back there." He gestures behind us, to another side hallway near where I killed the other creature. "Good job not burning the place down."

"Thanks," I say, catching my breath as I glare at the gnarled ceiling. "First order of business when I'm queen of the Ather is to eradicate this place and everything in it."

"Come on," Cassiel says, jerking his head toward the opening the demon child came out of. We step over the demon chunks, careful not to slip in the green blood seeping into the cracks of the planks. "The map indicates the scroll is through here."

The moment we step under the upheaved branches, they slam back down behind us, trapping us in a barely lit room. Chittering sounds all around us, and as my eyes are slow to adjust, it looks like the walls are...

Moving.

"Cass," I say as I shrink away from the walls. He does, too, our backs touching as we scan the room. "Tell me you're seeing that."

"Ather scorpions," he says. "Thousands of them."

I shudder as my eyes fully adjust. The walls are lined with the things, as dark as night, their barbed tails gleaming and dripping venom.

"I don't know if you know this," I whisper, "but I really *really* don't like poison."

"Is that so?" he asks sarcastically.

The creatures draw closer with each breath we take but stop a few inches around us, forming a tight circle, caging us in.

"Can we fly?" I whisper.

"They're all over the ceiling," he says. "Even if we could break through it, we'd be stung at least a dozen times, if not more."

"Got it. No flying." My fingers flicker with flames, the silver flecks in them casting the venomous creatures in bursts of light.

"If you burn us alive," Cassiel whispers, "I will never forgive you."

"Can you even die?"

"Yes!" He stands closer to me. "Not from old age or disease, but a fatal injury or a *firestorm* can absolutely end my immortal existence, and I'm really not looking to die right now."

I roll my eyes, swallowing hard. "Thanks for the vote of confidence."

Taking a deep breath, I mentally wrap myself around my power, willing it to do exactly as I say. I curl my fingers before darting them upward, making it rain thousands of tiny drops of flame. Then I take full control of that rainfall, moving the drops through the air wherever I command.

The chittering mounts as the creatures try to dodge the drops aimed for them. They scramble and scatter, fleeing up the walls and exposing a doorway. I rush for the door, trying to shove it open, but it's locked. I kick and kick, but it barely budges.

"On three," Cassiel says, standing next to me.

I nod.

"One, two," we say in unison. "Three."

We kick the door at the same time, and it flies open, the wood splintering as we sprint into the room. I slam the door behind me and do the heebie-jeebies dance like there's a scorpion in my hair.

I groan as I shake out my limbs. "*Ick*."

Cassiel arches a brow at me. "You about done?"

I flip him off. "Just because you have soul-stealing abilities and are more terrifying than those bugs doesn't mean—"

"Do you want to grab that scroll or not?" he asks, a gleam in his eyes.

I follow where he points, and the breath stalls in my lungs.

A raven-colored stump sits in the otherwise vacant room, and in its center rests a tiny brass container that almost looks like a super fancy rolling pin. Black roots twist and sprawl out from the center of the stump, looking a hell of a lot like pulsing veins as they crisscross over the scroll. They spear out in all directions, covering the floor we stand on and beyond as if the entire creepy tree house grew from this spot specifically.

I rush over to it, yanking the scroll from the black roots that slick across it. It's no more than three inches long, the bronze material embossed with intricate designs that sweep over it in swirls and sharp angles.

"The scroll is inside this?" I ask.

"There's a latch," Cassiel says, pointing to a tiny spot on the bronze.

Light flickers from inside the moment I run my finger over the latch, and power ripples from it.

"Don't open it here," Cassiel says.

Screams and stomps sound from the other side of the door, rocking the tree house.

"Time to fly," I say, quickly slipping the scroll inside Rainier's bag and securing it closed. I shoot my flames across the room through a small opening in the branch wall. The fire turns the wood to ash, giving us a wide view of the sage sky and gray forest beyond.

"One down," I say. Cassiel and I move in one fluid motion as he hauls me upward, lunging for the opening I created.

He flaps his giant wings, propelling us into the sky, leaving the roars of the tree house behind. He climbs higher and higher, and it's not until we're enveloped in silence that he grins down at me. "Six to go."

CHAPTER NINE

HARLEY

"We'll rest here for the night," Cassiel says, banking right toward a crumbling structure hugging the outskirts of the neighboring realm we've passed into.

I stare up at the building when he sets me down. "It looks like a palace," I say. "A burned-down palace."

He nods toward the building. "It'll provide cover for the night. The journey to the next scroll location is long. I need to rest my wings."

I follow him through a crumbling archway of stone that is only half complete, the other half dusting the ground at the base of the building. Windows are carved from the fog-colored bricks, the gray light from the sky casting it in an eerie glow.

"What was this place?" I ask.

"This realm used to be like Conilis centuries ago," Cassiel says. "The demons here had a talent for enchanting weapons and jewels with Ather magic, but living so close to the more unstable realms of the Ather ended up being their ruin."

My heart clenches. "They were killed?"

Cassiel shakes his head. "Scattered. When they couldn't defend against the attacks anymore. Theirs is a rare race now, living in various peaceful realms across the Ather. I used to come here to rest after carting souls to the Ather. I loved to watch them make the weapons."

He blows out a breath, his eyes going distant. There's a story here — I know it — but I don't want to push, so I quietly go back to studying the building. The ceiling is completely exposed to the sky as if some great dragon razed it ages ago, and from what Cassiel said, it very well could've been.

Something twists in my stomach—a mixture of regret and desire. Regret that I hadn't been here to help the people all those years ago, and a desire to not let any other peaceful realms suffer the same fate.

To my left rests a grand, winding staircase that leads to an upper level with an overlooking balcony. The floor is covered in debris—wood and stone and dust that shift beneath my boots as we linger in the entryway.

"Going up?" I ask.

Cass shakes his head. He nods toward a hallway curving around the staircase. "I'd rather not tempt the thing to cave in on us."

I follow him around the staircase, and we find a somewhat more solid room. The space is coated in dust that clings to the air, making it feel like we're breathing in ash, but it's miles better than the realm we just left.

The gash on my arm from the creeptastic demon-child thing stings. I wince, shifting Rainier's satchel over my head, and set it down on a stone bench that juts from the cracked walls. I draw on my earth power, reinforcing the long stretch of stone above the floor before settling onto it.

I grab a cloth from the bag and a vial of Revivify, the healing salve Wallace packed for me, and make quick work of slathering the pink stuff all over the wound. A cooling sensation tingles over the cut, and I sigh as my skin seals.

"I hope I don't catch some demonic infection from that thing." I shudder. The thing's *bones* were in my skin. *Bleh.*

"The Revivify will ensure you don't," Cassiel says as he drops next to me.

"Thank you," I say after I've cleaned up my arm as best I can and returned the rest of the salve to the pack.

He shifts so his wings are sprawled in the space between us. "For what?"

I lean my head back against the crumbling wall. "For

coming with me. I've done so many things alone in the past. Having people I can count on is a new thing for me."

"I understand that," he says. "It's been a long time for me, too. Beyond Draven, I don't have many friends. Not that there is a line for the spot."

I snort. "You *do* have the ability to steal souls. What if you're jamming out to a new song and accidentally snatch someone's soul just because you're vibing?" I tease. "*That's* pretty terrifying."

"Says the *literal* Antichrist." He cocks a brow at me, and I laugh. "And no," he continues. "I can't accidentally steal a soul just because I'm into a new band. Besides, it's not actual singing. It's more like controlling an ancient and powerful language, then directing it either at the soul in question or the soul's death song if they've already started to die."

"That's *comforting*," I say. "But if it helps, you don't scare *me*. If we survive this, I'll owe you one for your help here."

Cassiel chuckles, then leans his head back against the wall, too, his lids hanging heavy over his silver eyes.

My mind races with a million other questions, and my body is restless from the fight we just left behind. I fidget for what feels like half an hour before I give up. "Can you tell me more about the Dreamscape?"

"What do you want to know?" He keeps his eyes closed, as if he can restore his energy levels with that alone.

"Can only angels of death control it?"

"It's rare for any other supernatural creatures to be able to control and access the Dreamscape of others as we do, though some with great power can master it. I wouldn't be surprised if it's one of Rainier's." Meaning it could technically be one of mine. "Especially if the Dreamscape you're trying to connect with is open to you entering it."

I chew on my bottom lip.

"Why?" he asks.

"Ray," I say. "Everyone keeps calling her a seer." Aphian

wanted her for more than her connection to me. "She connected to Marid through her dreams. And she dreamed of you taking her back to Nathan after we defeated The Twelve." Panic over what my sister may be, what she might have to deal with growing into her powers, threatens to steal my breath. I glance at my empty lap, wishing Wrath's heavy head was there to keep me whole.

Cassiel furrows his brow. "I did feel something while I stood guard at your doors in The Bridge those weeks ago. She has untapped power. Seers were hunted in ancient times, by both the demonic and the divine."

I sit up straighter. "Hunted?"

"Their power is such a rarity gifted by the Creator. Wars were raged over possession of them. Where I came from..." His wings tense at his sides. "They were coveted. Worshiped, almost. Though they were few and far between. The divine were afraid of them because of their ability to see events and change the fated course of time. Many were executed centuries later, humans mistaking them for witches."

A knot forms in my throat.

"Anyone with the true sight hid it, and after years of persecution, a real seer hasn't been heard of in ages."

"Until my baby sister," I say.

He nods. "Aphian will want to test her abilities. He'll want to sway her to join his side. To help him with his plans, whatever they may be."

Flames flicker over my fingertips. Before we killed them, he was working with The Twelve to create supernatural weapons that can be devastating on Earth. "Whatever Aphian's plans are, I don't want my sister anywhere near them."

"I know," he says, folding his arms over his chest. "But her rare power keeps her safe, so that is something to hold on to."

I curl my fingers, shaping my black and silver flames into daggers, flipping them in the air only to catch them and do it over again. It's so easy now, shaping my powers, controlling them. I look at the ebony gem on my right-hand middle finger—my father's ring, the one he made for me from the sacred stone carved out of his mountain.

Accepting it has changed everything. At any minute, any one or *all* of Rainier's powers could unleash themselves inside me. Could be anything from telekinesis to shapeshifting, and yet, I still feel powerless to help Ray.

"She could access the Dreamscape of anyone she wants if she learns to control her powers," Cassiel says. "There is no telling what all she'll be able to do once she's trained."

I stop throwing my flame daggers in the air. "Will she be hunted by others? Like I have been for my blood?" Having blood that's the Key to opening the gates between the Ather and Earth is like wearing a *free refills* sign, and every malicious demon in a five-mile radius is dying of thirst.

A muscle in his jaw clenches. "If word spreads. If her powers grow until they're cast across the planes like a beacon and she's left unprotected, then yes. She'll be hunted just for what she is."

The ground shudders as my entire being rebels against the image of my sister being hunted for the rest of her life. For never knowing who she can trust because of what she can do.

"She won't be left unprotected," I vow.

"I know," he says. "And if we destroy the Seven?" His eyes lock with mine. "You and your father will be the strongest among us, beside the Creator."

I blow out a breath. "That's a relief." I think. I still need to deal with the fact that I've essentially unleashed the Devil on the world. I think Rainier feels similarly to me about the future of the Ather, but how well do I actually know him? Words won't be enough. He'll have to prove that I can trust him.

The Seven and getting back Ray and Draven are the only things I have the mental space to worry about right now. Especially when I thought all I'd have to worry about was farming in Conilis and slowly coming to terms with my birthright as heiress to the Ather. And I'd been doing just that.

Life in Conilis had been perfect.

Life with *Draven* had been perfect.

"Do you want me to help you sleep?" Cassiel asks.

"Hmm?" I try to speak around the spaces inside me that feel hollowed out.

"Another perk of controlling Dreamscapes," he says, waving a hand toward me. "I can ease you into a dream, if you'd like. You have to give me access to your mind, though."

I hesitate, terrified of what I may see if I shut my eyes for too long. I've had Kazuki in my head before, and the images he conjured still scare the shit out of me, despite him being a trusted friend. And Draven... He holds a permanent spot in my mind, a doorway just for him—

"It's all right," Cassiel says, looking away. "I know you don't trust me enough yet. Not many people do."

The words cut into my chest like a knife. Another case of pain and judgment, just for being what he is. How many people and creatures alike have written him off because of it? What must it have been like for him to walk the world before he found a brother in Draven? Alone and judged and feared?

"Actually," I say, sitting up a bit straighter. "I was wondering if we can try to reach Draven."

"Together?" he asks, tilting his head.

I nod. "Maybe if we use the mating bond..."

"It's worth a try."

"You'll just have to tell me what to do," I say, trying like hell not to let hope rise in my chest.

"Close your eyes," he says. "Open your mind for me. I'll come in and search for the doorway that leads to your mating bond. When I find it, we can try to channel that connection—kind of like hopping on a train to his mind."

I try to do as he says. It's...confusing. Nothing like letting Kazuki in, which had been because of a bargain we struck. And definitely nothing like when Draven is in my mind, which is effortless because of our bond.

I feel the sensation of someone knocking on my mental barriers. With effort, I peel my walls back, allowing Cassiel inside. His presence has a glacial strength that triggers my fight-or-flight instincts as he pushes further in my mind. I quell the urge to shove him out until the worries eating me disappear with each featherlight brush of his influence.

"Whoa," Cassiel whispers, but I hear his voice in my head.

"What?" I ask, panicked.

"There are…" He hesitates. "Way more doorways in here than I thought."

"Is that a bad thing?"

"No," he says quickly. "I need you to show me where the mating bond is."

I mentally nod, throwing my awareness deeper inside until I can see the blazing chain of gold that connects me to Draven. Arctic blue crystals grow from the gold links, pricking my heart. "Here," I say, my voice echoing in the chambers of my own mind.

It takes Cassiel's presence much longer than I expect to find me, but then he's there, his silver eyes churning with anger and pity as they trail along the rusted chain and ice. He reaches for the chain, nodding toward me to do the same.

I mirror his movements, gasping as I wrap my fingers around that chain—

Cedar and citrus and amber rush my senses, filling me with Draven's scent. A soothing sort of sensation rushes over me as I cling to that connection. "He's sleeping," I whisper.

"That's good," Cassiel says. "I'm trying to slip inside his Dreamscape now. Focus on that connection, Harley. Use it as a tether to follow me."

I narrow all my thoughts to the sensations surging from our bond—his scent, the deep rumble of his breath in sleep—but he still feels so far away, like a rubber band stretched to capacity, the material thinning and on the verge of breaking.

Pushing harder, I grip our bond so tight it *hurts*. I shove my mental awareness down it, pushing and pushing—

"Draven," I gasp as my eyes are filled with his image.

He's lying in a bed that's way too small for him, his long legs dangling off the end. A pillow is tucked beneath one arm, his brow furrowed in sleep. I reach out, but my hand smacks against a light blue wall that's as hard as ice.

"The divine commands," Cassiel growls, sliding his hand along the ice wall separating us from Draven's mind.

"Try sending him a memory," Cassiel suggests. "Something important to you and him specifically."

I nod and sift through a hundred good memories, not at all shocked there are so many even though we've only been together a short time. He's my best friend, my mate. Even when facing death, there's no place I'd rather be than with him.

I grab onto one, drawing it to the surface of my mind.

"Draven," I say, the breath catching in my lungs as he tugs me toward the edge of the pink river. Conilis's periwinkle sky is settling into a deeper purple color, the water sparkling where it flows near the obsidian soil. "This is amazing."

Draven interlocks our fingers, drawing me toward the bank, where he's laid out a blanket. "I thought you'd like this little secluded spot," he says, guiding me to the oversize blanket.

We settle onto the blanket, and I easily slide into his embrace, breathing out a deep, contented sigh.

"Did you think it could be like this?" I ask, his strong arms warm around me as we both look at the stunning view before us. Mountains pepper the horizon, the winding river snaking its way farther than we can see.

"Not even in my wildest dreams," he says, then kisses the top of my hair, pulling me a little closer to him.

I smile, shifting so I can look up at him. "When I joked about farming in hell, I never knew how wonderful it could be." I motion toward our view. "Conilis, the Ather, you and me... it's more beautiful than any future I could have ever hoped for. I know it probably sounds silly to someone who's lived and experienced so much of life —"

"*You're the best part of any life I've been allowed to live,*" he says, returning my grin, his golden eyes rich with love.

I manifest the memory into life until I can smell the crisp, earthy scent of the pink river, can feel the heat from his arms as he holds me, hear the sound of creatures cooing as the day ends. I unfold that memory, those sensations, and drape them over the chain connecting us.

And wait.

Cassiel holds his breath next to me but sighs after a few minutes. "It's not working," he says. "With this divine command, we can't reach him. It's too strong —"

"Draven!" I yell, slamming my fists against the ice. "Draven!"

My mind shakes, the wall before us trembling.

"Harley," Cassiel warns, but I'm past hearing him. I can *see* Draven, can almost feel him, and I want him to come back to me.

"You can hear me!" I shout. "I know it. Wake up. Remember —"

The ice wall thickens, frosting over with another layer of blue that makes it hard to see Draven. But I can just make out him struggling in the bed, like he's trying to wake up.

"*Please,*" I beg, tears biting my eyes.

The thickening along the wall spreads, blotting Draven from sight. A cold blast of air shoves against me so hard I'm knocked away from the scene, left breathless in my own mind, standing right where I was, gripping that mating bond of ours.

The one that now has more crystals spread across it than before.

I glance to Cassiel, whose expression is laced with worry. He's silent as he motions for me to follow him, and I do, pulling out of myself until I open my eyes.

Exhaustion clings to my body as I look at Cassiel. We haven't moved from our positions on the bench, but I feel like we've just traveled across the entire Ather and back.

"He's there," Cassiel whispers.

"But he couldn't hear me," I say, devastation in my tone.

"We'll keep trying," Cassiel says. "Your bond..." He considers for a moment. "It might be the one thing that will allow us to reach him."

"And if it doesn't?"

Cassiel purses his full lips. "Then we'll have to burn the divine command out of him."

CHAPTER TEN

HARLEY

I feel the shift between realms like someone turns a page in a book. One second, we're flying through gray skies, nothing but ruins beneath us, and the next, a chilly wind stings my cheeks.

Cassiel's wings flap harder against the brutal wind before I draw flames to linger closer beneath my skin. The heat instantly warms me and, I hope, Cassiel.

He chuckles. "That's handy."

"Being the Antichrist isn't always the end of the world."

He banks, readying us to land. "You made a joke," he says. "You *did* sleep well."

"Thanks to you," I say, once again grateful for him. After we tried to reach Draven in the Dreamscape, I was so exhausted I passed out. Cassiel made sure I didn't dream. Didn't get swallowed by nightmares. There was nothing but pure, numb bliss, helping me awake fresh and ready to get another scroll.

"I do what I can," he says. "I much prefer a blank slate to your nightmares."

I gape at him, but he keeps his eyes steady on where we're about to land. "You've seen my nightmares?"

"Once," he says, almost sheepishly. "When I guarded you and Ray at The Bridge."

My mind casts back to that time, and I cringe. I still haven't shaken my nightmares about killing Kai or him trying to kill me. "You knew I was lying," I say, remembering that I'd told him I'd dreamed about snakes.

"You had every right to. I didn't mean to slip into your mind that night," he admits, the frost-covered ground coming closer to us. "You were crying out in your sleep, and my powers responded. I woke you up as soon as I realized what was haunting you."

I blow out a breath. "A girl can't have any secrets with you, huh?"

He laughs, righting us as he lands on his feet. Snow billows up around his black boots, and mine crunch it once he sets me down. "I will take better care around your mind from now on," he says. "And since you've let me in willingly, that will be much easier."

I blink against the cold as I scan the area. We've landed on a frost-covered bank, a cerulean ice-coated river right next to it. Orchid-colored mountains eat up the horizon, their peaks covered in arctic white, a sky in a constant state of aurora borealis behind them. On our right is a city of ice—houses and larger buildings scattered about the line of the river, warm lights flickering from the insides illuminating all manner of creatures going in and out. Slick streets carve their way between the lines of houses and buildings, creatures gliding along them with ease. Fires dance in pits made of ice, the contradiction beautiful and fascinating.

I glance up at Cassiel. "I thought this realm was supposed to be terrifying."

"It was," Cassiel says, frowning at the laughter we hear ringing through the glistening streets.

"It doesn't *look* menacing," I say, but I keep my eyes narrowed. I know better than anyone that you can never judge anything based off of appearance. Still, there is nothing about the bustling city that has my fight-or-flight instincts flaring.

"Come on," Cassiel says, urging me toward the heart of the city. "We have to find the scroll either way."

He's right. It doesn't matter if this is a peaceful realm or a terrifying one. We have to get the scroll no matter what.

We walk through the snow, leaving the river behind us. I stick close to his side, using my flames to cast a faint heat around us both. Neither of us are dressed for this climate, and without my powers our T-shirts would likely be frozen right along with our arms. At least our boots and pants keep us from entirely shivering.

We reach what looks like a main street and timidly step upon its slick surface. I hiss when I lose my footing, and Cassiel darts an arm out to steady me. The motion casts attention our way, and a female with mint skin, toned limbs, and wide eyes shrieks when she notices us.

I swing around, my flames ready for whatever monster is about to burst out of the shadows and try to chomp our heads off. After all, that's the only logical reason for the female to be shrieking and running away.

But there's nothing.

Just Cassiel and me.

I turn back to her, raising my hands to show her *we're* not here to attack, but she grabs hold of a younger version of herself and hauls her inside one of the crystal buildings, slamming the door shut behind her.

"That's your fault," I fire up at Cassiel.

"Me?" He scoffs. "You're the one flailing around like you've never seen ice before. Aren't you from Chicago?"

I roll my eyes. "*Yes*. I've dealt with plenty of brutal winters before. But I'm not exactly wearing snow boots." I gesture at my worn-out moto boots, and he laughs.

In front of us, more creatures are fleeing the streets, slamming their doors behind them—presumably at the sight of us. What the hell?

At the apex of the main road rests the largest building, a palace of pure ice shaded in hues of cobalt and navy. A large crest is carved in the upper center of the palace, an intricate snowflake design that is breathtaking and screams authority.

"Guessing the boss lives there," I say. I take another step down the street and slip until I hit the hard ground. "Seriously. What kind of ice *is* this?"

Cassiel tries to cover his laugh with a cough.

I point a flaming finger at him. "I'll roast you," I say but laugh, too.

"You look like a baby deer," he says. "Come on." He glides toward me effortlessly as if there is no sort of terrain he hasn't dominated before. "I'll fly you to the door."

"If you don't, it'll take us hours to make it there."

"No doubt," he says.

We're on the front steps of the palace in no time, staring up at two wide doors covered in a light dusting of snow.

"Do we knock this time?" I whisper.

Cassiel shrugs. "The map says the scroll rests at the epicenter of the realm. And from what I saw from the sky view, this is it."

I suck in a steadying breath, nodding.

Cassiel bangs his fist on the icy door, the sound echoing throughout the now-quiet streets.

The doors groan open, two massive creatures taking up the entryway. They're tall with muscled bodies covered in grape-colored leathers. They have elongated ears, which taper into points near their hairless heads. Deep pine grooves shape intricate details on their mint-colored skin, and their eyes are matching shades of plum.

"What business do you have here?" the one on the right asks, his tone rough as he points a sharp spear of ice at me.

I eye the weapon but try not to immediately react. "We need to see your boss," I say. When both of them blink at me, I add, "Leader?"

"Who are you?" the guard asks, glancing between the two of us. I have half a mind to ask them who the hell *they* are. We expected to meet ruin and hell-legend stuff here, and yet we've found a city of ice. A beautiful one at that. With people way too skittish to be threats.

"Tell the leader Rainier's daughter needs to speak with them," I finally say, opting for civility over the smash-and-grab instincts brewing inside of me, especially with how well that *didn't* go last time. I need the scroll, and I need it fast. I don't have time for political bullshit, and if I have to pull my rank to get us seen, then so be it.

"You're the daughter of the king of the Ather?" the one on the left gasps, lowering his weapon just slightly when I nod.

"And guest," I say, motioning toward Cassiel.

They both barely hide a shudder as they take in his wings and eyes, no doubt feeling the gravitational pull of death that clings to his skin.

"Prove it," the one on the right says.

I sigh and snap my fingers, and my right hand is engulfed in the midnight and silver flames of my father. Then I show him the ring, and his stance softens.

"Come this way," he says, both guards sliding over the ice with absolute ease as they lead us deep inside the palace.

The air is just as cold inside as it is outside. The hallways twinkle under golden flames that dance in mini ice pits protruding from the walls. The ice is a bit more textured in here, so fortunately, I manage to stay on my own two feet as they lead us to a grand room through two more giant doors.

A male of the same likeness as his guards sits on a chair at the head of a giant oval table made of ice. It's polished and gleaming, but there are tomes and papers scattered all across it as the male looks over them.

"Sir," one of the guards says, and the male looks up. "You have visitors."

The male stands instantly, his chair nearly tipping over as he glides over the slick floor, skidding to a halt right in front of us. He's nearly as tall as Cassiel.

His skin is mint, too, but the grooves on his face are more distinguished than those of his guards, and I can feel power radiating off of him — a crisp sort of strength.

"She's the daughter of Rainier," his guard provides.

I don't know if I'm expected to bow or wave or do a little

figure skating, so I just try to make my face as calm as possible.

"Are you really?" the male asks, and I nod, demonstrating my flames again before he can ask.

He studies the ring on my finger before dipping his head just slightly. "Lysander," he says. "I rule over Pagos." He extends an arm to encompass the area around him. "The king has taken little interest in us over many cycles, so what business do you have here?"

I arch a brow at his tone. "Rainier has been trapped in his own realm since before you likely were born," I say coolly. "And forgive me, but my friend and I weren't exactly expecting a functioning realm when we came here."

The grooves on Lysander's forehead pull together, and then he huffs. "You wouldn't, had I not worked and *bled* to create what you see before you now." Pride ripples from him, and I can't really blame him. If he turned this realm into a peaceful one, then good for him. "Before I amassed an army big enough to push back the frost demons, Pagos was a realm of ruin. The one Rainier likely told you about because that's the last he heard news of it." He sighs. "I've tried to send many a correspondence across the realms to seek his council, but if he's been as you say—*trapped*—then now I know why those pleas went unanswered."

"What did you need from him?" I ask.

"Aid," he says, and I remember the Overlord mentioning certain realms requesting aid. "Or I did," he continues. "I suppose I still do in some regards, but in others, my people overcame. We carved out a life here for ourselves that doesn't involve death and bloodshed at any given moment."

"Your people ran from us the second they saw us," I say. "So, not *all* threats have been eliminated, right?"

His head bows to the floor. "No," he says, "though the attacks have been less frequent since we've driven the frost demons beyond our claimed territory." He eyes the two of us. "We're always prepared for an attack because of how close we live to their border. And strangers don't venture this far into the Ather. They likely saw you and immediately assumed a threat. But you two didn't come here to talk about wars and history, so I'll ask you again—what business do you have here?"

Cassiel and I share a look, a silent question of if we should lay our cards on the table or lie. After a few seconds, I decide I don't want to lie. I'll be taking the scroll either way; no need to play games about it.

"We're here for the scroll," I say.

Lysander straightens, eyes gleaming. "Of course you are," he says. "The very scroll that helped me create all this." He opens his arms, spinning in a graceful circle over the ice before facing us again.

"You're able to wield it?" Cassiel asks.

Lysander laughs, shaking his head. "No, decidedly not."

"Then how—"

"I don't know how the magic imbued in the scroll works," he says. "I haven't even seen it beyond its casing, and I certainly wouldn't be rash enough to try and pry it open and attempt to read something written by the Creator. But the scroll loaned its great power to me. Deemed me worthy." Pride twinkles in his eyes. "Deemed my *people* worthy, and my mission."

"And that was?"

"To create a place not of terror and death and carnage, but one of hope. Of peace. Create a place where the people of Pagos could love and grow and learn. The scroll created and gave us barriers that keep the frost demons away most of the time. Sometimes, they break through."

I study him but don't detect a hint of deception in his eyes. More than that, my powers are testing his, and they don't hold the tinge of evil I've felt in so many others.

"You've done amazing work," I say, "but I need the scroll."

"And you think because you're a princess you can just take it?" The grooves in his forehead bunch together.

Flames flicker in my chest at his tone. "I can take it because

I'm the only one who can. Me and my father."

"That may be true," he says, folding his arms over his chest. "But millennia change things. The scroll has assisted me on more than one occasion. It's bonded to me, and I to it. Without my approval, it will not be removed from its resting place."

I sigh, lassoing the flames at the edges of my fingers.

"See for yourself if you do not believe me." He spins around and glides through his grand room, gracefully stopping before a pillar of ice that connects with the ceiling. The pillar stands tall next to a crystal throne carved with delicate snowflakes.

Lysander extends a mint-colored hand toward the center of the pillar. My eyes instantly catch on a smooth, circular disk the size of my palm embedded in the pillar. It looks like some vintage compact the colors of teal and pearl, the piece of scroll we need no doubt protected inside. Thin white lines and dots decorate the top, the design looking like snow blowing in the wind.

I reach for it, smoothing my hand over the ice before wrapping my fingers over the compact. I tug, but a zap of arctic cold lashes through my bones, sending my flames hissing like a startled cat, and I yank my fingers back.

Well, shit.

CHAPTER ELEVEN

HARLEY

Lysander laughs, shaking his head. "I told you. You are not the first to try and take it from me." He moves before me, plucking the compact from the pillar. He tosses it up and down a few times before putting it back in its resting place. "Even the frost demons tried. I think that's why the scroll bound itself to me. It knew I would never use it for evil, like they would certainly try to do."

I look up at Cassiel, whose face is grim, before I turn back to Lysander. "I *need* that scroll," I say, desperation leaking into my tone.

Lysander studies me as he strokes the grooves along his chin. "I do not know you. Regardless of your bloodline, I don't know what your intentions are. How am I to hand over something so powerful, so *precious*, when you could use it for harm?"

I blow out a breath, anger rising in me like a raging current. I don't have time for this. I need that scroll to save my sister. My mate. I dig in the pack at my hip, retrieving the bronze casing and showing it to him.

"I already have one scroll," I say. "Doesn't that prove I'm worthy?"

"No," he says, though his eyes are wide as he looks at the casing. "It merely proves you are strong."

I pocket the bronze tube again, throwing my head back and inhaling deeply as flames engulf my arms. Lysander steps back, his guards skating over on nothing but their boots faster than I can blink to stand before him.

"I'm not going to hurt you." I grind out the words. The ring on my right hand pulses with power, almost like it's responding to my anger, to my panic, and supplying me with more power than I can handle. By the time I catch my breath, I have enough power rolling through me to light up this entire frozen city.

"Harley," Cassiel says, his voice calm, cool, soothing. "We'll do whatever it takes."

I nod, and a little of the overwhelming power settles back down in my veins.

"What's it going to take, Lysander?" I ask. "I am Rainier's daughter. I have say with him. And I'll be queen of the Ather someday."

"Being royalty doesn't prove your worth," he counters, his spine straightening.

I clench my jaw. All my life, I've had people tell me I'm worthless, useless, and won't amount to anything.

I'm over it.

"I've had many test my worth before," I say in a low tone. My ex-father. Marid. Rainier's damn Overlord and his weird desolate island. "I'm still standing," I say, extending my hands, balls of fire hovering above them.

Lysander and his guards eye them warily, and with half a thought, they're gone.

"Tell me," I say. "What can I do to prove it to you?"

He looks to his guards, and the three glide farther away, whispering to one another.

After several deep breaths, Lysander glides back over, hope lighting his eyes.

He motions to the table covered in papers. "The frost demons raided us last week," he says, his shoulders dropping. "We fought back, but they stole a handful of my people and an entire herd of pagles."

I frown. "What are pagles?"

He smooths his hands over his bald head. "Sacred animals that provide us with much-needed resources. We were strategizing a rescue mission," he says, pointing to the maps and papers laid on the table. "But my heart is heavy, as I know not all my soldiers will survive a battle with the frost demons on their own territory."

A hopeful gleam flashes in his wide plum-colored eyes. "But you... You're Rainier's daughter. You're strong enough to take a scroll from its resting place." A grin shapes his lips. "You could easily get them back with no casualties on our end."

My brows raise. "These frost demons—are there any among them that are innocent?" Because it would be so much easier if there weren't any. Then we could simply wipe them all out in one fell swoop.

Even as the thought fills my mind, I try to find the horror at where my mind went. But I can't. Maybe I'm totally and utterly broken. Maybe these powers are slowly transforming me into a hardened, unsympathetic thing. Maybe I just need my world to right itself again by getting my mate and sister back. I don't know and don't have time to figure it out.

"Hard to tell," Lysander answers honestly. "The only encounters we've had are with their soldiers, who have orders from their king to raid and steal and kill."

Great. "An evil king doesn't necessarily mean an evil people."

"Quite right, princess," he says. "But those who've attacked us? They're brutal, ruthless, and have little mercy." Something heavy flashes over his eyes. "I worry none of my people or animals are still alive. But I have hope and won't give up on them."

I glance at Cassiel, his dark brows scrunched together as he gives me one firm nod. Guess we're doing this, then.

I turn back to Lysander. "If I rescue your people and creatures, you'll give me the scroll?"

He nods once. "Yes."

"And what if we get there and there are no survivors?"

He flinches at my question, blinking rapidly before

straightening his spine. "Then I will commend you on your efforts to relay to the king that you are now my ally and it wouldn't be a good idea to cross into our lands ever again."

"Of course," I say, reaching out my hand so we can shake on it. It's not like I can have him sign a contract or anything to prove he'll actually do what he says. Just like he can't for me.

He eyes my hand curiously, then reaches out to clutch my left shoulder with his right hand, dipping his head slightly. I catch on, sending my left hand to grip his right shoulder.

If all Lysander is saying about the frost demons is true, then they're preying on innocent creatures, and that's never going to sit right with me.

"Show me the way," I say when he releases me.

"And me," Cassiel says, standing taller at my side.

"Show *us* the way," I amend, and Lysander's grin deepens.

"My guards will take you to the outskirts of Pagos that border the frost demons' city." He waves an arm, and his guards move toward the doors to the great room.

Cassiel and I follow the pair, something in my gut tugging at me, begging me to go back and snatch that scroll and run for it.

Fire is deadly to ice. I could destroy this city with a few sweeps of my power.

And the power inside me *wants* that.

I shut that shit down *real* fast. The Pagos people are peaceful, like Conilis. If I really am going to be the queen of the Ather someday, I can't rule with a fist of fire.

Still, the urge to raze this place is there. A temptation to use the growing powers in my blood to gain whatever I want, whenever I want, is tugging at the edge of my control, threatening to run rampant in my mind if I let it.

I squash it down, tamping on it until it's nothing but dust in my soul.

There is *nothing* I can't face, can't survive.

Except the loss of Ray, which I absolutely won't allow to happen.

An evil frost demon king and a rescue mission? Bring it on.

"I truly hope you don't die," Lysander calls when we reach the giant doors.

I glance over my shoulder at him. "You might be the first one to ever utter those words," I say, flashing him a smirk. "Have the scroll ready for when we return with your people."

CHAPTER TWELVE

HARLEY

"We go no farther," one of the guards says as he slows his vehicle over the ice.

The vehicle hovers by some sort of magic, and with snow seats, I'm more than happy to hop out of it.

He's spent the entire ride describing his people and the creatures.

In the distance, a distinct border separates the peaceful city from a much more desolate-looking piece of their realm—a stretch of ice wall that's superficial in size. It's miles from the city but close and easy enough to climb over that it's no wonder the people of Pagos live in a constant state of fear.

"Please bring our people home," the other guard says as Cassiel steps out of the vehicle.

"Any tips?" I ask.

"Be quick," the guard says. "If our people *are* still alive, the king is likely holding them in his palace on the lower levels. If you're lucky, only a leech servant will be guarding them. If you come across the frost demons, hit *hard*." He waves as he turns his ice vehicle around, leaving us in the snow-coated dust.

"Are you as worried about the *leech servant* thing as I am?" I ask, shivering. "I so don't want some giant creature latching onto me and sucking my blood. I mean, I was all for Klaus Mikaelson taking a bite out of my neck, but that was before Draven blew him out of the water."

Cassiel gapes down at me. "Sometimes it's like you don't speak English."

I laugh. "Ready?"

"Always," he says, and we clamber over the slick ice wall together.

If Pagos is a bright, idyllic ice city complete with a snowflake palace, this place is its exact opposite. The ice creating this realm is shaded in darker tones of denim, the snow a dirty-spruce color as we crunch through it. And there are no orderly buildings and homes—just tons and tons of deep blue ice jutting up from the ground to tower over our heads, their sharp points seeming to touch the sky.

Despite the gloomy look, I'm amazed by these realms of the Ather, and an appreciation I can't deny rises in my chest. This is my home—*all* of the Ather, regardless of the evil/non-evil status of the realms. I adore this place. I want to make it my true home with Draven.

We'd made plans those three weeks in Conilis. Silly, happy plans that involved a future filled with passion and freedom and fun. I wanted to take Draven to a Dermot Kennedy concert in the fall if we could sneak out of the Ather for a few hours. He wanted to find a legendary realm in the Ather, rumored to have the magical equivalent of hot springs and waterfalls.

But Aphian stole that from us.

Pain shoots through my veins, my power morphing into anger that thrashes like a wild animal demanding blood. Aphian's blood. The Seven's blood. I want to bathe in it, swim in it, splash around and laugh—

"Harley," Cassiel warns, pausing in the middle of a winding path. "Are you okay?"

I clench my eyes shut, casting out the murderous thoughts ripping through my mind. My soul feels like it's standing on the edge of some vast cliff and the power bubbling in my blood is there, ready to push me over.

"I'm fine," I say, my hand automatically reaching for Wrath but only finding cool air at my fingertips. The hellhound has been more of a support for me in times like these than I've realized, and I'm totally regretting not bringing him along.

"Are you sure—"

Footsteps crunch in the distance, and we dart behind a thick stalk of ice.

I hold my breath, peering around the wide edge of it. Thirty yards away, a fourteen-foot-tall giant dressed in nothing but a black loincloth lumbers by. Muscles upon muscles bunch beneath its royal blue skin, and some sort of crystal weapon protrudes from a strap on its back. Sharp ice juts from its shoulders, curving and tipping in serrated points, and I can just make out eyes of pure crimson as it turns to look behind it.

Which is when I realize there's not just one giant; there's a whole damn *dozen* of them. They're heading in a line toward something I can't see from this angle, and I'm just grateful they haven't spotted us. The ground shakes from their movements, and Cassiel and I stay silent until they're well out of sight.

"Holy shit," I whisper. "Lysander could've told us they were *giants*."

Cassiel smirks. "Would that have deterred you?"

I creep around the edge of the ice. "Not a chance."

The giants' footsteps are easy enough to follow. Cassiel stays close as we quietly trek along the path they left behind. Before too long, a winding palace dominates the horizon. It's made of the denim-colored ice, its exterior formed by chunks that twist upward in jagged spikes toward the dark sky. The base is surrounded by black soil that glitters underneath the torches lining the palace grounds.

We pause behind an outcropping, surveying the massive structure that's big enough to hold a thousand giants, let alone the dozen we saw before.

"There," Cassiel whispers, eyes trained on an opening that looks like a massive cave. It's on the left side and farther back than the dominating entrance in the front. "That looks like it lowers into the ground."

I nod, noting the slight dip in the cave's floor. Without further discussion, we work our way over to the opening in silence, using random spikes of ice as cover. We hesitate a moment at the lip of the entrance, and I strain my ears for any hint of the giant demons we saw before.

A few whimpers echo up from the cave, the sounds of anguish pricking my heart. I arch a brow to Cassiel, and we move inside.

The walls are blue-black and glistening, the smell of tepid water and mud hanging in the air. My powers hover beneath my fingertips as we venture deeper into the palace, this tunnel sloping down so much I have to walk at an angle to keep from slipping. Flames flicker from torches jabbed into the walls, but there isn't a single guard in sight.

Nothing but those whimpers growing louder the farther we make it down the cave.

"Something isn't right," I say as the ground levels out, indicating we've reached the lower levels of the palace. "This is too easy."

Cassiel grunts his agreement.

The space between torches lengthens until the distance is so vast we're plunged in darkness for minutes at a time. It slows our progression, but I don't dare use my flames to guide us, not wanting to draw attention to us if I don't have to.

A faint glow radiates blue ahead, and we head toward it, our steps slow and calculated. I take another step toward the light—

Crack!

I freeze, the sound halting the blood in my veins as I feel the ground shift beneath me. Flames roar on my hands, the silver flecks illuminating the room we're in.

We stand on a pillar of ice that is only big enough for the two of us, the strip we walked in on no wider than a rope bridge. Four different slides surround the pillar, plunging downward into a pit of darkness.

Cassiel's wings flare, and I blow out a breath. Having a companion that can fly is truly—

A scream rattles the walls around us, jolting me in the

silence. I raise my fists toward the roar that's only growing louder and nearly swallow my own tongue at the sight of the creature flying toward us.

Its wings and skin are the color and texture of oysters, with four spindly limbs hanging from its elongated body. Instead of hands or talons or claws, its arms fling about like they have no bones. They curl and flick like tentacles, and its face is nothing but a mouth with rows upon rows of serrated teeth.

Cassiel spins around so we're back-to-back, nearly slipping on the ice as another of the creatures flies toward us from the opposite side.

"Can they see us?" I whisper under my breath, trying like hell to keep my feet steady on the slick surface.

"I don't know," Cassiel answers just as quietly, his wings pressing against me.

"They don't have any eyes," I say. "Maybe they don't even know we're here."

"Wishful thinking," he says.

I draw my flames into balls, ready to chuck if they get too close. I barely even blink for fear of missing their flight patterns—

A sucking noise, like silicone against glass, sounds below my feet. I gasp as my flames illuminate another creature climbing up at us from below the pillar. It shrieks and lashes a tentacle around my ankle.

"Shit," Cassiel says.

I send a ball of fire at the creature, my dark flames slicing right through the tentacle. It wails as the thing slides off my ankle, then snaps its other one at me. I dodge on instinct—

And slip.

A scream climbs up my throat as I soar down one of the slides, my hair flying back from the speed. I scramble for purchase, but I can't grab hold of anything as I plummet down into the darkness.

"Harley!" Cassiel roars, and I look up. He's flying right for me, but a creature slams into him, hauling him in the opposite direction.

"Cassiel!" I call back, flipping around as I desperately try to stop my momentum.

The slide abruptly changes directions, and my head smacks into the hard side of it as it spirals down, spitting me out against a hard-as-fuck floor, and everything goes black.

CHAPTER THIRTEEN

HARLEY

Something cold and wet presses against my cheek, and I swear I can feel an axe lodged into the base of my skull.

Pain zings along my bones, shooting my mind with awareness. I bolt upright, scrambling away from a creature that looks like a mini mammoth, only instead of fur it has ice crystals hanging from its body. Two curving tusks peek from its mouth, a long blue tongue hanging past its lips as it chases where I retreat, its cobalt eyes glowing.

It leaps atop me, sliding that ice-cold tongue along my face again. "Hey, there," I say and gently push it off. These must be the pagles Lysander's guard described.

There are several more huddled in a corner of the cavern I'm tucked inside. I manage to get my feet under me, scanning the small space with ice walls and a dark soil floor. There are no doors, just a gaping hole high above me from where the slide ended, and there is no sign of Cassiel.

The pain on the back of my head flares from where I hit the slide, and I finger the wound. It's a knot the size of an egg, and it's bleeding.

The little mini-mammoth pagle at my ankles winds between them like a cat desperate for attention. The other six join it, and soon I'm struggling to stand as they swarm me. They aren't attacking me with those tusks, though, so that's something.

"It's okay," I say, soothing them and myself. "I'm going to get you out of here."

Anxiety claws its way through my veins as I remember

Cassiel being attacked by that flying leech creature. I need to find him.

I eye the opening high above me, then the slick ice below it, trying to calculate how I can climb out of here. My palms slide against the ice, but there's nothing to grip. Rainier's pack is still firmly strung across my chest, so that is a major relief. I don't know how long I was knocked out, but at least the pack didn't fly off when I fell down the slide.

The ground rumbles—not from my powers but from something else—and the pagles whimper and bolt to the farthest corner of the cave. I eye them as they huddle together, trembling, their glowing blue eyes blinking rapidly.

"What is it—"

The dark ice wall to the far left grinds upward, and six of the oyster-colored leech demons spill into the room.

"Shit," I hiss, backing up as they clatter inside, their long tentacle limbs sucking at the ground and their serrated teeth gleaming as they chomp at the air in front of me.

The whimpering I heard earlier mounts, the little pagles trying their best to tunnel through the walls with their tusks to get away from these things.

And I *hate* it.

Hate the way these creatures are so outmatched against the demons who took them. I shift my stance, placing myself between the leeches and the pagles, flames instantly roaring on my fingers.

The burst of power without delay is alarming, but fuck it. These things deserve to be torched.

"They're mine," I say, not entirely sure if these things can understand me.

From the way they hurry their pace inside? I'm betting they can.

Six on one aren't my favorite odds, especially with those seemingly never-ending rows of teeth, but I shrug and raise my fists.

"Who's first?" I ask, swirling the flames in my palms while also reaching for the ground beneath their tentacles.

The leech closest to me flaps its rubbery wings, launching its body into the air, tentacles flaring and reaching for me.

I hurtle a dark-flamed spear at the center of its neck, the fiery weapon hitting its mark. The leech plummets to the ground, a sickening *thwack* echoing off the walls. The remaining five roar so loud I almost cover my ears, but they're racing for me, so I do no such thing.

One on the left lashes its long tentacles at me so fast I have to tuck and roll to miss it. It tries to latch those teeth onto my leg, but I use my control over the ground to ensnare it, yanking it down and down until the dark soil swallows it whole. I grin, rolling back to my feet, only for a slimy tentacle to hit me right in the gut.

I double over, momentarily stunned. I can't breathe, but I manage to right myself as air slowly trickles back into my lungs.

A yelp sounds from behind me, and I whirl toward the sound. The leech who knocked me out of the way has a pagle in its grip, yanking it by its little ankle and dragging it toward its slobbery mouth full of razor-sharp teeth.

Oh, *hell* no.

I swing my arms, gathering as much dark flame as I can into a giant fireball, and send it crashing into the leech demon. It screeches, releasing the pagle, who scrambles back to its herd before the leech disintegrates from my fire.

I spare a glance at the herd of pagles, finding them all accounted for before I spin back around to face the remaining four leeches.

They've spanned out in a horseshoe formation, those long feelers rolling and cracking like whips at the ground near my feet. I lift my arms, drawing on my power to latch on to two more of the demons, jerking them beneath the ground until they're inhaling dirt.

Sweat pops from my brow, my body and power tiring

against the effort. I suck in a sharp breath, tipping my chin at the last two. The one on the right catapults into the air, its wings flapping and sending rancid-smelling air soaring past me. I duck, thinking it's aiming for my head, but it soars over me, heading straight for the defenseless pagles.

I race toward it, grabbing onto its wing. It snarls, whipping its head toward me, those teeth dangerously close to my hand. Flames lick over my skin, and the thing wails as I hold on, not letting it get one grubby tentacle near the pagles—

A wet, hot something wraps around my stomach, jerking me back so fast my vision doubles. I lose my hold on the leech and gasp for breath as I bash my flaming fists into the tentacle around my waist.

The leech I let go of crashes to the ground, its wing still engulfed in my flames. It thrashes as it tries to snuff them out, and I struggle in the other's hold, but its grip only tightens as it slowly curls its limb inward, winding me closer and closer toward its gaping maw.

The little pagles rush past the flaming leech, running straight for *me*. They spear and slash at the leech with their tusks, but they're no match for a thing that's made of pure muscle and teeth.

My vision splinters as I try to draw breath, but the grip is choking the life from my body, causing my flames to sputter on my fingers and my hits to lose strength. That rancid, hot breath rushes over my face as I'm drawn closer to that pulsating mouth, the teeth drenched in what looks like old blood.

I'm going to puke. Maybe if I aim for its mouth, it'll drop me.

Something dark spears into the cavern, yanking me out of the demon's grip before dropping me on the ground.

"*Cassiel.*" I choke out the word, relief barreling down my soul at the sight of my friend. He's bloody, his shirt ripped to shreds, but he's whole. I don't have time to ask what happened before the leech whose wing I'd set on fire lashes out at me. "Welcome to the party."

"I got held up." He faces the leech that just tried to make a meal out of me, shifting on his feet. "You good?"

"Yep," I say, sending a fireball toward its flailing tentacle, and it draws back. "You?"

"Yep."

He murmurs something under his breath, and the leech he's got a hold of wails like he's sliding a blade into its neck. Despite the cave walls being made of ice, I swear the temp in the room drops ten degrees. Cassiel raises his voice, and it's only then that I realize he's using his powers to call to the demon's soul. It's a language I can't understand and sounds a lot like Khal Drogo speaking Dothraki in *Game of Thrones*. It's all sharp and haunting and raises chills along my neck.

The leech in front of me snaps its feeler at me again, and with new breath in my lungs, I send a blade of fire straight over it. The tentacle falls to the ground, the leech wailing as its blood spurts from the wound. I send another blade for its head, silencing it.

I turn around, watching as the last remaining leech demon goes completely rigid as Cassiel towers over it. A whirl of sickly green air seeps from the demon, drawing toward Cassiel's raised palm. He jerks his arm back before punching the air toward the opening of the cavern, sending that green wind soaring up the slide until it's out of sight. The demon's body slumps to the ground.

"Was that the leech's *soul*?"

"Yes," he says, a muscle in his jaw ticking.

"You're hurt?" I ask, eyeing the blood on his chest.

"It'll heal," he says, then glances behind me. "You found them."

"Yep," I say, then crouch down to pet the pagles at my feet. "Thanks for trying to help me," I say as one leans into my hand. Its fur is a mixture of ice and wool, but I comfort it as long as I can before I have to draw my hand back.

"I found the residents of Pagos," Cassiel says.

I stand back up. "Close?" I ask, running my hand along my side with a wince.

He frowns. "I thought you said you were fine?"

"I *am* fine," I say, sighing. "But having a bloodsucker try to turn me into a Fruit Roll-Up isn't exactly a day at the spa."

He flashes me an incredulous look. "What?"

I wave him off. "Where are the people?"

"Another cavern," he says. "Just out that way." He nods to where the leeches came inside.

I head that direction. The pagles grunt as they follow me. Cassiel eyes the little creatures but shrugs and hurries to the front to lead the way.

We move down a tunnel that is way too narrow for my liking, twisting and turning until it finally opens up to another cavern. This one has no ceiling; instead, it's nothing but high walls of dark ice that open up to another area of the palace I can't quite make out and totally don't want to at this point. If the frost demons employ those leech demons as their servants? I'm not too keen on standing toe to toe with them if I don't have to.

"After that leech attacked me," he says, "I spotted them when flying to find you."

Gasps ring out as I step deeper into the room, finding it filled with eight people of Pagos, easily identifiable by the beautiful mint color of their skin and the deep grooves decorating their heads. Their clothes are filthy, and they look starved, some with wounds along their limbs while others just look terrified.

I swallow hard, wondering what the hell kind of abuse they've suffered at the hands of the frost demon king.

The pagles rush past me, hurrying toward their people. All but one—the same one who led the charge when the leech demon almost ate me for dinner. It stays close to my ankle.

"We're here to help you," I say to the people of Pagos as gently as possible.

"Who are you?" one of the females asks.

"I'm Harley," I say, then clear my throat. "I'm the daughter of Rainier."

Shocked stares roam over me, several of the Pagos people taking calculated steps back.

"Lysander sent us," Cassiel adds.

Some relief flashes in the female's eyes before she looks at the pagle near my feet. "She likes you."

"I'm pretty fond of her myself," I say, leaning down to pet the pagle again. A tiny purr rumbles from its chest as it leans into my touch. "She helped save my life."

The female nods. "Whatever plan you have needs to happen fast. The guards do rotations. Yank several of us out at a time and have us do the king's bidding."

Bile creeps along my throat. "When are they coming back?" I ask, chewing on my bottom lip. There is no way Cassiel can fly us all out at once. Even doing the trip one at a time would exhaust him by the end of it.

"Soon."

I eye the walls of the cavern. There is a crease along one, and I smooth my hand over it. "We'll have to hurry, then."

Because if we don't, I have a feeling we'll all die.

CHAPTER FOURTEEN

HARLEY

I push my flames against the wall. The dark fire spreads, melting through the thick wall of ice I know to be a doorway because it's identical to the one that rose when the leeches came after me.

The Pagos people are on their feet behind me as the doorway melts and opens large enough to let us pass through. Cassiel falls to the back, ensuring the Pagos people and pagles are guarded at the back as I take the lead.

Tunnels turn into stairways, and I know it's risky, but we can't possibly go back the way we came. If we're getting out of here, it'll have to be forward.

"Take a right at the head of the stairs," the female says to me. "That will lead you down the kitchen staff's hallway. There's an exit at the end of it."

"Noted," I say, pausing when we reach the top of the stairs. I carefully peek around the corner, checking that the pathway is clear.

Not a tremor of a giant rumbles the ground, and all I can see are the elaborate dark walls of the ice palace, so I wave my group onward. I turn to the right like she said, sighing at the sight of the opening at the end of the hall, exposing the brutal icy outdoors. We're so close. All we have to do is make it into the dark ice forest—then we can use it as cover as we make our way back to Lysander.

I step to the side when we're halfway there, ushering the Pagos people to move faster toward the exit. The little pagles' paws kick up the dark soil of the floors, but they're faster than they look, following their people with all the effort they can spare.

Cassiel's eyes are hopeful as he reaches me, and we walk side by side as the first of the Pagos people makes it to the opening—

Only for a slab of ice to slam shut before they can step one foot outside.

Adrenaline spikes in my blood, my powers pulsing as a deep voice shakes the space behind me.

"You dare steal from me?"

I turn around, my fingers trembling with the surge in my veins.

The giant before me is bigger than the dozen who stand behind him, and a crown that looks like it's made of shards of glass sits on his head. He holds a scepter in his right hand, the staff as long as his body, and he clanks it once against the ground. The frost demons behind him shift their stance with military precision, all retrieving their blades from the sheaths on their backs.

"Retrieve my possessions," the king orders his guards.

"No," I snap.

The king tilts his head, amusement flickering in his eyes as he raises a hand to stop his guards. "What did you say?"

"They aren't possessions," I seethe. I can't lose these people here. I *won't*. "They're innocents from Pagos, and you have no right to take them like you did."

The king laughs, the braying sound booming against the massive walls of his palace. "If they were worthy, they would fight for themselves." He motions to his guards. "You earn what you kill here. If they were meant to be anything other than my servants, then they would've killed me already and taken the crown for themselves."

Rage thrums through my blood, awakening something new. Something cold and vast and endless. My birthright ring sparks on my finger. "You will *not* touch them."

The king rolls his crimson eyes. A snap of his fingers, and his guards are before him, the tips of their blades aimed at my chest.

Cassiel's wings snap out, but I raise a finger to stop him.

The king notes the move. "Who are you?"

I eye the sharp points of the blades almost kissing my chest, then look back up at him. "I'm Princess of the Ather," I say. I feel the powerful whisper of something unlocking inside my soul, another piece of the puzzle that surrounds my heritage dropping into place.

Rainier's powers. They're unraveling like a spool of thread inside me, and my body is vibrating from the intensity of it.

"You have no authority here, little princess." His eyes glimmer. "But I do wonder what your father will pay to get you back from me. After I've used you as a pet for a while, of course."

I curl my lip at him, flames dancing over my skin as I move. The sharp tips of the guards' blades are an inch too close to my skin, but a burst of my flames sends the giants soaring backward, their blades clattering to the floor.

I gasp as those whispers inside me turn into all-out roars, and a new power unleashes itself inside me.

Ice.

Beautiful, deadly ice.

I flick my left hand, an arctic spear forming in a blink as I launch myself at the king, using my right hand and the earth in my blood to wield dark soil beneath me, gathering it in a pillar that propels me to the giant's eye level quicker than he can dodge. I hold that spear against the center of his chest.

"Yield," I say, my voice raspy with the power crashing open inside me.

He stumbles back a step. "Never." He jerks his scepter upward, the blade slicing the air right before my throat. I lean back enough to avoid being decapitated and shove the ice into his chest with all my might. It cracks through bone and muscle until I feel it scrape his spine.

The scepter clatters to the floor before he does, and I jump out of the way so he doesn't take me down with him. His huge body crashes to the ground with a thunderous *boom*, his crown rolling off his head.

I drop the soil at my feet, leaping back down, flames and ice at the ready for whichever guards are foolish enough to attack.

But the guards aren't charging us.

They're *bowing*.

"You killed our king. You become our new one," one of the frost demons says, daring to meet my eyes before dropping hers again.

I flounder for a response, then blow out a breath. "I am Princess of the Ather," I say loud enough for everyone to hear. "But I am not your leader. That duty goes to Lysander of the Pagos people."

I eye them, searching for hints of disgust, but find nothing but unflinching loyalty on their bowed faces. "You will abide by his rule. I'll be back to ensure you do."

"Yes, queen," they say in unison, and I cringe at the title, at their bowing, all of it.

"You," I say to the frost demon guard who spoke to me first. "What's your name?"

"Mina," she says, still bowing.

"Make sure your people know you are now ruled by Lysander and the people of Pagos are protected. Meet with Lysander at the border. He's your new king and will usher in peace."

"It will be done."

Cassiel nudges me with his elbow. "*Someone* sounds like a queen."

"I don't know what else to do," I grumble. "It's not like I can kill them all and be done with it. There could be innocents among them."

"And that's what makes you a queen," he says, pride in his eyes.

I wave him off, then turn back to Mina. "Do you have forms of transport?"

"Yes," she answers.

"We need them, please. I'm taking these people home."

Cheers erupt from the Pagos people behind me, and a little nudge at my ankle has me smiling down at the pagle who's been attached to me since we arrived.

It's not ten minutes before the frost demons supply us with our own vehicle, much like the Pagos ones, and we're speeding toward the border. We make it to the palace in record time, and I'm more than ready to wash the blood off my hands.

We slide into Lysander's grand room, his people rushing to embrace him. The little pagles do much of the same.

Lysander's eyes are lined in silver by the time he finishes with his people and heads straight for me, grinning widely. "You did it!"

"The king is dead," I say.

He gasps. "That makes you their new queen."

"I left that honor to you."

He blinks a few times. "You appointed *me* their leader?"

"I did," I say, stepping within an inch of him. "Tell me I didn't make a mistake."

Tears fill his eyes, but he blinks them away. He glides over to the pillar, plucking the compact from it and hurrying back over to me. "You could've taken the power for yourself, but instead passed it to me. I promise you here and now, you did not make a mistake," he says and plops the scroll's casing into my hand, closing my fingers around it. The sting from before is no longer there with his willing gift.

I uncurl my fingers, examining the smooth teal-and-pearl compact before tucking it safely into the pack on my hip.

Lysander steps back and bows deeply. "You are the true queen," he says. "And whenever you have need of me or my armies, we will answer your call."

Heat blooms on my cheeks, but I manage to nod. "Thanks,"

I say, sounding more like the eighteen-year-old I am than the queen everyone keeps expecting me to be.

The pagle at my ankles grunts softly, and I raise my brows to Lysander.

"Looks like you've earned a friend," he says.

"You're lucky to have them," I say. "She fought for me." I kneel down to give her a goodbye pat. "Thanks again. I'll try to come visit sometime."

The pagle grunts…unhappily? I frown.

Lysander laughs. "You couldn't shake that creature off if you tried. Pagles are loyal. Their ice crystals are medicinal, too, when melted down. She'll be a good asset to you."

"Wait, what?"

He smiles. "She's yours. Pagles are sacred, deeply intelligent creatures. They form bonds with certain people that cannot be broken." He motions between me and the pagle.

"She's mine?"

"And you're hers," he says.

Well, hell. Okay. Apparently, I'm collecting Ather pets.

"I'll take good care of her," I say, glancing down at her as she blinks her glowing cobalt eyes up at me. Wrath will have a field day when he meets his new baby sister. The thought almost has me laughing, but I manage to keep it in.

"Thank you," I say to Lysander, tapping the pack on my hip before turning toward the exit doors. The pagle keeps step with me, Cassiel at my right side.

"Two down," he says as we head out of the palace and onto the icy streets. Lysander must've spread the word, because his people are lining the streets, no longer fleeing from just the sight of us. "Well done, Queen."

"If you start calling me that, I'll start calling you Death Boy."

"Noted," he says, then glances down at the mini mammoth waddling at my side. "Now I have to carry it, too?"

"Please?"

"You're really taking advantage of the whole queen thing."

He gathers the pagle football-style under one arm and winds his other around my waist, then shoots us into the sky. "You'll have to hold on extra tight, since one of my arms is full of mini mammoth."

I grip him tighter. "I seriously hope one of Rainier's powers is flight and it surfaces soon, because I know this has to be exhausting for you."

The pagle, on the other hand, looks like it's smiling, its long blue tongue flapping in the wind.

"Not everyone can be as amazing as this," he teases. "But ice? That was brutal."

I swallow hard. "It came out of nowhere. But it feels natural, like I've always had it."

"More will likely come," he says, echoing Rainier's warning about what else my birthright ring will draw out of me.

Apprehension coils inside me at what else is lying in my blood, waiting to be unlocked, but I don't care what it is. "I hope they all surface. If it helps us get the scrolls—helps us give Rainier ultimate power so he can obliterate the Seven—I'm all for it."

Cassiel arches a brow at me. "And if it overwhelms you in the process?"

I feel the shift in the atmosphere as he passes us into a pocket realm. "Then I'll just have to take Aphian down with me."

I shudder at the sound of my name on her tongue. I release her wrist, and she shifts, timidly wrapping her arms around me. She lays her head on my chest, and I immediately return her embrace. Holding her feels like the most important thing I've ever done in my entire life.

So I hold her. Savoring each of her breaths as if the solid sound is music to my ears. Some unknown reassurance that as long as she's here, breathing and in my arms, then everything else will be all right.

After a while, she pulls back, reaching up to grab my neck, and draws me down until our mouths are only a breath apart. "If you don't kiss me, I may set the world on fire."

Her words have me cracking a smile, and her eyes light up as she focuses on my mouth.

"Say it again," *I demand, my heart racing.*

"Kiss me."

I slide my hands along her bare arms, savoring the feel of her skin beneath my fingers. She's not flinching or growing weak—my siphon powers don't harm her. If ever I needed proof this is a dream, then there it is. I haven't been able to physically touch anyone in ages. Not without draining the life from them.

She cups my cheeks and stretches up to crush her mouth to mine.

I growl from the taste of her, all mint and caramel and pure perfection. This is the best fantasy and the saddest reality.

I never want to wake up.

I'm content to stay here with this dream girl forever.

Tangling my fingers in her long hair, I tug her head back and kiss her at a deeper angle. A little moan slips from her lips as I slide my tongue against hers, teasing the edges of her teeth and bruising her lips until she's arching into my touch.

I groan, gripping her hip with my free hand and yanking her against me.

And then she's jerking her head back, her lips swollen from my kiss and her green eyes wild. She flashes me that wicked grin,

*then does a little hop, locking her legs around my hips. I grip
her thighs, relishing the way she feels in my arms.*

*"Fuck," I say as she arches against me, slanting her mouth
over mine.*

*"Draven." She says my name between our kisses. "I miss you
so much. I* need *you* to come back to me."

Something deep inside me wakes up at those words.

Sits up straight and listens.

Whatever this woman needs, I want to give it to her.

Anything.

Everything.

And if it's me she wants?

She's fucking got it.

*I kiss the corner of her mouth, the line of her neck, over her
collarbone, and lower. She tangles her fingers in my hair, nipping
at my bottom lip, and then she motions her head toward the bed.
I'm there, walking with her in my arms before I settle her on the
bed, and her smile makes me see fucking stars.*

Maybe that's what this girl is to me.

My night sky.

My ever-churning ocean.

My everything.

*She draws my mouth back to hers, and I devour her ragged
breaths. Everything in me narrows to the feel of her, the taste
of her.*

I've never felt anything as powerful, anything as sweet.

And every inch of me burns for this girl.

*"Tell me I'm still yours," she begs, drawing back enough to
look up at me.*

*"You're mine," I say, the words feeling more like a promise
than anything I've ever uttered before.*

*"You're still mine, too, Draven. You can't forget it. You have
to remember—" Her words bleed into breathless moans as I set
my mouth on her again, kissing every inch I can reach. "You've
got to remember," she whispers again as I make my way back*

up to her mouth.

Please don't wake up.

Keep me here forever.

I don't want to go back.

"What's your name?" I ask, hoping it will jar loose whatever this dream girl says that I'm forgetting, but she goes stiff beneath me.

Devastation colors her eyes. "Harley," she says, tears glittering on her cheeks now. I reach up and swipe a tear away with my thumb. "I'm Harley," she says again like I'm supposed to know that.

But this is my dream, and I didn't know her name.

She bites her bottom lip again, this time in worry, and I smooth my hand over her cheek.

"Harley." I test out the name, and it settles deep in my chest. "That's the most beautiful name I've ever heard."

She shudders, her shoulders shaking as she cries.

I sit up, holding her to me. "What's wrong?" I ask, desperate to take away her pain. Something inside me is churning like that ocean, demanding I help her. Soothe her. Make her smile again.

"I thought…" Her voice trails off.

A blaring sound beeps in the corner of my room. I ignore the sound, holding her tighter.

"I thought you knew," she says through her tears.

"Tell me," I demand, wiping away her tears as fast as they come. "Tell me what I'm supposed to know."

The blaring intensifies so much I can't hear her even though she's right next to me.

"You're my—"

I bolt upright in my bed, beads of sweat coating my body as I reach for my phone. I silence the alarm, chucking the thing to the end of the bed. Rubbing my palms over my face, I try to hold on to that dream.

But it's fading fast, and with it my chest feels like it's caving in on itself.

No, something is carving out my heart and roasting it on a spit.

There was a woman—a beautiful, perfect woman…

Already her face is fading from my mind. She had green eyes. Eyes that captivated me right down to my soul—

White-hot lightning shoots across my body and sears my mind. I bow back on the bed, grinding my teeth against the pain.

It ebbs, and I blow out a breath.

I note the crystal blue sky shining through my opened window and nod to myself.

Time to get to work.

I slide off the bed, hurrying to dress for the day. I graze my fingers over my lips, wondering at the tingling sensation there. The scent of fire and lilies lingers on my skin, and my mind stretches for a memory I can't place—

Electricity buzzes in my head, searing right down to my bones. I clench my eyes shut, straighten my spine, and breathe through it. I crack my neck, the pain subsiding, and head for the door.

It's a short walk to my charge's more luxurious quarters, and I don't bother knocking before striding inside.

Ray is sitting on the wide windowsill, her jean-covered knees tucked up to her chest, her long blond hair braided back and away from her face. She doesn't spare me a glance, just keeps her eyes trained on that ocean outside her window.

Something about it snags on that hook in my chest, and I can't help but rub at the spot like it can soothe that pain—

Fire lashes up my spine. Damn it. "Get up. It's time for your training."

Ray jolts as if she didn't hear me come in. She swings off the windowsill, tipping her chin up at me. Sadness flickers in her blue eyes as she looks me over. "Didn't sleep well?"

"I slept fine."

"You look like you were up all night."

I run a hand through my hair, the move carrying the damn

scent again—a crackling fire, a fresh vase of lilies.

"Training," I say, reduced to one-worded commands.

Ray sighs, nodding. "I hope we find out I can control fire or ice or maybe lightning like Ryder."

My brother's name clangs through me like a rock falling down a well.

She steps toward me, her eyes defiant as she looks up at me. "Because then I'm going to zap you so hard you'll remember me."

I glare down at her, my hands curling to fists at my sides. "You're no match for me, little seer."

She balks at my tone.

Then *laughs*.

She extends her hand toward me. "If you're so big and bad, then take my hand."

I jerk away from her without even meaning to, everything in my being yelling at me to back away. To run as far away as possible. But Aphian ordered me to train her under any means necessary, even if that meant using my siphon powers to motivate her.

She steps toward me, that hand reaching for mine, and I bolt away again. Because for some reason, the idea of harming Ray is abhorrent to me, and I have no idea why—

Acid trickles into all of my joints, blazing until my vision goes black for a second.

She halts, dropping her hand. "That's what I thought," she says, her tone drenched in sadness and a sort of determined resolve I can't even fathom. "Let's get started, then."

I suck in a sharp breath as it subsides, then nod to the girl. "Let's begin."

CHAPTER SIXTEEN

HARLEY

"Are you going to tell me what's bothering you, or are you going to just keep cringing every five seconds?" Cassiel asks as he flies us through the skies.

"Other than the fact that the Seven kidnapped my sister, blackmailed me, and turned my mate into a walking ghost?"

He cocks a brow at my tone. "It's more than that," he says, banking left. "I can tell. If you don't want to talk about it, that's fine."

I blow out a breath, the knife in my chest twisting a little deeper.

We slept in a pocket realm last night after leaving Pagos, and I'd been exhausted from the new power I discovered, too much to even test it further.

And then that dream…

The way Draven held me, gently and like he never wanted to let me go.

His smile; his kiss.

I groan, trying like hell to push the images out of my mind. It'd been so damn *real*.

Wait.

Heat explodes on my cheeks. "Cassiel," I say, my mouth dry.

"Harley." He mimics my tone, his silver eyes firmly on the sky ahead of us.

"You didn't…" My voice trails off, and I'm certain I'd rather jump out of his arms and plummet to the ground than ask this.

"What?"

"You didn't send me a dream last night, did you?" I blurt out the words on a rushed breath. The idea of him sending me into *that* Dreamscape—while amazing—is downright mortifying.

His brow pinches as he spares a look at me. "No, why?"

"You promise?"

He rolls his eyes. "You didn't ask me to. Why would I force you into a Dreamscape?"

I sigh heavily, the tension in my chest relaxing a fraction. "And you didn't, like, accidentally *see* my dream?"

He studies me for a moment, then bursts out laughing. It's the most real and raw laugh I've ever heard from him, but since it's directed at me, I end up smacking his chest on principle.

"Ow," he says, tapering off the laughter. "It just hit me. What you must've dreamed about to look that chagrined."

"God, you're ancient," I fire back. "No one says *chagrined* anymore."

"I do," he says. "So, clearly, *someone* does."

I roll my eyes, my cheeks still blazing.

"A good dream, then, I take it?" he presses, a barely contained grin on his lips.

I smack him again, and he free-falls just enough to make my stomach lurch. The pagle squeals and wiggles under his arm.

"*Ugh*," I groan when he finally levels out again.

"There is more to it," he says.

I arch a brow at him.

"You look like you're about to say something but keep stopping yourself," he explains.

I sigh. "The dream felt…incredibly real. And in it…" My heart twinges. "Draven didn't know me. I thought he did at first, with the way he acted." More heat sears over my skin, but I push on. "But he asked me my name. And I don't know, Cass. When I woke up…I swear I can still *feel* him. Smell him on my skin."

Cassiel clears his throat, focusing on the sky ahead of us more than necessary.

"Last time we tried to reach him through the Dreamscape,

a wall of ice blocked us. But it looked like the same room this time," I say. "Do you think I broke through?"

"I sure as hell hope so, Harley."

"Maybe it was just a dream, though," I say, not wanting to entertain the hope in my heart. "You said it was a power reserved for your kind and seers."

"I said extremely powerful beings can do it, too, with practice," he says. "And you're Rainier's daughter. There is no telling what other powers are going to crop up now that you accepted your birthright. Plus, you're Draven's *soulmate*," he says. "Do you know how rare and treasured that is among the supernatural?"

"Draven and I didn't really get a chance to dive into it," I say, biting my lip again. Sure, we talked about him keeping secrets from me, and then we spent the rest of the time exploring each other, loving each other, learning about the little things like favorite movies and books, the kind of music he liked. We thought we had time for everything else.

We were so wrong.

"You brought him back from death," he says.

I whip my head to him. "He told you about that?"

Cassiel nods. "Draven and I have known each other a long time," he says. "And when it came to you? He told me everything."

I think back to that night. To the way Draven had sacrificed himself to shut the gates on Marid and his brethren. To save the world. How I'd followed him into the dark, flying down our mating bond to yank his soul back to me.

"Your connection to him," he continues. "Being mates…" He shakes his head. "It's what allowed us to see him the first time we attempted to reach his Dreamscape, despite the divine commands trying to keep us out. Who is to say this dream of yours wasn't real?"

Hope flares in my chest, but it dies just as quickly. "He knew he was dreaming. And he had no clue who I was."

"He didn't hurt you, though, right?"

I shake my head.

"Then that means there is no standing order to harm you on sight. That's something."

I consider this. "Are you saying Aphian can use a divine command and Draven would hurt Ray?"

A muscle in Cassiel's jaw clenches.

"Draven told me a little bit about what happens when he's ordered to do things," I continue. "He told me that if Aphian ordered him to kill me, he'd have only enough time to tell me to kill him myself."

"It's true," he says. "Judges and those like me who are tied to the Seven's command can't refuse a divine order. However, not all the Seven like to inflict the commands as freely as Aphian and some of the others do."

"Fucking bastards."

Cassiel nods his agreement. "We're bound by a divine contract when we're called. Most of the time, our missions are willingly completed. I don't hate collecting souls," he admits. "I'm rather good at it. But there are times when I wish I could choose who *not* to collect."

I swallow hard, hating that their choices are stripped.

"So, if I piss Aphian off enough, he'll make good on his threat," I say, more to myself than Cassiel. "He'll force Draven to torture Ray."

"Could you do it?" he asks. "Could you kill him? If it came down to it? Like he asked?"

I recoil from the idea. Kill Draven? There's no way. I know what it feels like to watch him die, and to be the source of it? My entire soul rejects the idea so much my stomach turns over.

"I killed my best friend," I say instead of answering. "Did Draven tell you that?"

"He told me about Kai," he says.

"Did you know him?" He was a Judge, after all, before he turned on everyone.

"Not as well as Draven. But I met him once. I never liked him," he says, then glances at me. "Sorry."

"You don't need to be," I say, the old familiar guilt gnawing at my insides. How can I miss someone who was never real in the first place? "He fabricated our friendship. Violated my mind. I hated him for it, but even with that…"

"You miss him," he finishes for me.

"I miss the friend I thought I had."

"And he forced your hand," he says.

"I killed him before he could kill me, and I still have nightmares about it." Cassiel knows that better than anyone with what he saw that night at The Bridge.

He remains quiet, letting me sort through my thoughts.

"I thought he was my best friend—my *only* friend—and I killed him to stop him from bringing the world to ruin. But Draven?" I blow out a breath. "No. I won't ever be able to hurt him. And it won't come to that. I won't let it."

Cassiel eyes me but lets the subject drop. "After we collect all the scrolls, we have to be exceptionally smart."

"I know. We'll cross that bridge when we have them all." I nod toward the sky. "What are we facing in the next realm?" I ask, needing the distraction. "A split realm like Pagos, or something closer to the creepy-tree-house realm?"

He snorts at my description of the last one. "I wasn't expecting to find what we did in Pagos," he admits, sparing a glance at the little pagle's blue tongue flapping in the wind. "But if this realm hasn't changed—and I highly doubt it has—then we're facing something worse than the creepy tree house, worse than the leech servants of the frost demon king."

I groan. "Seriously?"

He dips his head. "It's rare, but I've ushered souls to this place," he says, his tone cold. "It's not a place I volunteer to go."

A knot forms in my throat. "What's its purpose?"

"You remember the purgatory legends?"

I frown. "A place where lost souls are taken to suffer until they're deemed worthy of leaving?"

He nods.

"But from what I've seen, the Ather isn't what the legends say."

"You're right. It's nothing like what historians have written about."

"Then why—"

"It's much worse," he says. "Wherever the scroll resides, it's no doubt guarded by the worst of the lost souls. The ones with little chance of ever escaping the realm. Whose crimes were so vicious in life, they will receive no freedom in death."

"You think we'll have to go through them in order to collect the scroll?"

"Yes."

Wonderful.

CHAPTER SEVENTEEN

HARLEY

"I've been thinking," I say as we cruise toward the barrier separating the realms in the distance. "The scroll in Pagos helped improve the realm. Granted Lysander power. If all of these scrolls were supposed to be in the worst places possible, why would the scroll help him gain peace? Do you think each scroll is capable of different things? If one can rest in a peaceful realm, the other a lawless realm. This one with so many lost souls around it…"

"I think it has to do with the piece of the incantation written on the scroll," Cassiel answers. "Whatever magic the Creator had to use to create a spell that will transfer an ultimate power to your father…it has to draw from all sources of power to be balanced. The good and bad and evil and pure."

"That makes sense," I say, sighing. "So, whatever piece of the incantation is written upon this scroll, it likely fuels the evil of this place? Just like the goodness imbued in the compact scroll fueled Pagos?"

"It's a theory. Brace yourself."

He dips low, flying us through the barrier. My ears pop with the transition, the breath in my lungs scattering for a few panicked seconds.

The sky is a smear of tangerine and bronze colors, and massive outcroppings of cedar-colored rock float in the sky. Waterfalls rush off of the mountains, an iridescent glow twinkling in the water as it plummets to the terrain far below.

"This place is gorgeous," I say, slightly awestruck. "But shouldn't purgatory be a lot more, I don't know, terrifying?"

Cassiel motions downward with his head. I scan it, noting it's an endless meadow of ash and pebbles bordering a river that's fed by the waterfalls high above, the river itself glowing white and winding farther than I can see. Still beautiful.

But then I spot them. Creatures, and what look like humans, gathered on the banks of the river, the sounds of their cries reaching us as we fly closer, twisting something in my heart.

"They're not crying because they're lost but because they're *damned*. They can't appreciate the beauty of this place or find any ounce of joy."

"We should help them," I say.

Cassiel's grip tightens like I might leap down there. "That's what they want," he says, his tone firm. "Don't be deceived by the beauty of this place. These souls are here for a reason. Reasons you don't ever want to know."

I blink a few times, forming a wall of ice around my heart. I trust Cassiel, and if he says these souls are meant to be here? Then I sure as hell don't want to get tangled up in it.

Still, if I ever do take over the Ather as its queen, I'll need to ensure all the realms' purposes are necessary and true. I'll have to right the wrongs the Seven inflicted on this place millennia ago when they folded it into the Earth where I was raised.

"What's this place called?" I ask, my voice a whisper as Cassiel navigates us through the floating mountains.

The closer we are, the more details I can make out. Bursts of color popping from trees as wide as buildings, and whines or groans from creatures that look prehistoric as they tramp through the foliage.

"This is the Death Striker realm," he says.

I gape at him. "As in...your realm?"

A muscle in his jaw ticks. "Legends have been handed down about this place through all the angels of death. Upon its creation, it was once ruled over by the strongest among our kind. She ensured it was never overrun and that the lost souls were able to fight or work for their passage into peaceful realms."

"What happened?"

"The stories say the angel of death fell in love with one of the souls and tried to redeem him before the Seven felt he deserved. They cast her out and declared no other angel of death would take her place to pass judgment here. They left this place to ruin, to be overrun with lost souls with no hope of ever finding redemption."

I chew on my bottom lip as we soar through the skies. Is this a realm I should try to save? If there once was a purpose, like Cassiel says, then could I enlist someone to work as the previous angel of death did?

My chest tightens with the thought. I'm so out of my depth with all this. I may be confused as hell about how to help the Ather, but I'm determined to educate myself. And, lucky for me, I have Wallace and Rainier to help do the teaching. They know more about the Ather and its people, and the more I learn from them, the better.

I can't help but wonder what Rainier plans to do now that his powers are restored and he can actually make a difference as king of the Ather. Wallace mentioned they were strategizing how to help restore impoverished realms, but what about these supposed *evil* realms? Where is the line? The determining factor on who deserves redemption and who deserves to be imprisoned and punished forever?

Fuck, maybe there's a *QuickStart Guide to being the Queen of the Ather* I can read.

"Sorry," I say, realizing I've spaced out on him. "I hate that the Seven decided to banish the angel of death because she fell in love. Because she saw redeemable qualities in a lost soul where the Seven couldn't even be bothered to look. I can't believe the Creator let them rule like this for this long."

Cassiel nods, banking left. "There must be a purpose."

"Or too many people have told themselves that and never

taken a stand against what is clearly, utterly wrong."

Cassiel sighs. "Or that."

"That's about to change," I say, determination coating my tone. Hasn't that been the case for so much suffering? Even among humans? People standing by in silence because they think there has to be a reason, a grand plan behind so much injustice?

Well, not in my world. The Seven must be stopped.

"How much farther?" I ask.

"See that giant floating rock?" He motions to the largest of the floating mountains, this one shaded in colors of seafoam and hickory with pops of glowing amethyst fanning out among the vegetation covering it.

"Yeah, it's pretty hard to miss."

"Rainier's map says it's there."

"And I'm guessing it'll be guarded by the strongest among these lost souls?"

"One would assume," he says, spearing us like a missile to a plateau on the upper level of the mountain.

"I'll have to kill it?" I ask, my stomach twisting. Ending the frost demon king hadn't been a hardship, not with the way he treated the Pagos people, but here? These souls may be damned, but what right do *I* have to condemn them?

Cassiel lands on a plateau, the space covered in colorful vegetation. "You can try bargaining with it," he says, setting me down, then the pagle, who immediately rushes around my feet as it sniffs at the ground with its trunk. "But seeing as this is a realm for the restless and evil, I doubt that tactic will work."

Ahead of us across the plateau, a white river races down the middle, parting around a giant tree that looks more like a jellyfish, its leaves like long billowing tentacles that glow scarlet, swaying on a blood-scented breeze. The water races behind it, falling over a sharp edge and plummeting into the endless sky below.

"That tree," Cassiel says as he examines his map. "The scroll should be there."

Sure enough, when we're close enough, I see a bright silver
tube jammed into the tree's red bark, one end of it sharp like
an arrow, and there are intricate flower designs carved into
the metal.

"Let's get this over with."

"Good plan."

I plunge my feet into the shallow river only to freeze when
a lone soul steps out from behind the tree. A soul I know very
well.

"*No*," I breathe, my heart lurching.

"Hello, Harley," Kai says. "Come to kill me again?"

"You're not real," I say, my entire body shaking. He's wearing that damn Thor T-shirt, the one he wore when I first met him when we were kids, but it fits his grown body now.

No, we didn't meet when we were kids. He planted that memory.

The pagle grumbles lightly at my feet, leaning against my ankle.

I frantically look at Cassiel, who stands on my left, his silver eyes crackling as he stares at Kai. "Tell me he's not real," I beg.

"Of course I'm real," Kai says, smiling as he waves me off like I'm the silliest girl in all the Ather. He paces in the river, keeping in front of the tentacle tree. "Do you remember the time I took you to the animal shelter in Chicago? I tried to convince you to pick out a mutt," he continues, eyeing the pagle at my feet. "I practically begged you to let me buy one for you. Told you I would pay for all its costs." He stops pacing, eyes back on me. "Do you remember? You wanted a dog so badly, but you didn't let me."

Angry tears bite my eyes. I refused because I knew my father would find a way to hurt it. The memory unfolds before me—I can smell the kennels, can feel the ache in my heart at so many dogs in need of rescue.

Wrath's image bleeds over the fake memory, and I hold on to that feeling. "I *did* rescue a dog," I say, even though Wrath is more an Ather hellhound than a dog.

Kai looks at the pagle as if I've lost my mind.

"*And* her," I say, pointing to the creature at my side. "You wouldn't want to meet Wrath."

I latch on to my anger to stop the grief sucking at the bottom of my heart. *He used you. Violated your mind. Tried to kill you and unleash Marid on the world. He's not your best friend. He never was. You were alone the entire time—*

"Why wouldn't I want to meet my best friend's dog?" he asks, his tone genuine, but there is something in his eyes, a flickering sort of malice I recognize from the night he stabbed me.

"You don't know the first thing about being someone's friend," I snap.

He forces a smile, but it's twisted. "You don't mean that. We were inseparable for years. I *loved* you—"

"You tried to kill me!"

He flinches like I slapped him. "You're the one who killed me, Harley!" he fires back, throwing his arms out to encompass the area around him. "After everything we'd been through. Do you know how many times you cried on my shoulder after your father beat you to shit? How many times you begged me to stay with you because you were too afraid to go home alone? And still, you sent me here! You're the reason I spend sleepless nights in this godforsaken place!"

His words hit me like physical blows, my heart battling against the memories of the boy I thought I knew versus the vile creature he turned out to be.

He cuts his eyes to Cassiel at my side, dropping his arms. "You traded up," he says. "But not by much. Tell me, is the angel of death better in bed than your precious siphon Judge? Did you kill him, too—"

"Enough," Cassiel says, his tone 100 percent *death*—ice-cold and as hard as steel.

Kai cocks his head to the side like he's listening to something we can't hear. A feral grin shapes his lips, and I shift on instinct, flames covering my hands.

"Move aside," I say, my voice cracking when I want it to be

as strong as Cassiel's. But Kai's death at my hands has haunted me more than I've ever admitted to anyone, and now his lost soul is standing between me and the scroll we need.

"No," he says. "You've taken everything from me, Harley. You will not take this." He gazes up at the silver tube with a power-crazed look. "The scroll whispers things to me. Constantly. Knowledge like you can't even believe. Knowledge is the true power here." He turns back to face us. "If you want to take that from me, you'll have to kill me. *Again*."

Cassiel steps forward, murmuring in that sharp, ancient language as he calls for Kai's soul.

"Stop!" Kai groans, clenching his jaw as he grabs his head.

My power mounts, adrenaline racing through my veins.

Kai drops to his knees, extending his arms as he releases some wild call.

"The scroll, Harley," Cassiel says. "I can only hold him so long. He's where he's supposed to be—"

"No!" Kai hollers, then laughs so hard spit flies from his mouth. "It has to be *her*, Death Striker."

Cassiel ignores him, locking eyes with me in support. "I've got him, Harley. You don't have to do this again—"

A roar cuts him off, the ground trembling beneath the weight of a creature bigger than the massive tree as it bounds toward us.

No, toward *Cassiel*.

Cassiel's words stop at the sight of the creature. It looks like a dragon, covered in teal scales, with gleaming red claws and a barbed tail.

"I've made some friends, too, and mine are so much bigger than your little pet there," Kai says, pointing at the pagle.

He unleashes a succession of guttural sounds and clicks, and the creature roars again, flapping its giant wings as it lunges for Cassiel.

"No!" I yell, but Cassiel bolts into the sky to dodge the creature's massive, sharp teeth.

The snap echoes around us before the thing gives chase, the two becoming blots in the sky as Cassiel tries to evade it—

A fist sinks into my stomach so hard I double over and stumble backward, the glowing river sloshing around my ankles.

"*Dick*," I cough out.

Kai laughs, stalking toward me. "You killed me. I think you deserve more than a sucker punch."

The pagle grunts, lunging for Kai's shin and driving her tusk into it. Kai groans and lets out a kick that I feel in my soul. The pagle yelps as she rolls onto the bank across the river.

I straighten, winding my earth power around my fingers. A vine from the ground near the river lassos Kai's waist, hauling him to the left so hard his back hits the ground with an audible *thunk*.

"*Bitch*," he snarls, ripping out of my vine's hold with a strength I can feel along my powers.

I leap over him, racing for the tentacle tree—

I'm thrown back, his fingers digging into my ankle. He yanks so hard my stomach smacks against the ground, air bolting from my lungs. Kai grips my shoulders, jerking me over as he pins me to the ground, one hand wrapping around my wrists and securing them above my head.

"You made a mistake coming here," he says as I struggle beneath his weight. He trails a hand down my cheek, settling it over my neck. "I've thought of a hundred different ways I want to kill you for what you did." He squeezes my neck, the breath stalling in my lungs. "You were supposed to remake the world with *me*. My best friend." His grip tightens, his words sinking into my chest like the blade he once sank into my side.

He was stronger than me then.

He nearly killed me.

And still, I've grieved his death like the loss of a loved one.

But I didn't know what love was beyond what I felt for my sister. I didn't understand there are a hundred different kinds of love.

Passionate, consuming love.

Supportive, companionable love.

Unmatched, unflinching love.

None of which Kai ever gave me. Not really.

I stop struggling against him, his eyes widening at the submission. I let him see every ounce of pity I have for him there.

Then I cover my body in black flames.

"Fuck!" he yells, scrambling off of me in a hurry. He falls frantically into the river, extinguishing my flames that cling to that fucking Thor shirt.

I jump to my feet, rushing for the pagle that's finally getting onto all fours again. Above us, Cassiel hollers.

"Cass!" The world seems to slow as I watch the creature clamp its teeth on Cassiel's leg, swinging him back and forth like he's nothing more than a doll. It releases him, and he falls toward us with such speed there is no way he'll survive—

I thrust my hands toward him like I can catch him, and something inside me explodes in a burst of power that crackles along my soul.

Air.

I don't think twice; I spear my awareness around the new power, wielding it as I would any other. I wrap him in wind and air, my knees buckling against the weight of not just him but his power, too. I groan, every muscle in my body straining as I slow his rapid descent.

He hits the ground next to me, but not nearly as hard. I crawl over to him, examining the teeth gouges in his right leg. Blood gushes from the wounds, and I clamp my hands over them to staunch the flow.

"Fire," he grinds out, pain etching every line of his face.

I balk at his request. "I don't want to hurt you."

"Do it, Harley," he says, silver eyes on the sky. "It's coming back."

I look, noting the creature banking and heading straight for us.

"Okay," I say, drawing my flames up slowly where I grip his wounds. I mentally demand my powers to seal, to heal and not harm. They bend to my will, searing his flesh closed as he releases a growl so terrifying I have to remind myself he's on my side. "There—"

I jerk backward, clawing at the hands in my hair hauling me away from Cassiel. Kai has me by the fucking roots, my scalp threatening to tear from my skull.

"Come on, bestie," Kai seethes, locking an arm around my neck and yanking me to my feet as he squeezes. "Watch my pet use Cassiel's bones to clean its teeth. Then it can have your pet for dessert."

The creature slams down on the mountain, stalking toward Cassiel with a hungry look in its eyes. Cassiel is no longer bleeding, but he limps as he clambers to his feet, facing the dragon head-on.

"Get the scroll," he says, and there is a finality in his voice that chills my blood. He heads for the monster, resolute and unflinching, and that's when I realize—

He's willing to *die* for me.

For my need to get this scroll.

Cassiel, who journeyed with me through the Ather to save my sister from Marid. Who didn't hesitate to take my sister to Earth when she needed to go home. Who stood by my side without question as we dove into the darkest realms the Ather can offer.

My *friend*.

No fucking way am I letting him die.

I grip Kai's forearm, raking his flesh with claws of black flame until he stumbles back. I dig my feet into the ground, racing in front of Cassiel too fast for him to stop me.

"Harley! No!" he bellows, but I've already fashioned an axe of dark flame and unrelenting earth. I use the air in my blood to propel it upward with all the strength I have, the blade slicing through the creature's muscle and bone.

A shriek wrenches from its mouth before silence chokes it. I knock Cassiel out of the way as the thing's head flies from its body, landing in a thundering heap right where we'd been standing.

"Are you kidding me?" He's shaking me by the shoulders where we kneel. "You could've died! You're my brother's mate; I'm duty bound to protect you—"

"You're my *friend*," I cut him off, my breaths coming in heaves from the use of power I expelled.

"Everybody has friends," he counters, silver eyes furious. "That doesn't mean—"

"I don't!" I shout. "I *don't*," I whisper again, my entire body shaking. "I'm not going to lose anyone else, Cass. I can't, I can't…" Tears roll over my cheeks. I'm thinking about the friend I thought I had and killed, thinking about Draven, my mate, now a ghost of the man he is, and thinking about Ray.

"Pathetic," Kai grumbles from behind us, and I whirl around. He's climbing out of the river, eyeing his pet with disgust rather than loss.

There is nothing in his eyes. No emotion. Just unflinching evil.

"Yeah, you are," I say, scrambling to my feet as I fashion daggers of flame. "And I'm done grieving over you."

His eyes flare as my blades of flame hurtle toward him too fast to dodge. Each one sinks into its mark, the sickening *squelch* sending waves of nausea crashing through my stomach.

"Harley?" he whispers as his knees hit the ground in front of me. He eyes the four daggers piercing his chest, then looks back up at me. Something clears in his eyes, some dense fog lifting. A gurgling sound chokes out of him, blood bubbling from his mouth. "Thank you," he whispers before bursts of light spring from his body so fast I turn to shield my eyes.

A fierce wind nearly knocks me off my feet, then silence.

I lower my hand, watching as a million sparkles of red light are drawn into the tentacles of the tree beyond, settling there like they were always one and the same.

My vision wobbles slightly, dizziness adding to the nausea as I try to process having to kill Kai *again*. I take a deep breath through my nose, focusing on the smell of the rushing river next to me to calm the fuck down.

Cassiel steps up behind me, urging me toward the tree, but I make sure my pagle is okay first. She's huffing but fine as she follows me. The water of the glowing river is ice-cold as we rush toward the tube lodged in its trunk, and my fingers tremble as I yank it out and shove it in my pack.

The long flowing branches of the tree surrounding us sway back and forth, their glowing red buds casting the entire space in crimson.

"I'm sorry you had to do that to him again," he says.

I stare at the river, then at the glowing red tree where his shattered soul flew. "I'm not," I say, feeling closure for the first time since he tried to kill me in Chicago. "All this time, I've felt guilty for killing the only friend I ever had, even though he'd proven that wasn't ever the case? I huff a dark laugh. "I didn't even know what true friendship looked like, Cass." I glance up to him. "Thanks for showing me."

I kick a stray indigo rock toward the glowing river, and my pagle chases after it with a happy little trot.

Cassiel visibly swallows. "No one has ever done that for me before."

I scrunch my brow. "What? Call you their friend?"

He chuckles softly, shaking his head. "Risk their life to save me."

My heart clenches as I see the emotion in his eyes, the loneliness that comes with being what he is. I spent years of my life feeling worthless and lonely, so desperate for someone to say those words to me. Cassiel may not be exactly like me, but we have more in common than I ever thought, and I sure as hell won't miss an opportunity to tell him what he needs to hear. "You're worth it."

Cassiel cracks a grin before grabbing me and the pagle, catapulting us into the sky.

"Being your friend is dangerous."

I laugh despite trying to look offended. "Probably more trouble than it's worth."

He chuckles again. "Oh, definitely." He free-falls, stealing the breath from my lungs. "But that's exactly what friends are for."

CHAPTER NINETEEN

DRAVEN

"Good," I say sternly as I pace the length of marble floor in front of Ray.

We've been in one of the various training rooms for four hours already, going over everything from meditation to the history of seers and their difficulties throughout time.

The girl has spirit—I'll give her that. There has been no task she hasn't met head-on, and I have to admire her tenacity to learn.

"I can see one of the Seven," she says, her eyes closed in concentration as she perches, legs crossed, on a royal blue cushioned bench tucked against a windowless wall.

The rest of the room is filled with bookshelves, herbs and incense, and a small corner stacked with wooden weapons and a practice mat beneath.

"Who?" I ask.

She pops her eyes open, glaring up at me from where she sits. "The pretty one is heading this way."

I purse my lips, doubting.

"What's the point of you training me if you're not going to believe me when I tell you things?"

I shrug, not really able to argue with that. "You're still young in your powers. It's okay to make mistakes—"

The door flies open, cutting off my words. "Esther?" I ask as she spills into the room, her pewter wings tucked in tight. She locks the door behind her, turning to face us.

"See?" Ray says, motioning to Esther. "The pretty one."

Esther grins at Ray. "Thank you, sweet one," she says, then

straightens as she walks to the center of the room.

I fold my arms behind my back, standing at attention to await whatever new orders she must be delivering from Aphian.

She clucks her tongue at me, shaking her head. Her long brown hair shivers with the movement. "Rest easy, Draven."

I shift my stance to let my arms hang by my sides. "Do you have Orders?"

Esther clears her throat. Blazing white light dances between her fingers. "Draven," she says. "I need you to look at me."

"I *am* looking at you," I say automatically.

"Do you remember when I stole you from Aphian? Taking you on as my student so he could no longer torment you?"

I tilt my head, a faint memory of what she describes fluttering through my mind too fast to grasp.

"How about the time I took you on your first real mission?" Her delicate oval face brightens with a full smile. "You had to vanquish a nest of cannis demons who'd escaped the Ather. The canine humanoids had torn through half a block in New York City before we got there. We worked as a team to eliminate the threat quickly. We had soft pretzels after."

I open and shut my mouth, shaking my head.

She sighs, closing her eyes for a moment before she steps closer and raises her glowing hands on either side of my head. "Remain still," she commands, all casual conversation leaving her voice. "*Remember*," she says, her tenor every bit the Seven she is.

I strain against the sharp pain pulsing behind my eyes.

"*Remember*," she commands again, and a barbed whip lashes against my spine, the pain splintering and dropping me to my knees.

Ray yelps at the sight, and Esther falls to her knees before me, her wings unfurling to their full length. "Draven, Judge, *Siphon*," she says, her voice calling to me over the blaring sound in my head. "Remember who you are!"

Tiny holes break through the roaring in my mind. Little

pieces of breathing space filled with things I can't understand—
the smell of lilies and a campfire, the taste of caramel and mint
on my tongue, a laugh that fills my soul with warmth and hope—

Electric currents buzz along every nerve I possess, and I
collapse, my body convulsing on the floor so hard I gnash my
teeth together. I can't hear her anymore. Can't see or hear or
feel anything other than the blinding pain.

"You're hurting him!" Ray's voice cuts through the chaos.
"Stop! Please!"

Esther cries out, jerking her delicate hands away from me
and landing in a heap on the floor beside me. Her white gown
blends with the cool marble I lie against, and I have to focus
on breathing before I can move.

"You were trying to bring him back?" Ray asks.

I'm too exhausted to question what she means.

"Yes," Esther says, breathless. "The wards in his mind are
more extensive than any Judge I've ever seen before."

"Aphian did this to him?"

"Yes," Esther admits.

The second I'm about to ask what she means, that searing
electricity is back, crackling along my muscles until I groan
on the floor.

"I want to help him," she continues. "But Aphian's powers
outmatch mine."

"What do we do?" Ray asks. "Please, how can we help him?
He's my friend—"

"I know," Esther says, waving her hand above my sweating
forehead. "He's mine as well. I thought maybe I could
counteract the commands, but the claws are in too deep. I
could kill him if I try any further."

I remain numb on the cool marble floor, willing my mind
to a winter sky—nothing but cold to keep the pain at bay.

Ray gapes at her. "So he's stuck like this forever?"

"No." Esther turns to face her. "I'm being watched carefully,
Seer. But I'm trying to awaken help. I'll do whatever I can, but

if Aphian doesn't release him—which I don't see him doing anytime soon—Draven alone can shake himself out of it."

"How?"

"He must fight through the pain. He has to return to himself," Esther says. "Willingly."

Esther rises from the floor, hovering over me with one of her glowing hands aimed at my face. "Forget."

I fold my arms over my chest, eyebrows raised at Ray, who's staring up at me with wide eyes.

"So?" I ask. "What do you see beyond that door?" I point to the closed training room door.

Ray parts her lips, then closes them.

I pinch the bridge of my nose. "Do your meditations again," I demand. "You need to create a safe space in your mind. A tangible place where you can go to access the full power of your sight."

Her eyes water.

I tilt my head at the sudden wobble of her bottom lip. "You're not giving up already, are you?"

She sucks in a sharp breath, shaking her head. "There are two Judges, both girls, walking down the hallway right now."

I head toward the door, cracking it open to peek. Sure enough, two Judges stroll down the hall, looking wrecked from a training session.

"Good," I say, giving her a firm nod. "Meditations. Now." She gives me a little huff, then situates herself back on the bench, closing her eyes. "Retreating to this place needs to become as easy and natural as breathing," I remind her. "Think of it as a safe haven for your precious power. Build a fortress that will keep it safe. Make it where only you can access it—"

"What if I want someone else to see it?"

"Like who?"

"You," she says. "I want you to see it. Tell me if it's good enough."

"How do you know I can see inside minds?"

She opens her eyes. "Do you want to check it or not?"

"Fine," I grumble.

She closes her eyes again.

I step toward her and close my eyes as I spear my mental powers toward her mind.

She's stronger than I thought, her mind a crystal palace of locked doors that shimmer with how much light shines behind them. And the *colors*. There are so many brilliant colors. A rainbow glistening over ice—cerulean blues and violet purples, emerald greens and apple reds. The space is filled with a warmth that reminds me of reading a favorite book by a crackling fire, snow glistening outside a nearby window. It's breathtaking, but it feels so damn...*suiting*.

"Over here." Her mental voice echoes off the crystal walls, and I follow it, twisting down several twinkling hallways until I reach an open door.

I step through it, diving deeper into her mind. *"This is the center of your palace,"* I say. *"Good work constructing it here. It's safer—"*

My words die in my throat as I step fully into the room.

That's not a room at all, but a *store*.

A vast store, the walls lined with colorful anime toys, backpacks, shirts, and shelf upon shelf of manga.

"Do you like it, Draven?" she asks, her tiny frame manifesting a few feet before me to stand in the center of the store.

My tongue is frozen, the words climbing up my throat too fast and too heavy to come out. Something tugs at my chest, my heart swelling.

"I've been here before?" I say, but it sounds like a question as I spin on my heels, scanning every inch of the place. We're the only two souls here, but I feel like someone is missing.

"You brought me here," she says. *"It was one of the happiest nights of my life."* She wears a sad smile. *"You changed everything for me that night. And my sister, but you didn't know it yet—"*

My heart is pounding against my chest, a dream I can't quite catch building inside me. *"Your sister…"* A phantom picture flutters across my mind.

Red hair and a smart mouth I can't get enough of—

"Gah!" I groan, lightning erupting in my brain, shaking the walls of her mentally constructed safe haven. The pain is searing, acidic. I can't breathe around it. The once warm, cozy air turns frigid, licking my skin with frost.

Something powerful shoves my chest, and I'm kicked out of Ray's mind so hard I stumble back in the training room.

"Draven?" she asks.

I blink until my vision returns to the present. "That place will serve you well," I say. "Being in the center of your mind palace is the safest spot. Now, you need to make sure you can instantly access it."

"What?" She's staring up at me like I'm tap-dancing instead of delivering orders.

"Your sight resides there," I say, sighing as I search for patience. "The core of your power. You need to be able to access it even while holding a conversation."

She gapes up at me.

"Again," I command. "I'll time you this round. Raise your hand when you reach it."

A tear spills over her lashes, but she closes her eyes.

And I draw up that winter sky, letting it blanket my mind, my damn *instincts*—the same ones roaring at me to say something funny, to do anything to make the tears go away and make her laugh. I bury the invasive feeling in a mountain of snow until I'm so cold I swear my heart transforms into a chunk of ice.

CHAPTER TWENTY

HARLEY

"Wrath!" I say, rushing across the grand library in Rainier's castle and dropping to my knees where my hound lounges in front of the roaring hearth.

He immediately leaps up and tackles me until I fall on my back, leaning his massive head against my chest in the most monstrous and wonderful hound hug I've ever had. I rake my fingers through his coarse fur, shifting out from under his weight as he settles back on the floor next to me.

The little pagle waddles over to me. She lifts her trunk, sniffing at Wrath. The hound goes completely still, allowing the creature to acquaint herself with him. "Wrath," I say. "This is Pagle." I pet her, the ice crystals clinking between her wool fur.

"You named the pagle *Pagle*?" Cassiel arches a brow at me.

I shrug. "I'm all out of creativity right now," I answer, turning back to my pets. "Pagle," I say. "This is Wrath."

Pagle sniffs again, then drops her trunk, her glowing cobalt eyes widening as she hops lower on her two front paws and shakes her ice tail back and forth. Wrath lifts one massive paw before slamming it down in front of her, and she tackles it without a hint of hesitation. Pagle hops around Wrath a few more times before leaning against his huge flank and snuggling down into a ball beside him.

I grin at him, scratching under his chin before I lean my head against his. I've missed him and the constant support and comfort he offers without a hint of judgment. I sigh, drawing back to look up at Rainier, who stands near the hearth.

He watches the exchange with wide eyes, something like

longing there, but it's gone in a blink.

"Oh sure," Wallace says, teleporting into the spot right next to me, her crackling indigo energy buzzing around her. "The hound gets all the love, and I'm just rancid ronc fruit over here." She nudges me. "I gave up a fried chocolate delight to be back here."

I jerk her into a side hug. "Such sacrifices," I tease as I release her, a warmth settling in my chest at being back here.

Home.

This feels a hell of a lot like home to me, but it's missing two vital pieces.

Cassiel is stretching his wings on one of the massive couches in Rainier's lounge, his head tipped back in exhaustion. He's still looking rough from the battle, and I seriously hope he can get some rest and heal before we head out for what will most certainly be another damn battle for the next scroll.

"For real," Wallace says. "I always forget how much I love Earth food. Y'all really know how to do chocolate."

I laugh.

"Are you trying to collect a pet from every realm?" Wallace asks, nodding at Pagle.

"She kind of collected me."

Rainier cocks a brow at me. "Is it my turn to welcome you now?"

I swallow a lump in my throat. I still don't know how to behave around him. Wallace earned my trust through life-and-death events we met on our journey through the Ather. Same as Wrath and Cassiel. As much as I'd love to hand out my trust freely, it's not in my nature.

"You were successful, I see," he continues before I can respond, pointing toward the pack I left on the coffee table near where Cassiel sits. The flap opens on its own, a simple flick of Rainier's fingers exposing the scroll casings inside.

"All three are accounted for," I say. "How did you do on your end?"

"Oh, boy," Wallace says, shifting next to me.

"What?" I ask, glancing between them.

Rainier sighs. "My attempts to contact my sister were unsuccessful," he admits, a muscle in his jaw ticking. He glares at the ceiling. "You think you'd listen when your *only* brother calls for you!"

I flinch from the power spearing through the room. Mine rises to match it, damn near overtaking it as I push back against his.

Rainier's head whips down, red eyes on me and wide with wonder. "More of your powers are manifesting," he says as he eyes the birthright ring on my finger. "You've *bonded* with it."

"Ew," Wallace says, then tilts her head. "What's he mean by that?"

"Um…" I furrow my brow. "I'm not sure."

"I mean you're accepting your role here as an heiress to the Ather throne." He smirks. "You're seeing the Ather as your home. The ring responds to that acknowledgment, only increasing your powers. How many more have you unlocked?"

I clear my throat. "Two more."

"Badass," Wallace says. "What's new? Can you move things with your mind or shapeshift?"

I call on the air in my blood, wrapping it around a book and carrying it over to her lap on a phantom wind. She flips open the book, scanning its pages quickly.

"Thanks," she says. "But Ather bird calls aren't really my jam."

I snort laugh, grabbing the book with my wind and placing it back where it belongs. I snatch the water glass from Cassiel's hands, flying it to Wallace's in a blink. I touch the rim, crystalizing the inside to an icy cold temp, and she instantly throws back the contents.

"Now that's more like it," she says and winks at Cassiel, who is glaring at me.

"She's hard to impress," I say.

"So am I," Rainier says, but he's almost smiling down at me. "And I would say that was quite impressive."

Cassiel grunts. "You should see what she does with an axe."

I playfully flip him off before returning to pet Wrath's massive head in my lap. Pagle is now snoring as she sleeps against him.

"So," I say, circling back to reality. "You don't know where the other scrolls are?"

"I know where *one* of the four is," he says. "Three are on Earth. I'm quite clear on that," he grumbles. "I just don't know *where*."

I sigh, my shoulders dropping. I know nothing in life is ever easy—nothing worth doing, anyway—but is it so wrong for me to wish for a damn break? I mean, sure, Cassiel and I survived getting the three scrolls from the Ather—hell, I even made a new friend along the way in Lysander, and got to bring home another beloved creature in Pagle—but it definitely wasn't easy.

"Excuse me, your highness?" The Overlord's voice cuts through my thoughts as he peeks in the doorway.

"Yes?" Rainier asks.

"Our research efforts have reached a standstill, I'm afraid," he says, eyes twitching from Rainier to me and back again. "Calls have been unanswered. I'm not sure what else to do—"

"Thank you," Rainier says, waving him off. "We'll re-strategize. I'll get back to you. We'll be traveling soon. Await word for me here."

The Overlord bows. "The leader of the Conilis realm sent a shipment of her finest fruit in thanks for your visit."

"Thank you," Rainier says.

"Where exactly will you be traveling?" the Overlord asks, lingering as those blue eyes scan the room. His hood is up, as usual, and chills rake over my skin. I don't know if I'll ever get used to this guy after he captured Ryder and me and forced us to escape his creepy island. "Earth?"

"I'm not sure yet," Rainier says a little sharply. "You'll know our movements when I do. You can have our allies ready if we need them."

"Of course." The Overlord bows and backs out of the room.

I raise an eyebrow at Rainier. "You told the Overlord about the curse being lifted. And you went to Conilis?"

Rainier shrugs. "The bonds on my realm lifted when you restored my powers. Naturally, I wanted to meet the leader of the realm you decided to live in these last three weeks. If I left without explaining it to him, there would be a lot more questions from anyone in the Ather who might see me out and about. He will spread the word that I've returned while we hunt for the scrolls."

"Is that really a priority right now?" I ask, regardless of the warmth flickering in my heart at the knowledge he wanted to meet Delta.

"I've worked tirelessly since you left," he says, that sharpness back to his tone. "My trip to Conilis was also to learn about what The Twelve subjected them to recently. And from what I learned about the Colis their mountains produce, I'm hoping Aphian was unsuccessful in securing large amounts of it from Marid. Though, from what Delta says, it sounds like he got a great deal of it." He shakes his head. "If he's used the Colis, weaponized it on Earth, he'll be an even bigger threat."

My chest tightens, and Wrath nuzzles deeper into my lap.

"What about you?" Cassiel asks, eyeing Wallace as he changes the subject. "Get anywhere with Ryder?"

She nods, her long locks adorned with trinkets and gemstones flickering in the glow of the fire. Her full lips are painted a pretty shade of purple today. "He's on our side," she says, and Cassiel cocks a brow at her. "He is. He doesn't have a clue where the scrolls are, though. But he's hell-bent on getting Draven back. Esther is close to bringing Ryder back in the fold, too."

Cassiel's jaw tenses.

"What is it?" I ask.

"I don't know if we should relay all our plans to him," he says. "He's too close to the Seven."

Wallace glares at him. "Because you all asked him to *spy* for you."

"I know that," he says. "His intentions could be the noblest in the world, but that doesn't stop the fact that he already made contact with the Seven before they flipped Draven's switch. What's to say they don't do it to him, too?"

I sigh, my heart sinking because it makes sense.

"I trust him," Wallace says.

"I do, too," I say. "But Cassiel's right. We can't tell him everything. Just in case. If Aphian gets even a hint that I'm going to betray him, he'll use Draven to torture Ray." I swallow hard. "I can't let that happen."

"We know," Rainier says.

"Right," Wallace says. "But he's still with us. We can let him help."

"Agreed," I say.

Cassiel remains silent, silver eyes wary.

"So," I say, heaving the heavy hound off of me and standing. "We need to go to Earth." I eye the pack on the table. "Maybe the scrolls will have some pull toward one another," I suggest, arching a brow at Rainier. "Since they're meant for you, maybe you'll be able to feel and understand their power better than me."

"Perhaps," Rainier says. "We can only hope we'll feel something up there."

Cassiel strides over to where I stand. "I can't take you all."

I wave him off.

"You don't need to take any of us," I say. "We'll go to Zion. He can't deny us now." I nod to Rainier. "Not when the *king* commands it."

A slow, mischievous grin shapes Rainier's lips, and he rubs his palms together. "It's been *ages* since I've been to Earth."

I grapple back and forth on if I should bring Pagle with

me on this journey, but it's not like I can leave her here all by herself, and we don't have time to take her to Delta—someone I trust to look after her. So, I wake up the little mammoth, and she groggily follows us out of Rainier's castle.

By the time we reach Zion, the Gatekeeper at the entrance of the Ather, my heart aches at leaving the Ather behind.

I grew up on Earth, was raised in a trailer by an abusive asshole who ended up not being my real father, but Earth is also where I got Ray. So I should be excited to go back—elated, even. But I'm not. And maybe it's because of the circumstances, but I can feel the shift deep in my soul, the one that solidified inside of me the second I set foot in the Ather.

This place is where I belong. I can feel that in my bones, and leaving it behind is only that much harder.

Zion's two gilded gold horns curl back from his head, his long white hair hanging like silk over his shoulders. Gold dusts his cheeks, and he dons his signature blazer with nothing beneath, his name tag tucked neatly near his chest. "Your Highness." He bows deeply at the waist toward Rainier and then, to my astonishment, to me. "Princess."

I arch a brow, unsure what to do, then cast a glance at Wallace. This would be the perfect time for her to start flirting with him like she did last time we were here—which felt like ages ago instead of mere weeks.

But she doesn't.

She gives him a small smile and hefts Pagle up higher in her arms.

"Where do you need to go?" Zion asks.

"The Bridge. Chicago."

Zion nods, flipping the massive metal book resting on his podium before him until he lands on the page that will allow him to transport us to Earth.

"Hold on to one another," he says, and we all reach out, forming one weird-looking circle between the king of the Ather, my hellhound and pagle, a leaper, the Antichrist, and an angel of death, but we make it work. "I'll feel your presence at any thinning, your highness," Zion says to Rainier. "Whenever you want to come home, simply find one, and I will bring you back."

Rainier dips his head, and then the sensation of a hook jerks the middle of my stomach, hauling me up and out like a fish caught on a line.

A thick layer of fog coats my vision, and I have to blink it away until The Bridge comes into focus. Smoke billows from the street-level windows, and it takes my mind a second to catch up with my body. My ears pop, the roaring in them finally clearing.

First, I hear a booming crack that turns my blood to ice.

Then I hear the screams.

Hundreds of them.

And it isn't until I inhale that panic truly sets in.

A metallic scent taints the air, sending bile racing up my throat as I sprint for the door to The Bridge only to screech to a halt outside of it.

It's busted in. Ripped completely off its hinges...

And it's covered in blood.

CHAPTER TWENTY-ONE

HARLEY

Shock racks my body, and I feel like my legs are filled with lead as I climb over the door and rush down the hallway—

A burst of orange light explodes against the wall, the white-hot energy of it soaring past my ear. I duck when another aims my way, just barely missing taking my head off completely.

"Harley!" Rainier calls to me from The Bridge's entrance, but I don't look back.

I can only look ahead, my heart lodging in my throat as the scene before me plays in slow motion.

The dance floor surrounding the neon square bar is in ruins. Creatures of all realms and cultures lie in pieces on the floor, their agonized wails curdling my blood. On the far-right side of the vast room are dozens of minions—the same skeleton-looking creatures who came after my blood on my eighteenth birthday—and each holds a weapon I've never seen. It looks like a futuristic version of a tommy gun, its casing a clear crystal that glows burnt orange from the inside. And in its epicenter, the rock powering it all—a piece of *Colis*.

Ohmigod. These are the weapons Marid was making for the Seven.

"Behind me!"

Kazuki's voice shatters my shock. He's in the middle of the dance floor, his emerald-topped cane raised. Waves of green energy pulse from the stone, creating a barrier against the minions shooting everything in sight.

The bartender, Crane, who was so smitten with Ray, rushes toward Kazuki's protective barrier. Another blast of orange light soars through the air, the light in the shape of a bullet. It sinks into the center of Crane's chest—

Dust.

Crane falls to the floor in a pile of *dust*.

Rage pulses and ebbs right alongside my collective powers, and I no longer duck or hide beyond the safety of the hallway wall.

I walk, hands shaking as they're engulfed in flames.

Daggers, axes, and flaming arrows. I fashion them all and catapult them at the skeletal bodies of the minions.

Growls and hisses erupt as my flaming weapons hit their marks, a dozen minions falling in piles of ash on the floor. They don't take aim at me; instead, they turn and open fire on a group of creatures trying to hide behind overturned tables and booths.

I curl the fingers on my left hand, darting an air shield around those creatures. I grit my teeth, using the cries and pleas for help to fuel my already adrenaline-riddled body as I make my way to Kazuki.

"I can't kill and shield at the same time," he says, no preamble. "Their weapons are too powerful—"

"Expand your shield. I've got this." I step in front of him, my dark flames flickering all the way up to my elbows as I raise my hands toward the minions still standing.

"Hurry!" Kazuki hollers at the last group of unshielded creatures.

I eye Wrath as he drops the skull of a minion at his paws. "Get them outside safely, Wrath!" I holler over to him, and he bounds toward those behind Kaz's shield, ushering them out the doors.

Fire surges from my hands, creating a wall of flames as the last of them make it to the safety of his shield.

"Out the back. Go!" Kazuki shouts when some are hesitant to follow my hound. Many are injured and all are crying as they escape.

Screeching wails fill the air, and I drop the fire wall. The minions are *pissed* at the sight of only Kazuki and myself standing there.

I feel the power of Kazuki's shield drop as he steps up to my right side and points his sleek cane at the minions. There are eight of them left, all snarling and pointing those weapons at us. "You'll regret coming here," Kazuki says in a lethally low tone, looking as intimidating as ever in his slick suit, his black hair and goatee in perfect order.

The minions roar, unleashing wave after wave from their weapons.

I duck a few, casting air up to divert the other shots while Kazuki swings his cane, cracking the energy back to a few of them like he's hitting balls with a bat.

"Don't let it touch you," Kazuki calls to me as I send a blast of flames toward a trio of minions.

"Thanks, Captain Obvious," I grind out as the trio turns to ash, their weapons clattering to the floor with their deaths.

"I'm more of a Sorcerer Supreme," he fires back.

A dark, twisted laugh rips out of me.

Obsidian wings dart behind two of the minions trying to herd Kazuki into a corner. Cassiel's hands crack skeletal necks before either of them can get another shot off.

"Their weapons legit dust you if you're hit!" I call to him and Wallace, who teleports next to him, her indigo energy crackling as she darts in and out of the minions.

Cassiel nods, then flies toward the ceiling to dodge a shot.

I groan as six shots hit my air shield at once. It feels like a semitruck smashing against cellophane, and my knees buckle, cracking against the hard floor. My shield drops, the air rushing out of my lungs from so many hits—

"Harley!" Kazuki roars.

My vision clears just in time to see him dive in front of me, a bright orange blast hitting him in his gut.

"No!" I gasp as Kazuki falls in a heap.

I stumble over a fallen stool to get to Kazuki as he groans, thankfully *not* turned to dust. More and more shots pop off. Wallace and Cassiel barely dodge them all.

And then the remaining minions train their weapons on *me*.

"Shit. Hang on, Kaz." I raise my flaming hands—

Rainier slams in front of me, my pagle rushing in behind him and crashing into my side. He shoves us both back with one fell swoop of his hand. His entire body is coated in the dark flames I've come to love, not daring to harm a hair on his body.

He snarls at the minions. "Don't fucking touch my daughter," he says, his tone a mixture of death and ice and fire.

One spits black ichor onto the floor at his feet and trains that weapon where I'm scrambling—

Rainier *explodes*.

I whirl around, diving to cover Kazuki and Pagle on the floor as waves of onyx fire blast across the room.

The sound is a terrifying, unexplainable thing—all power and crackling flames and terror rolled into one.

And then silence.

I gently shift off of Kazuki and Pagle, scanning the area.

The minions are just...gone. Ash. Even the weapons are dust.

In fact, everything is. There's nothing left standing.

Cassiel carries Wallace, his wings beating to keep them high near the ceiling, and Rainier? He's trembling as he turns to look at me, his red eyes filled with fear.

Not for himself.

Not for what he's just done.

But for *me*. I can see it there, the terror as he looks me over.

"There were more outside," he says, smoke curling from his lips. "I killed them before they could chase down the survivors out back."

"It's okay," I say, knowing he doesn't have to explain to me where he was, and yet he's doing just that. "I'm okay."

A groan jerks my attention away, and my heart plummets to my stomach.

"Kaz," I say, panic coating my voice as I run my hands over his chest and down his abdomen. A singed black hole is in his stomach, his blood spilling over his side and pooling beneath him. I press my hands over the wound to stop the blood.

He opens his eyes, the lavender color nowhere near searing like it normally is. It's dulled, the life ebbing away from him.

"No," I say, my entire soul shaking. "No, no, no. You can't die." He dove in front of that shot for *me*. And I'm sure his great power is the only thing that kept him from dusting, but he's bleeding out, and I don't know what to do. "Tell me what to do, Kaz."

He tries to say something, but a gurgling sound is all that comes out of his mouth.

"Rainier," I beg as he goes to the other side of Kazuki, red eyes on me. "Please. Tell me how to save him."

Rainier opens and closes his mouth a few times.

"You're the king of the Ather!" I say so loud he flinches. "Save. Him."

"I can't," he says. "We're not in the Ather. I can only bring someone back if they're in my world, and even then it's extremely difficult."

Kazuki moves, and I focus on him. His eyes are so damn hazy, and I can't stop the sob that wrenches from me as he reaches a hand toward me. It's covered in his own blood, and he smears it over my exposed arm, over the sorcerer's bargain tattoo marking my skin—the one he gave me in order to help me save my sister from Marid's control last month.

I gape at him as he keeps tapping it, each move weaker than the one before.

Electricity tingles every inch of my body, and shock rolls through me. "We're connected," I say, looking to Rainier. "We made a bargain." I throw my mental awareness toward him, and I nearly cry when I can hear him in my mind.

"Power," he says, even his mental voice weak. *"Share?"*

"Anything," I say mentally. *"Tell me what to do."*

"Willingly...give."

I nod rapidly, sliding my hands beneath his neck and hauling him half into my lap. Closing my eyes, I throw myself internally, diving deep into the source of my power. I can feel the mating bond between Draven and me, the icy, rusting chain flickering with life. And next to it, I can feel the bargain between Kazuki and me. It's like a little room in my mind reserved just for him and the power that allowed him into my mind when I first ventured to the Ather. It's filled with magic, glittering rows of nail polish, crisp suits, and more gemstones and vials of herbs than I can count.

But the contents of the room are flickering in and out of sight as he continues to bleed out on my lap.

I spear everything that I am toward those fractures in the walls. I fill the room with that power, mending it until I can *feel* him there—a spark of unmatched confidence and unflinching snark.

"Fuck." I hiss as the sharpness of his power blends with mine. It's ancient and strong and this side of terrifying. Kazuki's power is unlike the steady well of mine. His is a pulsing, thrumming web of silk strings connected to *all* things. It's as overwhelming as an ocean current ripping me out to sea.

"Stop fighting it." Rainier's voice sounds in my ear.

I blow out a shaky breath to calm myself. The minute I do, Kazuki's power meshes with mine with the ease of a stream mixing with a rushing river.

"Holy shit," Wallace says from somewhere far away. "Now they're both glowing."

I allow his power to tangle with mine to rebuild every inch of the room.

"That's enough, Harley," Kaz says in my mind when I try to triple reinforce the walls, terrified the warlock is going to die in my arms. "Enough," he says, his voice sounding outside my head. "You're suffocating me."

I relinquish the power share as I withdraw back to the

present. A choked laugh tumbles from my lips as I loosen my grip on the warlock. He raises out of my lap and up on his elbows, his searing lavender eyes examining the wound on his gut.

There's nothing but smooth skin and muscle there now, and I feel so relieved I'm sure I'll pass out.

"Bastards," he groans, and I gape at him. He sits up on his own next to me. "This was one of my favorite suits."

I laugh, then throw my arms around his neck, sighing into his shoulder. He hugs me back for all of two seconds before I draw away and punch his chest.

"Ow?" He tilts his head at me.

"Don't. *Ever*. Do that again."

He gives me a little smirk. "What are besties for?" he teases, eyeing the mark on my arm, which is covered in his blood. "Besides. I knew the weapon wouldn't irradiate me instantly. And I'd rather not find out if it would you or not."

I rise to my feet, offering him my hand and helping him stand, too. He leans on his cane, eyes filled with grief as he looks over his destroyed club.

"You risked your life for her," Rainier says, stepping toward Kazuki.

Kaz blinks a few times like he's only just realized who stands at my side. His lavender eyes flash between us a few times before he grins at Rainier, who stands eye to eye with him. "Of course I did, *Rainy*," he says, and my father's jaw ticks. "She's more important to the world than I am," he says, arching a brow. "Wouldn't you agree?"

Rainier dips his head. "I'm in your debt."

"Oh," Kaz says, grinning like a cat. "I *love* hearing that."

I roll my eyes. "First off, I'm not more important. Secondly," I say, glancing at Cassiel and Wallace as Wrath leans into my side. Pagle is reared back on two paws, her front ones pushing against my calf until I pet her. "Are we all whole?"

Cassiel nods, and Wallace waves me off. Wrath gives me a

throaty groan when I rub his ear, and at the sight of my friends safe and uninjured, I blow out a breath.

"Excuse me," Kaz says, his eyes flaring wide as he sees Pagle at my feet. He kneels down, grinning at her as she rushes right up to him and practically forces him to pet her. "How in the hell did you earn the love of a pagle?"

"Um," I say, shrugging. "I saved her and her kind from an evil frost demon?"

Kaz glances up at me as if he can't tell if I'm serious or not. I nod.

"May I?" he asks the pagle, fingering some of her ice crystals that are hanging low and by a thread of wool.

She shakes her body, the crystals clattering to the floor.

"Thank you, little one," he says, petting her once more before he gathers up the fallen crystals. "These will mend the injured." He motions over his shoulder, toward the back exit.

"Harley," he says, all banter and teasing gone from his tone. He reaches out to gently clutch my shoulder. "If you hadn't come when you did, so many more would've died. Thank you."

The room in my mind where our bargain lives flares a little at his touch, a supportive and warm sensation that solidifies our friendship. "If I had known, I would've been here sooner. What happened?"

"I don't know," he says. "One second, it's business as usual; the next, we were under attack. The weapons are unlike anything I've ever seen."

"They're what Ryder told us about," I say. "What Marid was working on with the Seven before I killed him. Using what he stole from Conilis to create these on Earth."

"If they can do that to demons…" Kaz eyes the piles of multicolored dust on the floor. "Then the amount of terror they can rain down on the humans would be unheard of."

Apprehension blooms in my chest like a flower made of glass.

"Why here?" I ask more to myself than to my group of

friends. I pace the ruined floor, the puzzle pieces coming together in a way I never wanted them to. "There are hundreds of Bridge clubs across the globe. Why *here*, Kaz?"

"I don't know," he says. "I haven't been at war in many centuries—"

"Aphian took Ray because I'll do anything for her," I say, my powers whispering through my arms, my legs, settling into an uncomfortable vibration in my chest. "He turned Draven into a walking shell because I love him."

"He what?" Kaz snaps. "What—"

The vibration shifts to anger, rising to simmer beneath my skin. "Why *here*?"

Cassiel moves like smoke over glass, Kaz flanking his side as they carefully step toward me like I'm a bomb about to blow.

"Harley," Cassiel warns, a hand raised.

"Let's just calm—"

"Because *you're* important to me. The Bridge is important to me." Which means—

My stomach plummets, the ground rumbling beneath our feet. I turn on my heels, sprinting through the ruined door.

"Where are you going?" Kaz hollers behind me, but I don't stop.

Can't stop.

Because I know where Aphian will strike next.

I tunnel into my well of power, my panic fueling it beyond a bearable degree—it's downright painful, but I use it. Draw on it and fashion wings of wind, mirroring every detail I've ever studied about Cassiel's.

And I launch into the air.

CHAPTER TWENTY-TWO

HARLEY

My body flails as I try to balance while I push those wind wings harder, faster.

"Dip forward!" Cassiel calls across the skies as he catches up with me. "Use your core to power every other muscle."

I do as he says, relief opening my lungs a bit as I find a good position. I concentrate on keeping the wind steady, holding those wings at my back in place. My shoulder muscles burn with the intensity of it, but I don't slow down.

I can't.

"If Nathan is hurt, you're going to have to knock me out or something, Cass."

"Draven would slaughter me—"

"I'm not joking!" Acid crawls up my throat, the powers inside me crackling and thirsty for blood. "I can't keep losing people. I can't—"

The words die in my throat as Miller's Deli comes into view. I tilt down, spiraling through the air as I lose my grip on the wings. I focus, managing to land on my feet in front of the deli.

"*No*," I whisper, eyes wide at the shattered glass doors to the deli. The inside is torn to pieces, just like The Bridge. "Nathan!" I rush through the broken doors, my boots crunching the glass. "Nathan!"

My breaths are too quick to catch, and black spots burst along my vision. Fire engulfs my arms, and wind races around me, whipping my hair in every direction. Ice crawls up the walls, a snapping sort of sound as it slicks upward.

Not him. Not him. Not him.

I hurry through the destroyed diner, a fresh pile of dust gathered near the kitchen halting me in my tracks. My mind scatters at the sight, at the thought of that dust belonging to *Nathan*. Nathan, who fed us when we were starving.

Aphian did this.

Ordered this.

My heart rips in two, bleeding and stuttering.

I'm done.

I'm going to go straight for his fucking throat.

Fire erupts along my body, a whirlwind creating even bigger flames as I rage and shake and—

"*Kiddo*." Nathan's voice slices through the roar of my powers.

"Ohmigod," I say, my powers instantly dying as Anka and Nathan come around the corner into the main part of the deli. Anka's indigo wings, armored with scales, are slightly drooping behind her, and her barbed tail swishes back and forth as she watches Nathan hurry over to me.

"A group of minions wanted this human's blood something fierce," Anka says.

I blink back the tears in my eyes as I race to meet him halfway.

Blood drips down his forehead, staining his gray T-shirt, but it doesn't stop me from hurtling myself against his chest. He groans but catches me and holds me tight. "You're okay," he says, relief coating his tone.

I draw back just enough to look at him. "Me?" I say, eyes scanning him. He's limping, bloody, but *okay*. "After they attacked The Bridge...I thought..." A knot forms in my throat. "And then when I saw that dust..."

They came for him.

They wanted to *kill* him.

And if Anka hadn't been here? They would've succeeded.

Grief and rage thrash inside me so hard I can barely breathe around it.

"Whoa, kiddo," Nathan says, his eyes wide as he stares at me. He cups my cheek. "I'm okay—"

"I left you unprotected." I shake my head as I hug him again. "I'm so sorry."

"It's not your fault."

"It is," I argue, releasing him to step back in case my flames decide to go all bloodthirsty again. "I should've never thought I could simply hide away from the people who wanted me no matter the cost."

"He wasn't exactly unprotected," Anka says from where she stands by Cassiel, kicking at a pile of ash with her thigh-high black boot. Her classic leather jacket is scuffed and singed along her toned arms, but she flashes me a smile like she's not even a little rattled.

"I don't know how to thank you," I say. "Anka, I—"

"Don't worry about it," she says, waving me off.

She's making light of the situation, but she saved Nathan, and I'll never be able to repay her for that. The warmth in my heart, that extreme gratitude at her saving Nathan…it helps lull my powers and keeps me just one toe outside of murderous rage.

"You were incredible," Nathan says, eyes on Anka. "The way you were with those knives?" He's practically awestruck but looks like a total goof as he mimes what I think is supposed to be an impression of Anka wielding her deadly blades. "It was awesome."

Anka smirks, and I swear Nathan's cheeks turn red.

I gape at him for a second before he clears his throat, dropping his arms, eyes serious when he looks to me. "At least Ray is safe," he says.

I flinch, glancing at Cassiel.

Nathan notices the exchange, the way Cassiel's jaw clenches in a mirror image of my own anger.

"Wait," Nathan says. "Draven said—"

"Draven has been compromised," Cassiel says, and I'm

grateful for my friend's ability to say the truth I can't face. "By the Seven. He took Ray because they Ordered him to, and now they're using them both to blackmail Harley."

"What?" he snaps. "Where are they? How do we get her back?"

I blow out a breath, my body and soul just…*heavy*.

Heavy with the added powers.

Heavy with the people I love in danger.

Heavy enough to suffocate me.

"I'm working on it," I say, but it feels a little like saying *I've got this* when trying to lift a car with one finger. "Grab some clothes," I say, forcing myself to focus on the next step. Just the one in front of me, not the hundreds I've yet to take. "Whatever you need. Pack fast."

"Okay," he says, not even bothering to question me. "Where are we going, kiddo?"

"The Bridge," I say, then silently convey to Cassiel to fill Anka in. He nods, and they talk among themselves as I stick close to Nathan. It's a short walk to his house from Miller's, but I'm not letting him out of my sight.

One stuffed duffel bag and a train ride later, I'm walking my old boss and the only real father figure I've ever known through the half-reconstructed supernatural club. Kaz must've used a *shit-ton* of his power in the two hours we were gone. He's cleaned up the interior and refashioned the entrance door—which opens immediately for us. I can even feel the magic in his protective wards around the building again, and the minute we're inside, I breathe a little easier.

"You brought more friends," Kaz says from where he's bent over the bar, plucking one of the only unbroken bottles from behind it. He turns, leaning against the bar as he dips his head to Anka, then Nathan. "Drink?"

"Aunt!" Wallace gasps, then launches herself at Anka.

"Niece," she says, pressing her forehead to Wallace's before they release each other. "It's been a while."

"Too long," Wallace says. "I'm here now."

"Wish it wasn't under these circumstances," Anka says.

Kazuki passes Cassiel the bottle, and he tucks his wings in tight to lean against the bar next to Kaz. He throws back the neon-green liquor, hissing slightly before eyeing me.

I shake my head even though I'd love to throw back the entire bottle and escape the hell I'm in. But I can't. I have to think. Have to work the problem—

"Holy hell, what is that?" Nathan steps in front of me as Wrath bounds down the stairs from the upper levels of the club. He throws a total dad-arm over my body, and I almost laugh at the way he's urging me back.

"That's Wrath," I say, gently nudging him out of the way. Wrath leans his entire body against me as I pet him.

"Wrath," Nathan says, eyes wide as he takes in the size of my hellhound. He *is* twice the size of the biggest dog on Earth. "And he's yours?"

"Yes—"

"Technically," Rainier's voice cuts me off. He, too, comes down the stairs, but his confident gait eats up every step versus Wrath's excited bounding. "He's mine. But seeing as how Harley is *my* daughter, the hound imprinted on her."

"Here we go," Kaz mutters under his breath, taking the bottle from Cassiel and throwing back another drink. Pagle curls between Kaz's legs, and he grins down at her.

I arch a brow at Rainier's tone. "*Actually*," I say when he stands right in front of Nathan, staring him down like he's some alien creature who poses a threat. "I saved him from the Pits in Machis. Pretty sure he just likes me better than you."

Rainier barely registers my words, too busy holding the staring contest with Nathan, who, to my surprise, isn't cowering an inch.

"You're Harley's biological father?" Nathan asks, tone hard and sharper than I've ever heard.

"*Father*," Rainier snaps. "No need for bio—"

"Nah." Nathan steps into Rainier's space. "Biological tag is *definitely* needed."

I shift closer, trying to reach for Nathan as he interrupts the fucking king of the Ather like it's no big deal. "Nathan," I whisper.

"I *am* her father." Smoke encircles Rainier's wrists. "You're just—"

"What's her favorite color?" Nathan cuts him off again, and now I downright gape at him. He folds his arms over his chest, his brow furrowed in challenge.

"I've got ten on Nathan," Kaz whispers not so subtly to Cassiel, who says, "You're on."

Nathan ignores them. "What's her favorite food?"

Rainier opens and shuts his mouth a few times.

"Do you know how hard it is to get her to ask for help? Or how she'll stay up all night if Ray has a nightmare, even if she has to work the next day?"

Rainier's brows draw together, the entire building trembling with his power as a growl builds in his chest.

"If you explode in my club and ruin the work I just did, I will transform you into a toad," Kaz warns.

Rainier blinks a few times, the fiery glow in his red eyes dulling a bit as if he's coming back to himself.

"I…" Rainier's shoulders drop just a fraction, and there is something like sadness in his eyes as he takes a step away from Nathan, then two, the retreat looking a hell of a lot like conceding a battle.

And it punches me right in the chest.

Because it's not his fault he doesn't know those things about me.

But it's not Nathan's fault he's trying to protect me, either.

"The chance to learn those things was robbed from me," Rainier finally says, folding his arms behind his back as he holds his head high. "If I could've raised her from a baby, I would've handed over my entire kingdom. I would've given up *everything*," he says, eyes on me, "just to know you."

Shock ripples through me. I swallow around the knot in my throat, my heart softening as I read the truth in his eyes.

"It's true," I say to Nathan, who doesn't take his eyes off Rainier. "The Seven put me in my father's hands—the one you know here," I explain. "Rainier didn't know about it until it was too late, and even then, the Seven had trapped him in his own realm."

Nathan's tense muscles relax a tad, his arms hanging loose by his sides. "I'm sorry, man," he says. "I didn't know."

Rainier's nod is almost imperceptible.

"Cheers to an unconventional family," Kaz says, holding up the bottle before taking another swig.

I blurt a dark laugh. "You *are* my family," I say, looking to each of them. "Each of you. I don't know what I'd do without any of you."

And I don't know what *I'll* do if any one of them is taken from me, or if I don't get Ray and Draven back. That notion scares me most of all. What I'll become if the Seven and their minions keep trying to take away what I love most.

"Do we get a choice in the matter?" Wallace asks, raising her hand like we're in class. "Because I never said I liked you, let alone want to spend holidays with you."

I laugh again. "Love you, too. And yes, you get a choice," I say to all of them. "I'm sorry for bringing you all into my world. My attachment to each of you puts you at risk." I gesture at the club. "Clearly."

"You said before you left that they came here because of my importance to you," Kaz says, placing the nearly empty bottle on the bar and nodding toward Nathan. "How did the Seven know about him?"

I sigh. "I don't know. Aphian said he didn't glean everything before he burned away Draven's memory of me. So, either he managed to take that from Draven's mind, or…"

"Or someone is betraying you," Kaz finishes for me.

I pinch the bridge of my nose. This is the second time that's been brought up. "The only people who know me well enough are in this room," I say, "and I highly doubt any of you are leaking deets to the Seven." I arch a brow at Kaz, but his lavender eyes are churning, seemingly unconvinced. "Can we—"

"Of course," Kaz cuts me off. His usually youthful appearance is looking downright haggard after tonight's events. I don't even want to think about what a hot mess I look like. "You're always welcome to stay here, Harley. And your guests." Kaz pushes off the bar, pointing his cane between Rainier and Nathan. "No fighting, though, you two," he says. "House rules."

Nathan nods, but Rainier purses his lips at the warlock.

"We'll need to continue our search tomorrow," I say, feeling totally exhausted. "But I need to rest for tonight."

"Agreed," Cassiel says.

"I call top bunk," Wallace teases, and I snort laugh.

"I don't do bunk beds," Kazuki says, looking astonished at Wallace. "I have plenty of rooms for each of you."

"I'll owe you," I say.

"You saved my life, Harley," he says. "I'm afraid I'm in your debt now. And I really hate being in anyone's debt."

"I'll take a bed as payment right now."

He laughs. "You are *not* a good negotiator."

I shrug, then glance to Anka. She reads my silent question and nods. "I will stick close to him," she says, then strides over to Nathan's left side, hooking her arm in his.

"What are we doing?" he asks as Anka leads him up the stairs to where Kaz keeps his private guest suites.

"Bodyguard duty," Anka says.

"I've got your back," he says.

Anka tips her head back in a laugh that carries down the stairs.

Some inner anxious piece of me relaxes knowing he'll be safe here.

Cassiel practically shoves me up the stairs, guiding me to

the same room I stayed in last time. My heart clenches at the connecting room beside it, hating that Ray isn't safely tucked away in there like she was before.

And the bed…Draven slept with me in this bed, kissing me and distracting me and loving me until I'd fallen asleep.

"Try to sleep," Cassiel urges after I've stared at the bed too long.

I blink out of the memories and rub my palms over my face as I sink onto the bed.

"We'll work on another location in the morning," he says, hand on the knob to close the door.

"Cass?" I ask, and he pauses.

"Yeah?"

"Before you go," I say, hating the apprehension in my chest. "Can we try to reach Draven again?"

His silver eyes glow in the darkness of my room.

"In the Dreamscape?" Heat flushes my cheeks. "Not like when I did it accidentally," I hurry to say. "If I even did. Maybe it's a ridiculous idea—"

"It isn't," Cass says, stepping into the room and shutting the door behind him. "I've been trying every night since we first attempted. I've never made it as far without your help."

After almost losing Kazuki, then Nathan, my soul is wire tight. Fear clutches every inch of me about who might be targeted next…

And what I'll do to whoever crosses that line.

I need Draven. I need my mate. Need him to ground me when all I'm doing is spiraling. Even if there is the slightest chance we can reach him in the Dreamscape, I *have* to keep trying.

Cassiel motions to the spot next to me on the bed, and I nod. He sinks down beside me, kicking his feet out over the bed, his wings tucked in tight behind him.

"Just like last time," Cassiel says, closing his eyes. I mimic him, slowing my breath. "Empty your mind of everything but your bond. I know the doorway to go to now, as long as you don't block me."

"I'll do my best," I say, and it takes me several minutes to work through the thoughts flashing like roadblocks in my mind—anxious, annoying little demons hissing and spitting every thought and worry I've gathered since Draven took Ray.

I mentally conjure my flames and send them soaring across every inch of my mind, letting them consume the demons until there is nothing left but blissful darkness.

"Good," Cassiel encourages, but his voice is a whisper from somewhere far away.

I venture deeper into my mind, in my soul, and relief slides into my veins as the chain linking me to Draven comes into sight. I smooth my fingers along it, not even flinching from how cold it is, how the rust has consumed more of the metal, or how many new crystals have sprouted from it since last time. I can smell his amber and cedar scent—can almost see his smirk and hear the fire in his voice.

Every muscle in my body relaxes, becomes so heavy I'm certain the chain between us is sinking me down, down, down into an endlessly ruthless ocean content to bury me in the sand beneath.

CHAPTER TWENTY-THREE

HARLEY

I step into a room made entirely of slick white marble, gold veins spiderwebbing along its surface. The air here is so frigid that when I breathe out, the fog turns to snow, little flakes fluttering to the pristine floor.

Rubbing my arms, I tense my muscles to stop the shivering as I walk deeper into the room.

A metallic clinking sounds from the right, and I hurry toward the sound.

"Draven," I say, skidding to a halt before him.

"Harley?" he groans, barely able to lift his head from where he hangs parallel above the floor. Black stone chains wrap around his wrists and ankles and across his hips, suspending him at eye height with me. He's shirtless, his pants torn and ragged, and there is a blue tint to his lips.

He looks like he's about to belly flop into some arctic ocean, and I tremble as I bring my hands to his cheeks.

"What are you…" A dry cough stops his words. "How?"

"Finally broke through, brother," Cassiel says, and I glance over my shoulder to see him striding toward us, obsidian wings fully outstretched—a blot of ink in this white room.

"We did it?" I ask, sliding my hands from Draven's face and along his arms. "We're really here?"

Draven groans as I tug on the chains at his wrist. "You shouldn't be here," he says, but his voice is devastated, not demanding.

"We're here to help you break free, Draven," Cassiel says, examining the chains at Draven's ankles.

"You can't," he whispers, then cries out when I try to remove the chains again.

I jerk back, gaping at the sight of his skin melting to the chains, the way it looks like acid is burning him every time I try to free him.

"Draven, please," I say, shifting to meet his eyes. "Tell me how to help you."

The usual blazing gold of his eyes is so drained of life, it feels like a knife straight to my heart.

"I've never seen anyone's mind this chained before," Cassiel says, gliding around Draven to stand next to me.

"You need to leave," Draven says, his eyes widening behind me. I spare a glance, noting a wave of white light bleeding from the corners of the room. It hisses and pops along every inch it touches. "It'll consume you, too. Leave! Now!"

"Not without you," I fire back, tears in my eyes. "We have to help you—"

"Kill me," he says, and a shudder racks my body. "Get out. Save yourselves. And kill me when you have to, Harley."

"No."

"You must," he says. "He'll have me..." He coughs again, groaning against some unseen assault. "He'll make me do such horrible things to you, Harley. Please. I can't. I can't do that to my mate. Please. Don't hesitate. Find me and end this—"

"No!" I yell, my entire body trembling now.

"Harley," Cassiel warns, reaching for my hand and tugging me away from Draven.

I jerk my hand free, rushing back to him. "You're stronger than this," I say, clutching his cheeks in my hands. "You're stronger than all the Seven combined." I crush my mouth against his, whimpering at how icy his lips are. But he opens for me, kissing me back like it's the last time. He tugs against his bonds, groaning between my kisses as he tries to reach me.

"Harley," Cassiel says. "We have to go."

I tear my mouth away, hating the defeat in Draven's eyes.

"I'm not." He breathes the words. "I'm not strong enough—"

"You are," I say. "Because you're my mate. Fate chose you, Draven. Mated you to the Antichrist. If you can survive that? You can survive anything."

I swear his eyes flicker with blazing gold as Cassiel tugs me away, racing for the only doorway in the Dreamscape. The white light crackles as we pass it, and just the graze of its power against my shoulder has me stumbling.

"Holy fuck," I groan, righting myself as we run toward the doorway.

"You got the holy part right," Cassiel says, gripping my hand and urging me to go faster.

I throw one more look over my shoulder, my heart in my throat as that white light washes over Draven...

And all I can hear is his screams.

CHAPTER TWENTY-FOUR

HARLEY

"Take me back!" I yell, thrashing against something heavy. "Take me back!"

"Harley, stop fighting me!" Cassiel demands, and I open my eyes.

Wrath is on the right side of my bed, his massive paws on my shoulder.

Cassiel is on the left, uncurling his fingers from my wrist, his hair disheveled and his silver eyes cast in panic.

I cringe against the screams echoing in my mind.

My mate's screams.

"We left him there, Cass." I jerk upright in bed. Wrath drops his head into my lap, whimpering softly.

"I know," Cassiel says, arms raised as if he might have to subdue me again. "I know."

I lock my muscles and my powers, focusing on the weight of Wrath's head in my lap to stop from shaking. "They're torturing him. Those chains, that acidic light?" I swallow hard. "It's mental warfare. Every time I tried to get him free, I only hurt him worse."

"And I'm sure it happens every time he has any memory of you," Cass says. "Any time he tries to come back to himself."

Rage builds and swarms inside me. "How are we supposed to get him free? Get him to come back to us?"

Cassiel shifts on the bed to face me, eyes wary. "We reached a part of him, Harley. There is hope for him. He's still there, still fighting—"

"You saw him," I cry. "Saw what those bonds were doing

to him." Sucking the life from him, burning away everything that made him *him*.

And I made it *worse*.

By going to him, reaching for him...I drew that light out, the light that was torturing him when we left—

"He's in there," Cassiel insists. "That means he still has a chance."

"But?" I ask when I can tell he's avoiding saying the word.

"But," he says, shaking his head. "He's going to have to do it himself."

"Draven wants me to kill him," I say.

Cassiel shakes his head, determination lining every inch of his face. "That doesn't mean—"

"Sure it does," I say, anger rising with my powers enough to make me see red. "You know exactly what that means."

Cassiel meets my gaze, defiant.

But I say the words he refuses to, every inch of my soul rebelling against the truth I'll never be able to face.

"He's already given up."

CHAPTER TWENTY-FIVE

DRAVEN

Navy blue water laps at an outcropping of concrete, all manner of shops and restaurants lining a vacant pier. A giant Ferris wheel spins around and around despite me being the only person standing here.

Salt and fried food and sweet smells carry on the slight breeze, and I fold my arms against a memory just out of reach. I walk toward the Ferris wheel, noting the lights illuminating in colors of red and blue and white as it spins. Somewhere, someone laughs, the sound scorching me right down to my bones.

I spin around, my eyes landing on Ray, but she isn't laughing. I jerk my eyes back to the Ferris wheel, training them against the setting sun.

There.

There *is* someone else here with us. Someone who is laughing in the very top cart of the Ferris wheel. I can barely see her—

"What do you think?" Ray asks.

"Impressive," I say, and I don't mean it lightly. The little seer is catapulting through her lessons. "You've mastered entering others' minds, and your illusion skills are fucking stellar."

"Language," she chides, but she's smiling. Something she's only done after mastering another facet of her powers. The little chide sends another scrape down my brain, an incessant itch I can never scratch. "Do you remember this place?"

"It does seem familiar," I say, scanning the area. "I've probably been here before," I say. "On a mission."

Ray sighs and folds her arms over her chest.

The laugh I heard earlier sounds again, and something inside me aches at the noise. "Who is that?" I ask. "Who have you conjured in here with us?" I keep my eyes on that Ferris wheel, my heart thudding as it brings the owner of that laugh closer to the ground.

I didn't ask Ray to conjure an actual person in my mind yet. That type of illusion is far more advanced, but the little seer seems to live to surprise me. I'll have to report to Aphian on her progress—she's moving much faster than I think anyone anticipated. He'll want to test her powers for his own purposes soon, and for some reason I can't understand, that pisses me the hell off.

Have I grown attached to the girl during our training? That's not possible. She's an assignment. A mission.

Then why do you want to lie to Aphian about her progress?

"A friend," Ray finally answers.

I hold my breath as the Ferris wheel stops, and a woman gets out of the cart.

"Whose friend?" I ask. And why is my mouth suddenly dry?

The woman walks toward us, clad in dark pants and a purple T-shirt, a pair of weathered black moto boots on her feet. Her hair is like liquid fire, and her eyes are too many shades of green to name. And she's looking right at *me*. Her smile is beautiful and dangerous and pure temptation as she stops to stand before me.

"Yours," Ray says.

"Mine?" I ask, unable to take my eyes off the woman.

"I've always been yours, Draven," the woman says. Something pulses in the back of my mind, a sort of frantic pounding that feels like my fist trying to punch through a brick wall.

"Mine," I whisper, unable to look away. I reach up, trailing my fingers above the line of her jaw. She leans into my touch, and I gasp at the contact. A bolt of electricity races through the center of me, clearing the fog clinging to my eyes. "*Harley*."

"Yes!" Ray says, her voice cracking on the word.

I whirl around, heart racing. "Ray?"

"You know me?"

I nod, the breath catching in my lungs. "Have I hurt you?" My bones twist against my clarity, agonizing pain rippling up my spine.

"No," Ray says, her eyes worried as she looks me over. "What's happening?"

I groan against the pain. "The bonds," I grind out. "The commands Aphian has given me. They come for me any time I remember—" I flinch as what feels like shards of glass spear into my skin. "Ray, I'm sorry. You have to find a way out. Your powers are immense. Use them—" Fire blisters along my nerves, stopping the breath in my lungs.

"Draven?" Ray asks, her little brow pinched.

"You must…" I collapse beneath the weight of pain, my fingers sprawled against the concrete as my vision goes black.

I blink a few times as I push to my feet. The water laps against the pier, the sound soothing as a lullaby.

"That's enough illusion for today," I say.

Ray gapes up at me.

"You'll need to rest," I continue. "This amount of conjuring must be taking all your concentration."

Her little shoulders drop before she snaps her fingers.

I wobble slightly as her illusion dissolves around us and we're revealed in the training room. I rub at my chest, wondering why I feel a pang of longing to return to the illusion.

"Good work."

Ray nods, but she looks anything but proud. "Are you going to tell Aphian now?" she asks after I've walked her back to her room.

I part my lips to say *yes, of course*, but something stops me. It's a heavy, hurting something, but I can't ignore the instinct in my gut yelling at me to stay with Ray.

"Later," I say, motioning toward her bed. "Get some rest, little seer."

A smile I haven't seen before lights up her eyes, but I quickly shut the door behind me, hating that I can't get a grip on my mind or emotions.

That I want to disappear there and never come back.

CHAPTER TWENTY-SIX

HARLEY

"I spent half the night resting," Kazuki says from across the room as he plucks a piece of fruit from the breakfast spread across the bar. "And the other half projecting."

I inhale the rest of my pastry before sinking down on one of the love seats. Cassiel is stretched out in an armchair to my right, Wallace and Rainier grazing over the food near Kazuki. Wrath pads toward me, climbing onto the love seat before plopping down in my lap while Pagle is beyond content to remain on the overstuffed bed on the floor.

"No animals on the furniture," Kazuki chides, but Wrath gives him a huff and settles deeper against me.

I shrug, smoothing my hands over the hound's head. "Projecting?"

Kazuki cocks a brow at Wrath, but then looks to me. "Astral," he says. "And thanks to power sharing with you, little Antichrist, I was able to reach farther than I ever have before."

"Really?" Wow. Kaz is one of the most powerful warlocks I know—okay, he's the only warlock I know, but still.

"Really, really," he says, his lavender eyes glowing extra bright today. He nods toward the birthright ring on my right hand. "That's not just a pretty adornment," he says. "It's unleashing more of your powers the longer you wear it. The fact that you can control so many already is fascinating—"

"She's my daughter, warlock," Rainier says from where he sips his orange juice at the bar. "Of course she can control them."

"Ah," Kaz says. "But not all her powers come from *you.*"

I blink between the two, raising my brows as I consider that. I've barely had two seconds to think about my biological mother, and with the revelation that my aunt is the Creator, plus all the other shit going on, I've been super distracted.

Swinging my gaze to Cassiel, I hope he'll have some kind of assuring look, but he's gone cold today. Colder than his normal angel-of-death setting. And I understand why.

Our venture into Draven's Dreamscape has me feeling completely hollowed out. I can barely shove the image of him in those chains from my mind long enough to think, let alone participate in conversation.

"What did you find during your projections, Kaz?" I ask finally.

Kaz smiles at the strawberry in his hand, his polished nails gleaming under the lights. "I found a lead on one of your scrolls, darling," he says, pleased with himself.

A thrill of hope shoots through me, and I gently wiggle out from under Wrath, leaving the hound dominating the love seat as I cross the space to hug Kazuki. "You're the wisest of all the warlocks," I say, releasing him. "Don't ever let me tell you otherwise."

Kaz rolls his wrist, urging me to continue. I eye him to say I'm done, and he laughs. "Fine, then," he says. "I've already sent the information to your cell," he says, and my phone in my pocket vibrates. "Seeing as this one is on Earth, I suggest you and Rainier venture to get it. There may be protection spells around it that take more than just you to break."

I glance at Rainier before swiping open the message on my screen. "London?" I breathe the word.

"London," Kaz answers. "One of my favorite cities. Had I known one of the Seven Scrolls was ripe for the plucking, I might've stayed there longer."

Rainier rolls his eyes. "You wouldn't have been able to take it."

"True," Kaz says. "But I bet my cane I could've siphoned

some pretty power off of it."

I can't deny that claim, especially after what I saw from the creatures surrounding the scrolls we collected from the Ather.

"Cassiel," Kaz calls.

Cassiel blinks for the first time all morning and grunts an answer at Kaz.

"You'll stay here with me and Wallace, yes? I could use those wings of yours to help me clean up this place. Might get dirty, though; better to lose your shirt." Kaz winks at Cassiel, but he just flips him off.

"I'll help clean," he says. "But I'm keeping my shirt on."

"Damn," Wallace says, snapping her fingers as she grins at Kaz. "You were *this* close." The two laugh in a conspiratorial way, and as much as I wish I could join them, it just doesn't reach me.

I'm too cold from the night before.

Cassiel, too.

"Wallace, you'll check on all the patrons mending from their injuries, won't you?" Kaz asks.

Wallace nods, finishing the three pastries on her plate. "I'll see how Anka and Nathan are before I head out."

"Stay safe," Cassiel says to me as he follows her.

I give him a reassuring nod. "Thanks."

Kaz studies his nails. "You'll want to use a doorway, I suppose?"

"Can we?" I ask.

"I don't know," he teases. "That would be twice, Antichrist. I don't normally allow that."

"I'll owe you?" I offer, and he waves me off.

"You're no longer allowed to owe me things, darling." He shifts his eyes to Rainier. "But you, dear Rainy. I'll take a favor from you."

Rainier's red eyes flare for a moment before he dips his head. "It's been centuries since I was worth asking a favor of, warlock," he says. "Deal."

"Right this way," Kaz says.

I give a quick hug to Wrath, asking him to keep a close eye on Nathan. His intelligent eyes indicate he will, and then he gives me a massive lick over my face for good measure. Then I make sure Pagle is good, noticing more of her ice crystals are almost ready to fall off. I'll have to make sure we collect them as soon as they do. With the way shit has been going? We'll definitely need their healing magic.

I have to jog to catch up to Rainier and Kaz, who have gone on without me.

And before I know it, I'm back in the hallway of doors in The Bridge, only this time I know how they work. There are *so* many of them, and a shudder runs through me at the thought of the minions who attacked last night getting through any of them.

They would've been able to take their weapons anywhere in the world with just the twist of a doorknob.

"Do you have extra wards around these?" I ask as Kaz slows to a stop in front of one of the doorways.

"Yes," he says, regret coloring his eyes. "The wards in place around the club below are lighter due to the admittance of so many different creatures. I can only protect it so much before the restraints would stop allowing certain species in. And, seeing as I'm an inclusive being, I couldn't have that." He sighs. "That's how those vile minions were able to slip through the cracks and attack us. But they would've been hard-pressed to get here."

Relief eases the tension in my chest just a fraction.

"This is it," he says, flicking his fingers toward the door, a cascade of green energy crackling over it. "Text me when you want to come back. I'll be waiting for you."

"Thank you," I say, then look to Rainier.

He nods down to me, folding his arms neatly behind his back like we're about to go to afternoon tea, not hunt for a scroll.

The door swings open, and I don't hesitate to step into the

darkness. It's all at once familiar and freeing, but it's over in a blink. Rainier and I silently wind our way through the London location of The Bridge, dodging all manner of creatures dancing and drinking around The Bridge's signature square neon bar.

We walk through the exit, sunset painting the sky in brushstrokes of butter and orange as we step out onto the streets of London.

London *Bridge* to be exact, and that has the smallest of smiles touching my lips.

"London," Rainier says in a nostalgic kind of way, slipping on a pair of sunglasses to hide his red eyes. He looks like he's about to pose for some editorial photo shoot with his immaculate black suit, his dark hair slicked back, and his smile growing as he glances back and forth.

"You've been here before?" I ask as we move to the side of the bridge and out of the way of foot traffic.

"Ages ago," he says. "Before the Seven trapped me in my realm." He smirks with a perfect combination of pride and mischief. "It was called *Londinium* back then."

I shake my head, baffled by how I can sometimes forget how old he is…like, older-than-time old. It's hard when he looks no more than forty.

"Yes," he says, grinning like a cat who's just caught a mouse. "Wild times back then." He rubs his palms together.

"What was wild about it?" I ask. "Wasn't it just a bunch of horses and crops?"

He gapes down at me. "Everything was fresh. Humans were on the brink of artistic explosion…" He purses his lips for a second, barely biting back a laugh.

"What is it?" I ask, marveling at how free he looks.

"I may have started a fire that lasted twelve days," he says. "But, again, wild times."

"You *what*?"

"It was *one* fire," he says. "And only a handful of people perished."

I gape up at him.

"I never said they were good people," he adds with a shrug.

The gesture is so casual and innocent. Apprehension claws up my spine. I'm standing not two feet away from one of the most powerful creatures in this universe, and he's newly unleashed from his cage. Add to that the fact I'm hunting down the very scrolls that will make him practically unstoppable. I swallow hard, hoping like hell I have some leverage as his one and only daughter to keep him in check.

"You…" I clear my throat, hating the nerves tangling in my stomach. "You can't do that here. You know that, right?" I tilt my head. "And by here, I mean Earth, not just London." Though, if I'm being honest, I don't want him to have any *wild times* in the Ather, either.

Rainier smirks, arching a brow at me. "Are you *worried* about me, daughter?"

I huff. "Worried about you setting an entire city on fire for fun? Absolutely."

He waves me off. "It was just a bit of recklessness. You should try it sometime. Rules are meant to be broken. Boundaries meant to be tested. You have a wealth of my powers inside you, and if you keep them shackled, they'll turn on you."

My stomach drops. I know exactly what he's talking about. The need to expel my growing powers is a constant sensation I can't shake—like an incessant itch.

Rainier claps his hands together. "So, where are we off to?" He eyes the cell in my hand curiously, as if he didn't just lay a truth bomb at my feet.

"This way," I say, studying the map on my phone and the twists and turns through the bustling city. "Just *once* I wish I was visiting places because I *want* to and not because life or death hangs in the balance," I grumble to myself as we set off.

"Once we rip out Aphian's spine, I want to see *everything*, both here and at home," Rainier says.

"Sorry," I say, taking another right turn. "Sometimes I forget you've been trapped in your realm for…"

"It's all right," he says when I don't finish.

This is the first time we've ever been alone together, and I'm suddenly unsure how to behave. He's my father, but I don't really know him all that well. At least we have a mission to keep us moving.

"Being trapped wasn't all bad," he says when I haven't responded. "The times with your mother…" He genuinely smiles, and I'm taken aback by the love radiating out of his eyes. "Those memories are the ones I relived when I thought I'd never see the outside world again."

I swallow thickly, focusing on the instructions. "You really loved her, didn't you?"

"More than she ever knew," he says.

Guilt sinks its claws into my chest. The only mother *I* ever knew left me behind without a second glance, fastening a power-sucking bracelet on my wrist before she did.

"What was her name?" I find myself asking even though I'm terrified to know the truth.

"Lila," he says.

My spine stiffens.

He cocks a brow at my rigid posture. "What's wrong?"

A gust of wind soars past my face, tossing my long hair back. "The woman I called mother…the one who left me with that abusive asshole and put that bracelet on my wrist. *Her* name was Lila."

Rainier's powers meet my own, lassoing the air before it can draw the attention of everyone around us. "Let it out," he says. "It's good for you to unleash a little hell every now and again." He looks ready to applaud me if I decide to rearrange the street we're walking down, and part of me *wants* to. Part of me craves to cleanse my anger through my powers. I mean, really, what would anyone be able to do about it anyway?

But there are innocent people walking all around us, so I clench my eyes shut, wrangling my powers until I'm able to look at him again.

Rainier sighs. "You shouldn't hate her."

"Sure I should," I say, crossing the street once traffic clears. We're only a couple blocks from the location Kaz sent.

"No," Rainier says, hauling me around to look at him once he's caught up with me on the sidewalk. "You. Should. Not." His voice is laced with power and his own dose of rage.

"She left me," I snap. "She knew what he did to me, and she *left*—"

"She had no choice." The sky above us darkens, and I whip my eyes to it. Thick black clouds roll in above us, the scent of rain coating the air, causing a few people on the street around us to quicken their steps before the storm hits.

I glance back to Rainier, and he takes a calculated breath, and the sky clears to its previous blue.

"How can you possibly know that?" I ask. "You've been trapped. You didn't even know I existed until recently—"

"I know it," he says, his voice lowering between us. He grips my arm, hauling me into a nearby alley so we can't be seen or heard. "Because your mother was a Judge."

CHAPTER TWENTY-SEVEN

HARLEY

My stomach plummets. "She *what*?"

"She was a Judge," he says. "With Orders from the Seven to spy on me. They wanted to know if I was trying to escape my cage. They had no idea they were sending me the one loophole to their curse. The love of my life that would lead to you, the one person who could set me free."

A knot forms in my throat. "You fell in love with a Judge."

And so did I.

Fallen for the very people sent to ruin us.

"I did," he says, taking his sunglasses off to fully look at me. "And I knew her. Knew her heart like I know my own. She would not have left you with that..." He bares his teeth. "*Man*. Willingly."

"Willingly," I repeat, and then my heart shatters with realization. "The Seven Ordered her away, didn't they?"

He nods, the muscle in his jaw flexing. "And then they killed her," he says. "My Overlord heard news of it. They found her trying to break her Orders, and they executed her for it."

A wave of his enormous power shoots past us. Cracks open up along the pavement where we stand, the sound of breaking concrete harsh in the late-afternoon lull of the day.

The brick of the buildings surrounding us starts to crumble, and I'm half terrified he's about to bring this whole building down on the alley we stand in.

His hands are in fists, trembling as a muscle in his jaw ticks. Smoke curls around his neck, almost looking like an intelligent entity all its own.

And I hate that I can't even blame him for his reaction. If Aphian killed Draven? Fuck, I don't even know if Rainier would be strong enough to stop me from razing the world.

A single tear slips over his cheek as he tries to suck in a deep breath, and I'm just as shocked by that as I am by the truth of what happened to my mother.

I step closer to him, hesitant at first, but then I wrap my arms around him.

He stills beneath my embrace, the smoke disappearing from around his neck, the sidewalk steady beneath our feet, the building no longer in jeopardy of collapsing. He holds his arms extended for a moment, almost as if he doesn't remember how to hug someone.

And maybe it's ridiculous that I'm comforting him, the king of the Ather, terrifyingly powerful and immensely unpredictable, but I do.

Because I can see his pain, practically feel it flowing off of him like waves in the ocean. And I know what it's like to love a Judge. To love someone who's not in control of their own fate.

He slowly wraps his arms around me, holding me to him.

"I'm sorry," I whisper against his chest, some inner part of me shifting to make room for this father I've never known. We're the same in so many ways, and yet we have so much more to learn about each other. But, I've suddenly realized, I *want* that gift of time. I want to be able to know him, to let him know me, but first...

First, we have to set the world right.

I release him, and he clears his throat as he awkwardly pats me on the back. I smother a laugh as he puts his sunglasses back on and we exit the alley.

"We were doomed from the start," he says after a little while as we keep walking. "Even if I wasn't trapped in my realm. The Seven separated the Ather long before they caged me, folding it into the Earth like a damaged piece of clay. Stripped my home of its original location along the globe."

"I hate that," I say. "What was it like before?"

"The Ather was a giant and glorious country all its own," he says. "We worked alongside humans. They didn't know a world where demons didn't live next to and among them. There were designated containment states for malicious demons and entities, just like there are for humans, but we lived in a relative peace." His brow pinches. "Then the Seven came, and everything changed. First, the containment states were tripled, with the Seven sentencing life punishments for even small crimes. And then they went further, deciding that the entire Ather needed to be contained and hidden from humans, even with our many peaceful realms. They banished my world from theirs until so much time passed that the humans forgot we were once allies and histories were written and shaped in different images, making us the stuff of nightmares instead of dreams."

My mind shudders at the span of history and time Rainier has seen. I try to imagine the world he's painting and wonder how it could even be possible. "Would you change it? If you could?" I swallow hard, smoothing my hand over my wrist. My blood could do it, could bring down the veil holding our two worlds apart—he knows it, and I know it—but neither of us says it out loud.

"I think the world would be better for it," he admits. "But only after opening a conversation with the world leaders. If you and I brought down the veil…if we sprung it on them, there would be panic. It would be hard to earn their trust in our people after that. Not impossible, but hard." He spares me a glance. "Would you? You grew up here. Do you think this world needs that kind of change?"

"If you'd asked me that question a month ago, I would've said opening the gates to what I believed was Hell would be the worst thing to ever happen to this world."

"And now?"

My heart swells. "Now I know what the Ather is truly like. I know how many wonderful, genuinely good things come out of it. Like Delta's innovative people. The hopeful people of Pagos. The passionate ones from Lusro." I slow my pace, my mind whirling with the possibilities. "Now I think *this* world would be able to learn quite a lot from our home." The medicinal benefits from pagles alone would change human history, but the displays of community and teamwork from the many peaceful realms could help inspire humans here, too. Pride flickers in his eyes, and I give him a half smile. "Of course, I have a divine army to stop before I can really think that far ahead."

"I'm going to make them suffer," he says, his voice low and lethal.

"As long as I get to help." We round a few more streets of buildings, stopping on the sidewalk when my phone tells us to. "We're here," I say, staring up at the large building.

Rainier looks up and laughs. "You've *got* to be kidding me."

CHAPTER TWENTY-EIGHT

HARLEY

I glance up at a building that looks plucked from history and plopped down in the middle of modern London. The stone building is decorated with small circular adornments, bordering a massive wall protecting an even taller building beyond it. Columns are carved into the rock, jetting up toward the sky, where it tapers off into a peak. Just looking at it is like taking a step back in time. "What is this place?"

"My sister always had a sense of humor," he says, sliding his sunglasses off, his eyes damn near twinkling. "This used to be an ancient culture's temple. A cult, really. Some Roman god, if I remember correctly."

"And why is that funny?"

His grin deepens as he looks at me. "Don't you see the humor?" He waves a hand at the historical-site-turned-museum. "My sister, the *Creator*, hid one of the scrolls in a temple that worshiped a different deity. It's funny because she's supposedly so against acknowledging any power other than hers."

"Oh," I say, mustering a small laugh. "That *is* kind of funny, when you think about it."

He nods, triumphant. "I'll have to ask her about it," he says, glaring at the sky. "If she ever returns my messages."

I shake my head. How is this my life? How can my biological father be who he is and have the ability to casually discuss *phoning* the Creator?

He extends his elbow. "Let's see what kind of damage we can do here, shall we?"

I slip my arm through his, and I swear something like relief flashes in his eyes as he guides me up the stairs and into the building. I can't deny my hesitance around him, but it's been disappearing the more time I spend with him. Life is short—I've learned that more since my powers emerged and half the world decided I was more useful dead. And while I have a hard time trusting people, I can't keep pushing him away. Any second could be our last, and I don't want to live with the regret of not giving my birth father a chance. Especially when his absence from my life wasn't his choice.

"We're closing in two minutes," the receptionist at the front desk of the museum says without even looking up from her phone.

"Oh, no," Rainier says, his voice coming out like warm honey. "That won't do at all, my darling."

Ick. I gape at him, wondering what in the hell has gotten into him when the woman quickly looks up from her phone.

And drops it when Rainier unbuttons his suit jacket and casually leans against the counter, flashing her a smile I've never seen before and I'm *instantly* sure I never want to see again. It's 100 percent flirty and just this side of *ew that's my dad*.

"Surely you can make an exception for us?" Rainier doesn't break eye contact with the woman. A flicker of power pulses in the atmosphere around us, but the woman doesn't even notice—she's too busy batting her eyelashes at him and giggling.

"I'm supposed to lock the doors…" She glances at the clock. "Now." She eyes the last stragglers in the museum making their way out of the exit doors, then looks back to Rainier.

He purses his lips in a faux pout. "But Marissa," he says, and the lady jolts a little at the sound of her name. She's not wearing a name tag, but she doesn't seem to care about that right this second. "I promised my daughter I would show her the museum, and this is our last night in town." He drags his finger along the counter, and she tracks the move, a shudder racking her body as if he were touching her.

Um, double ick.

"We can take a peek around, can't we?" he asks.

"Of course you can." She waves us toward the first exhibit. "Take as much time as you need!" she calls when Rainier tugs me along.

"What the hell was that?" I whisper once we're in the exhibit room and out of earshot.

"That?" he asks innocently, but there is that mischievous grin on his face again. "That was just a bit of fun, really."

I fold my arms over my chest. "What did you do to her?"

He rolls his eyes. "I convinced her to let us in."

"Convinced?"

"Trust me," he says. "I made sure her mind is very decidedly happy in the meantime. I spun an illusion for her. She's quite content, I assure you. One of her most favorite fantasies is playing in her mind and will stop once we leave. She'll think she daydreamed, and we won't be bothered."

"Wow," I say, unsure how to feel about that.

"Would you rather we broke in after closing?" he asks, the amusement draining from his tone.

"No, of course not."

"Or would you rather I simply toss her over my shoulder, haul her out to the street, and lock her out of her own building?"

Well, now he's just being an ass. "No."

"Perhaps you would've liked me to enter her mind and knock her out—"

"Okay!" I cut him off, throwing my hands up. "I get it. Jesus, you're dramatic sometimes."

He smirks again. "Oh, you have *no* idea. There was this one time before I was caged that an offender was sent to me because the demon had stolen from his own family and left them to starve. I made him live out his worst fear—which happened to be falling from a great height—for *weeks*." He chuckles. "It was hilarious. The *screams*," he says.

I open and shut my mouth a few times, completely at a loss. Considering who he is and what he can do, I suppose granting that woman her happiest fantasy while we do what we came to do isn't the worst thing that could happen.

I don't want to think about what *worse* would look like.

Rainier snaps his head to the right, all humor draining from his face. "Do you feel that?"

I shake out my thoughts, clearing my mind. There *is* something there, tickling against my power, almost calling to it. "Yes."

The first exhibit is bedecked in art pieces depicting the people who built and used this temple. A pang twists my heart as I note the colors sweeping across the canvasses. Ray should be here, seeing and experiencing all of this. Well, maybe not the life-or-death shit I'm sure is about to be thrown my way to gain access to the scroll, but the cultural stuff for sure.

We hurry through the next exhibit, Rainier looking a hell of a lot like a predator locked in on prey.

I gasp at the electrical shock that rushes through me when we pass a section of stone walls recovered from the original temple.

Rainier stops in the exact same place.

"Here," I say, nearly breathless from the power coursing through my veins. It's like I've chugged a supernatural Red Bull, and my heart is racing with the need to act.

Rainier examines the display I stand before, a large glass case filled with artifacts—stone tablets the size of flatscreens, polished and glistening jewels from the era, a variety of colored buttons, and even a few ancient-looking puzzle boxes are placed neatly along the case.

"There," Rainier says, eyes widening as he points to a bright red box the size of an apple, a thousand tiny carvings swirling over its surface, each dip or catch in the box a separate puzzle locking up whatever is inside.

I lean closer, touching the glass over the box. A bolt of lightning zaps down my spine, and I freeze.

Rainier tips his chin, then moves toward the lock on the

edge of the case. When he presses his palm against the catch, it hisses under his skin until the silver liquifies and slides down the glass like melted chocolate. He draws his hand back, opening the case and motioning me forward.

"Okay, now I'm seriously impressed," I say, stepping close to the opened case.

"If impressing you is that easy, wait till you see what I'm going to do to the Seven once we have all the scrolls."

There is a promise in his eyes that is equal parts pain and punishment, and I feel it in my bones. We're on the same page when it comes to how exactly we'll thank Aphian for sending us on this damn mission.

"I hope I get your illusion powers by then," I say. I'd make Aphian suffer for taking Ray, for making Draven forget me, and then I'd kill him. "Do you think I will?"

"It depends," he says. "But after this is all over, I'd be honored to help you uncover exactly what all you inherited from me and what all you inherited from your mother."

I clear my throat, my mind whirling at the new information about my mother. "I'd like that. If we can survive all this."

He straightens, an emotion I can't place filling his eyes before he looks at the puzzle box that holds the scroll.

"Take it."

I reach for it, then hesitate.

"What's wrong?"

"It seems too easy," I say. "The scrolls in the Ather all came with consequences." I shiver at the memory of the creepy tree house, at the leeches and their demon king, at the way Kai's lost soul had guarded the last scroll.

"Together, then," Rainier says, sliding his fingers next to mine over the box.

I nod.

Silently, we reach for the stone together, grabbing its small curves—

The display case before us disappears, the floor shifting

and popping so much that we stumble backward. I regain my balance, scanning the area.

We're no longer standing in a museum.

Instead, I perch on a piece of wood barely big enough for my feet. The floor is a twenty-foot drop below, and it's moving and…hissing. Covered in thousands of snakes I recognize as the Original Serpent breed—the one Marid set loose that nearly killed me.

"I *knew* it," I groan, taking in the rest of the room. It's a labyrinth of wooden contraptions, some as thin as the plank I stand on, others wide and jutting upward so I can't see around them. There are onyx blades swinging back and forth over a pathway on the opposite side of the room, and ropes hang all over from a ceiling I can't see.

"Daughter?" Rainier calls.

"Oh, shit," I say, my eyes widening at where he hangs in the center of the room, suspended above a snake-covered floor by a thin rope around his waist. The rope gives an inch, and he groans.

"My powers are useless here," he says.

I reach for my own powers. Nothing.

Goddamn scroll trials. "I'm so over this," I grind out, scanning the rope attached to Rainier. I follow its path backward, finding the other end secured to a hook on the totally opposite side of the room—beyond all the obstacles laying before it.

"All I have to do is get to the other side," I say, noting the thin planks, jutting boards, and other shit in my way. You know, like slinging blades and barbed baseball bats swinging at random in the hopes of knocking my ass to the serpents below. "Hang on."

"Like I can do anything else."

I huff before taking a careful step forward—

My vision goes black.

"Ah!" I jolt, freezing my steps.

"What is it?" Rainier asks.

I blink over and over, rubbing at my eyes, desperate to clear my vision. "I can't *see*."

"What do you mean—"

"I mean I *can't see*!"

Rainier groans, and I hear the snap of the rope again. "It's okay," he says, but his tone is panicked. "I can tell you where to go. What to do."

Panic rakes down my soul.

"Harley," he says, tone softening. "You're going to have to trust me."

CHAPTER TWENTY-NINE

HARLEY

*T*rust him.

"I know you don't know me that well," I say, muscles trembling as I stand poised above a pit of snakes with a long ass drop if I take one wrong step, "but that isn't the easiest thing for me."

"I *do* know you," he says. "You're my daughter, whether you ever acknowledge that or not. And the time I've spent with you has shown me your heart. You're a survivor. Stronger than me and your mother combined. You do not cower, you do not yield. Now, do as I say and we can get out of here."

I shudder against the faith in his words.

"I'll buy you a giant profiterole," he says.

"You're bribing me with desserts?" A half sob, half laugh rips out of me. "Maybe you really are a dad."

"I am a dad. *Your* dad."

Okay. I can do this. I can let go of all my trust issues if it means I won't die by snake. And I can't let that rope break and leave him to the thousands of snakes below, either.

"Fine," I say, my heart thundering in my ears. "Tell me what to do."

"All right," he says. "First thing is to step heel-to-toe thirty times."

I do as he says, focusing on the solid feel of the thin plank beneath me. Counting in my head, I make it to twenty-seven, confidence chasing away the panic—

My toe slips and I have to wave my arms to right my balance.

"*Twenty-eight* steps," he corrects himself. "Apologies."

I snarl in his direction. "*Apologies*?"

"Well, I'm not exactly holding a measuring tape!" he says. "Now, I need you to sidestep to your left."

"How far?"

"The length of your forearm."

I feel the sturdiness of the wider plank I'd seen before. "There's a wooden wall in front of me, right?" I ask, reaching my arms out before me.

"Yes," he says. "About ten steps directly ahead of you. You'll have to climb over that."

"Great," I grumble, then edge forward until my fingers hit the flat wall. I run my hands over it, trying to memorize the dips and grooves—

Rainier groans as the rope tears again. "Faster, Harley."

I fling myself at the wall. Gripping anything I can hold on to, I manage to find places for the toes of my boots as I propel myself upward. I grin triumphantly when I reach the top, swinging a leg over the wide lip—

"Duck!" Rainier shouts.

I immediately flatten my stomach against the edge of the wood.

A *whoosh* of air blows over my back, and I clench my eyes shut against whatever is trying to hit me. "What is it?" I call back, clinging to the woodgrain like my life depends on it.

"Slide down! Now!"

I roll off the other side, hurtling down until my ass smacks against another plank. I hurry to my feet, pressing my back against the wood wall to balance myself.

"Good," he says. "This is going to be the hard part."

"Did the others seem *easy*?" I can almost feel him rolling his eyes, but I don't really care right now. A cool breeze washes over my cheeks, almost like a fan is on the other side of the room. My stomach turns. "The swinging axes and bats with nails in them?"

"I'm afraid so," he says.

I can hear the concern in his voice. Great. If the king of the Ather is worried, I should probably be peeing my pants right about now.

"Let's do this," I say, acid bubbling in my stomach. Hey, maybe I'll puke all over the snakes below.

"You'll have to do exactly as I say here," he says. "They aren't swinging in a pattern; it's random. Run when I say, stop when—"

"I got it." I wave my hand in circles for him to hurry up.

"Run!" he yells.

I sprint forward, heart in my throat.

"Stop!"

I halt, sucking in a breath like that will make me a smaller target for the giant axe swinging my way. I can feel one behind and one in front of me, the air from their sharp swipes enough to kiss my cheeks—

"Run!"

I rush forward.

"Stop!"

I freeze to the spot.

Again and again, until sweat beads on my forehead and my heart feels like it will give out any second. Fear clings to me like a frozen blanket as I dance on the blade of death, taunting it with my inability to see where I'm going.

"Good," Rainier breathes. "You're free of that. One last thing, and then you're there."

I nod, curling my shaking hands into fists.

One more thing.

I can do that.

"You have to grab the rope in front of you," he says, "and swing to the other side."

"Swing?" I say and reach out, my fingers hitting a thick piece of rope.

"Yes," he says. "I'll have to tell you when to drop."

I swallow the knot in my throat. "Swing over the endless

pit of snakes?"

"I won't let you drop before you're clear of them."

A shiver racks my body. "Have I ever told you how much I *hate* snakes?"

"They're really misunderstood creatures—" His words choke off with the sound of his rope giving.

I whimper as I tug on the rope in my hands, testing its strength.

"Harley," he says firmly. "I've survived plagues, Atherscorpions, and the Seven's attempts to break me. I am *not* going to die in a pit of goddamn snakes, and neither are you!"

"Okay, *fuck!*" I'm full-on shaking as I step back with the rope in my hands, the visions of those snakes coiling and striking as I fall into them filling the backs of my eyelids. The memory of the venom coursing through my blood, nearly erasing everything that I was, burns my insides out.

I take a deep breath, burying the thoughts, and take a running leap—

The rope catches my weight as I swing through the air, gripping the rough cord for dear life.

"Okay," he says, but I can't let go.

"Okay drop or okay on the swing?" I ask, frantic.

"Okay on the drop," he says, then yells, "Not now!" as I loosen my fingers.

I grip them tight again. "What the hell?"

"You asked what I meant," he says. "Never mind. When I say *drop*, do it."

I nod, my muscles straining as I swing back and—

I fall, clinging to the rope before it jerks to a hold again. A shriek lurches out of me, and I wrap my legs around the rope. "Rainier!"

"It's breaking, too," he says. "Hold on."

Tears hit the backs of my eyes. "I don't want to die like this!"

"You're not going to die!" he hollers back, determination wrapping around his tone. "Almost," he says as my body sways back and forth. "Drop!"

I release my grip, free-falling through the air, my heart stalling—

I hit solid, beautiful wood, and the air rushes back to my lungs.

"Thank fuck," he breathes.

"Where is it?"

"Five steps ahead—" A crack bursts over his words.

I dive forward, reaching out in the dark. I feel the rope I spied when we first got here, and clutch it with all the strength I possess. Rainier's dropping weight snags against the rope I hold, propelling me forward. I dig my boots into the wood, hauling myself back and back. Grinding my teeth, I pull and tug on the rope, my muscles feeling like they'll rip against his weight until I hear him grab the wood I stand on.

"You did it," he says one second before I feel his arms around me. I sink into his embrace, shaking from the efforts of this twisted obstacle course. "You saved my life."

I blink as my vision bursts back to me. Rainier's red eyes are etched in concern and awe and pride as I look up at him, and I squeeze him tighter. My heart shifts, my soul making room for him in ways I never imagined before.

The obstacle course from hell wobbles beneath my feet, the planks dissolving like grains of sand. I gasp when I'm hurtled backward out of his arms.

He lunges for me, catching my hand in one of his, the other grabbing another rope hanging from the ceiling. The skin around my wrist burns from his grip, but I swing my other hand up to cling to him. My legs flail in the air as I look down at the awaiting snakes.

Rainier flexes against the weight, and I dart my eyes to his. "Please, don't let me fall."

"Never," he says as he lifts his arm, hauling me up and up until I can wrap my arms around his neck.

The rope breaks in two.

We plummet toward the ground, Rainier gripping me as if he can break our fall—

My ass hits the museum floor, the display case sealed before me, the lock untouched.

I gasp, heaving in air that feels like razor blades. Rainier hauls me to my feet as he looks me over. "Are you hurt?"

I shake my head, my body still trembling from the trial. I glance down at my left hand, eyeing the red puzzle box there.

"We got it," I say, stowing the box in my pack.

"You trusted me," he says, holding me at arm's length so he can look down at me.

Emotion clogs my throat, but if I can be courageous enough to swing over a pit of snakes, I can give him this. Still, I shrug like it's no big deal. "You're my dad, right?"

His brows draw together as silver lines his eyes.

"You earned that trust." I suck in a breath, stepping out of his touch as I arch a brow at him. "Don't make me regret it."

He clears his throat, smoothing out the wrinkles of his suit jacket. "Wouldn't dream of it."

I curl the fingers on my right hand, mentally hushing the powers coming back online inside me before I smile up at him. "I believe I was promised dessert."

Rainier laughs, then extends his elbow. "Indeed," he says, leading us out of the museum and onto the crowded streets of London. "Let's see who I can con to get you the best dessert London has to offer."

CHAPTER THIRTY

DRAVEN

I turn into the throne room, Aphian having summoned me moments ago, and halt two steps in.

"Ryder?" I resist the urge to cross the space to hug my twin, instead walking slowly to stand at attention before Aphian.

"Draven," Ryder says, his voice bitter as he looks me over.

I stare back. "Your hair—"

"Astonishing, isn't it?" Aphian grins at Ryder, his eyes glowing with pride.

Ryder was always his favorite.

"He truly looks identical to you now," Aphian says, crossing the marble floor. I don't dare budge from the golden compass design on the floor, remembering all too well the last time I broke attention before Aphian released me and the excruciating punishment that followed. "Except your eyes," he continues, assessing Ryder as he comes to stand next to me. "We'll have to remedy that."

Confusion coils my insides, but I keep my face as passive as possible.

"We're so glad to have you back, Ryder," Aphian continues. "We truly thought you were lost all those years ago."

Ryder bows slightly.

Buried memories rise to the surface of my mind. Ryder *had* been gone for a long time. How had I forgotten that? And it had nearly cost me everything to get him back. Everything being—

I hiss against the onslaught of pain ricocheting through my body.

"I'm glad to be back," Ryder says, his voice slicing through the pain until it ebbs. "I'm ready to get to work."

"That's my boy." Aphian practically beams at Ryder. "My finest Judge, returned and whole. And at a crucial time."

"Catch me up," Ryder says, folding his arms behind his back.

I want to turn and face him, want to ask him how he returned, how he's doing.

"From what we've learned," Aphian says, glancing at me, "the Antichrist is well and truly risen."

Ryder's brows raise, shock coloring his features.

"She poses a great threat to the world as we know it," Aphian continues. "We've received intel that she is collecting the Seven Scrolls." His wings flutter behind him like a shiver of disgust or fear shakes him. "She intends to drop the veil between the Ather and Earth, unleashing all of its realms upon our world."

Ryder's mouth drops. "Why would anyone want to do that? Millions of lives would be at risk from the shift alone—"

"Exactly why we've been constructing and amassing weapons that even the Antichrist and her armies won't be able to survive," Aphian says. "And why I've called you here today, Ryder. I know you're still adjusting to being back on this plane, but we're in desperate need of your help."

I swallow thickly, heat rising in my blood as Aphian carries on like I'm not standing right here.

"Anything," Ryder says, and something inside me twists at his eagerness.

"I need you to impersonate your brother," he says, and I can *feel* the divine command in his voice as he wields it against Ryder. "You must look like him, speak like him, walk like him."

"I don't understand," Ryder says.

"You must become him," Aphian answers, moving to grip Ryder's shoulders. "Draven is, *was*, an ally to the Antichrist—"

Ryder gasps.

I'm as shocked as he is. When? How? I riffle through my brain, panic leaving gouges along my soul when I can't find any memories beyond those of recent weeks.

"I know," Aphian says. "I burned the knowledge out of him before I could learn much, but he's constantly trying to reconjure those memories. He resists my commands on a daily basis."

I scrunch my brow.

No, I don't.

I follow Orders.

Always.

Don't I?

"You must go to her," Aphian continues. "Pose as Draven and learn her plans. She's likely already amassed a large army. We need to know the specifics so we can better protect our world." His voice rings with the divine command again, and Ryder's body goes rigid from the power of it. "Can you do this for me?"

"Yes, Master Aphian," Ryder says automatically.

"And you," Aphian says, turning to me. "The reason I summoned you…" He glances from me to Ryder and back again, studying my eyes with a focus that makes me want to shift my stance, but I remain still. "Yes," he says, more to himself than me or Ryder. He holds his right hand over Ryder's eyes. "Had to be sure I match them exactly," he says, a white light flaring from his palm.

Ryder flinches only slightly before Aphian drops his hand.

"Perfect match," he says, then grins deviously at Ryder. "Off you go."

Ryder dips his head, then heads toward the doors to the grand throne room. He pauses, looking over his shoulder at me.

Ice crystalizes over my heart at the sight of him—of *me*. His eyes match mine in all their shades of gold and amber, but I know I shouldn't be upset. It's part of the mission, and I'm a Judge bound by my duties, but a piece of me thrashes. It wails and screeches and rages, but I know if I dig into that feeling more, I'll be razed with pain.

So I keep far away from unpacking it, and note the smirk Ryder flashes me as he turns on his heels and disappears… wearing *my* face.

CHAPTER THIRTY-ONE

HARLEY

"I can't believe you've never had a pastrami sandwich and you've lived in Chicago this long." Nathan's voice stretches across the room as I round the corner into one of Kazuki's lounge suites above the nightclub.

We got back late last night, and I've been poring through Kaz's extensive libraries all day in an effort to figure out where the next scroll could be and found nothing. I'm beyond exhausted from the effort and even more pissed at having nothing to show for it.

Nathan sits on one of the plush leather couches, his arm outstretched over the back, and Anka is only a breath away from him, her legging-clad legs turned toward him as she laughs.

"Kiddo!" Nathan says once he sees me, crossing the room and crushing me in a hug. "Did you get some rest last night?" He holds me out far enough to look me over.

"A little," I say, patting his arm as he releases me. "Just exhausted from researching all day. You?" I ask, glancing from him to Anka.

"All good here," he says. "Been helping the wizard fix up the place."

"The wizard is a *warlock*," Kazuki says, his cane clanking against the floor as he enters the room. "And he has a name. For the hundredth time."

Nathan leans closer to me, keeping his eyes trained on Kazuki. "It's more fun calling him a wizard," he whispers.

I chuckle at that. "Anything happen while we were gone?"

Rainier joins Kaz for a drink at the bar across the room.

"Not really," Nathan says, but there is a hitch in his throat.

"Unless you count my aunt making moon eyes at the human the entire time," Wallace says from where she's reading a book in an armchair in the corner.

Anka shucks a tiny blade at her, the point lodging itself in the spine of the book.

"That's four hundred years old," Kazuki chides.

Wallace's eyes blaze indigo with her power as she grins at her aunt.

"It's on," she says, dropping the book and teleporting right behind Anka. The two start sparring, knocking into the overstuffed bed on the floor where Wrath and Pagle lay. Pagle grunts as Wrath gets up to come and lean against my hip, but my little Pagle Bagel is perfectly content to keep snoozing on the floof.

"Moon eyes, huh?" I whisper to Nathan, who folds his arms over his chest, trying his best to hold back a grin. "Where's Cassiel?"

"Right behind you," a voice says.

I jump, whirling around to punch Cassiel in his shoulder. "Don't *do* that," I say, a shiver racing down my spine. "Seriously, you're like the last person anyone wants sneaking up on them."

"Well now *I'm* offended," Rainier says from the bar, a glass hovering before his lips. "He's not scarier than me."

"The Antichrist has spoken," Cassiel says, and I swear he's holding back a laugh. "I win as scariest monster in the room."

Rainier glares at him, Wrath growls, and Anka and Wallace keep faux-sparring in the middle of the room. Kaz is the only one who doesn't care whether he gets the *big bad* award, and that might make him the most terrifying of all.

I snort out a laugh, waving the middle finger clad with my birthright ring at them. "Technically, I think *I* win. And the only prize I want right now is sleep."

"Some prize," Cassiel teases.

"I'll only be down for an hour or so," I say, yawning. "Come get me if anything changes, will you?"

Cassiel nods, and Wrath pads silently at my side, following me down the lavish hallways until we reach my designated room. He bounds through the opened door, leaping onto the bed so hard the frame groans under his weight.

"Careful," I say, stepping into my room. "Kaz will mount your head on the wall if you break any of his furniture—"

Strong hands whirl me around, slamming my back against the closed door.

Blazing gold eyes meet mine, and a choked sob climbs out of my throat. "*Draven?*" I gasp.

He parts his lips, but I launch myself at him, crushing my mouth against his. He catches me, a surprised yelp coming from the back of his throat as I slide my tongue between his lips. But he doesn't kiss me back. Why isn't he kissing me back? Frowning, I take a huge breath—

The ocean.

He smells like the ocean and sun and—

I shove him away so hard he stumbles back onto the bed, eliciting a growl from Wrath. "*Ryder?*"

He bursts out laughing, waving his hands in apology.

I snap my fingers, dark flames dancing on their tips. "I'm going to *fry* you!" I take a step toward him, and he leaps off the bed, retreating.

"You're the one who just attacked my face like it was your last meal!" he fires back, laughter still clinging to his eyes.

No, *Draven's* eyes.

My mind catches up with my body, and I extinguish my flames. His once shoulder-length hair has been cut *exactly* like Draven's. "Why do you look like him?"

"Aphian sent me," he says, lowering his hands as his features shift from amused to devastated in the span of a blink.

"What for?"

He slides his hands into his jean pockets. "To spy on you."

CHAPTER THIRTY-TWO

HARLEY

"He *what*?" I ask, wind whirling through the room as I walk toward him.

Blue-white lightning crackles between his fingers. "Obviously, I'm not here to do that, Antichrist," he snaps. "Put down your power and I'll put down mine. Then we can speak like civilized creatures of darkness, 'kay?"

I blow out a breath, closing my eyes for a second to soothe the powers inside me, and the wind stops. It's scary how quickly my powers are there, ready to fight at every change in my mood. Sometime soon I'll have to work on settling them. I need to harness my powers way better than I have been, but it's been kind of hard when every day brings new ones.

"Okay," I finally say. I look at Wrath, motioning my head for him to come to my side. He does immediately, and I pet him. If my hands are full of his coarse fur, they're definitely not catching fire. "Come on," I say, turning toward the doorway. "Whatever you have to say, everyone needs to hear it."

Respect flashes through his eyes. Eyes that should be turquoise like the ocean he smells like, not gold. He follows me down the hallway. "Is Wallace staying here, too, or did she go back to the Ather?" he asks, not at all casual.

"She's here," I say, then turn the corner and head into the same room I left not minutes ago.

So much for sleep.

We step into the room, and a flash of black darts past me, slamming into Ryder so hard he's pinned to the wall in seconds.

Cassiel's forearm is under his throat. "You are *not* Draven."

Blue-white lightning bursts between them, throwing Cassiel across the room. His wings flare, catching him before he can land atop one of Kazuki's glass tables.

"He's quicker than you," Ryder says to me, smirking as he rubs his throat.

Cassiel soars back over, but I hold up my hand to stop him. "He's okay," I say, and Cass drops to my right side.

"Ryder?" Wallace gasps, rushing across the room and skidding to a stop in front of him. "What happened to your hair?"

His hand twitches at his side as if he wants to reach for her. "Don't like the new look, Leaper?"

"I hate your eyes," she says, but she's grinning up at him like I've never seen her grin before.

"Good," he says, voice low. "They're not mine."

I arch a brow at the way they can't stop gazing at each other. "Yeah. They belong to *my* mate."

"Interesting," Kazuki says, strolling over to study Ryder. "Proper illusion, for sure. Your smell gives you away, though."

"Aphian didn't count on that, I guess," Ryder says.

"What the hell is going on?" Nathan asks from his spot on the love seat next to Anka.

Rainier huffs and makes his way over to our huddle. "For once, I'm on the same page as the human."

"Ryder was just about to explain," I say, blowing out a breath as I drop into one of the larger couches. Wrath settles by my feet, and I sigh. Exhaustion is a living thing inside me, but the adrenaline of Ryder's sudden appearance has my nerves frayed. Pagle perks her head up from the bed on the floor, looks me over, then settles back down.

Everyone follows suit, coming to sit in the lounge area. Cassiel perches on the armrest next to me, glaring at Ryder like he might steal his soul if he blinks the wrong way at him. Kaz and Rainier elect to stand, drinks in hand, and Ryder plops into an armchair across from my couch, kicking his feet up on the glass table in the middle.

"You must seek death," Kaz says coolly, eyeing his shoes on the table. He nods to Cassiel. "I'll hold him down for you."

"Sounds perfect," Cassiel says, silver eyes glowing.

Ryder rolls his eyes, taking his feet off the table. "Better?"

Kaz nods.

"I look like my brother because Aphian Ordered me to pose as him and spy on your little circle of weirdos," Ryder says.

Apprehension fills my chest. "He *ordered* you?" I ask. "Like, divine ordered?"

"Yep," Ryder says, smirking at me.

"We should restrain him," Cassiel immediately suggests.

"I wouldn't," Wallace warns, settling on the arm of Ryder's chair, her eyes flashing indigo.

Amusement covers the nerves tangling inside me just enough to send her a questioning look. She subtly shakes her head, telling me she'll explain later.

"You're not affected by divine orders anymore?" I ask. I mean, clearly he isn't or he wouldn't have told us, but I'm still confused.

"One good thing to come out of being tortured in Marid's realm for a century," Ryder says. "My mind can no longer be influenced. Aphian has no clue. It was easy enough to play my Judge role. He thinks I'm spying on you."

"So you're playing *both* sides," Cassiel says.

Ryder glares at him. "I'm on *her* side," he says, nodding to me. "She saved my life. Brought me to the land of cheese and endless bread. I owe her. And she's my brother's mate."

"You hate your brother—"

"I don't." Ryder rises from his seat at the same time Cassiel does. They're nearly chest to chest, Cass's wings flaring out so fast they almost clip me in the damn eye. "You are not his blood, Death Striker," Ryder seethes. "You don't get to make assumptions—"

"You nearly killed him."

"I did not."

"Every time he tried to set you free, he almost died. And how do you thank him once he *does* free you?" Cassiel snarls at him. "You lash out at him, blame him for your imprisonment, make him feel like more shit than he already did—"

"I apologized to him." Lightning crackles on Ryder's fingers. "We worked things out. Every time he visited me here before…" He sighs. "We felt like brothers again," he says, his voice softer. "Before Aphian claimed his mind."

Cassiel's jaw is hard as he glares at him. "I'll believe you're his brother again when you fucking act like it."

The blue-white lightning flares brighter as Ryder cocks back his fist.

"I dare you," Cassiel says, deadly quiet.

"Enough." I cast a blast of wind between them, shoving them apart until both of them relax. "Did you see Ray?"

Ryder finally looks at me. "No," he says, and my shoulders drop. "But Esther told me she's whole. Better than, actually."

"How?" I say, sitting up straighter.

"Aphian has Draven training her. Es tells me her powers are accelerating at a vast pace. She's learning quicker than most Judges do."

"She's not a Judge, though, right?" I ask, terror climbing up my throat at the idea of her being under the Seven's control.

"No," he says. "A seer for certain. And a strong one at that."

I blink back tears. "That's my sister," I say, hope building inside me like a rising storm. Hope that she owns every inch of her powers and uses them to keep herself safe until I can get her out.

"If you're not here to ruin us from the inside out," Rainier asks, his tone lethally calm, "then why are you here?"

"I came to gloat, obviously," Ryder says, sarcasm coloring his tone. I can't really blame him—Cass and my father aren't really giving him the benefit of the doubt. And Anka, Nathan, and Kaz are all playing the quiet game, as if they haven't made up their minds about him yet.

Cassiel storms toward him again. "Enough jokes. You're the Golden Judge. Who's to say you aren't playing us? Give me one good reason I shouldn't rip your soul from your body right this second."

"Cass," I say, exhaustion wrapping around my tone. We so don't have time to be fighting with each other.

"I can get Harley into the Seven's residence undetected," Ryder fires back. "That a good enough reason, asshole?"

CHAPTER THIRTY-THREE

HARLEY

Three days.

It had taken me and my crew three days to agree on a foolproof plan.

Three days for Kazuki to brew up an incredibly rare batch of *Telelumos*—or in non-warlock terms, teleportation dust.

Enough time for Rainier to update his Overlord and have him send messages across the Ather in case we need to call for help.

Now finally, *finally*, it's go time.

But there is still one thing I can't get over.

"*I* should be the one to get Ray," I say to Rainier for the umpteenth time. We stand in a circle in Kaz's lounge, each of us ready to play our parts in the infiltration of the Seven's residence.

Ryder will get us in through one of the Judge's entrances—tunnels beneath the main residence. Then he and Wallace and Cassiel will set off a diversion on the opposite wing from where they're keeping Ray.

Rainier comes with me and gets Ray out while I handle Draven.

Kaz will be our transport in and out.

Nathan, Anka, and Wrath will protect The Bridge while it's unguarded.

"Draven won't respond to me," Rainier says, red eyes pleading. "We've been over this."

"If anyone has a chance at getting him to remember who he is," Cassiel says, "it's you, Harley. His mate. You reached him in the Dreamscape. It has to be you."

Rainier shifts next to me, gently clutching my shoulder. "I will keep her safe."

"I know that." And I really do. As far as powerful beings go, the king of the Ather pretty much tops the list. He'll protect her, but I can't help it. She's always been my responsibility—no, that's not a good enough term.

She's been my *honor*. My heart.

Mine to protect.

It's hard to give up the reins.

Kazuki shakes the black velvet bag of *Telelumos*. "I'll be standing guard at our exit point, sending everyone back here as they come out."

My insides twist and coil. I chew on my bottom lip. "What if I can't get him to remember who he is?"

"Then you knock his ass out and bring him here," Ryder says.

"You are the only one who can touch him without getting the life drained out of you," Wallace reminds me. She stands close enough to Ryder that her shoulder brushes his.

"He'll remember you," Cassiel assures me. "It may take him a minute, but I know him. He won't be able to physically harm his mate. It goes against everything the bond promotes."

I blow out a breath, then finally nod. "Okay," I say, locking eyes with Rainier's. "Keep her safe."

"With my life," he vows, laying a hand over his chest.

"We're going to miss our window," Ryder says, shifting his weight from one foot to the other. "The Seven's high council meeting starts in ten minutes."

I look at each of my friends, hope and panic battling in my chest. This is a risky plan—going against Aphian's demands, trying to sneak out the two people I love most in this world without him knowing. The consequences if we succeed will be a shit show, but I'll deal with that when it comes.

We have to try.

And they're with me.

But if this plan goes south…

"Each of you still has a choice," I say. "This isn't your fight—"

Cassiel rolls his eyes.

"You've really got to cut that shit out," Wallace says. "We're with you, Firestarter. Get it through your thick head."

I arch a brow at her, and she smirks back.

"Quite," Kaz says, dipping his polished fingers into the velvet bag. He draws out a handful of shimmering iridescent powder. "And seeing as we really don't have time for pep talks or declarations of undying love…" He tosses the powder above our heads and the floor melts beneath my feet.

Warmth tingles over my skin, my entire being shifting into a million little bubbles as I propel through darkness—

My boots hit sand, my soul slamming back into my body with the force of a derailed train. Everything around me is doubled, my vision vibrating for a few seconds before things shift into a clear picture.

Ryder runs smooth and silent ahead of us, and I quickly mirror his movements until he stops in front of a mound of golden bricks with a bright wooden door inlaid between them. The sand is pearl white and the sky is a blanket of stars as it stretches over a churning ocean behind us.

I remember that ocean from Draven's Dreamscape and hope flares in my chest.

We're close.

So close to taking back what the Seven stole from us.

"I will be ready," Kaz says.

I squeeze his arm in a silent thanks, then follow Ryder through the door he's opened by pressing his palm against the center. Wallace is on his heels, Cassiel behind him, and Rainier behind me.

We're plunged in darkness as the door seals shut behind us, but golden lights flicker to life as Ryder passes iron sconces hanging from the stone walls. The air is damp and cold, the winding tunnel twisting and turning so much I have to repeat every direction four times to commit it to memory.

We won't all be coming back at the same time. Not if everything goes according to plan.

After what feels like an hour but is more like five minutes, Ryder pauses in the epicenter of the tunnels. Eight more tunnel entrances spread out from this center circle, looking like spokes on a wheel.

He points to the one we just exited. "Remember that mark."

I study the slash of gold paint above the tunnel exit—a thick brushstroke with three tick marks through it. "Got it."

"We go left, toward the council chambers," he says, then points to a tunnel on the right. "You and Rainier take this tunnel all the way down and out, then turn left. Ray is being kept in one of Aphian's private suites. The door is royal blue with a gold winged knocker, but Draven will likely be standing guard outside of it."

"Be safe," Cassiel says, reaching for my hand. "Bring my brother back to me, okay?"

Ryder glares at him for a moment, but then looks to me. "Try not to set the place on fire, okay, Antichrist? This isn't a revenge mission. It's stealth and rescue. Can you handle that?"

Wallace's brown eyes shift to indigo as her power crackles over her skin. "She's got this, right, Firestarter?"

"I'll do my best," I say, and really that's all I can promise any of them. Because if I run into Aphian by chance? I can't guarantee I won't roast him on a spit right then and there.

"Come on, daughter," Rainier says, urging me toward the tunnel Ryder indicated. "We have no time to waste."

Adrenaline slides like lava through my veins. I give my friends a parting glance and follow Rainier into the dark.

The tunnels do not respond to us in the way they did to Ryder—no beautiful sconces ignite to light our way, but my eyes adjust to the darkness well enough.

Each step we take toward the end of the tunnel has my heart thudding against my chest so hard I'm half certain it'll break bone. I inhale through my nose and out through my mouth, willing the powers thrashing inside me to calm, to keep me steady.

But my hands are *shaking* by the time Rainier stops before a wooden door, golden light peeking through the thin cracks. Earth and flame, ice and air spiral inside me, flexing and stretching with a need to be unleashed.

The mating bond inside me flares and groans, an internal tug on the rusting chain binding Draven to me and me to him. I gasp, instantly covering my mouth. Rainier cocks a brow at me, and I blow out a shaky breath, concentrating on that bond.

"He's close," I whisper, sliding my hand over the center of my chest. "I can *feel* him," I say, tears biting the backs of my eyes. The chain is crumbling at the edges and so, so cold.

Rainier growls, his red eyes flickering like flames as he reaches for the door.

I nod to him, my entire body buzzing with the need to *move*.

He slowly pushes against the door, only allowing it to open enough for him to survey the hallway beyond. He urges me to follow him after a few moments, and I have to blink against the stark light as we move out of the tunnel.

Gold-framed pictures decorate the smooth stone walls, a lit sconce in between each illuminating the polished marble floors. We move silently, following Ryder's directions. The area is quiet, giving some hope that our plan will work. The Seven will have their meeting, then be drawn away by a distraction, we'll get my sister and my mate, and all will be right in the world again.

Yeah, because that's how life works.

I silence the inner bitch in my mind, shutting her out and focusing on nothing more than taking the next step in front of me.

Rainier pauses at the end of the hallway where we need to turn left, and I hold my breath. He glances down at me, shaking his head. We round the corner, and I immediately note the royal blue door with the golden wings in its center.

No Draven.

Rainier silently asks me what I want to do, and I urge him forward. Stick to the plan. Get Ray.

What if Aphian forced Draven to go to the meeting? But why would he include Draven in a meeting meant for only the Seven?

We make it to the door, and my heart is ready to burst from my chest as Rainier swings it open. The room is dark, the only light coming from the opened windows lining the farthest wall, the moonlight glinting in beams across a massive bed—

"*Ray*," I whisper, racing to her. Rainier is on my heels, but I'm sliding my arms underneath her and hauling her to me.

"Harley?" she gasps, throwing her arms around my neck.

"Ohmigod," I whisper-cry, tears rolling over my lashes. I can't help it. Relief barrels down my soul at the sight of my baby sister. "I can't...*Ray*."

"I need to take her now," Rainier whispers.

I cup Ray's cheeks in my hands. "You're going to go with Rainier now, okay?"

"What about you?" she asks, eyes wide with panic.

"I have to find Draven," I say, hating that I have to let her go. "Do you know where he is?"

"He's—"

"Right here," Draven's lethal tone answers.

Light floods the room. I spin around, gaping at Draven, who stands near the closed door, hand poised over the switch.

"Rainier," I warn, and he scoops Ray into his arms.

"You're not taking her anywhere," Draven snaps, and flicks his wrist toward Rainier. Shadows burst from his fingers, spears of smoke aimed at Rainier's neck.

I leap in front of the shadows, casting air around me in a tight shield to push them back. The dark tendrils recoil from the hard air around me, and Draven's golden eyes widen.

I shift on my feet, hurtling my air at Draven so hard he slams against the opposite wall. "Go!" I yell, keeping my position in front of Rainier and Ray as he hurries them toward the door.

"Harley!" Ray calls as Rainier gets the door open. "He knows. He *does*!"

"Get her to Kazuki," I say, then mouth *I love you* to my sister before they disappear into the hallway.

I turn back to Draven, my air still pressing him against that wall. "I'm sorry."

A twisted grin I've never seen before shapes his lips.

He lashes against my power with his own, spearing shadows beneath my air and snuffing it like blowing out a candle. A blink, and he's crashing into me, a dagger of pure shadow pressed against my throat.

"Not as sorry as you're going to be, Antichrist."

CHAPTER THIRTY-FOUR

HARLEY

"Draven," I say, the kiss of the shadow blade sharp against my skin. "Please, look at me."

But he *is* looking at me.

And he has no clue who I am.

"I will not let you destroy this world," he says in a voice that isn't his at all.

I eye him then the dagger and back to him again. "Then what's stopping you?"

Something flickers in his golden eyes. "Aphian will want you."

"That's the only reason?" I ask, and he grips my arm, hauling me to my feet. "Draven, you're my—"

"Shit!" Rainier shouts from the hallway outside Ray's room. I move that direction, my heart racing.

Draven jerks my arm so hard it burns, keeping me from the door.

I glance down at his hand. "Feel that?" I ask, and he glares down at me. "Nothing, right? Why do you think you can touch me, *Siphon*?"

He blinks a few times, then cringes against some invisible pain. My heart twists. He's trying to remember me and the commands in his head are torturing him for it. Just like when Cassiel and I found him in the Dreamscape.

"Trick." He groans out the word, his dagger disappearing as he grabs me with his other hand, his eyes blazing as he looks where he touches my bare skin. "It's a *trick*. Aphian will just have to forgive me for killing you."

Draven conjures two shadow axes. He swings them toward me, and they crash against my flame, the smoke hissing and sputtering as I shove my strength into it. We're almost nose to nose as we battle to shove a blade one way or the other, and I grit my teeth.

"You are my *mate*," I say.

"Liar. *Deceiver*."

I gain the upper hand, hurling him off of me so hard he stumbles backward. I point my sword at him as we circle each other. "You play piano," I say, matching him step for step as he studies me for a weak spot. "You have a secret air-handshake with Ray." I block the swing of his axe with my sword. I shift my arm, showing him the black flame and leaf tattoo. "You gave your *blood* to buy this mark for me." I dodge another swing. "You died!" I yell, anger rising in my throat. "You *died*, and I refused to let you go. *I* brought you back, Draven. Because you're mine and I'm *yours*."

Draven goes rigid, his back straightening so quickly he jerks against it. His eyes shift, his expression momentarily so lost, my heart aches.

"It's me," I say, stepping toward him timidly. His axes hang loose by his sides, and I extinguish my flaming sword. "It's *Harley*. You know me. Better than anyone has ever known me before." I reach up, shaking as I place my hand over his heart. "This is not who you are," I say, watching as the gold in his eyes churns—

He slams a palm against my chest, propelling me across the room. I hit the wall next to the opened door so hard I see stars. I slump to the floor, the sounds of a battle raging in the hall penetrating the fog in my head. Ray and Rainier. Are they in trouble? I try to get up, to go help, but Draven is already sprinting across the room, axe raised and aimed right at my throat.

I cringe against the hit I know is coming, my powers weak and wobbly as I reach for them through the stun of the hit—

A blade of pure gold blocks the swing of his axe, the reverberation sending a shockwave through the room. Draven's thrown back, and a woman steps in front of me, her long hair a red the same shade as mine, and she's wielding that beautiful sword.

My eyes clear and my stomach drops. "Mom?"

"Get up," she orders.

I'm on my feet in seconds. A million memories race through my mind—her sneaking me an extra roll behind my father's back at dinner, her blowing raspberries against my palms to make me laugh, her tear-soaked eyes as she wrapped that bracelet around my wrist and made me promise never to take it off.

My mind catches up with my body, and I blink off the shock of seeing her.

"Your dad needs me," she says. "Help this one." She points at Draven, then flashes me an apologetic look before sprinting back out the door.

Shit, shit, *shit.*

Draven rises to his feet, and I brace myself to face him. I can hear the fighting from the hall and every instinct is screaming at me to run. To help protect them. But Draven, my mate. He needs me right now, and I feel split down the damn middle.

"Draven," I say, using the space I've always left open for him in my mind. *"You're stronger than this. Your powers are greater than all the Seven combined. You answer to no one but yourself."*

I reach for him, and he snarls at me like a wild animal.

And my heart sinks at the sight before me.

My mate—lost and empty and raging.

"Draven—"

The word chokes out of me as he rushes me, slamming the force of his weight into me until my back is against the wall and his fingers are wrapped around my throat.

I grip his forearms, trying like hell to dislodge his grip without truly hurting him. "Draven," I gasp as he squeezes harder. "I don't want to hurt you." My powers surge, begging for release. Begging to protect me.

His brow pinches as I drop my hands, let them hang weak at my sides.

I focus, doing my best to project memory after memory at the spot for him in my mind—the first time we danced, before I knew anything of this world, the first time he kissed me, the first time we slept together.

"You're…" I barely get the words out. "Killing. Me."

I mentally wrap my fingers around the golden chain between us, the one covered in ice crystals and rust. The mating bond that's suffered under the divine command to forget me. Forget his mate. I jerk it as close to me as possible as I coax my onyx fire around it. Burning it, melting it, shaping it into something more powerful than any command or order.

Draven jolts against me, groaning against the searing heat I send down that bond—

"Harley," he gasps, his grip instantly dropping.

I barely get a chance to suck in a lungful of air before his mouth is on mine.

His tongue parts my lips, stroking me until I'm no longer trying to push him away, I'm tugging him closer.

"I'm sorry," he breathes between our kiss. "I'm so fucking sorry."

CHAPTER THIRTY-FIVE

DRAVEN

She tastes like honey and caramel and everything right in the world. I keep kissing her, drinking in her gasps, devouring the whimpers from her throat.

"I'm sorry," I say again, moving from her lips to her jawline, to her neck, and back again. Holding her to me like that alone will heal the wounds I've caused. "Did I hurt you?" I ask, drawing back.

Her green eyes are filled with light and hope and *fuck* I never thought I'd see them again. My mind is a spinning, spiraling mist of fog and memory—a tornado of images from the second Aphian had taken control to the minute she freed me.

"No," she says.

"You found me," I say.

"I'll always find you," she says, grinning, tears shining in her eyes. "Are you with me?"

I nod, claiming her mouth again and groaning at the feel of her body against mine.

My *mate*.

Aphian almost made me kill my *mate*.

"I'm here," I say, shaking my head as I cup her face in my hands. "I've been trying to fight it, Harley." I swallow hard. "And there were times I remembered, but the Orders drove me away again."

"Can you still feel the commands?" she asks.

"Yes," I say. "But you...the bond. It's different. Stronger. The chain shattered those commands and isn't letting them rise again."

She closes her eyes, two tears rolling down her cheeks as she sighs.

I can feel the relief from her barreling down our bond. I wipe away the tears with my thumbs. "Look at me," I say, and she opens her eyes. "I'm with you."

She crushes her mouth to mine before jerking away. "Don't," she says. "*Ever*. Do that to me again."

I capture her lips, stealing the breath from her lungs before pulling back. "Never again."

CHAPTER THIRTY-SIX

HARLEY

I pull out of Draven's embrace.

Now that I've saved him, all my instincts are roaring about the battle raging outside. I can't ignore them, can't stop for one second to formulate a plan. I just go, racing out the door, an unflinching need to protect my sister, Rainier.

I jerk back one step outside the door, dodging a massive body hurtling through the air.

Rainier is on one end of the wide hallway, hands raised as he wields his powers.

My mother is behind him, her golden sword clanking as she battles two Judges. Ray is behind her, forced into a small alcove, my mother protecting that one spot of shelter.

"You will regret coming here," a masculine voice says. The male who Rainier threw down the hall. No, not a man at all. He's on his feet, massive gray dapple wings stretched to their length. A menacing smile shapes his thin lips as he glances over his shoulder.

Another winged male steps up behind him, his wings a burnt orange.

And *Aphian* stands to his right.

I bristle at the sight of him.

"Looking a little singed there, Hillel," Rainier says to the gray dappled-winged male. He smirks at the patches of black along the angel's feathers, the spots still smoking from a hit Rainier delivered.

Hillel glares at him, flexing his chest beneath identical robes of white that Aphian wears.

"You can't possibly take all of us out," Aphian says. "You know you're no match for the collective power of the Seven." But there is a hint of fear in his voice, and he's not moving an *inch* closer to Rainier.

"Maybe not," Rainier says. I can feel the power snapping from him as he shifts on his feet. Something like pure excitement flickers in his red eyes as he raises his hands again. "But I sure as fuck can take *three.*" Flames pop along his hands and arms. Smoke curls around his shoulders, growing larger and wider until he's blotted out the space behind him where my mother battles the Judges. Where Ray is safely tucked into that alcove.

"Hillel." Aphian says his name like a command. "Kill him."

Hillel visibly swallows before harsh white light fills his eyes.

"Yes, Hillel," Rainier says, laughing. "Do try." He waves his hand, beckoning him forward.

Hillel rushes Rainier, his bare feet lifting off the ground a few inches as his wings propel him faster.

"You too, Judah," Aphian commands.

The other Seven next to Aphian lunges that direction, too, and my heart lurches.

I move before thinking about it, crashing into him. We fall to the floor, his left wing covering my entire body as he pins me with it. It smells like rotten oranges and its heavy as fuck. I thought feathers were supposed to be light, damn it. How does Cassiel fly with two of these things on him?

"Two on one isn't a fair fight," I snap, shoving at the wing.

"Look at the cute little Antichrist trying to save her worthless daddy," Judah says.

Half a thought.

That's all it takes to engulf my entire body in flames.

And then I lose my ever-loving shit.

Judah screeches, flinging himself off of me, his feathers curling to ash against my flames. White light blazes, snuffing the fire as he stumbles backward. I hop to my feet, smirking at the Harley-sized scorch mark along his wing.

"Yes!" Rainier calls behind me, dodging a blow from Hillel. "Let it out, daughter! Put them in their place!"

I glance over my shoulder to grin at him, but Hillel takes the moment of distraction to hurtle into Rainier, tackling him to the ground.

I move to help, but Judah's white light brushes my skin, and every muscle in my body locks up like I've just dropped a toaster into a bath I was enjoying.

"Harley!" Draven turns to shadow, spiraling around Judah. The white light releases me, bursting in sparks between Draven's shadows.

I turn to Aphian, chest heaving as I catch my breath.

He looks down his nose at me, nothing but disappointment in his eyes. "Thaddeus," he calls, and within seconds, another winged male is flying into the room.

Adrenaline bursts beneath my skin at the power in the hallway. So damn much of it. Four of the Seven. I take a step back, my instincts telling me now is the time to go.

Draven's shadows shift to my side as he materializes next to me. Judah's knees crack against the marble floor, but he's rising to his feet faster than I'd like.

Judah and Thaddeus stand wing to wing as they advance, their white light combining as they swing it in a wave that hits both of us dead center in the chest.

We hurtle through the air, landing in a heap behind where Rainier and Hillel still fight. Bursts of white light and onyx flame bash against each other, the smoke wall behind Rainier faltering in spots.

I whimper as pain lashes through my bones.

Aphian, Judah, and Thaddeus start speaking in unison, the words low and unintelligible.

"What are they doing?" I ask Draven, panicked at the thought of them trying to control him again or put him into the Divine Sleep.

"It's a spell." Draven hauls me to my feet, a muscle in his

jaw flexing. "A containment spell." He looks at Rainier.

"Fuck," I groan, stumbling toward the three Seven.

"I put Lila into the Divine Sleep," Hillel spits at my father. "I can do it again as simple as this." He waves a hand behind Rainier, and I hear her gasp through the smoke wall.

"No!" Rainier roars, thrashing his arms. Hillel jerks into midair, a silent scream on his face as Rainier holds him there. His body isn't even trembling with the effort to contain a Seven as he saunters up to him, nothing but hatred clinging to his red eyes.

"You're done," Rainier whispers as he looks up at Hillel. He punches his hand through Hillel's chest, turning to look at the three Seven still chanting that damn spell. "*All* of you are done fucking with my family."

I freeze, gaping, as Rainier jerks his arm back.

His fist squeezes Hillel's *heart*.

The Seven drops to the floor, his wings disintegrating into a pile of ash before his body follows.

Rainier squeezes that dead muscle in his hands, and it crumbles to black at his boots. He wipes the ash from his palms as he steps forward. "Who's next?" he asks, the words almost as casual as if he's asking them out to lunch.

Aphian's eyes are wide. "Bartholomew!"

A second, and a male with brown wings flies around the corner, landing at his side.

Rainier glares at the four of them, moving toward them—

They chant again, louder this time, and Rainier pauses.

Then roars against some invisible pain.

"No!" I hurry to his side, but I'm thrown back the second I get within an arm's reach of him.

Draven catches me before I fall, steadying me on my feet as Rainier's smoke wall drops completely.

Six Judges lay unconscious on the ground, my mother heaving for breath as she turns to face us.

I whirl back to look at the four angels.

"Stop!" I yell. Rainier is on his knees now—his fucking *knees*. He's roaring against their spell, his teeth bared, looking every inch the king of the Ather. Flames shoot from his body, smoke snapping from him like a whip. Cracks splinter up the marble walls, the ground beneath our feet rumbling—not from my power, but from his.

That's my *dad*. And they're trying to fucking trap him again.

These are the ones who took Ray.

Took my mate. Nearly had him kill me.

They attacked The Bridge and Miller's. Everything I love. My *family*.

"*Stop*," I say again, but this time my voice sounds like a combination of fire and ice.

But they don't stop.

And my powers rise like a tidal wave.

Smoking flames and glittering ice swirl together, shooting at the four angels who have threatened so much, and they crash into a wall of harsh light that sends my teeth rattling. I flinch against the blowback, clenching my jaw as I push my powers harder.

Bartholomew breaks from the pack, soaring over our heads and behind me. He snatches Ray up so fast I barely have time to breathe as he hauls her back toward Judah and Aphian and Thaddeus.

"Cease your powers, Antichrist," Bartholomew demands as he plops Ray on her feet. She kicks him in the shin, and he growls at her. "Or you'll end up killing her, too."

I lasso my powers, my storm of fire and ice evaporating.

My mother yelps as she's yanked on some invisible string, crashing against Rainier, who's still on his knees. Encased now where he's trapped, too.

Chunks fall from the ceiling, cracking against the floor in massive shatters. Draven hauls me back before one can cave in my skull.

"Ray!" I scream as Draven tugs me back.

A female with pewter wings flies up behind the four, her delicate wings graceful as she dodges the building coming down on top of us. She opens her arms for Ray, and Ray rushes into them willingly.

"Ray!" I gape at the pair as she takes to the air again, flying out of sight.

"Harley," Draven says, tugging me back. "This whole section is coming down. We have to go!"

I jerk out of his hold, my powers snapping as they aim for the four. "I have to get Ray!"

A chunk of the stone ceiling clips my shoulder, and I yelp, the pain sharp and searing. But I don't stop. I keep walking, keep sending my fire at the four as my dad roars on his knees.

A band of shadow wraps around my waist, yanking me back and out of the way of another massive chunk of the building. The debris pelts my ankles, and I bite back tears from the pain.

"Esther has Ray," Draven says, replacing that band of shadow with his arm. He hurries us back and away from the four, from the falling building. From Rainier and my mother, trapped by the Seven's spell. "You can't save her if you get yourself killed!"

"Damn it!" I cry out, struggling as he continues to yank me out of the room.

"*Esther is on our side,*" Draven says into my mind. "*I promise. She will keep Ray safe. But if you die here, there's no saving any of them. You die, your family dies. Because no one else is strong enough to go up against the Seven.*"

His words hit me like a hammer.

Because he's right.

If I die, who else will be able to find the scrolls and stop them?

My heart feels like it's being sliced in two as I stop fighting Draven and instead turn on my heels and run with him.

We race through the tunnels, Draven keeping pace right behind me.

Kaz breathes out a half-annoyed, half-relieved sigh as we skid to a halt in front of him. "About damn time," he says, fisting a handful of the powder.

"We're behind you!" Ryder calls out, orange bursts of energy crackling behind him as the familiar sound of weapon fire rings out. "Go! Now!"

Kaz tosses the powder over our heads, and we're spiraling through the world, failure snapping at our heels as we leave with fewer people than we came with.

CHAPTER THIRTY-SEVEN

HARLEY

We slam against the slick floors of The Bridge, Draven's strong hands hauling me to my feet.

The ground trembles as Kazuki, Cassiel, Wallace, and Ryder hit the floor next to us, shaking their heads to clear the effects of the teleportation.

I eye the spots where Ray, Rainier, and my mother *should* be, and panic makes the breath in my lungs tight.

"What the hell happened?" Ryder asks.

"Your diversion didn't work," I fire at him.

Lightning crackles in his eyes. "It was a trap."

I'm moving before I can help it. He retreats as I advance, only stopping when he hits the wall.

"You were supposed to distract the Seven. But *five* of them came straight for us. They trapped Rainier. My mother." I clench my eyes shut. "They still have Ray."

"They knew we were coming—"

"This was *your* plan." I grip his shirt, fire rippling up my arms. "How the fuck did they know we were coming?"

Draven steps up to my left, and Cassiel is on my right.

"Harley," Cassiel says. "Let Ryder go."

"She's fine," Draven says. "She's in control."

The fact that Draven is reassuring Cassiel that I'm not about to become a living bomb makes me check myself. I release Ryder, taking a calculated step away from him. I inhale deeply, latching on to my mate's scent of cedar and citrus, using it to calm the powers inside me.

"I'm sorry," I whisper.

"I don't know what happened," Ryder says. "Honestly. I have no idea how they knew we were coming."

"Maybe a spell?" Cassiel offers. "For detection?" He looks to Kazuki.

"I wasn't close enough to confirm that theory," Kazuki says.

I blow out a breath, turning to Draven. His amber eyes lock with mine, and I don't need his mind reading powers to know how sorry he is.

"It wasn't your fault," I say. "You were right. Even if I hate that you were." I shake my head. "I would've died trying to get them out." And then I'd really be the useless piece of garbage my nonbiological father always told me I was. "I can only protect my family if I'm alive."

"If we could've done anything different —"

"I know." I wrap my arms around Draven, trembling with exhaustion and loss.

A buzzing sounds from the pocket of Draven's jeans, and I pull out of his embrace.

"I don't remember having my phone on me," he says, golden eyes wary as he draws it out. He answers the call, his hand shaking as he presses it to his ear. I tilt my head, and he lowers the phone, putting it on speaker.

"That was not part of our bargain, child." Aphian's voice rings loud and clear over the line. "The only reason your sister is still alive is because Esther got her away from the damage your father caused. And because you gave me something so much more valuable in exchange for the worthless soldier you took."

Fire courses through me.

"Though, the death of one of my Seven can't go unpunished…" The sound of something shifting rustles over the line —

Rainier roars, an agonized scream I can feel in my bones. And a woman is crying in the background, yelling against something I can't see.

My mother.

"Stop!" I beg, body shaking from how powerless I am. "I have your scrolls! Stop!"

Rainier's roars cease, and the crying from my mother fades until all I can hear is Aphian. "Be grateful they were closest and not your sister."

I grind my teeth so hard they almost crack. "If you hurt her—"

"How many scrolls do you have?"

"Two," I lie. He gave me three weeks, and we've managed to get all but three in half the time. "They're harder to get than you might think," I continue. "I'm distracted. If you give me Ray, I'll work faster." Silence eats up the seconds between us. "You have my mother. And my dad. Give my sister back."

"Hmm," Aphian muses. "No. You have Draven and Ryder. Unfortunate about Ryder. I adored that Judge. His betrayal will leave marks on my soul for centuries."

You won't be alive for centuries, I silently vow.

"I will keep Ray and your father and mother. And trust me when I say that not only can I send her right back to the Divine Sleep she's been in these past years, but I can flip her as easily as Draven. And she will not be swayed like he was. She barely remembers you. All it will take is one Order from me, and her blade finds a home in your father's heart."

"Bastard," I seethe, and Draven looks equally as murderous.

"Time is ticking, child," he says. "You have a week and a half left. I'd hurry if I were you."

The line goes dead. The silence snakes into me like an oil, slicking over my heart until I'm sure I'll suffocate from it.

My friends are quiet, calculating and waiting. Wrath pads past all of them, leaning into my side. I pet his coarse fur until my fingers stop shaking, until I can breathe without it feeling like my chest is caving in.

Cassiel shifts his leg when Pagle waddles close to him.

Draven arches a brow at the creature.

"That's Pagle," I say.

"You and your pets," Draven says, a soft smile on his lips.

Cassiel turns to Draven. "Aphian planted you with that phone on purpose. He knew there was a chance we'd get you out."

I sigh, my brain searing from the questions racing through my head. "You're sure he won't hurt Ray—"

"He won't. *I* know he won't," Draven says.

"Tell me again."

"Esther is our ally. She was trying to break the commands while I was there. She won't let anything happen to Ray. Plus, Aphian Ordered me to *guard* her, train her. The power she possesses is precious to him. He won't risk damaging what he hopes will be a growing relationship between them. He wants her to choose him in the end. To stand at his side and be his divine seer for eternity."

I curl my lip. "She would never—"

"I know. Trust me. She fought me until she realized honing her gifts may be the only way to help me." He visibly swallows, shaking his head, the ghost of a smile playing at his lips. "She's incredible, Harley. We advanced to illusion casting because she blew through telepathy—"

"She can read minds like you?" I gasp. "What kind of illusions?"

"All kinds," he says. "She's as powerful as you. She made me see things. Subtle clues. She triggered my true self several times before the divine commands tore me away again."

Pride swells in my chest. "She fought for you."

Cassiel laughs. "Little seer was always stubborn."

"Aphian won't risk hurting her," Draven says again. "He wants you to believe it, so you'll do what he says."

A little relief untangles the knots inside me. "But now he has Rainier and my mother." I pace the length of Kazuki's room. Wrath follows me step for step as my friends settle on the edges of the couches and chairs.

"We all thought your mother was..." Ryder's voice trails

off as he glances at Wallace.

"Dead," Wallace finishes for him. She shrugs, never one to beat around the bush.

"I did, too," I say. "So did Rainier." Didn't he say his Overlord had heard news of it? I guess I wouldn't put it past Aphian to spread the lie about her death, but for what? Just to hurt Rainier, who was already caged?

"She's a Judge," Draven says, shaking his head as he rests his elbows on his knees from where he sits in a chair. Cassiel is in the one next to him while Kazuki takes up an entire couch on his own as he stretches out.

Draven's eyes meet mine and I stop pacing. "I should've seen it. I knew it didn't make sense for your mother to leave you with that asshole. But you can't refuse a divine order and before she even had the chance to fight, Aphian put her to sleep."

Fire spirals around my fingers, but I work with them instead of against them as they feed off my anger. I shape them into tendrils of black and silver and send them dancing across the air between us.

"This has to stop," I say, shaking my head. "The Seven's— well, Six, now—control over the divine soldiers is horrific." I swallow thickly. They stole my mother's chance at knowing me, just like they did to Rainier. And how many more have they done this to? How many more people have they ripped apart? Forced them to do things against their will?

"You're close," Kazuki says. "Only three left to find, and you'll have the power to stop them for good."

"Right," I say, dragging my fingers through Wrath's fur. The hound leans his massive weight into my side. "But I'll still have to play Aphian's game. I can't risk him hurting my family."

"And you can't risk actually giving him those scrolls, either," Ryder says. "You know what he wants with them, don't you?"

"Beyond the power they give?" I ask.

Ryder looks at me—still with Draven's eyes, which is creepy as hell. "They aren't just powerful scrolls with an incantation that grants ultimate power," Ryder says. "They'll grant him the ability to bend the veil."

"But my blood—"

"Is the Key, yeah. But those scrolls were made by the Creator. Wielding all seven of them?" He shakes his head. "Aphian wants to drop the veil entirely, blend the worst parts of it on Earth to cleanse who he considers weak. Then he'll rid the world of those creatures who did his dirty work and the remaining survivors will be his new loyal subjects to usher in a new world order." He shrugs. "After that, he could destroy the rest of the Ather, if he wanted."

My blood runs cold. "He could do that to the world *and* destroy the Ather?" The one place that feels like home to me? "Is there anything this asshole can't take from me?"

"We'll take it before him," Draven says, eyes like golden fire as he looks up at me. "And *you* decide what you want to do." He rises from his chair to stand before me. "You'll stop him. And you can set the good parts of the Ather free, if that's what you want."

"Oh?" Kazuki chimes from behind me, and I turn to look at him. "Is that on your bucket list, darling?"

"Maybe," I say, thinking about my brief conversation with Rainier about the way the world *used* to be. Demons and humans living together in one endless world. "Rainier and I spoke about it in London, but…" I blow out a breath. "Let's stop Aphian first. He's not only blackmailing me, but he's testing those weapons." I glance to Draven. "He attacked The Bridge, or his minions did. The weapons made from the Colis he stole. They're horrific, and one almost killed Kaz."

Draven's eyes widen on the warlock.

"Harley had perfect timing," Kaz says, grinning at me. "She power shared with me to heal me," he continues, cocking a brow at Draven when a low growl rumbles from his chest. "Jealous, Judge?"

I slide my fingers into Draven's, squeezing gently.

Cassiel grunts from his chair. "More like disgusted. Who *knows* where all your power has been."

"Whenever you want a taste, Death Striker, all you have to do is ask." Kaz's lavender eyes blaze.

"Keep dreaming, wizard," Cassiel says.

A small, broken laugh flies past my lips, and the tension mounting in my chest eases, but Cassiel's word triggers something inside me.

"Dreaming," I say, my heart racing. "Draven, you said Ray is advancing in her powers." He nods, and I turn to Cassiel. "Cass, can we try and reach her through the Dreamscape?" If we can reach her, then we can plan better, and most importantly, I'll know if she's okay.

Cassiel purses his lips. "We can try."

"Now."

We don't hesitate as we slip effortlessly into the roles we played while trying to reach Draven.

The room grows quiet as we work. I concentrate on every memory I have of Ray, everything that makes up who she is—colors and hope and optimism. Laughter and joy and light.

Cassiel follows me as I cling to those thoughts, a rainbow forming in my mind. It winds and spirals and even has slides as we shoot our mental awareness down it—

We slam into a wall of pure, harsh white light.

"Shit," Cassiel grumbles out loud. "Aphian has her mind shielded from you."

I keep my eyes clenched shut, shifting gears. "Let's try Rainier."

"Okay," Cassiel says, not a hint of hesitation to try and break into the damn Devil's mind.

I don't have memories of Rainier to draw on. Not enough. I gasp as we dive deeper and deeper. I keep pushing, sifting through what feels like an endless well of power, not all of them revealed to me.

Rainier. Rainier. Rainier.

I repeat his name in my mind, clinging to the powers his blood gifted me —

And slam into another white wall that stings my entire soul.

"Fuck!" I snap, drawing out of myself.

"Aphian must've done it right after we left," Cassiel says, slumping into his seat a little deeper.

"Harley," Draven says, pulling me to him before I fall over. "You need to rest."

I take a few solid breaths. "We need to get the next scroll," I counter. "But I don't have a clue where it is."

"I can help with that," Draven says, a crease forming in his brow. "Esther...she spoke about one, but I wasn't myself." His eyes go distant like he's wading through muddled memories. After a few minutes, he blinks back to the present. "I know where to go."

Hope blooms in my chest.

"Are you sure you don't want to rest first?" Draven asks. "We can —"

"Point the way." I give him a look that says there is absolutely no use fighting me on it.

"We're going with you this time," Ryder says, rising from the couch, Wallace right behind him.

I don't bother arguing.

"I'll stay with the wizard and your human," Cassiel says, referring to Nathan. "Work on leads to the last two scrolls."

"Thank you," I say, hugging him, then rub Wrath's ears. "Stay with Cass."

"Here," Kaz says, crossing the distance to us. He hands me the velvet bag of *Telelumos*. "You must have a clear image in your mind when you use it," he explains. "Let one person conjure the location in their mind, and the rest of you just make sure you're touching."

"Got it," I say, handing the bag to Draven. "Thanks, Kaz."

He bows slightly. "I'll put it on your tab."

I look to Draven as he dips his fingers into the bag, drawing out the fine powder. Wallace grabs my shoulder with one hand and holds Ryder's hand with her other. I step up and wrap my free arm around Draven's waist, and Ryder grabs my hand, since no one else can touch Draven.

"Ready?" Draven asks, and we all nod.

"Show us the way," I say.

CHAPTER
THIRTY-EIGHT

HARLEY

"It's a *door*," Wallace says, cocking a brow at me, then Draven. She leans closer to Ryder, who stands on her left. "Does he know he just teleported us on the *wrong* side of a door?"

Draven glares at her. "I've never been on the other side of this door." The massive structure in front of us is as tall and wide as a wall with tons of iron bars and ancient-looking locks strewn over it. "I could only picture what Esther planted in my mind."

"She put this in your mind when you were under Aphian's control?" I ask.

"Yes," he says. "She tried to undo his commands, too, but his powers are greater than hers." He visibly swallows. "She left this memory in my mind. A scroll is behind this door, I know it."

I chew on my bottom lip. "She's *good* then? I know you told me she was your ally. But honestly, after Aphian and the Orders the Seven agreed to…"

"You're ready to slaughter them all," Ryder finishes for me, and Wallace jabs him in the stomach with her elbow. He flinches, then pins her with a look that is more playful than angry, and I can't help but smile at the two.

"Yeah," I finally answer. "I am."

"Not her," Ryder says. "She's on our side. Playing both roles, like I was supposed to before Aphian figured out what I was doing."

I sigh, rubbing my palms over my face. I glance behind me, noting there looks to be like a thousand steps leading down from the landing we stand on. They disappear into a thick green forest that's cloaked in darkness.

"Where are we?" I ask.

Draven is studying the door, his golden eyes darting from lock to lock and back again. "Rome," he says all casual, like he didn't just teleport us across the damn globe.

"Great," I say, stepping closer to the door. I clear my mind, forcing out the anxious thoughts threatening to choke me. An electric current hums in my blood, growing stronger the closer I get to the door. "You're right," I say, adjusting the pack on my hip. "There's definitely a scroll behind there."

"Let's go then," Wallace says, her body twinkling with the indigo energy of her power. She smirks at me, then blinks out of sight—only to appear on her ass two feet behind us, nearly falling down the endless stairs. "*Shit.*"

Ryder hurries to help her up, and she dusts off her black leather pants, glaring at the door like it bit her.

"That was adorable," he says.

She arches a brow at him. "Keep joking, Judge, and I'll teleport you to the sky and then drop your ass."

He grins at her, his fingers on her wrist as he draws her closer. "You'd have to shake me off first," he says, almost a whisper between them. "And I'm known to be quite...*clingy.*"

Wallace laughs, shoving him away, and my heart swells for them. There is some serious chemistry flying between them and I'm here for it. They both deserve happiness, especially in this fucked-up time.

"It's locked," Draven says, apparently oblivious to what's going on with his brother.

"I think Wallace already figured that out," I say. "How do we open it? Did she leave that information in your head, too, by chance?"

His features twist in an apologetic gesture.

"It's fine," I say. "She probably didn't know. Every time we've gotten a scroll, it's been different."

"When we get this one, you'll have to tell me about all the rest."

I nod, beyond elated to have him by my side but also so fucking angry that Aphian still has Ray, and now Rainier. My mother. I shove the thoughts down, focusing on the giant door before me. It's nearly as big as the ones in the frost demon king's palace and my stomach twists. If I have to deal with giants one more time…

"These don't look like normal locks," Wallace says, shifting one closest to her and examining the bottom. "Not any I've seen before, anyway."

Ryder follows suit, checking out the one nearest hers. "What kind of lock doesn't have a keyhole?"

Draven scrunches his brow, heading to the other side of the door, studying one at his eye height. "Maybe whoever sealed the door didn't want anyone getting in."

"That would make sense," I say, stepping to his left, eyes roaming over the door. "Seeing as how every scroll comes with its own set of consequences." I purse my lips. "What will it be this time?" I reach for a lock at my hip level, right as Draven reaches for another—

A surge of energy blasts through me, my vision blurring like I'm soaring too fast through the sky. Stars barrel past me, and I snap out my wings of wind, trying like hell to slow my momentum, but the force of the pull is too strong.

Omph! I tumble onto a cobblestone path, rolling from the speed of my fall until I land on top of someone.

"Harley," Wallace groans, shoving me off of her.

"Sorry," I say, scrambling to my feet, and helping Wallace to hers. Her hand is still in mine when her eyes go wide.

"Look out!" she says, pointing to two dark spots headed straight for us.

I raise my hand, slowing their fall with air.

Ryder and Draven land more gracefully than Wallace and I did, but they look equally confused. Ryder looks like himself, long black hair dusting his shoulders, and turquoise eyes as stark as the ocean. I head straight for my mate.

"You good?" I ask.

He slides his hand along my cheek. "Yes. You?"

I nod.

"What the hell is that?" Wallace asks, and I spin around to see what she's pointing at.

"Holy shit," I say, looking up at the massive circles of light that are shimmering at the end of the cobblestone path. Cerulean and lapis circles overlap and intertwine in a constant state of motion while little purple symbols dance in the small spaces the overlapped circles create.

"Oh no," Ryder says, hands in his hair.

"What?" I ask.

His eyes dart from me to Wallace to Draven and back again. He shakes his head, wagging a finger crackling with lightning at the circles of light ahead. "I've seen something like this before."

"What is it?" Wallace asks, her hand on his shoulder.

"It's a *mylo circle*," he says, and I'm relieved when Draven and Wallace look as confused as I feel. Ryder barks out a laugh. "It's a cerebral spell...it links minds together."

Wallace's gaze widens. "We're in each other's minds right now?"

"More like our consciousnesses are together in a completely separate plane," Ryder explains. "But in our consciousnesses is all we are and all we possess, so technically, yes, we're in each other's minds."

I raise my hand like that might help me sort through what he's saying. "Can you run that by me again?"

Ryder groans. "We're linked," he says, then smacks his palms against his chest. "This may look like my body, but it's not really my body. It's my mental projection of it."

"How certain are you?" Draven asks.

"I have my eyes and hair back, don't I?"

"That doesn't mean anything," I say. "How do you know this isn't just some illusion we've fallen into cast around the scroll? Rainier and I were teleported to a trust-test from hell with the last scroll, maybe this is—"

"It's not. Look, I'll prove it to you. You all know what my powers are, right?"

"Divine lightning," Wallace says. "We get it. You're cooler than Thor."

"And like ten times more handsome," Ryder says, then raises his hands. "But here, I can use any of your powers because we're linked." He curls his fingers and Draven's signature shadows spring to life from them. Draven gives him a warning look, but Ryder ignores him, instead lighting himself up with indigo energy until he teleports right behind Wallace, making her jump. "See?"

I gape at him.

"Oh, I have to try this," Wallace says, a wild grin shaping her full lips. She snaps her fingers and her hand is engulfed by *my* dark flames. She jolts a little before laughing as she turns the fire this way and that. "Badass!"

I stretch my mind, finding an infinite well of selections in my power stores. Draven has siphoned a lot over the years. More than I expected. I pluck one out and a whip of liquid silver manifests in my hand. I grin at Draven, blown away by the way his power feels. And there are *so* many more of his to choose from, but his gold eyes are cast in a warning, no amusement anywhere to be seen.

"No one touch the siphon power," he warns, and I instantly let go of the liquid silver in my hands. It disappears in a blink. "Trust me," he continues. "None of you want to feel that."

The grins on Wallace and Ryder's faces melt off, and I step toward my mate, sliding my hand into his.

"Okay," I say, turning to Ryder. "We believe you. How did you know, though?"

"I spent a century trapped in Marid's realm. He used this spell on me all the time," he says, then shrugs. "He kept trying to figure out a way to transfer my power to him, but it never worked. He could only wield it when we were linked by the spell."

Wallace grazes her fingers over his, just barely.

"If we could kill him again," I say, "I would."

"I know," Ryder says.

I glance at the energy circles at the end of the path.

"So in order to gain the scroll, we what?" Wallace asks. "Mind share until it decides to present itself?"

I walk closer to the circles and study them. There are four distinct keyholes in equal spaces along the third inner circle. "No," I say. "I think there is more to it than that." I trail my gaze down, noting the cobblestone path forks left and right from this spot. "Ryder, how do we get out of each other's minds?"

"Unlocking that mylo circle is the only way we'll be unlinked."

"Have you unlocked one before?" I ask.

"Marid always kept the keys to himself. No matter how hard I fought or tried to get them from him, he never let me have them. He maintained full control."

I swallow hard. "But no one is controlling this one. This is a spell cast by the Creator ages ago to protect the scroll."

"Looks like it," Ryder says.

"Where are the keys then?" Draven asks.

I point to the two paths leading into the darkness. "I'm guessing we'll have to take one or both of these to find out."

"All right then," Wallace says. "Age-old question. Do we go together or split up?"

Ryder steps closer to her, and she grins up at him.

"Together," I say before anyone else can. "I'm not losing any of you here."

"Door number one or two?"

I shrug, walking to the one on the left.

Draven's shoulder brushes mine as we head down the cobblestone path, which grows darker the farther we leave the light of the mylo circle behind.

"All those powers, Draven, and you don't have like a flashlight that works if you boop your nose or something?" Wallace asks.

I snort a laugh.

"Did you just say boop?" Draven asks, glancing back where she and Ryder follow close behind us.

"What?" she asks. "It's pitch black—"

A pop sounds, the space around us illuminated in the span of a blink.

"Whoa," I say, scanning the area. "How did you do that?"

"I didn't do anything," Wallace says.

I'm grateful for the light either way. "What is this place?"

We're in a room with walls lined with hundreds of shelves. All manner of containers are filled with bric-a-brac that screams *Ather*—everything from baskets of ronc fruit to smoke orbs to blades to books. Even more shelves create an almost mazelike pattern in the center of what I can only guess is a store. The place smells woodsy but comforting, and I instantly love it.

"Kypsel," Wallace says, turning around in a full circle before she meets our eyes again. There is a weight I've never seen in hers before.

I step toward her. "What is it, Wallace?"

She smiles softly, tears lining her eyes. "This was my parents' store. Before one of Marid's Twelve stole everything we had and killed them in the process."

"Shit," Ryder says.

My stomach twists. "I'm sorry."

"I was eight," she explains. "Anka raised me until I was fine on my own." She shrugs, but the smile is back on her lips. "I dream about this place all the time."

"You touched the lock first," Draven says. "On the actual door in Rome."

"And?" she asks.

"There are four keyholes on the mylo circle. You touched the first lock on the real door, and now we're in a fully constructed memory from *your* mind."

Wallace's eyes dart around. "You mean there is a key hidden here?"

"It makes sense," Ryder says, eyes scanning the shelves for a key. "The incantation around the scroll that linked us all likely pulled from our own memories and hid our keys to freedom in them."

"Nice," Wallace says, stepping around a shelf and reaching for the basket of goods closest to her. "Then all I have to do is find it—" The basket melts into a puddle of metallic ore, the thick liquid moving to secure her ankles and feet to the floor. "What the hell?"

"There's always a catch," I say, motioning for Wallace to stop trying to yank out of the liquid. Every time she does the stuff only climbs higher up her legs.

Ryder reaches for it, clawing at the metal-colored liquid in an attempt to free her.

"Wait!" I say, but it's too late. His hands are being yanked to the floor so hard he falls to his knees at her feet.

"Well, that worked," Draven says.

Ryder rolls his eyes. "What's your grand plan, brother?"

Draven's eyes narrow as he reaches for the basket of ronc fruit closest to him. Carefully, he reaches just a finger out to touch it—

It falls off the shelf, clattering in a mess on the floor. No ore, no traps.

If I ever get to meet my aunt, I'm going to tell her what a pain in the ass her little protection maneuvers are. "We have to work together," I say. "Wallace, this is your memory, but if you touch anything, it'll turn to ore. I'm assuming even if it's the key we need."

"Well shit," she says, standing a bit awkwardly with the trap and Ryder on all fours at her feet. "Let's hope it wasn't in that basket." She glances down to Ryder and smiles at him. "You're kind of cute like that."

"*Leaper*," he warns, and I bite my lip, unable to hold back the laugh at the sight of them. Ryder turns his glare on me and Draven, who's joined in on my laughter. "Laugh it up. We'll see how amusing this all is when we hit one of *your* memories. Imagine how fucked-up they'll be."

For some reason, that makes both of us laugh harder.

"He's not wrong," Draven says.

"I know," I agree, barely reeling it in.

"These two are fucking nuts," Wallace says, but her tone is teasing. "Hello!" she shouts over our laughter. "Kind of welded to the floor over here. Do you mind looking around for a damn key?"

I clear my throat, swiping at the tears from the corner of my eyes. Draven winks at me, and we split up to search the store.

"Any hints, Wallace?" I ask from across the room. "There are like a zillion different types of products in this store."

"My parents liked to cover a broad spread."

"Not helpful," Draven calls from the other side of the store where he riffles through a crate of weapons.

"How am I supposed to know?" Wallace fires back. "I was eight!"

"This is your memory," Draven says. "Did you have a favorite thing in this store? A favorite place?"

"I don't know," Wallace says, flustered. "I barely remember my parents, let alone this store. The only time I ever came in here was to help—" She cuts herself off abruptly, and I spin around to look at her. Her eyes are distant, but she blinks and looks at me. "The till," she says, motioning to the far back corner of the room where a little counter sits, tons of miniature sculptures scattered around a large metal box. "I helped take the units sometimes!"

Draven gets there first, with me reaching him seconds later. The metal box is sealed shut, but he snaps his fingers, lighting them up with my flames. He grins at me, and my heart warms at the sight of my powers all over him. A quick swipe of the flame along the seam and the box pops open.

"Yes!" I say as he pulls out an iron key in the shape of one of the keyholes on the mylo circle.

"*Umph!*" Ryder groans, and we head back over to them, finding him sprawled on his stomach from the ore disappearing so fast. "Don't laugh," he warns, but there is a smirk on his lips as Wallace helps him stand up.

Draven pockets the key, then motions to the door across the room. "Who touched the next lock after Wallace?"

"I did," Ryder says, eyes wary as we head toward the door.

Ice crawls along my skin. "Shit, I hope we don't see Marid out here," I say, then flash Ryder an apologetic look.

He nods at me, hand on the door to push it open. "No," he says. "That's fair." Then he clenches his eyes shut and shoves the door open.

CHAPTER THIRTY-NINE

HARLEY

We file through the door, not stepping onto a main street like I assume an Ather store would sit on, but instead, a quaint room with hardwood floors and cream-colored walls. Piano keys twinkle, filling the air with a beautiful melody that's slow and uplifting.

Ryder is frozen two steps into the room, gaze riveted on the person playing the piano tucked against the wall farthest from us.

The *child* playing the piano. A boy no more than nine with messy dark hair and golden skin, his fingers flying over the keys in a graceful rhythm. Another boy is sitting next to him, same dark hair but falling to his shoulders, and he sways slowly on the bench to the music.

"Ohmigod," I whisper. "That's…"

"Us," Draven says, a crack in his voice.

I move deeper into the room, unable to stand still when child Draven and Ryder are right there. They don't even notice me as I move past the bench to see their faces—and since this is a memory, I guess they wouldn't—still, I'm blown away by the smiles they wear. They're so…happy. Just two brothers, playing the piano to pass the time on what I'm guessing is a slow afternoon.

"God, you were even a show-off back then," Wallace says, winking at Draven.

He smiles, but both him and Ryder are watching the memory with a weight in their eyes. This was before everything happened—before they were Called to be Judges, before Ryder was captured by Marid because the Greater Demon mistook him for Draven, before Ryder was tortured for a century and Draven was sent to kill me.

This was a time when they just...*were*.

I swallow the lump in my throat as I watch the youthful twins, unhindered by the realities of a world they don't know exists yet. I glance between the two beside me, and I can almost feel their grief gnawing my heart. They once had this unbreakable connection—they were even Called to be Judges together—but they were torn apart. They've been working toward regaining that connection, but it's clear in both their eyes right now—they'll never be those nine-year-old boys laughing and playing games, sharing secrets, and trusting each other without hesitation.

"Ryder," Draven says, and Ryder blinks out of the trance the scene held him in.

"I'm not going to touch anything," he says, shoving his hands into his pockets. "The key is most likely in that piano bench," he explains, something heavy flickering in his eyes. "I used to love listening to you play," he says, almost as if he's talking to himself. "I could sit on that bench for hours. The one place we weren't pitted against each other."

"You never had any interest in playing," Draven says, and Ryder laughs.

"I didn't want Mother to compare us in yet another area," he says. "Not playing meant you could shine and I could just be your brother."

Draven visibly swallows, then glances to me. "Our mother used to set the same tasks upon us, using our competitive nature to drive us to do better."

"Twisted," Wallace says.

"There are worse parents," Draven says.

Nerves tangle right along the sadness, making my shoulders slump. I bite my lip, hoping my memory isn't one of my abusive ex-father. I had enough of that when I was stuck in Marid's mind, desperate to break the tether he created in Ray that allowed him to possess her. I really, really don't want to do it again.

"Almost done," Ryder says, and the song young-Draven is playing mounts to a crescendo that makes young-Ryder clap.

A sliver of happiness breaks through the heaviness in the room. Ryder clearly cherishes this memory despite all his snarky jabs at Draven, and it gives me hope that one day they'll have the close relationship they used to.

The song ends and the twins giggle as they rush out of the room, rounding a corner in a hallway we can't see.

Draven lifts his hand like he might touch his brother's back, then thinks better of it, quickly dropping it. "Ryder."

They have a silent exchange, and I do my best to focus on Wallace, wanting to give them space but that's kind of hard when we're in such a small room.

"Thank you," Draven says.

Ryder flashes him a small smile before turning to Wallace. "Will you?"

She hurries toward the bench, wrenching it open. "There it is," she says, grabbing a key and showing it to us before pocketing it.

Draven points toward the main door we came from. "Guess it's my turn," he says, and hesitates in front of the door, his hand frozen on the knob.

"Whatever it is," I speak into his mind. *"I'm here with you."*

He glances over to me, gold eyes panicked. And I understand why—our pasts are riddled with dangerous memories and experiences that neither of us want to relive. It may have been funny a little bit ago, but now that we're about to actually face it? There isn't an ounce of humor in either of us.

"Wallace's memory was a happy one," I say. *"And Ryder's."* I motion to their childhood home.

He inhales deeply before he nods. *"Okay. Stay close to me just in case."* He shoves the door open, and we all follow behind him.

Lights flicker and pop over a crowded dance floor I recognize, a sultry voice singing from the stage to our left.

Draven huffs out a laugh, reaching behind him for my hand. "This is…"

"The first night we met," I finish, grinning up at him.

"This singer is amazing," Wallace says, swishing her hips to the beats Bishop Briggs is belting out.

Dancers crowd the floor of this memory, the music pulsing to a rhythmic beat that begs my soul to *move*.

"Is this your memory or hers?" Ryder asks Draven.

"We touched our locks at the same time," Draven says, glancing down at our joined hands, and sending a flicker of heat down the bond stretching between us. "Our memories must be linked."

"Okay," Ryder says. "Where the hell are we going to find keys here?"

I bite my bottom lip.

"What is it, mate?" Draven asks me, a wolfish grin on his lips.

"If this is a combination of our two memories from our first night together," I say, heat flooding my cheeks, "then my key is probably over there." I point to one of the club's storage rooms near the back of the building.

Draven's lips part, his gold eyes blazing.

"I might've dreamed of that night ending differently like a zillion times," I admit, and Draven tugs me closer.

"And it ended with you two in a storage room?" Ryder asks, then something clicks behind his eyes and he curls up his nose. "Gross."

I elbow him in the ribs.

"What?" he asks. "That's my brother."

Wallace rolls her eyes. "Since you two can't touch anything," she says, gently pushing on Ryder's chest. "We'll just hop over there and take a peek."

Ryder's eyes light up, all ick factor from me fantasizing about his brother replaced with undiluted mischief. "Yeah.

That's a fantastic idea, Leaper." He grabs her hand, tugging her in that direction, but stops short, looking at his brother. "Wait. Where would yours be, then?"

Draven points up at the VIP balcony overlooking the stage. The space filled with secluded little pockets of space with plush couches and lounges.

"*Wow*," Ryder mouths dramatically.

Wallace laughs. "We'll check there next," she calls over her shoulder when Ryder tugs her toward the storage room.

Draven pulls on my hand, whirling me around until I'm pressed against his chest. He glides his fingers over my arms, slowly moving to the beat of the music. I laugh as he spins me out again, turning me so my back is against his front. "Since we have to wait…" he whispers in my ear.

Warm chills burst along my neck. I rock my hips in time to his, falling easily into the dance as one song transitions into another. I close my eyes and lean my head back against his chest, gripping his hands, which clutch my hips.

"Tell me what you pictured," I say up to him, opening my eyes and finding his on me as our bodies move together. "When you thought about that night."

The first night we met. At the Bishop Briggs concert Kai took me to for my birthday. The night Draven crashed into my life and changed it forever.

Draven grazes his hand up from my hip, over my ribs, and all the way to my chin. He grips it gently, leaning down to trace his lips over mine in the lightest of kisses. "I kept dancing with you," he says, using his other hand to tuck me closer against him. "I didn't let you go." He brushes his lips over mine in a teasing kiss, and I gasp, white-hot heat flaring down my spine.

He drops his grip on my chin, grabbing my wrist to uncurl me from against his chest only to draw me back in so I'm facing him. He slides a leg between my thighs, rocking us back and forth to the beat, a carnal smile shaping his lips. "And then I ask you if you want to watch the concert from up there," he says, nodding to the VIP balcony.

My heart races as his hand slides to the small of my back, him dipping me slightly before drawing me flush against him.

"And of course, you say yes."

I laugh. "Cocky as ever."

He arches a brow at me. "Always. We go upstairs," he continues, unraveling the way he wanted this memory to go. "And we…talk."

I gape at him, the shock enough to stop my movements until he laughs and gets me dancing again. "*Talk*?"

He grins down at me, not missing a beat as we continue to dance. "Yes," he says. "You talk to me, and I listen. Then I talk, and you listen. We laugh. We use the late-night hours to get to know each other like we should've." He visibly swallows, holding me a little tighter. "No demons." He trails his knuckles over my cheek. "No siphon draining." He leans his forehead against mine while we dance. "Just us."

Tears bite the backs of my eyes. The picture he paints is beautiful. And slightly tragic. "We should've done that," I say. "But you're here. We're together. That's what matters."

"Aphian almost robbed me of all that time with you," he says, a growl in his tone. "But you brought me back."

I huff. "Yeah, well, I don't like people taking my stuff."

He grins, pushing me out to sway me in one big circle before bringing me back to him.

"Tell me about how you wanted the night to end," he says.

I have to hold back my grin. "No way."

"Why not?"

"After that ridiculously amazing, sweet story you just spun? Hell no. I'm not following that."

"Come on," he begs. "Tell me and I promise when this is all over, we'll do the Marvel marathon you've been wanting to do."

I grin up at him. "In the proper order?"

He nods.

"*All* phases?"

"Every single one." He smirks.

"You're cruel," I say. "You know how much I love Marvel."

"A good siphon works with whatever is available."

"You've got a deal," I say. "But instead of telling you, I'll show you." I open that spot between our minds just for him.

I conjure the much more physical way I pictured the night ending all those months ago when I met the mysterious, broody, cocky, and delectable stranger that was Draven. A series of hot kisses and tangled limbs.

"Damn," he says when I finish playing the scene for him in his mind. "I wish I'd known that. I would've kissed you way sooner."

"No you wouldn't have," I laugh, shaking my head. "You were certain one touch would kill me and you couldn't decide if you liked or hated that idea."

He shrugs, the muscles in his broad chest flexing with the move. "How was I to know you were the one person immune to my siphon abilities?"

I shake my head, my heart soaring. "Mate," I say, leaning my head against that delightful chest. "I missed you." My voice is thick with emotion. I haven't really had one second to process getting him back, instead diving right into what needs to be done to save my sister.

Draven fingers the strands of my hair, holding me close as we sway back and forth to the music. "I missed you, too," he says. "Even when I couldn't remember you. Something was missing. I felt it, your absence."

The hollow ache in my heart from when he was gone flinches like it's afraid this is all a dream. I fist his shirt, using his solid *real* presence to ground myself before I can spiral into a puddle.

"Got them!" Ryder's voice cuts through my thoughts, and Draven and I break out of our dance as we eye the two keys in his hand.

Wallace's hand is gripped in his free one, her purple lipstick slightly smudged and a wicked grin on her face.

I eye her. She purses those lips, and seeing her happy, seeing both of them that happy, chases away the darkness clinging to my soul. It gives me hope, the sight of those keys and their joy, hope that I can finish this soon and they can live the amazing life they deserve. One free of Orders and death threats and everything in between.

We hurry out of Draven's and my memory, my heart tugging slightly when we wind back up on the cobblestone path. I could live in that memory forever, but there is a real life to live.

And we're missing it.

The lights from the mylo circle come into view and we all jog to get there quicker. We each grab our respective keys, finding the matching keyholes. "On three?"

Everyone nods.

"One," I say, lining my key up. "Two." We all slide them in. "Three." We turn our keys in unison—

I'm pulled back through the sea of stars, through a black wind tunnel that threatens to rob me of consciousness before I hit solid ground again.

The door in Rome is wide open, revealing a single wooden table inside. And on that table is another key, only this one is the size of my palm with a swirling design at the top and a thick spine leading down to tapered teeth at the end.

I carefully scoop up the key, just in case there are more wards in place, and run my fingers over the grooves at the head, feeling where it twists open.

The scroll inside calls to the powers in my blood, a familiar zap of electricity at the recognition. My powers react, testing the scroll's. This one is different. It's a soothing, comforting sort of power that radiates warmth and understanding and isn't nearly as overwhelming as the others have been. And since the trial around it wasn't all doom and gloom, I can totally understand why it feels that way.

I walk back outside, showing my friends. "One step closer,"

I say, pocketing the key.

Ryder wraps his arm around Wallace, tucking her into his side. Draven links our hands, and I reach out to grab Wallace's until we're all linked by touch instead of mind.

"When this is over," Wallace says as Draven pulls out the powder that will teleport us back to The Bridge, "we *have* to hit up the clubs in the Ather. The ones in Lusro are incredible."

"I'm in," Ryder says.

"Me too," Draven says, grinning down at me.

"It's a date," I say just as my cell blares from my pocket. Draven pauses with the powder in his hand as I fish out my phone, frowning at Kaz's picture flashing on my screen.

"Kaz?" I ask by way of answer, heart in my throat. We may be close, but the warlock wouldn't call for a gossip sesh when he knows we're collecting a scroll—

"Another attack," Kaz says, breathless. The sound of crackling weapon fire and Cassiel's roar sounds from the background.

"The Bridge?" I ask, heart pounding as I leap to my feet.

"No."

Then I hear the screams. Human screams.

"Myopic."

CHAPTER FORTY

HARLEY

The smells of sulfur and blood fill my first breath as we land outside Myopic—my favorite bookstore in Chicago.

"Holy fuck," Wallace says.

Bursts of energy crackle from inside the store, the exterior windows and doors shattered. Wails and whimpers come from inside along with hollers from Kaz and Cassiel, who I can just see battling among the shelves.

I plow inside, my boots crunching against shards of glass and an endless stream of shredded paper. An explosion of books that rains in strips of covers and dust...

Human dust.

Customers and employees alike take cover behind Kazuki's shield, others outright running from the angel of death who is knocking them out of the way of the minion's weapon fire.

"*Please*," a feminine voice cries from my left. "Don't. I have kids!" She's sobbing, her hands raised in submission as a minion trains its weapon on her, its skeletal feet *click-clacking* against the floor as it advances on the helpless human.

It pulls the trigger, and I dart toward her, a wall of pure, arctic ice erupting from my raised forearm. The energy smashes into the ice, the hit reverberating all the way down to my bones, but it holds.

"Run," I say to the woman. "There's an emergency exit to the back left. Take everyone you can with you."

She hurries to her feet, eyes bulging at the sight of my ice. "Thank you," she breathes, then rushes where I directed, grabbing people on the way.

I don't have time to think about her shocked face. Don't have time to wonder what the veil showed her when I blocked the shot or if she saw the truth. Too many minions have spotted the ice and are now firing in my direction, the place exploding with orange light.

"How many are left?" I call out, cringing against the power hitting my temporary shield.

"Nine," Cassiel says. The floor trembles as he lands next to me, the beat of his wings sending more whirls of shredded paper around us.

"We took out six," Kaz says. "We need to get the rest out."

Cassiel nods, flying to help.

Wallace's indigo light flashes, shocks of color among the wreckage as she disappears from sight, then returns in a blink. "Make that eight," she says, dropping a minion skull at my feet. The thing's jawbone falls off and clatters on the floor.

"Show-off," I say, then cringe again as hit after hit sends fissures spiderwebbing through my ice.

"Drop the shield," Draven demands, his golden eyes blazing as he raises his hands, power crashing off of him in waves.

Ryder is on his right, his divine lightning crackling in his eyes.

I nod, then punch the air before me, shattering the massive block of ice and sending its shards hurtling toward the remaining minions.

Screeches and wails accompany more weapon fire as scores of the brutal orange bullets propel toward us—

And *stop*.

Full-on, midair, stop.

Sweat pops from Draven's brow, and I know he can only hold each power for so long before it drains the life from him.

I unleash a wave of flames. Four minions combust in seconds, while another two are shot back from a lightning strike so bright, I have to shield my eyes.

Wallace teleports, appearing right behind a minion and

snapping its neck as it falls to the floor before disappearing again.

The last remaining minion wails, firing its weapon over and over again, each burst stopped by Draven behind me. He drops to his knees, jaw tight. He's waning.

The sight has my instincts flaring as I rush to help my mate. I draw my hands together, spinning flames until I've gathered a vortex of fire between them. I jerk them apart, flinging as much power as I can into the hit.

"Shit!" Ryder yells, jumping over Wallace to cover her body as a wave of pure, onyx flames rushes from me.

It turns everything in its path to ash—the deadly orange energy, the last standing minion, its weapons, even the glass and destroyed books lining the floors. It eats and razes, hungry and relentless until I draw it back and smother it between my hands.

I drop to my knees with the relief of ushering the power back inside me, then I whirl around.

Draven is on the ground, eyes closed.

"*Draven.*" I shake his shoulders.

He blows out a breath, peeling open his eyes. "Couldn't let me have a win, could you?"

"Next time," I say, laughing through my concern. "You can kill them and I'll hold their fire, deal?"

He reaches up, placing his palm over where my hand rests on the center of his chest. "Deal."

The store I love is in ruins, and blood spatter paints the far walls red. Ryder is helping Wallace up, smoothing his hand over her cheek.

Kaz and Cassiel rush through the stacks, coming from the emergency exit as they skid to a halt among us.

"How many?" I ask Kaz.

His shoulders drop. "They killed six before we got here."

I clench my eyes shut, my heart aching. An image of John, the elderly owner who always gave me discounts on books, pops into my mind. He never once complained about me hiding in here for hours while Ray was in school because I didn't want to go home earlier than necessary. I didn't see him in the group of survivors, and the idea of him being reduced to nothing but ash makes tears bite the backs of my eyes.

"But you saved twenty," Cassiel adds, and I open my eyes. "Kaz felt the break in the veil, and we called as soon as we got here. You coming so quickly saved way more than we would've alone."

I nod, but it isn't enough.

"Those people didn't deserve to die," I say, swallowing thickly. Another place *I* love. Hit. Targeted. "Kaz," I say, pleading. "Can we protect other places they might hit? I'll give you whatever power you need, I just can't do nothing—"

"We'll start tonight," he says without hesitation.

"This is personal," I say, helping Draven to his feet when he shifts on the ground. "Aphian doesn't just want to blackmail me—he wants to hurt me. He's going to learn what happens when you try and hurt the Antichrist."

Draven slides his fingers into mine.

I look at the innocent blood splattered over shelves and the spines of books. "And I'll use *his* blood to decorate."

CHAPTER FORTY-ONE

DRAVEN

"Did they cover everywhere?" Ryder asks as I find him at the abandoned bar downstairs. The dance floor surrounding the main bar in The Bridge is deserted and downright eerie without its usual array of delighted creatures.

"Everywhere Harley could think of," I say, settling onto the barstool next to him.

Ryder leans over the bar, snags another glass, and slides it toward me. "Where is your Antichrist now?" He opens the large bottle of sparkling water before him and pours a healthy amount into my glass.

"She's researching in the library, pretending she's relaxing." It had taken me a good hour to help her come down from power sharing with the warlock, and it had taken me twice as long to silence all my instincts while they worked.

Power sharing isn't exactly an intimate or off-limits thing between supernatural beings, but it definitely requires a healthy amount of trust and friendship. And while I'm thrilled she's gotten close to Kazuki and Cassiel and the others, I can't turn off the jealousy triggered by my mate power sharing with anyone other than me.

"The more she pushes herself, the worse off we all are," Ryder says.

"I know. But *you* try convincing her of that." I take a drink of the bubbly water. Some of my aching muscles unwind. I should probably be resting after nearly draining myself at Myopic. But after Aphian stole my mind...the way he nearly burned Harley out of my memory...

Sleep isn't the easiest thing to achieve.

Ryder is right. After I've given Harley a little space to sort out what happened, I plan to do something just for her. Something that will help take her mind off her overwhelming mission, if only for a few moments.

"You scared me," Ryder says, tone low and quiet between us.

I cock a brow at him. "This coming from the man who spent an eternity in Marid's realm?"

A shudder racks his body, lightning crackling in his eyes. "I mean it, Draven."

The humor dies on my tongue as he turns to look at me. My twin, even more so now that we're back in the real world, Aphian's spell making his eyes and hair identical to mine.

"That day in the apartment," he says, shaking his head. He visibly swallows. "I thought I lost my brother again."

Ryder's childhood memory of us from the mylo circle plays out in my mind, and my lungs constrict. Marid separated us when he took my brother to his realm a century ago, and before that Aphian always gave us missions with oceans between us. I finally freed him from Marid's realm, and then Aphian nearly broke us apart again.

"I didn't have a choice — "

"You do now. Why do you think I'm not their puppet anymore? Because I spent years undergoing mental torture from Marid, and I survived. I adapted. I willed my mind to be stronger than my body, my powers." He presses his finger to his temple, then points to mine. "Your little Antichrist did the same for you. She burned you out, Draven." He huffs, wrapping his fingers around his drink. "I owe her my life for bringing you back."

"You don't," I say, but my voice is off, hoarse with emotion. Ryder spent the time I saw him in the weeks before I was taken telling me he was sick of my apologies. Sick of my constant begging for forgiveness for him being taken by Marid in my place. But the urge to say sorry again climbs up my throat. "I'm—"

"Don't," he cuts me off. "Don't fucking apologize again. I may have blamed you in the beginning, but it was *funny*. It's lost its humor now with your groveling." He sighs and stares at his water. "I thought Aphian took your mind to *kill* you. Even as I worked with Wallace to find intel on you, I thought you were destined for his chopping block. I spent nights awake, thinking about all the things I didn't get to say to you when you and your girlfriend ripped me out of the Ather…"

My stomach twists. This is the most Ryder has spoken to me since we found him, and I can feel my heart inflating with the hopes of getting my brother back. The one I knew before all this shit happened to tear us apart. "Like what?"

"Like…" Ryder lifts his drink, the thing poised before his mouth before he grins. "Like your taste in furniture is atrocious. My spine is ruined from your horrible mattress."

Shock ripples through me, and I bellow out a laugh. "I gave you that apartment for *free*, brother. You can't honestly be complaining."

"After spending the night in one of Kazuki's suites? I may never go back to it."

I chuckle, shaking my head. "I haven't had as many years on this Earth to amass endless wealth like the warlock has. And you know how little allowance the Seven grants for missions. If you want a better bed, get a job."

"That's an idea," he says. "I could list *soldier drone* and *fight club expert* on my resume. I'm sure I'll be climbing the corporate ranks in no time."

"Touché," I say, and we clink glasses again. Something settles in my chest, a sense of connection I haven't felt in ages. That long-dormant magical bond between me and my twin breathes to life inside me, filling me with more hope than I usually allow myself. "I've missed you." I whisper the words, almost afraid to look at him, to set him off with any more apologies or excuses.

Ryder clears his throat. "I always missed you. There were times Marid would conjure these intense illusions where you were the one torturing me, but I always knew it wasn't really you. He could never get your eyes right, for one. And when he grew bored with me, releasing me into Sage's 'care'..." He scowls at the mention of the Pit master in the Machis realm. "They would have team-fights sometimes, and they'd always pair me with the worst partner." He sighs. "I remember always wishing it was you and *not* wishing it was you. I didn't want you trapped with me, but I knew if I could've picked anyone to survive that hell with, it would've been you."

Angry tears well behind my eyes, but I grunt them away. "We'll make up for that time lost, brother. I promise, we will."

Ryder nods, then looks to me. "You know this is going to end bloody," he says. "Even if we play every angle right, this is the Seven we're talking about. Even with the loss of Hillel. Aphian has been on this plane for millennia. He won't go down without a fight."

"I know," I say, apprehension coiling in my gut.

"And Harley," he says. "She's growing immensely more powerful now that she's accepted her birthright ring. Rainier should be *here*, helping her control that power. It's too much for one person alone. And she's only two away from completing the Seven Scrolls. Rainier said she wouldn't be able to translate the incantation without him, but if she somehow figures it out and tries to take the ultimate power for herself? It will change everything," he says. "It could consume her. And I'm terrified of what she'll do if you or Ray are harmed. She may not be able to come back from it—"

"She will." I understand his concern, but he doesn't know my mate like I do. "She brought me back," I say. "I won't let her lose herself. I've got her."

I hope.

Ryder holds my stare for a few moments, and it's weird as shit staring into my own eyes, but there are such subtle differences in his mannerisms that he's still *him* despite looking like me. Then he cracks a grin, nodding before draining the contents of his glass and smacking it on the bar.

"I need to sleep," he says, pushing out of his seat.

I smirk back at him, finishing my drink as I stand, too. "Is that with or without the Leaper?"

Lightning crackles in Ryder's eyes.

"I'm your brother," I say. "It doesn't take a mylo circle linking our minds for me to see you're into her."

Ryder slides his hands into his pockets, eyeing the stairs that will take him to his room. "You know I can't resist a sharp tongue and a wicked sense of humor." He sighs. "But it's more than that. She *sees* me. Not the trauma I went through in Marid's realm. Not the madness that still lingers from that place. Just *me*."

"I'm happy for you," I say, following him up the stairs.

He stops at the landing, both of us needing to go different directions. "Thanks," he says. "I can't shake this feeling though…"

"What?"

"Like if I let myself be too happy, I'll lose it."

I press my lips in a line, totally understanding that feeling. "Every second I spend with Harley feels like I'm stealing from Fate and she'll come to collect any moment." I run my fingers through my hair. "But it's worth it. No matter what happens. Every breath is priceless."

"Would you do it all over again?" he asks. "The Orders, the pain, the fear…would you do it all over again if it led you to her?"

"Without question," I say instantly.

He smiles. "Yeah," he agrees, then his grin turns facetious. "Wallace tells me every night how much she hates your eyes."

A laugh rips through me, and I flip him off as he walks

backward toward his room.

"Turquoise is just better," he says, flipping me off in return before whirling around.

I head toward the kitchen, silently vowing to do whatever it takes to fix Ryder's eyes, even if I have to slice off Aphian's fingers one by one until he undoes his spell. But for now, I have a mate to spoil.

CHAPTER FORTY-TWO

HARLEY

"Will you come somewhere with me?" Draven asks from my spot on the purple couch in Kazuki's library, my little Pagle Bagel at my feet and Wrath curled up by the fire. He grins, hand extended toward me. "As long as it's okay with your protectors?" He glances between Pagle and Wrath.

"They trust you." I laugh, grabbing his hand and leaving the book behind. Pagle waddles over to Wrath, spinning in a few circles before settling down next to him. He grunts at the chill from her ice crystals, but closes his eyes soon enough.

"Glad to hear it," Draven says, guiding me out of the library and toward a set of stairs I've never explored before.

We climb the winding staircase until it deposits us into another elaborately decorated hallway, this one with a fuchsia color scheme.

"Where are we going?" I ask when Draven stops in front of a sleek black door.

He winks at me, then opens it and tugs us through it.

"Whoa," I say, the cool night air kissing my cheeks as Draven leads me onto the roof of The Bridge. "Draven," I say, my heart expanding at the sight before me.

Candles flicker in the center of the roof, sitting atop a small wooden table, a plate of treats next to it. Two lounge chairs are on either side of the table, and they're piled high with cozy cashmere blankets.

"You need a break," he says, motioning to the beyond romantic spread. But he looks sheepish when he gazes down at me. "Is this okay?"

I press my lips together, emotions swirling inside me. I reach up on my tiptoes, kissing him quickly before smiling. "This is perfect."

I settle down in one of the chairs, tossing the luxurious blanket over my legs before I reach for one of the chocolate macaroons on the plate. "Mmm," I moan around the bite. "My favorite."

"I know," Draven says as he settles into the other chair. He grabs a thermos, spinning off the cap and pouring what looks like hot chocolate into two emerald-colored mugs.

He hands one to me, and I clutch the warm mug, inhaling the rich scent before taking a drink. "Does Kazuki know you raided his kitchen?"

"No," he says, arching a brow at me as he sips from his mug. "Are you going to tell on me?" He chases a few stray drops of hot chocolate from his lip, and a warm shiver races down my spine.

"Never," I say, then grin. "I'm just shocked the warlock doesn't have a protection spell around his goods."

Draven laughs, placing his mug next to mine. "I have no doubt the ones around his suits and jewelry are solid."

"Ohmigod, could you imagine trying to steal his eyeliner?" I grin, munching on another macaroon. "He would go nuclear."

"Have you thought about it before?"

"Have you seen his makeup?" I ask. "Kaz has the best of *everything*."

Draven grins at me, and a comfortable silence settles around us as we snack on the decadent treats he stole from our warlock friend. Once I'm done, I lean back against the lounge chair, looking up at the night sky scattered with stars.

Draven follows my gaze, sighing deeply. "I wish I could've been with you when you gained the first four scrolls."

"You're here now."

"You're going to stop them," he says, a muscle in his jaw

ticking. "I know it. And you're going to change so many things, Harley. Right so many wrongs."

"*We* are."

"You're the one," he says, shaking his head. "The one who has the power to end this."

"We're stronger together," I say. "You know that."

He gives me a soft smile, but I can tell he's stopping himself from arguing that fact. He's never given himself enough credit.

"And besides," I say, reality pinching in on this perfect moment. "The incantation on the scrolls is meant for Rainier, not me. Once I have them all, we'll have to get to him before Aphian finds out. Have to read the scrolls together and grant him the power to end this. It won't be *me* in the end." A smile shapes my lips. "But I'm sure as hell going to watch."

"And I'll be right there, by your side," he says, reaching around the table for my hand. The muscles in his arm bunch as I take it, him squeezing my hand in a silent vow that sends warm chills all over my skin. "Come here."

Heat flies in my blood from the command. I stand up, and he lifts his blanket, allowing me to slide into the chair next to him before he drapes it back over us. He wraps his arms around me, and I settle my head against his chest, relishing the scent of him curling around me, the solid feel of his strong chest beneath me, the sound of his heart beating.

"Thank you for this." I look up at him, our mouths an inch apart.

He takes my chin in his fingers. "Thank you for finding me," he whispers, before leaning down to kiss me. His lips are gentle and soft against mine as he drops his hand from my chin to slide around my neck.

I tremble under his touch, leaning deeper into his embrace. "When you were gone," I say, pulling back to meet his gaze. "I could barely breathe around needing to get you back."

"I'm here now," he says against my lips. "Thanks to you. And I'm staying. As long as you'll have me."

I whimper when he crushes his mouth to mine. Warm shivers dance down my skin as I fist my hands in his shirt.

"Tell me you don't feel it," he groans. "Tell me I'm not the only one who's being driven by this bond between us." He raises himself up above me, just enough to glide his hand between my thighs, his fingers teasing me over the black yoga pants I'd found in Kazuki's wardrobe in my bedroom after we'd gotten back from Myopic.

"I feel everything," I gasp, my nerves tangling.

"And this?" he asks, his voice confident. He moves beneath the blanket, situating me until my back is fully against the chair and he's grinning down from above me. He grips my pants, guiding them down and off my body in one easy motion.

My heart stutters with the move. We're outside, the busy city bustling far below, the night sky stretched wide above.

His golden eyes blaze as he looks down at me. "Do you like the way this feels?" He dips his fingers between the apex of my thighs—

I bow off the chair, arching into his touch. "Yes," I breathe as he glides those fingers straight through the heat of me, pumping and curling until I'm a coiled spring at his mercy.

The cool night air teases my skin, and I can't help but bite my lip to keep from being too loud. Anyone could find us up here, wrapped up in each other like this, and it sends a shot of pure, delicious adrenaline straight down my spine.

Draven leans back down, eyes on my mouth, a cocky little smirk shaping his lips. "Do you want me to stop?"

I nip at his bottom lip. "Don't you *dare*." I rock against his hand, instinct pushing me toward the edge of release I can feel building there.

He grins, and I tug his mouth to mine. He tastes like mint and cinnamon and I can't get enough of him as I swipe my tongue against his. I gasp between his kisses as he pumps those fingers inside me, flattening the heel of his palm over that sensitive bundle of nerves—

"Draven!" His name is a plea as I tumble over the edge, my body clenching around him in delightful little shivers.

He kisses me, drinking in my breaths as he works me through the throes of it, before he gently draws back his hand and grins down at me.

I'm liquid and heat and I'm so not even close to done. I smirk up at him, pushing against his chest until he switches positions with me. I get rid of his clothes, and he laughs at my frantic touches as I try to hold the blanket around us in the process.

"Impatient little Antichrist," he says as I settle over him. The humor dances right out of his eyes and is replaced with a carnal need that matches my own.

"Would you rather wait until we go inside?" I ask, running my hands over his stomach, relishing the feel of muscles under his golden skin as I lean over him. We're chest to chest, my thighs on either side of his hips.

"Not a chance," he says, a hand sliding into the hair at the base of my neck. "I want you here, under the stars." He kisses me again until I'm trembling above him. "I want you now. *Always*."

I shudder at the sincerity in his words, at the intensity in his gaze. The golden chain between us goes taut, flames licking the mating bond up and down as I draw out this moment between us. I want to stretch it out into forever, a place of pure bliss and unflinching love.

I slide my fingers along his strong jaw. "You have me," I say. "Then. Now. And always."

I slowly sink atop him, dropping my hand to his shoulder to balance.

"*Harley*." His hands fall to my hips, drawing me closer, the move sending shockwaves of heat dancing up my spine.

I'm breathless as I move on him, the blanket falling from my shoulders. And I don't even have a second to worry about it. I'm too wrapped up in Draven, in the way he looks beneath me, all muscles and gold eyes and the moonlight shining down around us.

Our bond flares with life, gilded in darkest flame and purest shadow, the golden links of the chain encircling us, pulling us closer together than ever before.

Draven sits up straighter in the chair, aligning his body with mine so no inch of space is between us. His hands move from my hips to beneath my shirt, lifting it up and over my head. He lets it fall to the side before he palms my bare breasts, lowering his mouth there.

"You're so beautiful," he says, kissing every inch of skin he can reach.

I meet his eyes. They're wild and liquid gold and shadows snake out from all around us, his powers stretching wide. Mine perk up at the feel of his, and I unleash them as I move above him, arching back enough that my flames use his shadows as pathways until the entire roof is a devastatingly beautiful depiction of flickering darkness.

"This is," I say, breathless as he thrusts upward just as I sink down on him.

I throw my head back, and he leaps on the opportunity, feasting on my neck and making everything inside me tighten with a searing heat.

Ice crystalizes along the roof in sweeping snowflake patterns and a gentle breeze raises chills on our sweat-slick skin.

The other chair, table, and candles lift off the floor with Draven's mounting power, and I can feel the endless well of it along the bond as we blend together in a never-ending share of power.

This is completely different and unique to *us*. With every roll of my hips, with every plunge upward from him, we're solidifying that connection between us.

Glittering darkness swirls around us as I up my pace, needing to feel more of him against me, in me. He slides his arms around me, holding me as close as two people can possibly be, and I shudder at the way he's never cowered at my power. The way he's never been afraid of me, content to draw me closer and follow me into whatever darkness surrounds us.

"*Draven.*" I say his name, a plea and a promise as we clash together, clinging to each other beneath the stars as every tight and knotted thing inside me unravels. I tremble against him, flames crackling around us as I fall completely apart in his arms.

His growl nearly shakes the building as he follows me over that sweet edge.

I lean my forehead against his shoulder, catching my breath.

He tugs on my hair, tipping my head so I can meet his eyes. A carnal smirk shapes his lips. "Do you think we're done?"

My lips part on a gasp, anticipation rippling along my soul. "Aren't we?"

"Not even close," he says, then starts all over again.

CHAPTER FORTY-THREE

HARLEY

K azuki slides a porcelain mug of coffee across his grand dining room table, lavender eyes rimmed in kohl.

"How do you look that perfect in the morning?" I ask, sinking into the chair to his left where he sits at the head of the table. His emerald-green suit is immaculate and it's not even dawn yet.

I take a sip of the black coffee, sighing as the warmth dances on my tongue.

"I'm over a thousand years old," he says, grinning over his own coffee. "I have to look this good or I'll show my age."

"Yeah, right." I roll my eyes, and he waves his free hand over the table. A spread of epic proportions appears complete with a variety of pastries, breakfast meats, and fruit. "I. Love. You." I immediately dig in, snatching up a pastry and moaning around its taste.

"I'm sure you're *famished*, what with nearly taking out my roof last night," he says.

Heat bursts beneath my cheeks. I nearly choke, swallowing too big a bite.

"Relax, darling." He laughs, waving me off. "No one, including myself, went near the roof last night. But the wards around the building alerted me to a spike in power." He arches a brow at me. "I can't even imagine what being mated would be like," he says sort of wistfully.

I manage to get some more coffee down before I'm taken out by a pastry bite.

He isn't wrong. I'm starving. Draven helped burn through

my energy stores in the most amazing way last night. But I'm also…strong. I can feel it. I'm more refreshed and recharged than I've felt in days and I know that has everything to do with getting my mate back. Since accepting the bond unconditionally, like I did in the Ather, it's like we signed a supernatural contract that ensures we're stronger together. And these days he's been away from me have been more damaging than I even knew and only realized once I got him back.

"*Anyway*," I say, grabbing another pastry and totally ignoring the fact that a spell alerted him to what Draven and I were doing on the roof. "I've figured something out."

Change of subject is *so* the mature way to take this conversation.

"Oh?" Kaz leans closer over the table, his black polished nails gracefully wrapped around his mug. "I've never been with a Judge, darling, so please do tell."

I laugh against the sip I'd been about to take, the hot coffee sloshing in my mug. "You're terrible," I tease but smirk a little behind my mug. "But I do *highly* recommend it." Even though I know what Draven does to me has nothing to do with him being a Judge and everything to do with him.

"That was saucy," Kazuki says, smiling proudly at me like I've just won a gold star for something, which makes me laugh harder.

I clear my throat, sinking back into the reality that can't be kept at bay forever—no matter how hard Draven worked to carve out some totally detached, blissful time for us last night.

"I think I know where the next scroll is," I say, setting down my coffee.

"How?" He gives a little wave to Wallace, Ryder, and Cassiel as they spill into the room.

"There's always food here," Ryder says half astonished as he sits next to Wallace. "I *love* it."

Kazuki blows Ryder a kiss, and Cassiel steals the last chocolate croissant before Wallace can grab it.

"Judas," she spits, but laughs as she lunges for a strawberry Danish instead.

Cassiel winks at her.

Lightning crackles in Ryder's eyes. I barely contain my laugh. Poor jealous Judge.

Draven saunters into the room, all sleepy-lusty-eyes and his hair mussed from me tangling my fingers in it so much last night. He's donning a satisfied sort of smirk that has my cheeks flaring again. He settles next to me, popping a strawberry in his mouth, a promising look in those golden eyes that sends a warm shiver down my spine.

"You were saying?" Kazuki asks as Anka, Nathan, Wrath, and Pagle are the last to fill the room.

I take a moment to look at everyone, more pieces of my heart clicking into place. My found family. Almost all of them are in this room.

But the three people missing are what have me sucking in a breath and returning to my earlier conversation. "The next scroll," I say. "I had a dream about it last night."

Draven tilts his head, as if he's trying to calculate when I could've possibly had a dream when he kept me up half the night. But there were a few hours at the end where we'd passed out in delightful exhaustion.

And I had a nightmare, naturally.

Cassiel's wings ruffle as he sits up straighter. "Did you go into the Dreamscape again?"

"I'm not sure," I say. "It was more like diving into a memory." I swallow against the churning in my stomach. "My ex-father," I say, because I really don't know what the hell else to call him. Saying *that asshole* can get confusing and we don't really have time for questions. "He didn't have much money because he drank away any we ever got. But he had this gold stone paperweight that he treasured. He used it to bash my head on more than one occasion."

Draven slides his hand over my thigh until he clutches my

hand beneath the table.

"Bastard," Cassiel growls.

"Agreed," Kazuki adds.

"I would clean the place while he was gone," I continue. "Whenever I touched the stone, I'd feel sick. I used to think it was because of the negative way it had been used against me, but I had the bracelet on—the power-draining stone that my mother had put on me when she left. I think my powers were reacting to the stone because of what it is. A scroll."

Draven squeezes my hand, and I blow out a breath. Shame coils like a snake around my skin, but I keep my chin held high. I don't have anything to hide from the people at this table.

"There's a chance I'm wrong," I say. "But there was something about the dream. It felt…important. And Aphian gave *me* to him. Maybe there is a reason it's there."

Wrath sits in the space just behind me, his massive wolf chin perched on my shoulder as he huffs. I chuckle softly, reaching for a strip of bacon and feeding it to him. His massive fangs snap and chomp the meat right next to my face.

"Spoiled hellhound," I coo, scratching beneath his jaw. Then turn to see a lot of arched brows at the interaction. "What?"

A collective laugh goes through the room before it gives way to crunching breakfast and sipping coffee with a side of contemplation.

"There is only one way to prove your theory correct," Kaz says after taking a few bites of his fruit.

"I need to go get it," I say, hating the idea of stepping one foot back inside that trailer. But if it gets me closer to putting Aphian in his place? So be it.

"I'll find a tarp," Ryder says, eyes crackling with power.

Wallace taps the table. "I'll bring the shovel."

"I can steal his soul," Cass offers.

Draven growls, shadows swaying behind him. "If anyone is going to kill him, it's going to be Harley."

"We'll hold him down," Kazuki says.

"I'm with the wizard," Nathan says, and Anka laughs.

Emotion clogs my throat. They're with me. A real, solid, unflinchingly loyal family is with me no matter what. I've never felt that before, and I'm nearly crushed by the intensity of it all because I know how precious and rare this is. And I'll do everything in my power to protect it, to protect *them*.

"We're all going, then?" I finally manage to ask.

"Hell yes," Wallace answers for all of them. "But *I* call dibs on kicking his teeth in."

CHAPTER FORTY-FOUR

HARLEY

"I'll go in by myself," I say, stomach churning as my old trailer comes into view. It hasn't even been a year since I walked out, but it feels like an eternity has passed as I head toward the half-rotten wood steps. A huge part of me doesn't want my found family to see this, to get a peek into this ugly past. "You all can wait here—"

"Fuck that," Cassiel growls.

"Not a chance," Wallace adds.

"Agreed," Kazuki says. "I want to see where you grew up, Dark Princess."

Draven grazes his fingers over the back of my hand. "Whatever you decide," he says, and the rest of our group *boos* him.

At least I'd talked Nathan, Anka, Wrath, and Pagle into staying behind. After every trial surrounding the scrolls, I didn't want Nathan anywhere near one that I hadn't earned yet.

"Fine. At least let me go in first. He may be passed out drunk, anyway," I say, but every warning in my body is blaring. I shove off the sensation, knowing I'd never have warm-and-fuzzies coming back here.

My crew nods as I reach for the door, finding it unlocked. I push through, keeping my pack tight against my hip, the rest of my friends filing in behind me as we step into the pitch-black trailer. The smells of sweat and vodka hang in the air with just a hint of mildew, and I'm immediately thrown back in time—a helpless little girl trying to earn love from a man who was incapable of compassion.

"Is there a light switch?" Kazuki whispers somewhere near the door. "Or shall I illuminate the space?"

"To the left and up," I answer, and I hear him fumbling on the wall until he finds it. A *click* sounds, then the trailer is flooded with harsh white light.

"They warned me you'd come for this someday."

My ex-father's voice shakes the entire room, or maybe that's just *my* reaction to it. He stands right next to that same threadbare couch he always passed out on. The same rug on the floor with my bloodstains still spattered across it.

I eye the gold stone paperweight he's tossing in the air and catching, over and over again just like my dream. "Give that to me," I say in a voice that sounds way more confident than I feel.

And I know it's ridiculous—the fear frosting over my soul at the sight of my abuser.

I *know* I'm stronger than him.

I *know* I owned my self-worth when I left him behind, but it doesn't matter.

Seeing him has every scar and healed bruise trembling.

He studies the gold stone paperweight in his hand. "You know, when they gave you to me as a baby with instructions on how to raise you and orders to keep your mom in line, too, I thought it would be an easy payday. A check every month. But about six months in, *this* showed up in your crib." He shook his head. "And your *mother*. Fuck, she about swallowed her tongue when she saw it. Told me it was sacred or some shit. That we had to keep it hidden." He tosses it again. "I can't even count the number of times she tried to hide it from me, but every time she touched it, it burned her. Even that guy that gave you to me, the one who told me to make sure your life was miserable…"

I swallow hard, my fingers curling into fists.

"He tried to take it from me and couldn't." He laughs at that, then puffs his chest a bit. "But *I* could always hold it just fine," he says, throwing it in the air again for emphasis.

"I remember," I say through clenched teeth. The side of my

head practically throbs from the memory of how many times that stone drew blood.

He folds his arms over his chest. "Wonder why that is?"

"Probably because you're not smart enough to figure out how to wield the power inside," I clap back.

He cocks a brow at me, his eyes skirting over my friends standing in support behind me. "You should've brought more," he says. "*I* did."

A collective groaning sound rumbles from outside, and I hurry toward the door to fling it open. There are at least thirty skeletal minions surrounding the trailer, weapons poised in their bony fingers.

"*Shit.*"

CHAPTER FORTY-FIVE

HARLEY

I bolt out the door, rushing to meet the minions on the grass. I send flame-daggers soaring toward the ones closest, and the sound of falling sand fills the air as I drop minion after minion outside my ex-home. I hurtle spears of ice on an unchecked wind, severing their skeletal heads from their bodies.

My friends instantly rush outside after me.

Shadows erupt to my right as Draven battles his own handful as he dodges the blast from their weapons.

Green bolts of pure energy crackle as Kazuki thrashes his cane around him, sending ashes flying into the air and weapons plummeting to the grass.

Wallace glows bright indigo as she zaps in and out of sight, bringing a skeletal head or two with her each time.

Ryder slams that pure-white light into the chest of any who approach him, filling the air with a melted, searing smell.

Cassiel is a sight to behold as he soars on his great wings, plucking heads from their bodies as he dodges the rain of weapon fire.

And in the middle of it all—my ex-father. Watching from the wooden steps of our trailer, his eyes wide as my friends and I match his little army with the powers we own.

"Hand it over," I say, having fought my way through the minions surrounding him, leaving nothing but piles of black dust all over the steps.

He glares at me. "Everything you're doing is pointless. You know that, right?"

My fingers dance with flames. "I stopped listening to you

a long time ago." I extend my hand when I've reached him, hearing the battle rage on behind me. "Give it to me or—"

"Or what?" He backs up a step toward the closed door behind him.

"I'll send you to the darkest parts of my *true* home."

More minions are pouring in from around the trailer, but I know my friends have this. The sooner I get the scroll, the quicker we can get out of here.

"The guy told me," he blurts out when I raise my flaming hands toward him. "He told me years ago why he wanted this so badly."

I hesitate. Did Aphian really tell him? "And?"

"He said it was a key piece in a puzzle that will change the world."

I roll my eyes. That sounded like Aphian all right. I take another step forward, forcing him against the closed door. "Nowhere to run."

"He also said the final piece of the puzzle was somewhere you'd never be allowed to set foot," he continues, his eyes wide with terror with how close my fire is to his bare skin. "So coming here—pointless. You'll never get the last one—"

Wallace shrieks, an agonized yelp that has my bones turning to ice.

I whirl around just in time to see her hit the ground, clutching her thigh. Blood spills between her fingers, and black scorch marks scar her skin.

A sharp smack hits me over the back of the head, wobbling my vision as I spin back around. He holds the stone, fresh speckles of my blood splattered over the top. I manage to stay on my feet, but a wave of sickness washes over me.

I lash out, not even bothering to cover my hands in flames as I grip his neck. I use the full force of my strength to squeeze and squeeze. I could end him here and now. Kill him and never look back.

Cries pop in my ears, and I leave my cowering ex-father

behind, rushing toward Wallace on the ground.

Ryder is relentless, sending bolt after bolt of lightning at anything that comes his way. Draven is at his side, finishing the remaining minions around them with searing hits from liquid silver whips.

Kaz and Cassiel finish their group, and the world falls eerily silent as I sink to my knees beside Wallace.

"Never a dull moment with you, Firestarter," she chokes out, the sparkle in her warm brown eyes fading as she looks up at me.

"You wouldn't have it any other way," I say as I shift her hands away— "Shit." My heart plummets to my stomach at the sight of the fist-sized hole in her thigh. Fear makes the breath in my lungs thin.

"It clipped her Leaper energy." Ryder drops beside me, eyes frantic. "You saved Kaz. Save her. *Please*."

I don't hesitate before I push my hands against her wound, her blood warm and soaking my fingers.

"That *stings*, bitch," Wallace says, but her snark is almost all gone and that terrifies me more than the hole in her thigh.

I close my eyes, diving into my powers, into the elemental ones, the Dreamscape one, and pushing further, searching, begging to find something to help her. Some hidden talent from Rainier that has passed to me. I focus on the warmth radiating from my birthright ring and silently plead for help.

But there isn't anything—not like when air and ice surfaced, or even when I could control the Dreamscape. I can't find anything. And I have no bond or bargain with Wallace like I do with Draven ánd Kazuki that allows me to power share.

I can't save her.

Terror flashes across my soul.

"Here," Kazuki says, hurrying over to us and reaching for the pack on my hip. "I stored the rest of Pagle's melted crystals in here." He yanks it open, digs for a second, then pulls out a tiny vial filled with just a few remaining drops of melted pagle ice crystal. He uncorks it, dumping the contents into Wallace's mouth. Her eyes flutter back open as she swallows.

"Whoa," she whispers. "That tastes like champagne."

We watch in awe as the medicine takes effect, knitting her wound together until nothing but smooth skin and a half-burned shirt remains.

Wallace's head drops back and her eyes close, but her breathing is steady.

Ryder slides his arms beneath her and hauls her up against his chest. He stands, cradling her there. "Thank you," he says to Kazuki. "That pagle has just earned an endless supply of whipped cream from me," he adds, referring to my pet's favorite treat.

I eye Kaz, silently thanking him, and make a mental note to check for more crystals we can use when we return to The Bridge.

I spin around, finding the porch steps empty, and the door to the trailer half open.

I race up the steps, flying through the door—

The gold stone hits me in the nose so hard I fling backward, crashing the door closed as I try to right myself. Pain ebbs from my nose, blood trickling down to my chin. I swipe at it, feeling the break and wincing. My legs give out, my head spinning, and my ass hits the floor.

He's there in a blink, cracking that rock across my skull so hard I see stars.

And I'm that same powerless little girl again.

Begging for strength to save me.

Reaching for powers I couldn't possibly understand.

He grabs my arm, hauling me away from the door, and tosses me in a heap on the floor.

"Even with fancy-ass powers, you're still a weak, worthless piece of shit," he says, pressing his dirty boot onto my neck. "And now that I'm no longer getting paid to keep you? I won't lose a thing by killing you."

I gape around the pressure on my throat, my mind whirling as I try to shake off the hits. This is where he's always tried to kill me.

This damn trailer.

The same trailer where he nearly let Ray and me starve to death.

The same one where he hurt Ray, thinking she was me.

And I'm *not* going to fucking die here.

"Harley!" Draven's voice is pure rage as he rushes inside.

But he's too late. I don't need saving.

My ex-father does.

One move—that's all it takes to knock his boot off my neck. Another, and I'm on my feet, my powers surging like a tidal wave. I lash out, kicking his feet out from under him. His back hits the floor so hard the stone falls out of his hand and rolls behind me.

"Get that," I command Draven, my voice not wholly my own as I stand over my ex-father.

"Draven," Cassiel says from somewhere behind me. "She's going to—"

I can't focus on anything but the man on the floor. The one who ruined my life. The one who, even now, coats my soul in fear. Because I spent a lifetime under his beatings, his verbal abuse, and every memory is racing through my mind right now.

My powers roil, the ground shaking so hard the trailer rocks back and forth.

"You want to know what it felt like growing up with you?" I kneel over him. He tries to scramble away from me, but I lasso his arm with a slice of air so strong I hear his rib break.

He yelps through clenched teeth.

"Like this," I say, heart pounding furiously against my chest as I stand up and hurtle a kick into his side. He curls in on himself, trying to block my attack. But I'm already back down there with him, wrapping my hands around his throat.

"Please," he whispers.

I squeeze harder. "How many times did *I* say please? Huh?"

Onyx flames lick up the walls in great waves, filling the trailer with a searing heat.

"Draven!" Ryder snaps from behind me. "You need to stop her before she explodes beyond this place!"

I glance over my shoulder, my gaze murderous as it meets Ryder's. How can he try and stop me from ruining the man who hurt me my whole goddamn life?

Ryder gapes at me, lightning rolling in stark waves along his body as he rushes toward me. Draven's liquid silver whip wraps around him, hauling him back before he can touch me.

"Harley," Cassiel says. "Please."

I send a warning flame his way, and he dodges it as I turn back around. My grip tightens around my father's neck. His nails dig into my hands, trying to stop me.

But he can't. His eyes fall closed, his body going slack beneath my fingers. My power rages and pulses, feeding off every emotion coursing through my soul.

Ice splinters over the floor, bursting through the flames already razing the walls, and shooting out of the windows. The earth beneath the trailer shakes harder, the sound like a rockslide outside the trailer.

"I can contain her," Kazuki says from behind Cassiel.

"*Contain* me?" I whirl around, finally standing to face them.

"You're not going to touch her," Draven snaps as he makes his way through them.

My entire body shakes as I glance at my ex-father unconscious on the floor.

Anger and hate and anguish and fear swirl inside me like a maelstrom.

In that second, I feel every hit. Every kick delivered by the man I believed was my father.

I feel my heart being ripped from my chest when my mother left me behind.

I feel the sickness consuming me when Draven took Ray

and was lost to me.

I feel Aphian wielding Ray as a bargaining chip, keeping her from me.

I feel...everything.

And it *burns*.

Flames engulf every inch of my body, the foundations rattling in my soul. I want to crush and sear.

I want to feel Aphian's feathers turn to ash beneath my fingers.

I want to kill—

"Shit," Ryder's voice growls above the roaring in my head. "*Run!*"

Air spirals throughout the room, sending all the furniture hurtling across it. My flames eat them in seconds.

"Mate," Draven says, using his own powers to push through the thrashing of mine until he stands before me. His face is scrunched against the pain of the flames flaring off my skin, from the brutal wind stinging his eyes. "I'm here."

But I can't stop it.

Can't stop feeling every single thing that has happened since I turned eighteen.

Kai and Marid and the Ather.

Ryder and the Pits and Draven's Winter-Soldier debut.

Cass almost dying.

Kaz almost dying.

Wallace injured.

Nathan hurt, his place destroyed.

Ray being targeted again and again.

"I can't stop it," I cry, my knees hitting the floor. "I can feel it, Draven. All of it. All the shit that's wrong in this world. The *pain*." My powers pulse and burn and expand, stretching and reaching across the entire damn world. Every ounce of evil, every pile of dust from Aphian's weapons is a spark of ash hitting my soul like a bullet.

Draven's shadows spill from him, soaring around me in

a tidal wave of citrus-and-cedar-scented smoke. His shadows wrap around us in a never-ending spiral of soothing darkness, stilling my soaring air and smothering my relentless flames.

Silence fills my head in his cocoon of dark and tears spill over my lashes as my chest heaves. He interlocks our hands, drawing them to his chest as he pins me with that golden gaze, not allowing me to look away. I can feel the chain between us arching into the warmth he's sending down it.

"You weren't chosen to be the Antichrist because you're evil and destined to ruin the world," he says.

A silent sob racks my body.

He draws me closer until we're knee to knee, my hands still locked in his and pressed against his beating heart. "You were chosen because you're the only one strong enough to save it. To bear the weight of that burden. Don't you see? You're the Key to everything. You always have been." His mouth draws closer to mine, my heart slowing, my rage and power ebbing at his words. "You, my mate, my Antichrist, will not be broken."

His lips graze mine, and I melt into his kiss. Every place we touch erases the hate threatening to consume me. Every pass of his hands along my cheek, my neck, a soothing balm to the rage demanding blood. He holds me, kisses me, soothes me in the shade of his shadows until every dark thought trickles from my soul, and I can think clearly again.

Draven gently grips the back of my neck, holding me away enough to study my face. "There she is," he says, eyes scanning mine like he's looking for something.

"Did I hurt you?" I ask, voice hoarse as I scan him for any sign of where my flames might have burned him.

"No," he says, his shadows still spiraling around us, hiding us from the world in a perfect pocket of darkness. "But you almost roasted Cassiel like a chicken."

I laugh, leaning my forehead against his, my palms pressed against his hard chest. "I'm sorry," I breathe.

He shifts until he can look at me again. "Flames or ice or

brutal wind," he says, offering me a broken smile. "I'll love you through all of them."

A shudder racks my body, and I stroke the hard line of his jaw. "Winter Soldier or siphon," I say, and he bites back a smile. "I'll love you through all of it."

He draws me closer until there isn't an inch of space between us. I rest my head on his shoulder, the pieces of myself that belong solely to *me* sliding back into place where my anger and rage tried to obliterate them.

And I find I can breathe again while he holds me in the dark.

CHAPTER FORTY-SIX

HARLEY

"What do you want to do with him?" Draven asks when he's dropped the shadows, revealing us to our friends who are making their way back into the trailer.

My ex-father is twitching as he comes to on the floor.

I flash Ryder, Cassiel, and Kazuki an apologetic look. Ryder is cradling an unconscious Wallace in his arms, but he dips his head. His eyes are no less wary, but I'll have to deal with that later.

"You need to save that unleashing for someone far more worthy of it than this garbage," Kazuki says.

I blow out a breath, grateful they aren't running away from me screaming in the other direction.

"Cassiel?" I ask, looking to my ex-father on the floor. "Can you hear his song?"

Cassiel wrinkles his nose. "It's not even a melody," he says. "A pattern of horrid clicks and slashes."

I nod, not surprised at all.

"Just kill me already," my ex-father groans as he fully awakens.

"That's too good for you," I say, glaring down at him.

This is the man who beat me since I was younger than Ray.

The man who told me I was worthless my entire life.

The one who hurt Ray the night we walked out.

He doesn't deserve a quick death.

"Will you take him to the Death Striker realm?" I ask Cassiel, not wanting to bark orders at my friend. He always has a choice with me.

"With pleasure," Cassiel says, stomping over to him and hauling him up by his shirt.

My ex-father's eyes go wide with terror, and I grin, pointing at his face. "*That*," I say. "That look. You feel it? You *feel* that helpless terror? *That's* what it was like growing up with you." I choke back tears. "What it was like every time I tried to be the best daughter for you so you would love me, only to be met with hate and hits and kicks."

His whole body shudders.

"Think about that," I say. "You'll have an eternity, after all."

I nod to Cassiel, who gives me a predator's grin. A crack of silver lightning engulfs them both, and they disappear. Kazuki collects the fallen weapons, storing them in some invisible pocket of space next to him, and we all barely make it two steps outside the trailer before Cassiel's silver lightning strikes again.

"It's done," he says.

I expect joy to flood my soul, or at least some sense of satisfaction knowing my ex-father will spend an eternity suffering in the Ather's version of purgatory, but it's not there. He earned his fate, but I only feel a hollow sort of closure. The only thing I can do is breathe a little easier knowing he'll never lay a hand on another innocent person ever again.

"Thank you," I finally say to Cassiel. "I'm sorry I lost my shit."

"You stopped," Cassiel says. "That's what matters." He casts a glance to Draven, and we both know that the only reason I didn't keep raging against the world is because of him. My mate.

"Like I said," Kaz says. "Save it for the remaining Six."

"I'll do my best," I say, and Draven interlocks our fingers as we leave the trailer behind for good.

CHAPTER FORTY-SEVEN

DRAVEN

"Damn it," Harley snaps just as I come through the door to our bedroom at The Bridge. She throws a book across the room, the old tome smacking against the wall.

"Bad ending?" I ask, shutting and locking the door behind me. I set down the snacks and drinks I grabbed from Kazuki's kitchen on the nearest table. We've barely been back an hour since the incident at the trailer, and I knew trying to get her to sleep would be pointless. Snacks seemed like a better option.

"No," she finally answers, but her back is still to me.

I cross the distance between us, gently turning her around to face me. Her eyes are frantic and flickering with her onyx flames. They ripple across her body, too, and I hiss against the sting, but I don't dare move away. "How are you feeling?"

She blinks a few times, and her powers withdraw.

"It won't stop," she groans as she tries to back away from me.

I release her instantly, knowing if she needs space, then she gets it.

"What won't stop?" I ask.

She huffs as she paces the sitting area in our room, and lifts her right hand to examine the birthright ring on her middle finger. "This thing," she says. "It's been unlocking more and more powers in my blood. And after what happened today?" she sighs. "It's like I can't *breathe* around them. And if I even think about Ray for a *second…*" She sputters at the end of her words.

"Ray is safe," I assure her. "I know it. If I thought she was in real danger from Aphian, I would use every single drop of my power to kick in the Seven's door."

She closes her eyes, nodding.

"Let me help you," I say. "Let me take the edge off."

"How?" she asks, finally halting her frantic pacing.

I approach her slowly, reaching out for her. When she steps into my touch, I sigh. Her body is riddled with tension, and I can almost *taste* the powers crashing off of her. I step behind her, drawing her back flush against my chest, and relish the little gasp she inhales at the position.

"I don't want to hurt you, Draven," she says. "What if I lose control again—"

"You won't." I glide my fingers over her bare arms, eliciting chill bumps as I make my way to her hands. "I'll never get over this," I whisper in her ear.

"What?" she asks with equal quiet.

"Touching you." After being Called to be a Judge and awakening my siphon powers, I never thought I'd be able to touch another person again without draining the life from them, let alone be able to touch someone as magnificent as Harley.

She trembles against me as I intertwine our fingers and lean down to press my cheek against hers. "Close your eyes," I say, and she does. I lift our joined hands, drawing them upward and pointing toward the bare wall across from us. "Do you feel that?"

I concentrate harder, using that spot in her mind she leaves open for me to magnify our connection. Heat ripples along the chain connecting us, that beautiful, unbreakable mating bond.

"You're there," she gasps.

I smile against her cheek. "May I?" I ask as I run my mental fingers through her stores of power. She shivers, wiggling her hips against me. I growl, planting a kiss on the line of her jaw.

"Yes," she says, and I dive into her powers.

"Fuck," I gasp as she lets me all the way in until I'm drenched in powers so deep and so heavy, I don't know how she's standing, let alone functioning as well as she is. No wonder she reacted like she did at her ex-home. The place is a standing trigger for all the trauma she's suffered, and with the powers she has? She could've easily turned every inch of that place to dust.

And everyone in the path of her power, too.

For a moment, I thought I wouldn't get her back. I was terrified I'd lose her to those consuming powers. And now that I can feel them? Things could've gone so much worse.

But I was there, helping her. Just like I always will be.

I swim through her powers. They're ancient and thrumming with intensity—ever the daughter of the king of the Ather, the Antichrist—but I manage to grip onto one, then another and another, until I'm pulling on them like a thread from a sweater.

"Open your eyes," I say, and she does just as I force power from our joined hands.

Shadows and flames swirl together, creating a crackling tornado of darkness. Green vines and liquid silver whips coil around the chair across the room. Snowflakes hover in the air, shaping and sculpting until the wall is decorated in intricate snowy designs.

"It's incredible," she breathes as I guide our melded powers, siphoning off the overwhelming stores of hers in the only way I know how.

"*You're* incredible," I say, continuing to work and create and mix our powers until I feel each of her muscles relax against me.

She spins around, hooking her arms around my neck as I relinquish our powers. She sighs in a satisfied sort of way as she looks up at me. "See how much better this is?"

I tilt my head, my hands gliding over her hips as I bring her closer. "What?"

"Working *with* me instead of against me," she says.

"When have I ever worked against you, honey badger?"

She gapes up at me, laughter in her eyes. "Oh, I don't know," she says. "How about the time you lied to me about who and what you are?"

I press my lips into a line.

"Or how about the time you didn't tell me about your brother, or the fact that I was your soul mate—"

"All in efforts to protect you," I counter, but I know it's a bullshit excuse.

She arches a brow at me, closing her eyes for a moment as she envelops our connection in the powers roaring softly inside her. Even with the amount I helped cast out of her, she's still the most powerful creature I've ever felt.

"Protect me from big bad you?" she asks in a teasing tone.

I give her a warning growl. "My worst fear *did* play out before my eyes," I say, cringing against the foggy memories of when Aphian stole my mind from me. Turned me into his favorite killing machine.

She reaches up, tangling her fingers in my hair. "I know," she says. "And big bad *me* brought you back."

I can't deny that.

"So," she continues, tugging me down to her level with that tight grip in my hair. "Let's agree we're two monsters who are made for each other. We'll always be stronger together." She's a breath away from me, and I try to capture her mouth with mine.

"I agree," I say as she pulls back, and the smile that she gives me is radiant, dark, and downright delicious.

"Good boy," she teases.

"Good. *Boy*?" I growl the words, gently nudging her away.

Her eyes dance with liquid fire as she tips her chin up at me in challenge. "You heard me," she taunts, retreating as I advance on her.

"Well then," I say, caging her in with my arms when her back hits the ice-decorated wall. I trail a fingertip over the line of her jaw, down the center of her chest, and go lower still. "Let me show you just how *good* I can be."

CHAPTER FORTY-EIGHT

HARLEY

"Why would Aphian force me to get these scrolls if he already knew I wouldn't be able to get the last one?" I ask as Draven holds the door open for me at a popular coffee shop around the corner from The Bridge, Ryder and a perky Wallace following in behind us.

"Aphian's plans are a convoluted mix he's likely been plotting for centuries," Draven says.

We order and then take our coffees to a secluded table in the back of the shop. Kazuki had been in full research/astral projection mode this morning, so we didn't want to bother him. Plus, I needed to take a peek at the real world, checking the news after what happened at Myopic. The survivors who did interviews spoke of a random group of civilians helping them escape what they were calling a mass shooting, but none of them could seem to remember who exactly helped or how. So the veil was in full force with its work to soothe humans' minds when they saw or experienced something unexplainable to them.

My body is—thankfully—fully relaxed as I settle into the chair next to Draven, despite the questions piercing my brain. And I owe that to the devious siphon on my right.

Draven leans casually back in his chair, a wholly satisfied look on his face that makes my heart race. Power sharing with him, blending our gifts together to help me release the pent-up energy threatening to consume me from the inside out, had been incredibly intimate...but not as intimate as what we did after.

And I'd thought our night on the *roof* had been hot.

I clear my throat, hoping my face isn't as red as it feels. "How are you feeling, Wallace?"

She rolls her eyes. "How many times are you going to ask me that?"

"Probably at least a dozen more," I say, hands around my own cup. "You bled all over me." I glance down at my clean hands, hating that I can still feel the stickiness of her blood there. I don't know if I'll ever forget the feeling, and I'm getting really fucking tired of feeling my friends' blood on me.

I need to do better. *Be* better, so I can better protect them.

"She's as bad as you." Wallace elbows Ryder, who sputters around his coffee from the jab.

He slides an arm around her shoulders, tucking her in close. "I'm much worse and you know it," he says, leaning down to plant a kiss on her forehead. "If I never see you harmed again, I'll die a happy man."

I grin at the two of them, my heart expanding despite the worry clinging to my soul. Good things happen, even in the midst of such awful events. I hold on to that little sliver of joy, if only to stop my heart from spiraling into the darkness from missing my sister.

"Do you have any ideas?" I ask Ryder, drawing back to our earlier conversation.

Ryder rubs his hands over his face, and for the umpteenth time I wish Kaz could fix his eyes. They aren't his, they're *Draven's*, and they don't suit him at all. "Aphian amassing the weapons and testing them against places you love makes sense," he says. "Don't get me wrong—it's awful. But I've known since Marid's realm when he worked with the Greater Demon that one of his priorities was creating an unstoppable power, hence the weapons."

"But for what?" I ask. "He also gave me to my ex-father in the hopes he'd abuse me so much I'd be a weapon, and yet he sent Draven to watch me and *kill* me if I showed the signs of being the true Antichrist."

"Who is challenging him?" Draven asks. "The weapons," he clarifies when we glance at him in confusion. "He started working with Marid before you ever stepped into your powers, Harley. So who is challenging him that he'd need these weapons to defeat?"

That's something to consider. "Rainier would pose a threat," I say, a pang of longing hitting me in the chest. I never knew I'd miss my actual father as much as I do until he was taken from me. "But he's been locked up tight."

"The demons that slip through the cracks between the veil?" Wallace offers.

A shiver races down my spine. So many of those demons had tried to take a bite out of me when I first came into my power. They wanted to use my blood to open the gates of the Ather, set it free.

"What is it?" Draven asks after I've fallen silent too long.

"It's no secret that the veil between this world and the Ather doesn't exactly sit right with me," I say. Rainier and I had spoken about it before...the dream of a world where the Ather is free to live in peace alongside the human world, as it was in the beginning before the Seven turned it into somewhere they dumped their garbage. "I understand the need for securing malicious souls, entities, and demons, but it should be as it started—a totally separate space. Rainier told me the Ather was once laid out right next to our world, like a different country, and everyone lived in relative harmony regardless of human or demon or other."

"And?" Draven asks.

"And," I say, "with each scroll we get, each new power unlocked inside me due to accepting my birthright ring...the urge to bring down the veil grows more and more in my mind."

"Holy shit, Firestarter," Wallace says, her coffee poised before her lips. "Are you going to do it?"

"I don't know," I say. "Part of me wants to, part of me doesn't.

But every part of me is wondering what Aphian would *gain* from the veil coming down."

"Aren't the Seven the ones who put it up in the first place?" Wallace asks.

"Yes," Ryder answers. "So why would he need the scrolls to take it back down?"

"That's what I'm asking," I say. "Rainier told me these scrolls definitely have the power to do it. Aphian wouldn't even need my blood." I shrug. "And he wants them. He took my sister so I would get them for him, and I think it has more to do with a grand plan than to simply take them off the chess board."

"You're right," Draven says, eyes churning. "None of what he's done makes sense. Placing you with that asshole as a child, Ordering your mother away, giving Ray to him, too, and then sending me out there to kill you if it came to it…" His voice trails off and the gold in his eyes blazes. "Unless…"

"Unless what?" Cassiel asks.

Draven's eyes are wide when they meet mine. "Unless *you're* what doesn't make sense."

I blink at him. "Um…offended?"

"Think about it," he says. "Aphian ordered me to kill so many creatures who showed signs of the precursors to becoming the Antichrist. But no one expected you to turn out the way you did, Harley. Who else would have a heart as big as yours under the conditions of your raising?"

"That's not fair," I say. "There are too many people on this earth who suffer the same or worse fate than I did growing up. That doesn't make them bad—"

"I know," he says. "I'm not saying that. I'm saying that you were abused and unloved almost every single day in your life. Then you came into your powers and every demon around you tried to kill you."

"Thanks for the recap."

He closes his eyes. "What if Aphian wanted you to feel all that so that when *he* came to you or Ordered me to bring you to him, you would be *grateful* to be in his presence?"

Yeah, I can't see that ever happening. "I'm not following."

"He would've given you a home and a safe haven for Ray. He would've trained you in your powers, would've praised you, would've *coveted* you. You and Ray would've been fed every day and slept in a safe, warm bed. He wanted to be the savior in your story so you wouldn't hesitate to be the weapon in his when he needed it."

"Fuck," Ryder says. "That sounds like something he'd do."

I swallow hard. I went to work at Miller's Deli when I was thirteen just to feed us. Nathan giving me a job was the only thing that kept Ray and me from starvation. Would I have been able to say no if Aphian had offered constant access to food and shelter? Especially for Ray?

"But," Draven continues, drawing me back to the conversation, "he didn't count on Marid forming a connection with Ray. Didn't count on you venturing into the Ather—your *true* home—to save her, and by doing so meet your true parentage."

"He had to switch gears," Ryder says. "So he stole Draven's mind and blackmailed you."

I blow out a breath. "Okay, so one part of this puzzle makes sense," I say. "Rainier said the incantation is meant for him, but just like in Pagos, if Rainier chooses to gift the scrolls to Aphian, the power will transfer to him. And, just like you told us before," I say, glancing to Ryder, "he'll use that power to keep the good parts of the Ather under his thumb and unleash the evil realms on the humans to weed out who he views as weak."

"Oh sure." Kazuki saunters up to our table, Cassiel behind him. "We didn't want a delightful caramel macchiato or anything," he says, sliding a chair and tucking it at the head of our table. He motions to Cass, who does the same, sitting next to him. "If this is a couples-only exclusive, then consider the angel my plus-one."

I bite back a laugh, and Cassiel glares at me from where he

sits. "Sorry," I say. "You were projecting, Kaz. We didn't want to bother you."

He waves me off. "Catch us up, squad."

I chuckle again, but the humor is gone in a blink as the severity of our conversation stomps all over my laughter. I quickly shift gears and fill Kaz in on our conversation.

"So why do you think that asshole claims you'll never be able to get the last scroll?" Cassiel asks.

"I don't know," I say. "The last scroll is somewhere I can't step? What does that even mean?"

"I think I know the answer to that," Kazuki says. He studies the emerald atop his cane thoughtfully. "Rainier and I were working on a spell. One that would allow him to communicate with his sister."

I gape at him. "And?"

"It's a complicated spell, darling," Kaz answers, dropping the cane over his lap. "One meant for Rainier." He leans forward. "Think hard, Harley," he says. "Where would an antichrist never be allowed to set foot?"

"Heaven?" I joke, but there is no humor in Kazuki's lavender gaze. My blood runs cold. "You're saying the last scroll we need is in *Heaven*?"

Kazuki nods.

"And where do we have to go to enter there?" I huff. The first time Kaz snuck me into the Ather, I had to go through the back of a McDonald's. "A Taco Bell?"

"Unlike the Ather," Kaz says, "there aren't many entrance points to Heaven. So, no Taco Bell for you. Just me and my potions."

HARLEY

"Hold up," Wallace says, pointing at Kazuki. "You have enough power to send someone to Heaven?"

Kazuki beams at that. "Only with the right blood," he says. "Rainier's is one and the same as the Creator; hence, the spell will only work for him."

"That's not true, though," I say. "*I* have Rainier's blood."

"That's correct."

"So I *can* go."

"Like hell," Draven growls. "It's too dangerous."

I splutter a laugh. "Wait, going to the Ather, going to Marid's realms and the Death Striker realm, and battling my Winter-Soldier boyfriend is *less* dangerous than a trip to Heaven?"

"Boyfriend?" he grumbles.

"Fine, *mate*," I amend, but he's still not having it.

"Do you not remember what Rainier said about the Creator's realm?"

I rack my brain. "I've had like a millennium of history shoved in my face in the last few months," I say. "I can't remember everything everyone says."

"The Creator keeps the worst of all offenders close to her," he explains. "So she can better keep them contained."

"Worst offenders?" Wallace asks. "You're saying there are worse creatures out there than Marid and his Twelve?"

"Rainier said as much," Draven says, "which is likely why he didn't tell you where the last scroll was. He didn't want you anywhere near that place."

I rub my palms over my face. "Well, I'm sure he didn't intend on finding my mother alive and getting captured, either. I'm going," I say with finality.

Draven sinks back into his chair.

"Heaven," I say, shaking my head, then glance at Wallace. "Is that what it's called?"

"Don't look at me," she says. "I'm an Ather girl through and through. I have no idea about any of that mess."

I glance at Draven, who looks like he's trying to figure out the right words to convince me not to go, then to Ryder, who looks equally baffled, and finally to Cassiel.

"You know," I say to him. "Don't you? You have to carry souls there, too, sometimes, right?"

Cassiel's silver eyes are sharp as he looks to me. "I answer to Orders," he says, voice low. "And I've only ever carried a handful of souls to the Creator's realm."

A shiver races over my skin.

"I wasn't there long enough to hear it called by any other name, nor learn about it."

"Well, you've been entirely helpful, Angel, thanks," Kazuki says, rolling his eyes.

Cassiel's obsidian feathers ruffle as he glares at the warlock. "My powers and strength are more often used for those entities who like to fight death." He leans his elbows on the table. "If anyone can handle journeying there, though, it's Harley."

I beam at him.

He flashes an apologetic look to Draven, then shrugs. "She can do this—"

"I never doubt what she's capable of," Draven says. "It's the fact that she has to do it *alone*."

I slide my hand over his thigh. "I'm not afraid of being alone anymore."

"That doesn't mean I'm not afraid *for* you." He leans his forehead against mine.

"I know," I whisper, leaning back to look at him. "But it's Ray. And Rainier and my...mother. We need the last scroll to get them back, to finish this. It's not even a question, Draven. I'm going."

CHAPTER FIFTY

HARLEY

"This is cold," I say, hissing against the smooth black table Kazuki tells me to lie back on.

The warlock purses his lips at me from where he stands on the right of the table, shifting bowls and vials around. "You, Dark Princess, have control of all four elements, the Dreamscape, plus a wealth of other unknown magic inside you, and you're complaining about a cold table?"

Grumbling, I draw my flames to hover just beneath my skin, effectively chasing away the chill.

"I still don't like this," Draven says from my left.

Wrath whimpers in the corner, voicing his own dislike of the situation, and I sigh at both of them. "I'll be back before either of you can miss me."

"Doubt it," Draven mutters.

"It's not like I'm actually leaving anyway," I say, tapping the table. "I'll be here the whole time. Right, Kaz?"

"Not technically, no," he says.

I glare at him. *Way to have my back, dude.*

"This level and depth of astral projection is highly frowned upon," he continues, grinding up some herbs in a mortar and dropping in a thick red liquid that looks a lot like blood. "Rainier had no qualms because he's the king of the Ather, the Creator's only brother, and well, infinitely powerful." Kaz mixes and grinds until he pours the mixture into yet another vial. "Your body will be here but your soul will take this journey. Whatever happens to your soul will reflect upon the body."

"Sounds comforting," I say, apprehension tingling along my nerves.

Draven squeezes my hand tighter. "Send me with her," he says, eyes pleading as he looks to Kaz.

"Can't," he says, swirling the red liquid in the vial. "Rainier only gave me enough blood for one ticket, love," he says. "Sorry."

Draven releases me, raking his fingers through his hair. "I'll ask Cassiel—"

"Don't you dare," I cut him off. "Don't put our friend at risk like that. Please, Draven. I just need you to trust me."

"I trust you more than anyone," he says, dropping to his knees so that he's eye level with me on the table. "But that doesn't mean I want my mate venturing into the unknown without me."

"If I could take you, I would. But this is my *aunt's* domain we're talking about here. Who doesn't love a visit from their long-lost niece?"

Draven sighs, and I can feel the resolve rattle across our bond. "You come back to me, you understand?" he says, his voice lethal. "You come back to me and we finish this. Together."

"I will," I say.

"Promise me, Harley."

"I promise," I whisper.

Draven grazes his mouth over mine like he can make my promise more binding with a kiss. And the heat of it razes all the way along my bones, making my body arch with need—

"Sure, we have time for that," Kazuki grumbles. "Scoot, Judge." He flicks his fingers at Draven like he's a fly buzzing around his workshop, and I have to bite back a laugh.

Scowling, Draven clicks his tongue and Wrath pads over to his side as they linger in the opened doorway.

I love you. Draven mouths the words, and I silently say them back before he takes my hellhound and disappears around the corner.

"Sorry about that," I say to Kaz.

He flashes me a knowing look. "No, you aren't."

"Not even a little bit," I laugh.

Kaz raises his emerald-topped cane, and the lights in the room blink out. Candles flicker along shelves on the walls, casting everything in a muted, golden glow. He leans over the table, holding the vial with the red liquid before me. "This potion will help split your soul from your body. I've spelled it with instructions from Rainier. You will be catapulted through space and time and across the many planes of this universe until you find the Creator."

A chill skates over my skin. "Sounds easy enough. So why do I feel a *but* coming on?"

"But…"

I smack the table and groan. "Why is there *always* a *but*?"

He *tsks* me, tapping my forehead with the vial so I pay attention. "*But*," he says again with more emphasis. He uses his free hand to prick the skin between my thumb and forefinger with a sharp needle, and I hiss against the pain. "I've secured a drop of my own blood here," he says, pressing his thumb against the hurt. "Squeeze this, and you'll shoot straight back here. Understand?"

I glare up at him. "Understand you like inflicting pain, you twisted, demented warlock? Sure."

"Lean all the way back," he says, voice lowering, and I do as I'm told, staring up at his dark ceiling. The smell of incense coils through the air, hints of jasmine and orchids curling in puffs of smoke all around us. "Let your arms and legs grow heavy at your sides," he says, his voice almost melodic with its soothing rhythm. He uncorks the vial and poises the opening at my lips. "Drink."

I open my mouth, and he dumps the contents in. I swallow, the liquid much thicker and spicier than I was anticipating. I cough, unable to control it as my chest heaves for a clear breath. But my body is heavy and drifting, and my eyes widen on the once-dark ceiling.

"So many stars," I whisper, finally able to breathe. "How did you paint so many stars on your ceiling?"

"I didn't," Kaz says, but he sounds so far away.

I try to turn my head to look at him, but I'm too busy sliding backward down a long, dark tunnel, those shimmering stars growing brighter and brighter until all I can see or think or feel is their shine.

CHAPTER
FIFTY-ONE

HARLEY

Smells hit me first.

Rubbing alcohol and plastic and sanitizer.

The moment I think about opening my eyes, I do. There is no lag between response times, no aches or pains or tension in my muscles. Even the overwhelmingly heavy powers in my blood seem lighter here.

Here.

Stark white lights illuminate what is clearly a hospital room—there are all kinds of equipment beeping steadily next to a lone bed across the small room. A single elderly patient lays in the center of the bed, eyes closed and tubes snaking from her arms that hook up to fluids in bags hanging from silver racks on the other side of the bed.

A female nurse is checking the equipment, her clothes covered in bright blue plastic that cinches at her wrists and ankles. She wears a face shield and a hospital mask, but I can see the seafoam color of her eyes as she spares me a glance before returning focus to her patient.

"Ah, Niece," she says, her voice like a melody. "Can you pass me an extra blanket?" She points to a little bundle of blankets and pillows sitting in the chair next to me.

I glance down, shocked to find I'm outfitted exactly like her, face shield and all, my pack resting on my hip underneath it all. My limbs move automatically as I grab a blanket and hand it to her.

"Thank you," she says, unfolding it. "The fever broke, but she's still a little cold." She tucks the blanket atop the one already covering the sleeping patient, then turns around to face me. "Half of the job is making sure they're comfortable," she says, then motions for me to follow her out of the room.

I do, dumbfounded as we emerge into a busy hallway with more bright white lights. Nurses and doctors and staff alike are rushing this way or that, paying us no mind as they go about their duties.

"In here," she says, holding open a door for me, and I slip in. She shuts the door behind her.

This room is different than the one previous. It's empty except for supplies and a giant light board on the wall I stand before.

"I've been waiting for you," she says, shucking her gloves into a trash can, then untying the blue plastic covering her body and disposing of that, too. I mimic her movements, and we both lose our face shields and masks last.

She's a little taller than me, wearing lavender-colored pants that hug her long legs, and a rose-colored shirt that shows off her curves. Her hair is a variety of colors—blush and violet and lapis and emerald all shimmer in an elegant updo, secured by five golden bird adornments. Each gold piece has wings outstretched, all looking to fly in different directions while pinning her hair in place.

"So you're the Creator," I say. The particularly chill and put together Alexis Rose—like being in front of me is the last thing I pictured when I envisioned my aunt. I don't know why, but I was expecting something more along the lines of a giant ethereal creature with golden wings and sunshine sparkling around them.

She beams at me, a smile that is equal parts genuine and warmth. "That I am, my dear," she says, winking at me before she heads across the room. She fingers several transparent pieces of plastic before she flips on the light board hanging on the wall next to her.

"If you've been waiting for me," I say, stepping closer to her as she continues to sort through those plastic pieces, "then you must know why I'm here."

My words still her movements, her eyes softening a bit as she nods. "I wish we were meeting under different circumstances. You know, like for a lunch date. I could really go for a banh mi right about now."

"Couldn't we all," I say, crinkling my nose at her. "But the world doesn't work that way, does it?" I can't keep the fire out of my voice. Not when I'm standing before a Creator who seems more interested in X-ray scans and sandwiches than helping me, you know, save the world.

She gathers up a stack of the plastic pieces, hugging them to her chest as she looks at me. "Do you think I'm unaware of how this particular world works?"

"This particular world?" I ask.

"Earth," she says. "And the Ather. They're a couple diamonds in a mine of millions of different universes spread across the mountain of existence." She reaches up to touch a lock of my hair. "And too many of them are in peril all at once. And I know I'm almighty and omnipotent and all that, but I can't be everywhere at once."

Okay. I didn't expect there to be a million different universes, let alone that she'd be in charge of all of them. I mean, I'm all for the Marvel multiverse when there are enough Bucky Barnes and Loki variants to go around, but in my reality? Yikes. I swallow hard. "But you're the Creator. Can't you snap your fingers and fix every mess?"

A soft smile plays at her lips, but there is a sadness in her eyes. "That does sound sort of fun, doesn't it? But what would be the point in creating anything if what I created has no choice in any of it?" She sighs. "The thing about being the Creator is it comes with its own set of rules. Rules that ensure the universe stays balanced—"

My mouth drops open. "You call what's happening now *balanced*?"

Her eyes flare. "When I created humans and creatures of all kinds, I did so under the condition that once they sprang to life, they'd be governed by *free will*. They do as they feel and please. I have no power over them or their destinies any more than my brother or you do over those in the Ather." She shakes her head, and turns to the light board, sliding piece after piece into the clips. "What do you see?"

I step closer to the board, examining the illuminated pieces. They don't look like X-rays at all. In fact, they don't even look like a human body or bones. "It looks like tree branches," I say. "Thousands of them." I furrow my brow when she points to the first picture—a single slash of white against the black backdrop.

"Pretend this is a being—human, demon, any creature in between. I can see its endless possibilities for the future, but I can't *force* any one future to happen in particular."

She moves to the next picture, which has dozens of smaller branches stemming off in different directions from the main one. "All I can do is be an influencer," she says. "Place opportunities in the path of the being that can lead to an ideal future. But it's up to the being to make the right choices."

She trails her finger along one stemmed branch, following its path all the way to another picture with even more branches spread across it. "If they chose this path, it leads them here." She follows it, turning and jutting where all the lines connect. "Then here and here and here and so on." She drops her hand, returning to the first picture.

"So you're saying if we don't choose the right path the first time, we can never recover from that choice?"

"Look at how many options there are," she says, pointing to the line of pictures. The branches grow along each picture, increasing every time until the last one looks like a spiderweb made of millions of pieces of thin silk thread.

"Of course there isn't only ever one choice," she continues. "I place thousands of different opportunities and choices everywhere I can to try and help the being get to where they want to be. But..."

She snaps her fingers. Some of the branches turn sickly green, illuminating an entirely new path across the pictures. "I'm not the only influencer out there. For balance, there must be a counteragent to my desire for happiness and joy. The demons you know from the Ather—the ones the Seven tried to imprison there—they are influencers, too. And the being in question has the same rights and opportunities as everyone else. They choose. Not me. The beings of the universe are not my puppets, nor am I a puppet master, swiping my hands and cleaning the world of its ick."

"Would you?" I ask, eyes darting from the pictures to her. "Would you get rid of all the evil in the universes if you could?"

"No one should have that kind of ultimate power," she says.

"But you made the Seven Scrolls with Rainier." I arch a brow at her. "Whatever incantation you created will grant *Rainier* ultimate power."

Curiosity glimmers in her seafoam eyes as she narrows her gaze at me. "Again, balance. I created the scrolls for the future that's unfolding in the present."

I clench my jaw to keep from groaning. "The Seven—well, Six—*divine* beings you sent to earth to protect it are abusing their power. They're killing innocent people, both from the Ather and Earth alike. Aphian wants the scrolls for himself. But you already knew that."

She blows out a breath. "I know everything," she says. "A blessing as much as a curse." Her eyes go distant as if she's seeing something very far away. A blink and she's back to me.

"Aren't you upset that Rainier killed one of the precious Seven?"

"I don't grieve for Hillel. His choices led him to that end." She shakes her head. "I *do* grieve the circumstances of your life ever since you came into existence."

I roll my eyes. "Gee, thanks."

"You're so your father's daughter," she says, a little

exasperated. "I didn't want your life to unfold like it has, but it was the only way."

"The only way for what?" I snap. "Aphian gave me to a ruthless man who beat me every day of my life. Who told me I was nothing. I was worthless..." Emotion clogs my throat, and I jab toward a sickly-green branch on one of the pictures. "Is that my life? My destiny? To be steeped in the evils of the world only to, what? *Die* trying to save it?"

Tears line her eyes, but she swipes at them with her fingers. "Every step of your life has been leading you to what comes next."

"That's incredibly vague."

"Not every detail has been bad. You have your sister, and you found your soul mate."

"My sister was taken from me. And Draven..." I step back. "Did you do that? Did you...put him in my path?" I ask, eyeing the branches displayed before me.

"I've done everything I can to ensure the world I love so much does not fall into peril."

"Everything you can," I repeat.

"I *know*, I watch, I listen, I see. I influence. I cannot change the course of time or turn it backward."

I narrow my gaze, then motion to the door behind me. "This is a hospital," I say, and she nods. "Aren't you and all the real baddies supposed to be in Heaven?"

"My realm and the beings in it are totally fine. I have a guy. He's watching over everything for me." She winks, but then her expression sobers. "This place, however, is overrun with people in need and it is dangerously understaffed. I go where I'm needed to do what I can."

"As long as you walk that thin line of balance?"

She breathes out slowly, a look of relief on her face. "Yes," she says. "What I can do, I do. What I can't, I rely on the good beings scattered across the universe. The ones making the hard choices, the painful choices. The ones taking the harder path that leads to a result for the greater good."

Adrenaline surges in my blood, thinking about the paths that have led me here. "That seems incredibly unfair."

"I never said life was fair," she says. "If anyone says I did, they're horribly misquoting me."

"What would you say, then?"

"Life is *yours*. To shape, to wield, to throw away. To enrich, to wallow, or to sleep away."

"Fine," I say, not needing to hear any more about her stance on balance and free will. I get it. I really do. But I'm—

"I know you're tired, Harley," she says, and the way she says my name with such familiarity and warmth makes my eyes sting. "You've amazed me with each decision you've ever made in your life." She spreads her fingers along the pictures, smoothing them over the branches. The lines all disappear, leaving clean slates along the light board.

Whatever. I don't have time for weird family dynamic flattery right now.

"Can Aphian gain control of the scrolls if the incantation was meant for Rainier?"

She presses her lips together. "If you or Rainier gives them to him, yes."

"Can you tell me how to defeat him? How to get my sister and father and mother back?"

"It all depends on the choices you make," she says. "There are a million and two outcomes to any given situation. I've always given you the power to decide." She looks to me over her shoulder, then back to the blank board. "Isn't language the best? I've always loved words. They have so much power. They can hurt or ruin. Or they can heal or uplift or fill. Words don't judge or discriminate. They are to be read, regardless of language or type. Words revive as quickly as they slay. Illuminate as fast as they can keep the reader in the dark."

The change in subject is jarring. Apprehension coils around my heart as I listen, wondering suddenly if I should be taking notes or if my aunt just needs someone to wax poetic words to.

She taps the board, and the word *infectious* scrawls across it in bold letters. "How would you describe this word?"

I arch a brow at her. "Um, bad?"

She smirks and taps the board again. The word *joy* scrawls right next to the first.

"Infectious joy," I read aloud.

"See how quickly words can change the outcome?" Hope builds in her eyes as she looks to me. "The most balanced weapon or healing magic in all the universe. Words hold the key to everything." She reaches her arms behind her head, unclasping one of the golden birds from her hair and handing it to me.

I smooth my fingers over the palm-sized adornment, a familiar zing of electricity ricocheting in my blood. "The final scroll?" I gasp. "Will I be able to read it on my own? To translate it without Rainier and still give him the power?"

Something anguished passes over her features as she steps up to gently clutch my arms. "You'll have everything you need to do what you have to."

"That's ridiculously cryptic of you," I say, but I'm hopeful as I hold the final piece of the puzzle in my hand. I quickly slip it into my pack with all the rest, more than ready to get home and finish this.

"I know," she says. "And it'll all make sense in the end." She leans down, pressing a kiss to my forehead. Warmth radiates from the caress, a soothing kind of awareness washing into my mind, spearing into my soul like sparks of light. "I see a couple banh mis in our future," she says, stepping back slightly, her hand falling to mine. "If the choices line up."

"When—"

She presses the spot between my thumb and forefinger, jolting me out of this reality and sending me spiraling back to my own.

CHAPTER
FIFTY-TWO

HARLEY

A low whine has me popping open my eyes. Shock hurtles through me, and *pain*.

The black stone table I laid on is now in chunks around me, the smell of smoke and ash making my eyes water.

Another whimper, and I shove a slab of stone off my leg, wincing at the throbbing ache in my ankle as I crawl through the debris to where Wrath is whining.

"What happened?" I ask my hound as he licks my face. Blood is matted in his fur, but he limps over to a pile of rubble in the corner, nosing it furiously. I hurry over to it, my heart stopping dead when I see a hand peeking out among the rock.

"Nathan?" I gasp, shoving away the rocks until I uncover his body. He's bleeding from various cuts along his arms from the fallen rubble. "Nathan!" I shout, arms trembling as I haul him into my lap.

Wrath whimpers again, nudging him with his massive snout.

Nathan sucks in a sharp breath, and I nearly cry from the sound of it. "Kiddo?" he groans, his eyes peeling back to focus on me.

"What the hell happened?" I ask, and Wrath swipes his tongue along Nathan's cheek until Nathan pats his head.

"I'm okay, boy," he says, flinching as he sits up on his own. "They blew the place to bits," he says. "There were too many of them. Wrath wouldn't leave you. He herded me in here, and Anka locked me in before Kaz warded it. Wrath stood guard even after the place caved in on us."

Angry tears bite my eyes, but I lean my forehead against

Wrath's. "Thank you."

"Anka?" Nathan calls her name, climbing to his feet. He's limping as he navigates the wreckage, his blue jeans stained with red from a wound on his calf. "Anka!" He wrenches open the half-collapsed door and stumbles through it.

Wrath and I are on his heels, leaping over chunks of what used to be The Bridge.

"Here," Anka says, my Pagle Bagel tucked under her arm as she gracefully navigates her way to us over the debris. Her hair slightly disheveled, her signature leather jacket dusted with ash, but otherwise she looks unharmed. "I fought off the minions trying to take her, too," she says. "I didn't realize who else was storming the place. Until it was too late." She sets Pagle down and she waddles over to me.

"What the hell? How long was I out?" I ask Nathan.

"Two days," he says.

Holy shit. I was with my aunt for two days? It felt like half an hour, max.

"Wait," I say, my mind circling back to Anka's words. "Who else came here beyond the minions? Where is Draven? Cass?"

"The Seven," Anka says. "They took them all."

CHAPTER FIFTY-THREE

HARLEY

"You can't go alone," Nathan says, stomping behind me as I head for the exit door.

"He's right," Anka adds, her giant indigo wings outstretched behind her, the scales over the top gleaming as her barbed tail swishes back and forth. Pagle is at her feet, her cobalt eyes glowing brightly as she looks up at me, too. I'm beyond glad she wasn't harmed in the attack. "You need us."

I snap my eyes to hers. "You expect me to bring Nathan into the Seven's residence?"

"Yes, that's exactly what she means," Nathan answers for her.

"Nathan," I say, shaking my head. "You're hurt." I motion to the blood staining his clothes, the way he's flinching when he limps closer.

"I'm fine," he argues. "A few scratches."

"We're dealing with powers here that you can't possibly fight—"

"You think I don't know that? I know how strong you are, how strong Anka is. I know that you're best friends with a wizard and *Death*. That you're mated to a scary powerful siphon and that you choose monsters for pets." He steps close to me. "And I don't care. I don't care that Ray can see into the future or that you shoot fire from your eyes."

"I don't shoot fire from—"

"It doesn't matter. *You* matter. You're the world to me, you and your sister. I know I can't fly or heal or cast spells. But I'm here. I'm with you. You're not going without me."

I shake my head. Despite his faith in me, despite his support.

I can't lose him.

"What do you think you're going to do?" Nathan asks. "Take out all six of those things by yourself?"

"Yeah, that's exactly what I'm going to do." I grab the last of the *Telelumos* powder I have.

"You can't go alone," Nathan says, stepping closer to me, Anka on his heels.

"I'm not going alone," I snap. "I'm taking Wrath."

I lay my free hand on my hound, and toss the powder into the air, the picture of the Seven's residence clear in my mind.

Nathan glares at me, grabbing ahold of Wrath with one hand at the last second, his other interlocked with Anka's—

My boots—and theirs— hit the sand along the ocean in front of the same entrance through which we infiltrated the Seven's residence last time.

"You did *not* just do that!" I gape at Nathan. "And you left Pagle to fend for herself at The Bridge!"

"She'll be fine," Nathan says.

"That was the last of the powder I had," I say. "I can't send you back—"

"Then let us help you."

My mind spins with how I can protect them now. I'm half tempted to use my earth powers and lock them on the beach until I can finish this. At the thought, my powers eagerly surge to the surface.

A *clanking* sounds next to us, and I finally scan the doorway that leads into the Seven's residence.

It's open, but guarded by two Judges. *Brainwashed* Judges, based on their glazed-over eyes. And they're armed to the teeth with two swords each.

Wrath growls, baring his gleaming, razor-sharp teeth.

One of the Judges steps forward, a sword pointed at my hound.

"Touch him and die," I say with finality. I'm two steps beyond caring, and the lack of empathy for them should probably jar loose some shred of humanity I have left, but it doesn't happen.

Between the cryptic Creator talk with my aunt and the power-hungry, overstepping asshole that is Aphian, I'm just so fucking done. I feel like I've been done since my damn eighteenth birthday, and I'm about to buy a break with blood.

The Judge glares at me, stepping forward, jabbing that sword toward Wrath regardless of my threat.

I flick my fingers as my power surges. Spirals of sand whirl around both of the Judges, flinging them backward against the entrance so hard they slump to the ground. Dropping my hold on the sand, I step toward the open door.

"Harley!" Nathan says, gaping at the two Judges on the ground, eyes closed.

"They'll live."

His eyes widen.

The concern in them niggles at the corner of my mind, but I focus on the cold need for revenge instead. I can't worry about what this might turn me into, I can only move forward. Get my family back.

We step into the tunnels, and I illuminate the area with my flames, the flecks of silver casting everything in a moonlit glow.

"We need to split up," I whisper when we reach the hall of pathways that spreads out in a giant circle like spokes on a wheel. I point to the hallway that leads to Ray's chambers, hoping like hell she's in there. "You two head toward where they've been keeping Ray. If she's in there, you get her out. Do not—and I really fucking mean it, Nathan—do not come looking for me." I hurry to give them a description of her room.

"You're joking, right?" Nathan asks.

"Not even a little bit. I'll handle Aphian and his cronies. If Ray's there? Get her out safely."

Nathan looks like he wants to argue, but Anka gently tugs on his arm and they head down the path.

I wait until they're out of sight before I survey the other options. I have no clue what each golden tick mark means or what it might indicate, so I try and center myself enough to *feel* something.

The mating bond is warm inside me, but it feels like it's been hit with a shot of Novocain. A fuzzy *otherness* swarms around the chain that only increases when I step toward a tunnel to the left.

"Okay then," I say, looking to Wrath at my side before we plunge into the tunnel's darkness.

"Draven?" I speak into the spot in my mind I always leave open for him, but nothing but a vast sea of emptiness answers me back. Emptiness and that strange numbness.

Adrenaline courses through my veins as we reach the door at the end of the tunnel, my heart pounding so hard it hurts. I reach for the doorknob, hissing at how damn cold the handle is.

"All this power, you think they'd heat the damn tunnels," I grumble as I shove the door open.

"Always with the sharp tongue."

Aphian stands in the middle of a grand room in front of me, his blood-tipped wings outstretched and white robes billowing over his bare feet. Thaddeus and Judah are at his back.

Wrath growls at my side.

I sneer at them before scanning the rest of the room.

And everything in me goes quiet.

Kazuki hangs suspended from the ceiling by black stone chains, his arms and legs outstretched as he hovers above a slew of sharp, gleaming blades pointed right at him. His eyes are closed, his expression serene. Unconscious? Or is the warlock up to something?

Cassiel's wings are stretched to their limit, two massive iron spikes driven through each that pin him to the balcony. He struggles to lift his head as I cross the room. The silver of his eyes is a dull gray, but the hatred and death radiating from every pore of his body sets me back a step.

Ray — my sweet, beautiful sister — is bound and gagged on her knees on a dais next to Rainier. Ray looks terrified, but unharmed. I can feel her power from clear across the room.

Draven was right. My sister is a badass.

Rainier is bound in tons of power-draining chains, his broad shoulders strained against whatever invisible containment Aphian holds him in. The muscle in his jaw ticks, his red eyes feral as he struggles against his chains.

Beside him, Lila, my mother, is perched on a white columned pedestal, a thick band of rope around her neck, her mouth gagged, and her wrists tied behind her back.

Wallace and Ryder are on the opposite side of the room, their mouths taped shut and black stone chains cutting into their bodies so tightly they draw blood. Ryder's face is swollen and bruised but he's himself again, his eyes a sparkling turquoise and his matted, bloodied hair hanging to his shoulders.

Wallace looks far better. I suspect Ryder's injuries have a lot to do with that.

The remaining Seven are lucky she's contained, because the rage in her eyes promises the most painful kind of revenge.

The ground trembles beneath my feet as I turn around to face Aphian, my blood boiling. Draven is bound and gagged with those power-draining chains just behind him, Bartholomew standing guard.

"Come on, Harley," Aphian taunts. "Say something funny. Say something defiant. I *dare* you."

CHAPTER FIFTY-FOUR

HARLEY

"Oh, you don't have to dare me." I send a wave of fire toward Aphian, feeding it with wind until the flames tower over his head.

He blocks it with his own power, that acidic white light bursting from him.

Wrath bounds across the room, going after Bartholomew near Draven.

I race toward Aphian, using the wind wings at my back to propel me faster. Shaping swords and daggers out of my fire, I send them hurtling at him. He backs up a step, but his white light casts away each hit I try and make.

Switching tactics, I send spears of ice toward Judah and Thaddeus. They dodge the ice, just like I wanted, and run right into a wave of fire. Hissing, they flap their wings, flying up and over my flames, some of their feathers falling singed to the floor.

"You are no match for us," Aphian says, wielding his white light like a bat as he swings it at me. "Give me the scrolls."

I slide to my knees across the marble, ducking the light. I flick my wrists, whirling wind around him until his light falters. I pop up in front of him and send a flaming right hook across his face.

Judah and Thaddeus land right behind me, each one grabbing an arm as they yank me back. Thaddeus reaches for the pack on my hip, but meets a blade of ice instead. He draws back, gaping at the bloody icicle shoved through his hand.

"Don't touch my stuff," I snarl, jerking against Judah's hold. His strength is relentless, so I become a living flame.

He jumps back, smothering the flames catching along his robes.

Free, I race for Aphian, flapping wings of wind as he flies toward me, too.

We crash together, the force like being hit by a car. I manage to grab hold of his shoulders, spinning us as we crash toward the floor. His back hits the marble, and I grin triumphantly as I stand over him, sending waves of flame over his body.

Never again. He'll never hurt my family again—

A crack of white light hits me dead in the chest, throwing me across the room. I hit the marble wall so hard it knocks the breath from my lungs. I smack against the floor as I try to catch my breath, but Judah is there, kicking my stomach until I double over.

Rainier and Draven roar, the sounds muffled by their gags.

Air slips into my lungs, and I draw on that precious power, wrapping it around me like a shield. Judah's foot snaps against the harden air shield, and I laugh darkly as I manage to get my feet under me. He stumbles back a few steps, jaw clenched in pain.

Thaddeus hits my shield with his power, the white light cracking against it hard enough to hurt. A few hits and my shield falters, that stinging light searing my skin as it wraps around me like ropes.

I fight against the bonds, panic flaring over being trapped. I send my fire scorching around them until I'm free, allowing me a moment of precious control. My flames follow the light all the way back to its source, eliciting a delightful scream from Thaddeus.

I race toward Aphian again, a sword of black flame in my hand. I bring it down, prepared to slice his head from his neck, but my blade bounces off his own made of the purest white light.

But I keep swinging.

And he keeps blocking me.

Exhaustion creeps in with each blow, but I fight through

the pain. My family's lives are at stake. I will *not* fail them.

Judah and Thaddeus surround me, herding me into a tight circle until I can barely see around their wings.

"Child," Aphian seethes. "Give up the scrolls."

"Never." I encase myself in a wall of flames, forcing them all back several feet.

Aphian glares at me, his sword disappearing.

The collective power of these angels swirls around me so much it makes me dizzy, but I can sense the defeat on Aphian, just a flicker of hesitation in his power. I use that as I lift my arms, directing my flames to swarm them, raze them until they're nothing but a pile of bone and ash—

"Antichrist!" Bartholomew yells.

I spin around and my stomach plummets to the floor.

Wrath is across the room, limping as if he'd just been thrown. And Bartholomew is holding a black stone knife to Draven's throat, blood trickling down his neck. "Stop now. Or your mate dies."

CHAPTER FIFTY-FIVE

HARLEY

Everything inside me coils at the sight of Draven's blood welling around the point of that black blade. I draw my flames back until they linger beneath my skin.

"Thought so," Aphian taunts, eyes churning with malice as he looks down at me.

The Judge standing behind Ray and Rainier shifts toward them, eyes glazed and sword drawn. Wrath is growling, one paw poised to run—

"Tell that beast to stand down," Aphian commands. "Or I'll put him down."

My eyes dart from Aphian to Judah to Thaddeus to Bartholomew. They blocked me at every turn. No matter how much power I threw at them, and now...fuck, what was I thinking?

"Wrath," I choke out his name, and he halts, tense as he limps to my side. Ray's blue eyes are wide as she looks to me. My fingers tremble as I scramble in my mind for a way to save them all.

"I told you she was up to much more than she says," the Overlord's voice carries to me as he steps into the room, coming to Aphian's side. "She wants the scrolls for herself. That's why she came in here with the plan to destroy you."

Rainier glares at him, struggling against his bonds.

"*You*," I breathe. "You're the one who told Aphian about our plan to get Ray and Draven out. You're the one who—"

"No need to recant it." The Overlord's black robes are in direct contrast with Aphian's white ones, but the two look thick as thieves. Rainier looks utterly betrayed, rage in his eyes as the Overlord sneers at him.

"You're an idiot," I say. He glares those arctic blue eyes at me. "Aphian will never give you anything you want. He's a selfish bastard who doesn't want anything but power and control—"

"There once was a time I wanted you to willingly serve at my side," Aphian says. "Once a time when I wanted everything from you."

His words trigger a domino effect leading right back to some of Kai's last words to me. Another power-hungry soul throwing a tantrum for not getting their way. For not being able to control *me*, shape and mold me to fit in their ideal of what I *should* be instead of who the fuck I am.

"I never thought it would come to this." Aphian turns to the Overlord. "Go. Prep the veil room. I will be along shortly."

The Overlord bows, disappearing through the grand doors.

Veil room sends spiders down my spine. The blood in my veins grows hot as if merely hearing the word *veil* has it prepping for defense.

"Was it your plan to shed innocent blood in your search for ultimate power?" I ask. "Your efforts to *hurt* me because nothing went according to plan? It cost people their *lives*. You're supposed to be the best of us. Chosen by the Creator—"

"Don't speak of the Creator to me," he snaps. "You know nothing—"

"I know *her*," I say. "My aunt. I paid her a visit, Aphian. She's very disappointed in you. Stop this now, and you may be able to get back in her good graces."

But you'll never be back in mine.

I'm willing to try anything to sway him. To get him to order Bartholomew to drop that knife. To give me a minute to think my way out of this.

Draven's eyes widen on mine, but I can't tell what he's

trying to silently say, and our mental connection is weak under the weight of the power-draining chains.

"Please," I beg, focusing on Aphian again. "Let them go. You can have me and do whatever you want with me. Just let them go. They don't deserve this. Show mercy, and maybe the Creator will show you mercy when she returns."

"She never showed me any mercy!" he yells.

I cringe against the tone in his voice, the power radiating from his wide, outstretched wings.

"She chained us to this wretched world and *left.*"

"So that gives you the right to wage war on the world?" I ask. "To amass weapons and steal Conilis's resources and unleash them on innocent people here? To force me to get the scrolls for you?"

He clears his throat, tightening his lips. "Being abandoned here opened my eyes to the injustice of the world in which we dwell." His feathers stretch and flutter behind him. "We are the superior beings. We have the ability to remake the world. I had hoped you'd be a willing participant, Antichrist, but no matter. You will assist me in balancing the scales whether you like it or not."

"I won't let you unleash the darker parts of the Ather—"

"Half the world deserves far worse. Those who survive will be worthy. They'll be strong of body and mind and the new world will have *order.*"

"The world will never have the order you seek," I say. "Demons or humans and everything in between—we have free will. We have desires and choices and needs. Those create a beautiful sort of chaos that can't be controlled. That *shouldn't* be—"

He waves me off. "You are young and infantile in your powers. And I won't take advice from someone who is content in the company of siphons and warlocks and angels of death." He sneers at me.

"I don't know what twisted you," I say, stepping closer, "but

I can arrange a meeting between you and the Creator. I can make sure she listens to you. All you have to do is stop this. Let my family go, and we'll figure this all out—"

"Enough! Give me the scrolls," he demands, eyeing the pack slung across my body. "Or I'll let Bartholomew take his time carving out Draven's heart."

CHAPTER FIFTY-SIX

HARLEY

I look at my friends, pinned and beaten and bound.
I am alone.

No one is going to rush in to stop this.

No one is coming to save us.

Hopefully Anka and Nathan did what I said and left me here the minute they couldn't find Ray.

There's just me and this choice stretching on an endless moment. Another branch, another path.

If I willingly give Aphian the scrolls…if he can translate the incantation, he'll be nearly unstoppable.

The world will be at risk.

But if I say no, he'll kill Draven—my mate, the half that makes me whole.

And when I break it down into those terms, it isn't such a hard choice.

"I'm sorry," I say, tears lining my eyes as I look at Draven. "I told you I've never been a hero," I say, shucking off the pack and handing it over to Aphian.

He snatches the pack with his free hand, flipping it open to see all the scroll holders inside. "For him?" he asks, astounded as he looks to me. "You hand over the *world*, for this…Judge?"

I tip my chin up, tears rolling down my cheeks. "I would give up everything for him."

Aphian rolls his eyes, walking to a nearby slick, marble table. I follow him step for step. He dumps the contents of my pack on its surface, the scroll holders and empty vials spilling across it.

"Beautiful," Aphian says. He scoops up the closest one—the smooth compact from Pagos—and smashes it against the table. It shatters into pieces from the force of his hit, a tiny piece of parchment unraveling in the carnage.

One after the other, he shatters the holders, revealing all the scrolls I've bled for over the past two weeks.

"You have them," I snap, looking to Bartholomew. "Now let him go."

Draven struggles against his shackles, trying like hell to break them.

Bartholomew holds the knife harder against Draven's throat, stilling Draven's movements.

Aphian smooths his free hand over the pieces of parchment, ignoring my outburst. As he unrolls the pieces and lines up their edges, a golden light bursts from them as they seal together to make one piece barely bigger than his hand. He draws it up, eyes roaming over every inch of the paper.

"What is this?" he roars, frantically flipping over the parchment forward and backward. He whirls toward me. "There's nothing here!"

I gape at him, heart thundering in my chest. I look at the scroll then back to him. "I—"

"You *lied*. I have your family, your mate under a blade, and you *dare* to try and trick me with this?" His voice is booming now.

Draven swings his chained arms, trying to dislodge the knife from Bartholomew, trying to get free. But with the power-draining chains, he's weak, and Bartholomew jerks him closer.

A tiny, almost imperceptible voice sounds in my mind, the only one strong enough to be heard over the panic swamping my body, dragging me under a tidal wave of fear.

"*Harley*," Ray says directly into my mind, her voice growing stronger by the second. *"We have to help get everyone free. Take out the guards but don't kill them. They don't know what they're doing."*

My heart nearly stops at the sound of her voice, at the way she's broken through whatever wards Aphian had on her before. I do as she says, conjuring and weaving elements that I send soaring straight at the Judges wielding weapons over my friends, knocking them down like dominoes.

"*Good,*" she says.

I can sense her there in my mind like I can sense Draven. Her presence is full of good things—hope and sparkling light and healing energy. I want to bask in it, wrap myself in the warmth my sister has always embodied.

"*Free Cassiel first,*" she says. "*He'll get everyone out of the chains.*"

I draw in a deep breath, then catapult my air toward the spikes in Cass's beautiful wings, plucking them out as quickly as possible. Cass falls, but I catch him on that same wind, depositing him softly on the floor. He rolls over, gasping as he struggles to his feet.

I turn back to Aphian, shooting a blast of icy air toward his chest.

Aphian raises his free arm, acidic white light blazing from it, turning my roaring wind to nothing more than a whisper.

Weak shadows sputter around Draven's chains as he desperately tries to break free of Bartholomew.

I drop my wind, regrouping for another tactic when Aphian flies over to Bartholomew, slamming down hard enough to shake the floor.

"You will regret trying to trick me," Aphian says, ripping the blade from Bartholomew's hand.

And slams it into the center of Draven's chest.

CHAPTER FIFTY-SEVEN

HARLEY

Agony rips through every piece of my soul as Aphian shoves Draven toward me so hard I fall to the ground under his limp weight.

"You're next." Aphian takes one step toward me, but is jerked back by a female with pewter wings.

"You will not touch her," she says, wielding her own white light against his.

"Esther," Aphian growls. Another winged male with butterscotch wings lands in front of Judah. "And Efrain. I always knew you two were traitors. And now you've proven it."

He tries to move around her, but she stops him, shoving him with her light, her wings pushing them farther and farther away from us.

I haul Draven into my lap. "No, no, *no*." Blood bubbles from his lips as my hands jump from the blade buried in his chest to his face and back again. "I'll fix it," I sob. "I'll fix it."

Wrath howls at my side, nosing Draven's limp arm.

I'm shaking, trembling, as I fling my awareness inward, reaching for our mating bond. The powers in my blood stutter, flickering in and out with the power-draining blade so close. Draven's blood is warm as it slides over my thighs where he lays.

"No," I growl, my mind splintering. I know I read somewhere that if you're ever impaled, you need to leave that shit alone. It'll keep you alive longer. But the power-draining stone is stopping me from even trying to heal Draven, and I won't just sit here and watch him die.

I reach for the blade in his chest and pull, then hurry to

gather up the chains too, shucking the wretched things as far away from us as possible. If I can just get to our bond, I can save him. I did it once; I'll do it again. He *can't* die.

His body spasms from the removal, and I throw my hands over his wound to staunch the bleeding. I can give him everything he needs by power sharing. We've done it so many times, it should be as easy as breathing. It'll work. It *has* to work.

My powers flood back with the absence of the draining blade, and I push them against his. I stumble inside his powers, my heart guttering at how weak they feel, like wisps of smoke. I spill buckets of ice and caches of fire into him. I give him tons of my wind and vine, giving him everything I can until the wound in his chest is at least sealed.

But he's not waking up.

He's barely breathing.

I cling to that beautiful golden chain between us. But it's melting, disintegrating right through my mental fingers.

And I swear I can feel my soul bleeding.

"Draven!" I yell his name, shaking him as I try to wake him up.

But he's limp in my arms, our mating bond nothing but golden grains of sand strewn between our two souls.

A shadow looms over me, and I glance up. Thaddeus's wings are outstretched as he reaches for me—

Cassiel slams down in front of me where I kneel over Draven.

A wave of power snaps through the room as Cassiel speaks in that eerie angel-of-death language.

Thaddeus's face pales as he steps back, clawing at his chest. "What are you doing?"

Cassiel's murmuring grows louder, his hand a fist as he reaches toward Thaddeus.

The angel goes rigid, eyes bulging right before Cassiel rips his soul clean out of his body. A mess of sickly green and yellow air snaps into his raised fist, and Thaddeus's body slumps to the floor. It disintegrates into ash, and Cassiel sends the soul spiraling out of sight.

He growls. "I believe it's called *fuck around and find out.*"

"Hurry up!" Rainier yells, struggling against his own chains, desperate to break free.

But Cassiel doesn't move, devastation shaping his features as he stares down at Draven. He tilts his head as if he's listening to something before his panicked eyes snap to mine.

I shake my head. No. No, no, no. I slip into Cassiel's mind. The faint sound of piano notes trills in my ear—

A searing cold chain snaps around my throat, yanking me into the air so hard and fast my vision blacks out for a second.

"No!" Rainier roars, the entire room shaking from his rage.

Cassiel shoots into the air after me, only to get blasted by white light. The hit sends him sprawling back toward Ryder and Wallace.

I grip the chain around my neck, legs flailing. Below us, Esther is sprawled lifeless along the floor, a gaping wound across her throat, the gash smoking as if she were burned.

Efrain bellows, sinking to his knees beside her.

The chain jerks hard around my neck the higher we get, and I force my gaze up. Aphian holds the other end of the chain, his enormous wings flapping as he propels us higher. My powers race backward in my blood, the ancient stone draining the life right out of them.

Aphian hisses, and we're jerked downward so fast I yelp against the pain.

I glance down. Wrath's sharp teeth sink into the tail end of one of Aphian's wings, his back paws sliding along the slick floor as he tries to bring Aphian down.

My lungs burn with the need for air. I tense my muscles, doing everything I can to relieve the pressure, but I'm growing weaker by the second.

"Filthy mutt." Aphian swings out a leg, clipping Wrath right in his throat. My hound whimpers as he loses his grip and crashes to the floor in a heap next to my mate.

I try to scream.

I try to catch hold of any piece of Aphian I can, but he's flying too fast.

The chain at my throat is too tight.

Aphian spears through the hallways, turning into a room so large I can barely see the ceiling. He finally stops, hovering us at least twenty feet in the air, a massive golden compass decorating the slick marble floor beneath us.

And then he drops me.

CHAPTER FIFTY-EIGHT

DRAVEN

Fog lifts from my mind, a painful pulling back of a curtain made of spikes. It feels like there's a hole in my chest, and it's festering with something I can't explain.

I blink, lids heavy and thick from the throbbing at the back of my head.

Ryder is gripping my hand, and Cassiel is across the room, unshackling Rainier. Cassiel growls, whipping his head in my direction. He's walking over to me with jerky movements, or more like he's being *pulled* and is trying to resist.

Kazuki hovers his emerald cane above my forehead, the green light glowing as it rushes over my body. "I took his pain, Ryder, but he doesn't have much time left. I'm going after Harley," he says before disappearing.

"Ryder," I say, voice hoarse.

"*Brother*," Ryder says. "You're going to be okay. We'll get something to heal you."

The length between my blinks grows longer. I'm so cold.

Cassiel's knees hit the ground next to me, and that's when I see it.

The unrelenting grief in his eyes.

"Who died?" I try to joke, because I can feel it. My soul is tugging toward Cassiel like a magnet.

"You're going to be fine," Ryder repeats, defiant.

"I can't hold out much longer, brother," Cassiel says through clenched teeth.

Panic ripples up my spine. "Where's Harley? Why are you still here? Help her, Cass. She needs you. Leave me—"

"I can't," Cassiel says. "I have to take *you*."

"Ryder," I say, looking up at my brother. "Please. Go to her."

My mate. Fuck, she's going to be so pissed when I die. Again.

He grips me harder. "I'm not leaving you."

"Cassiel has me," I say, and in that, there is a little comfort in death. I suppose, if I have to go out this way, having my best friend take my soul is the best way to do it.

A wet cough rasps out of me as Wallace pops up near Ray, glowing with her indigo light, ready to teleport her out of there.

"I just got you back." The words wrench out of Ryder.

My breaths are coming shorter, quicker, and I shudder uncontrollably. "Did I do okay? Did I fix things between us, Ryder?"

Ryder nods, his brow pinched as tears line his turquoise eyes.

"At least you don't look like me anymore." I cough out the words. Cassiel reaches for my hand, taking it out of Ryder's grasp. "Do it quickly, Cass," I say. "And get back to Harley. Both of you."

Ryder presses his forehead against mine. "We will," he says. "I love you, brother."

"Love you," I say. "Tell her…" I cough. "Tell her…"

"I will," Cassiel promises, his eerily cold influence sliding beneath my skin, stealing all my pain. My vision loses what's in front of me, replaced with just the image of my mate, my Harley, standing on the beach, the night sky twinkling behind her.

And as I slip away, I think it's not the worst place to die.

CHAPTER FIFTY-NINE

HARLEY

I free-fall, my head tipping forward from the weight of the chain.

I rip it off, unwinding it from my neck and throwing it as far away from me as possible. My powers gasp to life, and I manage to create my wind wings, flapping them only twice before I crash to the floor.

Aphian soars down just as I get to my feet, swooping in a circle in front of me. With lightning quickness, he lashes out with a blade of white light, slicing over my forearm. I hiss, jerking away from him, the motion sending my blood splattering along the floor.

Which is exactly what he wanted.

I hurry to cover the gash on my arm, spiraling my flames to seal the wound. Maybe that wasn't enough blood. If I can just stop it… I grind my teeth against the sensation, but manage to quell the bleeding.

But it's too late. The walls tremble, the floor creaks—

Inside me the mating bond shatters in a sharp burst of pain that has me gasping for breath. I grip my chest like I can hold my heart together as I try to reach for the broken chain linking us, but my mental fingers go through the links like grains of sand.

Draven.

They couldn't save him. *I* couldn't save him.

The foundation of my soul crumbles, waves of numbness erupting from its depths until I feel nothing. See nothing. Static fills my mind.

"Can you feel it?" Aphian asks from where he hovers above me. "The veil? It's such a flimsy thing, isn't it?" He lands, pacing along the outer lines of the golden compass, eyes feral as he looks to me.

The veil is the last fucking thing I want to think about right now. My mate is gone, damn it. Ripped away by the asshole in front of me who's gloating about the end of the world. My soul screeches through the numbness, my powers begging to be set free.

But I do feel it. The veil. Around us, the building is shaking.

"I wanted to be able to control whatever comes out of here with the scrolls," he says. He's so caught up in what's happening, at what my blood is doing to that thin spot of the veil. "But the Creator lied about those blasted scrolls. They never had any power. A diversion. To keep us thinking, guessing, hoping." He curls his lip at me. "It was you. Always just you. I should've just slit your throat the minute you came into your power."

"Say that again," Rainier snaps, stepping in front of me. "I dare you."

Relief floods me. My dad's here. Cass got the others free. But Draven...

Aphian grins at Rainier, not at all deterred as he lands on the other side of the compass. He extends his arms. "I caged you twice, *Devil*," he spits. "I can easily do it again."

"You're down by three, permanently. Fucking try me." Rainier flicks his wrist, and Aphian flies backward from some invisible hit, his back smacking against the hard wall.

The ground shakes again, a crack spiderwebbing right through the center of the compass, the force of pressure releasing from the split throwing me and Rainier back on our asses.

"You *killed* her," a male voice says from right behind me, and I turn to see Efrain soar over our heads, tackling Aphian to the ground.

Clacking echoes from the massive open doorway behind

Aphian, minions marching into the room.

Hundreds of them.

Some of them are armed with those horrific weapons—those crystal tommy gun-looking monstrosities fueled by Colis—and others have swords or daggers or flails.

Judah and Bartholomew fly through the same doorway, landing at Aphian's back.

The Overlord snakes in on a dark purple smoke, gathering himself near them.

Kazuki appears on my right, clanking his cane against the floor. Ryder races into the room, eyes grief-stricken and murderous.

And that look shreds what little pieces of the heart I have left.

Because if he looks like that and Cassiel isn't *here*…

Something large flies toward me, and I duck, barely missing being taken out by Efrain, his butterscotch wings soaring over our heads before he slams into the wall behind us.

"What are you going to do, Rainier?" Aphian shouts across the room, the gaping split in the compass dividing us. He motions to Judah and Bartholomew. "We may not be able to trap you the same way, but you can't stand against us three."

Rainier's dark power fills the room, searing as he paces the length of floor between us. "You will die today," he says. "Even if we have to go through every single one of you." He eyes all the minions standing in position, weapons trained on us and waiting for orders.

"I'm with you," Efrain says as he walks toward us.

Silence encompasses the room as Aphian steps forward, slicing his gaze over one of his kind standing by me and my father, my mother and Kazuki and Ryder on the other side of me.

"Where is Wallace?" I ask Ryder.

He doesn't take his eyes off the enemies before us. "She's with Ray."

I nod, unable to feel gratitude or relief. I'm too cold, too hollow for that.

Rainier inches closer to me, lowering his voice so only I can hear. "Aphian is right," he says. "I can't do this alone. I can't do this without you."

I'm so tired. I want to sleep. Want to escape the never-ending nightmare that's become my life. It would be so easy to give up. Curl into a ball on the floor and let this battle end everything—

"*Harley*," Rainier says, red eyes widening as if he's read my mind. "You are stronger than this. Stronger than any single one of those evil creatures. You are the Key—not to the end of the world, but to saving it. You are my daughter. My blood runs through your veins. And *we* don't give up."

I glance at the overwhelming numbers on Aphian's side, and then the way too few numbers on ours. Draven should be here. He should be right next to me as we fight. But he's gone and I feel empty. Draven believed in me most. Never doubted my strength.

"We will finish this," Rainier urges. "For the Ather. For children like your sister. For Draven."

His words break through the shield of numbness around my heart. Draven wouldn't want me to give up. He would want me to end this. For him, I can be strong a little longer. For my sister, I can hold on.

A fire ignites inside me, drawing my powers right to the surface. I've lived my life against the odds, and I sure as hell won't let it stop me now.

"Together?" I ask.

Rainier grins down at me. "Together."

CHAPTER SIXTY

DRAVEN

The vision of Harley beckoning to me on the moonlit beach dissolves, and I spiral deeper into my own mind.

Cassiel is with me in the vast darkness that now bleeds over my mind. I can feel his presence, can almost feel the beats of his wings as he carries my soul to the beyond.

"Cassiel," I say, my voice clear and unhindered from the fatal blow I took. "Where are you taking me, brother?"

His voice echoes in my mind. "Where you deserve."

"Where—"

A snap of light illuminates a room.

A hospital room.

"I'm beyond saving, Cass," I say, my heart saddened for my friend. He's trying to drag this out, but I can feel it in my soul. There is no saving me. I'm already dead.

"That remains to be seen," an elegant female voice says, and I turn toward the sound.

She's beautiful, whoever she is. Her hair is a mess of rainbow colors that Ray would love to sketch. But there is an ancientness about the woman's seafoam eyes that has me taking a step away from her.

"Cass," I whisper this time, leaning closer to him. "Where the hell are we?"

"Please," is all Cassiel says, but he isn't looking at me.

"You've never *once* visited me, Angel of Death," the woman says, amusement crinkling the skin around her nose. "Why risk doing so now?"

"You know why," he says. "You know everything."

She sighs, her shoulders dropping like the weight of the world rests on them. She turns toward a backlit X-ray board, examining what looks like thousands of broken branches.

"I knew you'd come," she finally answers, returning to look at us. "But the circumstances aren't always so clear. It all depends on the choices made, the actions taken."

"Shouldn't I be on that beach for the rest of eternity, Cass?" I ask, my mind spinning with the conversation between the two. "I mean, it's my death. The first time I went to Rainier in the Ather. I think I've earned that beach this time."

The woman laughs, the sound both sharp and fleeting. Chill bumps explode along my neck, my soul recognizing the power in the room. I take a step closer, suddenly unable to stay away. "*You.*"

She arches a brow at me.

"You're...you're the Creator? You're Harley's aunt?"

She nods.

"You're *awful.*" I spit out the words.

Cassiel gapes at me, darting his arm out to draw me back, but I dodge him.

The Creator doesn't flinch at my words, merely keeps those eyes locked on mine.

"You are the worst aunt in history. You made me her mate. For what? To give her hope only to rip it away in the end?"

"Draven," Cassiel warns, but I'm beyond caring.

I'm dead. Who gives a shit what the Creator thinks of me? What more can she do to me?

"Are you saying you wish you weren't her mate?" the Creator asks.

"Never. But she deserves more than the path you put her on."

She tips her chin up, motioning to the light board, the branches there. "There are infinite paths, Draven. Who says I can forcefully put any of you on any given one?"

I narrow my eyes.

"I can't. I can merely lay them out and see which ones your actions and choices take you on."

I fold my arms over my chest. "Well. She deserves better."

And I hate that I'm not there for her right now. Fuck knows what Aphian is doing, the lengths he's going to in order to get what he wants. But I do know one thing—she doesn't need me to save her. She'll survive this. She'll own her power and herself and make the world a better place. I *know* that. I just wish I could be there to cheer her on.

A small smile plays at the Creator's lips. "So you wouldn't race back to help her if you were given the chance?" she asks, clearly having read my mind. "Because she doesn't need your help?"

Cassiel arches his brow.

"It's not an option," I say.

"What if it was?" she asks casually, like we're discussing a lunch menu, not my life.

I drop my arms to my sides. "You can send me back?"

"Perhaps," she says.

"What's the price?"

"Do you think I deal in prices like your warlock friend? Or even like the Seven?"

"I don't know anything about you other than you've sat on the sidelines for longer than the world needs."

Her eyes flicker to Cassiel, then back to me. "I deal in *choices*." She sighs again. "I can't interfere. I can only inspire. Changing one thing can change a million."

"So sending me back wouldn't be worth the price."

"You think sending you back will change things?" she asks.

"You just said—"

"I said it *can* change things. But some things were predestined."

I don't let hope rise in my soul. Not one inch of it.

The Creator steps toward me, infinite knowledge and power radiating from her. And sadness, loneliness, but slivers of hope,

MOLLY E. LEE 349

too. "Why do you think I put Cassiel on your path, Draven? Maybe so he could bring you here, not ready to lose his best friend?"

Cassiel goes still at my side.

"If that's the case, then you already know the outcome," I say.

She shrugs. "Not true."

"What do you want from me?" I splay my fingers over my chest. "I've given my life to the Judge Calling. I've served under the torture of Aphian for longer than I can remember. I've been forced into the Divine Sleep longer than I've been allowed to live. I took a blade in the chest from the very creature who you appointed as protector of the world. My *mate* has had to watch me *die*. Twice. What more can I give?"

"What more would you give to go back? To be with your mate, even as she fights for her life. For the lives of her family. The world."

My lips part, the words tangling in my throat.

"Would you give up your Calling?" she asks.

"Yes," I answer automatically.

She steps closer. "Would you give up your powers?"

"Yes."

"All of them?"

"Without question."

She stops only two inches away from me, looking up at me with hope in her eyes. "Would you suffer through all of it again?" she asks. "The Calling. The Divine Sleep. Aphian's torture. All he made you do at his command. Would you live that life again, in order to go back to her now?"

"I would live that life a hundred times over if it meant that I got to be with Harley in the end."

A flicker of pride sparkles in her eyes. "For her," she says. "You'd do all that?"

"I'd do anything for her, *give up* anything," I answer. "She's worth everything."

"Would you?" The Creator turns back to the light board, examining the pictures there. "One branch disappears, but another can take its place."

Hope, traitorous, wonderous hope flares in my chest.

The Creator's eyes go distant like she's looking at something very far away. A blink and her eyes are on mine as she reaches out her hand, laying it over my heart. "You are the mate I always knew you'd be."

Electricity like ten times that of Ryder's divine lightning soars through my body, the taste of metal and fire burning on my tongue.

Cassiel moves to stand next to the Creator.

"What are you doing?" I reach for him, ready for him to take me back. "Let's go."

"You've always been the brother I never thought I'd have," he says, his eyes glistening. "I love you, but Harley *needs* you."

Shock catapults through my soul.

One branch to replace another.

His soul for mine.

Horror rises up in me. "No, you can't. *Cassiel—*"

"Don't let me down." He smiles at me.

"Cass," I say, my words choked. "I love you—"

My soul is yanked backward, hurtling me back to the real world.

CHAPTER SIXTY-ONE

HARLEY

"Kill them!" Aphian commands. "Kill them all."

The minions screech, the sound grating as it bounces off the walls as they rush toward us. The ones with the Colis weapons squeeze the trigger, sending a wave of orange bullets right for us—

Rainier waves an arm, and the bullets fling upward, redirecting their path and soaring down on the ones who fired the shots. Pops snap as the minions turn to ash, leaving dark little piles for their friends to run through as they race for us with daggers and swords and flails.

I swirl my hands together, shaping balls of fire and earth, and send them hurtling at the first wave of minions that make it over the ravine separating us.

Aphian remains on that other side, watching, waiting with his winged buddies.

"Cowards!" I spit. "Fight—"

Three minions crash into me while I'm focused on Aphian, and we hit the floor. I shift right, dodging as they try and sink blade after blade into me. Ice spears from my hands, shooting through two of the skeletal creatures' rib cages, cracking their spines before they turn to a litter of black dust above me. I cough, rolling to miss the third one's attack by inches.

Rainier is battling over twenty on the other side of me, barely looking like he's breaking a sweat as he makes the space rain ash.

Ryder is lighting up the room with bolts of lightning finding homes in the minions' skulls.

Kazuki is a wave of emerald power, aiming for the winged creatures behind the minions, working with his magic to bring down their defenses.

Efrain is deadly grace as he cuts down his own group of minions.

I scramble to my feet, blood trickling from my nose. I swipe at it with the back of my arm, and with a flick of my fingers, my favorite sword of black flame manifests.

The minion hisses, raising its own dagger and rushing for me. I block its blade with my own, the heat from mine melting through its in seconds. I slash my arm down and across its neck bone, severing its head from its body. Another pile of ash at my feet—

"Duck!" My mother's voice fills the space next to me right before I feel her hand on my back, jerking me down to the floor.

A minion's flail flies over us, barely missing my mother's body over mine by inches.

She hurries off of me, offering her hand to help me up. I take it, and we stand, chests heaving.

"Thanks," I say.

"Anytime," she says, raising her golden sword as another minion rushes her.

Rainier fights on my left side, a slew of minion dust bursting wherever he looks.

I cut down a minion launching for me, and something pulses in my powers as I stand between them.

Between my *parents*.

The Overlord shifts into his smoke form, flying across the massive crack in the floor, the one that is sputtering and hissing, the sounds of the darkest parts of the Ather echoing up from the depths below. He leaves Aphian behind, manifesting a few feet away from Rainier.

"I've served under you for far too long." The Overlord draws a silver dagger from his cloak, the ghost of a smile twisting his lips beneath his hood as he aims that dagger at my dad and lets it fly.

Rainier snatches the dagger before it can sink into his neck. He shakes his head, letting the weapon clatter to the floor. "Pathetic."

The Overlord rushes for Rainier, aiming his smoke powers at him. He gets lucky, grabbing one of Rainier's arms enough to haul him off the floor.

But Rainier just laughs. "You picked the wrong side."

An arrow of onyx flame spears from his free hand so fast I barely register it. It tears a hole through the center of the Overlord's chest. He doesn't even have time to scream before he drops in a limp heap to the floor at Rainier's feet.

"Holy shit," I say right before a minion crashes into me. I manage to stay on my feet, shoving at the thing's skeletal body before turning its rib cage to cinders.

More and more come, until each of us is fighting six or more at a time. I can barely breathe long enough to steady myself, let alone check on my friends. My family.

Every time I turn a minion to ash, another crops up until we're all being forced to the back of the wall, hordes of minions crowding us in. My body trembles from the exhaustion of wielding my powers this hard and this long, but I don't stop.

"Fetch the girl," Aphian yells over the sounds of the battle to Bartholomew. He doesn't hesitate to fly over the minions, slamming into me as he hauls me an inch above the floor.

Not again.

I conjure my wind wings, pulling and tugging in the opposite direction as I try and wiggle out of his tight hold. I struggle, my eyes cast downward as I see Rainier battling thirty minions, and half that for each of my friends.

Ice bursts from my skin like spiked armor, and Bartholomew wails as he starts to lose his grip on me. I use the power of my wind wings to send us crashing back to the ground.

He lands on top of me in a heap, his weight suffocating. I push against his chest, trying like hell to get air between us to shove him off, but his powers are considerable as white light battles everything I throw at him.

My muscles go weak with every sweep of that white light, my powers stuttering out. I'm exhausted, barely able to catch my breath. My vision wobbles in and out as he shifts atop me, moving to yank me into his arms. To fly me back to Aphian so he can do who the fuck knows what to me.

I lash out with another wave of power, but it disintegrates against his light.

This is it. Rainier is overrun. Kaz and Ryder, too. I can't see my mother.

I want to. I want to look at them one last time. Tell them I'm sorry—

A whip of liquid silver wraps around Bartholomew's throat.

The mating bond flares to life inside me, that chain of gold purring as it snaps into place again.

Bartholomew jerks backward, clawing at the silver before his hands go limp at his sides. All the color rushes from him. Even his brown wings turn gray, like the life is being drained from him. My heart stops as Bartholomew disintegrates to ash, revealing the source of his captor behind him.

"Draven!" I gasp, racing to throw my arms around his neck. "How are you here? How are you alive?" I'm shaking at the sight of him.

"Didn't I tell you I'd always find you?" he says, but absolute devastation twists his voice. He holds me tighter, his body trembling against mine. "Cassiel. He gave his soul for mine."

A ball of emotion clogs my throat. I look up at Draven, wanting him to deny it, but I can see it in his eyes. The pain.

"Cassiel is gone?" Tears bite my eyes, my soul whiplashing between the joy of my mate being alive and the anguish over losing my best friend.

Draven can't even speak. He just gives me one solemn nod.

Aphian roars, the sound shattering the bubble of grief we're wrapped in. He commands the rest of his army to span the ravine in the floor and wipe us out.

I whirl around, watching as a thousand descend upon us.

"Do what you need to do," Draven says, moving in front of me. He raises his hands as he sends waves of power toward them. Holding them back for as long as he can.

The floor trembles beside me as Rainier rushes to my side. He draws up his forearm, taking calculated steps back as I feel his power press out and up—

The minions hit an invisible wall, but they don't stop coming. They claw at his shield. Some slam their weapons into it over and over again, taking off each other's limbs in the process.

Kaz rushes to Draven's side, raising his cane, waves of green energy pouring into Rainier's shield. "Relentless little bastards," he says. "Aren't they?"

"Indeed," Rainier says. "Keep it steady!" he commands Draven and Kaz as he drops to one knee, using his free hand to dig in his pocket.

"You pulling out a supernatural grenade?" I ask.

"Something like that," Rainier says, showing me a handful of parchment.

"The scrolls?" I shake my head. "But there was nothing on them."

He smooths out the united pieces, cringing as the minions keep hitting his shield. His red eyes are wide as he darts them over the parchment.

"See?" I say. "Your sister spun a pointless tale about power. Probably for some balance bullshit reason—"

"No. She made them for me." A smile shapes his lips. "That has to be the reason Aphian couldn't read it."

He presses his palm against the parchment, his fingers stretching bigger than the piece as he closes his eyes. When he opens them, there's no change. His brow furrows as his red eyes scan the blank piece over and over again.

"You sure about that?" I glance at the minions attacking his shield. At Kaz and Draven, who are helping with their own power.

And just behind them, coming up from the gaping crack in the floor—*talons*. The dragon creatures from the Death Striker realm are clawing their way up and out of the hole in the veil. "We don't have time for this!"

"Daughter," Rainier says, breathless. "Your hand."

He grabs my right hand before I can open my mouth, and smacks my palm flat against the scroll.

Heat singes my skin, a golden light blazing from beneath my fingers. Rainier releases me, and I yank my hand back, gasping at the beautiful script scrawling all on its own along the paper.

For the one who is so like the power of words.
Balanced in strength and softness.
Capable of destroying and rebuilding.
Survives in all conditions.
Thriving in good and bad.
Close your eyes.
Count to seven.
And make a choice.
Only you can decide what you become.

CHAPTER SIXTY-TWO

HARLEY

My fingers tremble as I read the words over and over again, hearing the voice of the Creator as easily as if she were speaking in my mind.

"I thought they were meant for you," I whisper to Rainier.

Rainier visibly swallows. "It appears they were meant for someone stronger. Do it. Take what's *yours*."

I look to my mother.

"We're right beside you," she says.

I never knew how much I needed to hear those words until she spoke them.

Tears spill over my lashes as I close my eyes.

One.

I'm Harley, Ray's big sister.

Two.

I'm an abuse survivor.

Three.

I put an end to The Twelve's evil.

Four.

I'm Draven's mate.

Five.

I'm Rainier's daughter.

Six.

I'm the Antichrist.

Seven.

And I'm going to change the world.

Golden light erupts from the scroll, spearing straight through my chest so hard and fast it almost knocks me over. I remain steady, even as every power and then some awakens in my blood, so sharp I can taste it. My mind and soul whirl with the intensity of it, the all-encompassing strength, the endless well. Reality manipulation. Telekinesis. Mind control. It's a never-ending list. All I have to do is mentally dip my fingers into it and I can draw out a wealth of power that outshines even Rainier's. A slew from my mother, too—a divine power for healing and strength that feels like liquid gold.

"Harley." My mother's voice cuts through the chaos in my mind.

I open my eyes.

Draven and Kaz are still holding the line, but exhaustion lines their features. More creatures are climbing out of that crack in the floor—snakes the size of alligators, dragons, and massive furry things that look like a cross between a grizzly and a buffalo.

And through the chaos, I see Aphian, his mouth parting as those monsters come through the crack in the ground. He stumbles back a step, then turns on his heels and runs through the doorway.

"Harley," Draven says, a strain in his voice. "You have to go after him."

"I have to help you first," I say.

"He *can't* get away," Rainier says. "I'll help hold them back!"

Rainier dives into the fray, just in time to take a hit from one of the dragons. The sound reverberates along the walls, crashing against my ears.

I glance from the army whose sole goal is to take our blood to the demons spilling out of the crack between our worlds, then back to him, Draven, and Kaz. There are too many. There's no way the three of them can hold them back for long. "When that shield comes down—and it will—I'm going to be right here. With you all. Fighting to the end—"

"There will be *no* end," Rainier snarls. "None. Except for Aphian's at your hand. Now go!"

"You can't boss me around. I'm stronger than you now—"

"I'm your father!" His voice is ever the king of the Ather. "You *will* do as I say."

"And because you're my father," I fire right back, "I won't leave you alone—"

"He's not alone." Wallace's voice soars over the rumbling of the minions against the shield as she races into the room, but it's what's behind her that steals my voice.

An army.

An army comprised of Delta and the people of Conilis.

Lysander and the people of Pagos.

Ore and the people of Lusro.

Even Sage and her fighters from the Pits in Machis.

They stand behind Wallace, armed to the teeth.

And they're *bowing.*

To me.

To Rainier.

He gives me a Cheshire grin. "See?" he says, nodding toward Wallace. "The Leaper has my back."

"Always," she says, her shoulder brushing Ryder's as she stands next to him.

I part my lips, eyes on Draven. I can't leave him again. What if something happens? Another argument is on the tip of my tongue, but he slides into my mind.

"Go," Draven says. *"We can't let Cassiel's sacrifice be for nothing. I'll be right behind you once I help here. You're the only one strong enough to take on Aphian."*

"I'll open a space just for you, daughter," Rainier says, twisting one of his hands to the right. His red eyes meet mine, determination and pride churning there. "Make sure he *suffers.*"

CHAPTER SIXTY-THREE

HARLEY

I sprint down the space Rainier carves out for me between the slew of minions in my way.

Forming my wind wings, I propel myself over the crack in the marble floor, aiming my hands at its gaping center. I latch on to the power unraveling between the veils, holding it with my own. It's strong and fast and hard to cling to, but I draw it toward me as I hover there, using every ounce of strength and power I possess to mend the crack between worlds.

Slowly, the breath heaving from my lungs, the gap in the floor seals itself, and I land on the other side as Rainier drops the shield and all-out war breaks between the minions, the monsters, and my family.

"Aphian!" I roar with all the rage and hurt in my heart as I race through the door he bailed through. I catch sight of a slip of his robe as he rounds another corner down the hallway, and I push my legs to move faster.

I punch the air, sending a fireball soaring straight for his back.

He spins just in time, waving a hand before my flames, stopping them cold. "You truly are the Antichrist," he snarls. "You ruin everything."

I draw my hands together, weaving fire and ice into a sharp, bubbling contraption I hurtle at his head. His eyes flare, but he ducks, missing the first, but the second throw catches him on the shoulder, singeing his perfect white robes there.

"You're pathetic," I seethe, twirling my fingers, gathering more and more flames there. "Hiding behind an army of minions. Ripping the world in two regardless of the cost." I throw the balls of flame and ice his way so fast he can barely dodge. Some hit; others miss him by inches. "And you killed my mate." Rage ripples up my spine, my new powers bursting to life. I fling a hand toward him, latching on to the power welling inside me. Half a thought sends him to his back.

It doesn't matter that Draven came back to me—we lost Cassiel as a direct result of what Aphian did. He deserves to suffer for what he took from us. I span the distance between us, leaning over him as I wield that power, keeping him pinned to the floor.

"Tell me," I say, spearing my mental awareness toward his mind. Rainier told me in London this is what he liked to do to malicious offenders. So I slice into Aphian's mind as easy as a warm knife through butter. "What's your greatest fear?"

Aphian struggles beneath my invisible hold, his great power sending stings of pain up my own, but I stand firm.

I close my eyes, racing through his mind, nearly drunk on the power of it. Fuck, if this is what Rainier feels all the time? It's a marvel he hasn't reshaped the world to his liking. Because why the hell not? Who can stop him? Who can stop *me*?

"Tell me," I growl, pushing harder, deeper into Aphian's wretched mind. I flinch against the malice coating every thought. The selfish, power-hungry desires clinging to every corner of his mind. He sees himself as a god, someone better than all the rest, but just behind that posturing, that arrogance—

"There," I whisper, the taste of victory filling my mouth. I could kill him right here and now, but I want him to swim in his pain for as long as I can. I want him to cower and beg for his life. I want to repay him every ounce of anguish he caused me when he shoved that knife into Draven's chest. When he took Ray. When Cassiel didn't come back.

Aphian's fear flutters to the surface of his mind, and I snatch it up like catching a buzzing fly. With all the grace and talent of my little sister, I paint a mental picture in his mind.

Aphian, his wings pinned with blades to a marble slab. The Creator is there, and Rainier, too. Each one takes turns plucking out his feathers and laughing while he screams. The Creator saying he's nothing. He's weak. A mistake.

Rainier, using blades of fire to carve him up from the inside out.

"Help me!" he cries to the Creator. "Help me. Spare me. Please. My Creator. I've only ever served you!"

"You've only ever served yourself," she says and turns her back on him.

Rainier's smile is feral and sadistic, his red eyes glimmering with delight as he slides blade after blade over Aphian's skin until he's flayed him alive.

It's gruesome, but no more than he deserves.

"Stop!" Aphian shouts from outside our linked minds.

And it's my turn to smile cruelly as I draw out of his mind, clearing his vision to the present. He slackens under my hold, sweat beading from his skin. "Should I dig a little deeper?" I ask, my voice laced with the power making me drunk. "Should I make you live out your worst fear over and over again for the rest of your existence?"

I can do that, I realize. Keep him alive for centuries. Trap him like he trapped my dad. Lock him in a cage in his own wretched mind. I'm that strong now.

The choice is mine.

Acid splays over my skin, Aphian's white light bursting in a desperate and frantic blow. My hold on him slips as I stumble away from the light, glancing down at where it's burned my skin.

Aphian clambers to his feet, watching with terror in his eyes as my body heals itself. He spins on his feet, darting down the hall and into an open doorway.

"Come out and face me, you coward!" I yell, chasing him into the room—

I freeze two steps in.

"You were saying?" He aims one of those Colis-fueled

weapons at me, and the walls behind him? They're lined with the things, all buzzing with the energy from the Colis he stole and configured in the most horrific way possible. "Oh, that's right," he says. "You were just saying *goodbye*."

He squeezes the trigger, my eyes widening at the blast of orange blotting out my eyesight—

The blast hits a wall before me, one made of liquid silver and shadow.

Draven's growl fills the room as his powers absorb the blast.

I spin around, finding him just inside the doorway, dropping the shield once the blast is absorbed. A flick of his wrist, and the weapon flies out of Aphian's hands. "I'm here," he says, eyes on me. "What do you need?"

My heart swells, all the shattered pieces reconfiguring to something stronger than I've ever felt before.

"Stay with me," I say.

"Always."

At that declaration, I spin back around, hands curling as I extend my arms horizontally.

Aphian flinches before he realizes I'm not aiming for him.

Flames snake up the walls, melting and consuming every weapon poised there.

"No!" Aphian roars as he lifts his hands, trying like hell to stop the flames.

But he can't.

Because his power is *nothing* compared to mine. To what I've unlocked inside me. There is little that will be able to put out my flames now.

I crack a flaming fist across Aphian's perfect jaw, his head snapping to the side as we tumble to the ground. He rolls atop me, hands going for my throat, but I'm ready, blocking him with a wave of ice that has his fingernails scraping backward against it.

"Men like you always go for the throat," I snarl.

Aphian returns my hit, and my head cracks to the left. I

spit blood on the floor, but grin up at him with bloody teeth.

Draven growls, stepping toward us, but I hold up my finger to stop him. I shake off the hit as I glare up at Aphian. "My drunk ex-father hits harder than that."

Aphian seethes as he swings again.

I dodge, landing a blow to his stomach that has him flinching. He digs his fingers into my arms, white light melting through my shirt. Ice storms my blood, soaring out of me and clamping over his wrists and ankles and wings, yanking him down and pinning him to the floor.

He cries out, struggling against my thick ice bonds, hissing at me like a caged animal.

I punch him again until I feel his blood on my knuckles. "That's for taking my sister," I say, standing up to rise above him. I draw my boot back, and send it flying right into his junk. "That's for killing my mate. For costing me my friend." I haul my leg back and do it again, relishing his cries of pain. "And brainwashing my mother," I say, my breaths rushed and frantic.

I look to Draven, who is watching with a sense of pride in his eyes. "Draven," I say. "He's all yours."

His eyes are liquid gold as he cocks a brow at me.

I nod. This is the creature who tortured Draven for years just for being a siphon, keeping him in the Divine Sleep longer than he let him live. Who sank that blade into his chest and almost took him from me forever. Who forced Cass to make the ultimate sacrifice.

I step aside, letting Draven take what's his.

He fashions a blade of pure shadow in his hand, reaching back for mine with his free one. I interlock our fingers instantly, not hesitating as he connects with my power and forges that shadow dagger with my flames. "This," he whispers, pressing the tip of his blade over Aphian's chest, "is for Cassiel. And *me.*" He plunges the dagger in.

Then Draven lays his palm flat against Aphian's skin.

Agony rips from Aphian's lips, but it is drowned out by

Draven's roar. I grip his other hand, feeling every inch of his pain as Aphian's siphoned powers roll through him.

The angel's blue eyes turn white, his red-tipped feathers wilting as they shift to a fog color. His body sinks in on itself, folding up and in until he bursts into a pile of grease-colored dust.

I jerk against the rush that hits me like a tidal wave.

Aphian's considerable power combined with Draven's endless well and mine, powered by the gift from the scrolls.

This.

This is the stuff of Biblical legend.

It's too fast, too heavy.

I can't breathe around it.

"Draven," I whisper, drowning in power, a nuclear weapon counting down in three, two...

One.

CHAPTER SIXTY-FOUR

HARLEY

The room erupts in bursts of dark flame and ice, vines and wind as the power sweeps me into the air. I hover high above the floor, a tornado of power surging around me and inside me.

The veil is coming down like you asked, master of the scrolls, the blood Key, an ancient voice whispers inside my head. And through Aphian's power now filling my veins, it shows me what he started when he used my blood to open spaces in the Ather.

I see the Death Striker realm and Marid's realm and those of his Twelve Brethren. I see more evil realms containing malicious entities and bloodthirsty demons. And they're all coming, the force of Aphian using my blood to bring them closer to blend with the world as we know it.

And then to wipe it out.

I cringe against the vision. I may have sealed the opening in the marble room, but my blood in this holy spot has unlocked so much more. Everything Aphian wanted is about to spill into the world.

So much pain inside you, the voice whispers, drawing up more and more images. *So much anguish.* A flash of my ex-father, kicking me in the side when I'm already down. A burst of Ray flying across our trailer, her little body hitting the wall so hard it knocks her out.

Kai sliding that knife into my side.

Marid slipping inside my sister's mind.

Ryder in the Pits, fighting for his life.

Wrath, broken and bloody as he's outnumbered.

Rainier, trapped and forced to believe the love of his life is dead.

My mother, Ordered against her will to abandon me.

Cassiel, trading his soul for Draven's.

Draven, that knife digging into his chest.

Disasters striking across the world—earthquakes and hurricanes and viruses and sickness and shootings.

A Creator who can't control anything, only inspire and influence. She can't fix things for those crying out for help. The ones I can hear ringing in my ears. There are so many of them, countless souls and creatures across this world and the Ather who need *help*.

Who need *hope*.

But hope doesn't live here, the voice whispers, streaming those terrible memories and thoughts and calls for help on repeat. Over and over again until rage and helplessness are all I can feel, can taste. The bitter tang of failure. Because the world is cast in shadows of regret and selfishness and there will be no changing it. No fixing it.

Not without a reset.

Let them come, let them cleanse it, the voice says. The seduction in the ease of allowing this all to play out is overwhelming.

Why shouldn't I let the evil of the Ather overrun an unforgiving world? Why shouldn't I succumb to this great power? The Creator gave it to me, made it for me, after all. Why can't I drown in it until there is no more pain, no more suffering. Why should I make a choice—

A choice.

An image of a sickly-green branch stemming from a hundred other branches fills my mind.

Life is filled with a million choices. Some of them more important than we realize. And this is mine.

"Harley." Draven's voice is in my mind. *"You are more than your past. It forged you into the person you are today. A good,*

strong person who knows the world is worth more than its faults."

Tears stream down my cheeks, the power crashing through my soul. It feels like it's hollowing me from the inside out, but I can feel Draven there. Clinging to his powers that have braided with mine, clinging and yanking them back. Trying like hell to unravel them to give me peace.

"You have the power to change the world for good, Harley!" He's roaring in my head now, my mate. Returned to me by our friend when I thought I'd never see him again. Reaching down our bond and drawing me to him. *"Change this. Set it right!"*

"Why?" I ask. *"There's so much pain, Draven. So much hate and selfishness and greed. People like the man who abused me my whole life. People like Marid and Aphian and—"*

"And there are good people, too," he says. *"Like Ray and Wallace and Rainier. Like Nathan and Anka. Ryder. Cassiel. You,"* he says. *"You* are *good. And I will follow your goodness anywhere. I will fight for you and with you for as long as I am breathing."* His awareness scatters in my mind, in my soul, as he unbraids our overwhelming powers, as he shakes loose him from me and me from him.

I sigh against the feel of it, helping him from my side, drawing the scrolls' infinite well back until it's settled and calm inside me.

I am the Antichrist, I say to that whispering voice. *I am the reader of the scrolls. I am the one who wields you and you will do as I say!*

I shift my fingers, turning them in a rewind motion as I call back every order Aphian had sent into the universe with my blood. Like a sculptor folding a pile of clay, I force the evil Aphian tried to unleash back into its cage. The effort is like trying to lift a bus out of quicksand, and I can feel the screech and wail of every evil creature fighting against my commands. I focus every ounce of power I have to keep them from coming out to ruin the world as we know it.

It drains me, this divine battle to undo what he did, and

I'm unable to stop the rest of the veil from coming down. But happiness sparkles in my soul as I feel the joy from every good and wonderous creature set free from the Ather's previous bonds. The pagles and people of Conilis and Pagos. All of them, their cries of joy reaching some internal piece of me that assures me even though it wasn't planned, it's all going to be okay.

As you wish, the voice finally says, and it sounds so much more like the Creator than the whispering tempter before. And then all falls silent in my mind.

A great rush of power bursts out of me, shattering the marble walls around us. I plummet to the floor, only to fall into strong, familiar arms.

"I've got you," Draven says, cradling me to his chest.

I cling to him, relishing the feel of his strength beneath me, the smell of cedar and citrus filling my nose. Exhaustion clings to my bones with the scrolls' power settling deeper into the depths of my soul, making a home for itself next to the rest of my power.

"Is it over?" I ask, barely able to hold my eyes open as Draven caresses my cheek before planting a kiss on my forehead. He carries me through the wreckage and into the hallway.

"No," he says. "This is only the beginning."

CHAPTER SIXTY-FIVE

DRAVEN

"Efrain didn't make it?" I ask Ryder, who stands next to me in the throne room of the Seven's residence.

He shakes his head.

"And Judah?"

"Rainier finished him after we fought the minions back," Ryder says.

I blow out a breath, a mixture of sadness and relief sliding through my body. The Seven are gone. Finally. But it cost us almost everything.

Harley is sleeping off the effects of our joining powers, but Ray assured me she'll wake soon. She checked her Dreamscape, making sure she was whole. The effort it took to erase Aphian's order nearly killed her. Nearly had her unleashing an evil onto the world it would not survive.

But I drew her back.

I'll always draw her back.

That's why Cassiel made sure I got a second chance. Not to help her fight Aphian's army, but to be Harley's anchor. Her new powers are too much to handle alone, and I've always been willing to be whatever she needed. An enemy, a friend, a lover, a mate.

I rub my palms over my face, my mind racing and splintering between what happened. Cassiel, my best friend throughout Divine Sleep and too many battles to count—he's gone. The hollow spot in my heart where his friendship should be flinches every time I think about it.

"Draven." Ryder comes to stand next to me. He's bruised

from the battle, but at least he's had time to clean the blood from his face.

Kazuki and Wallace are likely doing the same thing. From the way Ryder tells it, it was a close battle, but with Rainier, they won. It would take us days to clean up the wreckage if we wanted to make this place a real safe haven for Judges now. But that would be up to my mate. With us taking out the Seven and her being the new ultimate power, she would be in full control of the Judges, the angels of death, and the rest of the divine creatures who are Called. Unless her aunt makes an appearance any time soon, which I don't see happening.

"I'm sorry," he says.

"For what?" I ask, my voice grief-stricken.

He folds his arms over his chest, shaking his head. "I wasn't there when you needed me, but Cassiel was."

I swallow the rock in my throat.

"Without him—" Ryder's voice cracks and he has to clear his throat. "I'll never stop being grateful for what he did. What he gave. And I know I can't replace the brother he turned out to be, but I'm here."

My mind is still trying to wrap itself around everything that happened. Dying. Again. Coming back. The cost of it all. It's never going to sit right with me, but I can't let his gift go to waste. "You're my brother. My twin," I say to him. "And I love you."

Ryder shuffles his feet. "You going to stick around this time?"

"I could ask the same of you."

"I'll stay if you do."

"I'll be wherever Harley is," I say. "But I'm here, Ryder."

"I know," he says. "And since our girls are friends, looks like you're stuck with me. Good thing I love you, too." He arches a brow at me, a small smile tugging at his lips. "Speaking of, I should probably go check on Wallace. She may need help in the shower."

I wave him off as he heads out of the room. We'll be okay, Ryder and me.

I head upstairs, too, navigating the halls until I come to my old rooms, and swing open the door. Harley is still asleep. When we combined our two wells…fuck, I can still feel it. The endlessness of it. We stretched across time and space and I was terrified I'd never get her back.

But I can feel her, across our bond. She's in full control now, not the other way around. When she wakes? She'll have entire control over what the Creator gifted her through those scrolls, what she inherited from Rainier and Lila.

I settle against the windowsill, watching as night blankets the ocean far below while I wait.

"Draven?" She finally shifts in the bed an hour later, sitting up as she blinks sleep from her eyes. "How long was I out?"

I'm across the room in seconds. "A few hours," I say, settling on the bed next to her. "How do you feel?"

"Like an ancient power tried to use me to bring the world down," she says, shaking her head. "Like I lost my mate and one of my best friends in the span of a blink, and only one came back." Her shoulders slump.

I can see the battle raging in her eyes, the happiness I came back to her and the loss she feels over Cassiel. I relate completely. I smooth back some of her hair, and she leans into my touch.

Harley's eyes go distant for a moment, and I wait patiently for her to come back to me, lost in my own emotions, too. After a few minutes, she blinks, turning to face me. "The world," she says. "I can hear whispers…the Ather, the best parts, they're free."

I can't imagine how overwhelming that must feel. Panic coats her eyes, and I scoot closer. "Tell me what you need."

"I just unleashed a world of magic and wonder and the humans…they will need help adjusting." She fists my shirt, drawing me close. Her lips crush mine in a frantic, desperate kiss that sears along every inch of my body. I meet her stroke for stroke, relishing the taste of her before she pulls back. "Will you help me, Draven?" she asks. "Will you help me figure all this out?"

I slide my hands along her body until I grip her hips and haul her into my lap. "I go where you go, mate," I say, kissing her again.

She shudders against me, melting into my kiss, and soon we're a tangle of breathless kisses and languid touches, each fiery graze reminding us both what we've fought for. What Cassiel gave his life for. What we will continue fighting for as long as we live.

CHAPTER SIXTY-SIX

HARLEY

"Harley!" Ray cries as she races for me across the newly reconstructed Bridge's upper dining room.

I catch her against me, dropping to my knees so I can hold her tighter.

"You're okay," she says.

"So are you."

She gives me a soft smile, but it's ringed in sadness. Everyone is feeling the sting of Cassiel's loss and none of us have had proper time to process it yet. I don't know if there will ever be enough time to heal that wound.

Wrath pads up beside her—Wallace told me he never left Ray's side after he healed from the hit Aphian gave him during battle. Not even when she teleported her, Anka, and Nathan back to the safety of The Bridge before she went to the Ather to call our armies.

The hound nuzzles my neck, and my little Pagle Bagel isn't far behind, her trunk tickling Ray's hand.

"We've been waiting for you," she says. She motions to the table where my family sits, all but one.

Wallace is perched on Ryder's lap, the two looking battle weary but content as they support each other. Nathan and Anka on the other side of the table, Kazuki next to them.

I walk around and take a seat next to my mother and Rainier, Draven settling on my left.

"What do we do first?" I ask, unsure of our next move. We accomplished what we set out to do—minus the unplanned unleashing of the good parts of the Ather. But we lost someone vital along the way, so my mind is split between wanting to sleep for two weeks straight and knowing we absolutely have to start planning for the new world.

"I'd like to get to know you," my mother says.

A knot forms in my throat. "I do have some questions for you."

"I'll tell you anything you want," she says, blinking tears out of her eyes.

Rainier's hand is linked with hers under the table, and there is something hopeful about seeing him reunited with her after being torn apart.

"We'll have to create a new order," Draven says. "For the Judges and other divine creatures now that the Seven is gone." He flinches on the last part.

He's not grieving the other five, but Esther was his friend, and Efrain, too, in the end. Their loss paired with Cassiel's will sit heavy on him for a long time.

They're all looking at *me* for an answer, and my stomach churns.

"First thing I'm getting rid of is the Divine Sleep and brainwashy stuff. The choice to serve will always be priority."

Draven slides his hand along my thigh. "The Creator still has final say over a majority of that."

"I know," I say, and glance to Rainier. "And my aunt will just have to come and meet with us if she wants a say."

Rainier arches a brow. "She'll come," he says. "She told you she would. But her sense of time is different than ours. It could be years before we see her."

"Well, until she does, I'm taking full control of the divine warriors. They will have a choice in what they do from here on out."

Pride ripples along the bond, and I grin softly at Draven.

"You'll have to make a public statement soon, darling," Kazuki says, and apprehension flares in my chest. He grins at me. "The world knows something happened, but they'll need specifics. You'll have to work with the world's leaders on integrating the realms and to help stop a panic."

My eyes widen as I look to Rainier.

He dips his head. "You have the scrolls' power now," he says. "You're the new queen of the Ather. I will help you however you need."

I blow out a breath. He's been a ruler for far longer than I can imagine. I'll definitely need his help, need all of their help.

"Thanks," I say. "*Dad*," I add just to make him smile.

"And I'll help with your wardrobe," Kaz says, eyeing the leggings-and-sweatshirt combo I have on. "Can't have a queen going live to the world in a *Stranger Things* sweatshirt."

I chuckle. "I just saved the world, Kaz," I say. "Cut me some slack."

"Never," he says before blowing me a kiss.

I look around the table at my friends, my family. "I want each of you to have an important role going forward," I say. "We're stronger when we work together. And I'm still so new to this world. I'll need your help. But it's always your choice."

Wallace raises her hand. "Consider this my formal application for New-Ather princess."

She's making jokes, but I fully intend to let her take whatever position she wants in this new world. She's beyond earned it, and she's more than fit for any job.

"I vote for the title Sorcerer Supreme," Kazuki jokes, and then everyone chimes in with a more ridiculous title than the next.

"As long as you're with me," I finally say, reeling in my laughter.

"We are," Draven speaks on behalf of our little family.

And for once, I settle into the day stretching out ahead of us with a hope I've never felt before.

EPILOGUE

HARLEY

"It's almost time," Draven says as he steps behind me. I catch his gaze in the mirror I stand in front of, nerves tangling as I look at myself.

Kazuki selected the gown for the occasion, and I can't decide if he's the smartest warlock on the planet, or the deadest.

The gown is fashioned from black and silver beads and silk, the halter neckline a succession of intricate flame designs that taper to a point over my bellybutton, the back nothing more than two crisscross straps holding it in place. The skirts are black and glittering silver, billowing in a pool around my feet. And atop my head, holding back my waves of red hair, is a crown carved from the slick black stone of Rainier's realm and accentuated with black diamonds that wink like my birthright stone in the light.

Draven is my perfect counterpart in an outfit of jet black, his own simpler crown poised on his head. It suits *him* with his golden eyes and dominating presence, but me?

"You look stunning," he says when I haven't responded to him. He grazes his lips over my bare neck. "My queen."

Molten heat soars through my veins.

It's been three weeks since the veil came down.

Three weeks since Rainier handed over his kingdom to me, staying on as my advisor.

Three weeks since the known world changed.

When the veil dropped, all my power went into containing the evil parts of the Ather. The good pieces were unfolded next to the world as we know it, a vast country popping up on the map right next to those already established. Territories transferred still intact—Conilis and Pagos and Lusro and so many more—the realms now laid out like states on a map.

And today is the day I address a confused and scared world in a livestreamed conference that will be viewed across all nations.

"You'd tell me if Kazuki was going to make me look like a fool, right?"

He grins that wolfish grin at me, and my toes curl in the heeled black boots beneath the gown's skirts. "You could never look like a fool, Harley."

"You've seen me almost trip headfirst into a garbage can full of old pastrami," I counter. "Don't patronize me."

He laughs, the sound refreshing after weeks of grieving. The hole Cassiel's death put in our hearts will never fully heal, but we're doing our best to not waste his sacrifice. He would kick our asses if he knew how much wallowing we've done on his behalf.

Draven shakes his head as he extends his arm. "You look amazing," he says. "No matter what you wear. But this?" He eyes the gown. "It sort of looks like armor fit for the queen of the Ather."

I sigh, some of the tension in my body unraveling at his words, his touch. I slip my arm into his and he guides me through the room, along the hallways carved from dark stone, and toward a balcony overlooking Rainier's realm—well, my realm now.

"We are incredibly grateful for each of the world leaders tuning in tonight to hear our queen's statement." Rainier's voice rings loud and clear from the edge of the balcony, and my heart leaps to my throat. "As well as the rest of the world. We know you all have questions and concerns and we will do our best to answer each of them." He glances behind him, winking at me. "So, without further ado, here she is, Harley, queen of the Ather."

Applause and cheers erupt from over the balcony, and it's

not until Draven starts tugging us toward the edge that I see the massive number of creatures lining the streets below Rainier's castle. Those from Pagos and Lusro and Conilis are front and center, their support considerably louder than the rest.

Projector screens are set up all along the borders of the crowds, many with split screen views of myself, Draven at my side, and the world leaders tuning in live. Camera crews are situated all over the place, catching every angle, every breath… every chance I might fuck this all up.

"You've got this," Draven whispers in my ear.

I close my eyes briefly.

I can do this.

I *have* to do this.

"Thank you all for coming tonight." I address my people first, then smile at the cameras to include those watching from around the world. "I know you are confused. I know some of you are worried I'll be declaring war against you."

Some of the world leaders shift uncomfortably in their chairs, their own camera crews catching everything there, too. We'd intercepted several attacks those first two days after the veil dropped, Rainier's and my combined power is enough to stop other countries from dropping bombs on us. I forgave their rash actions, if only because I understand how alien the New Ather looks to them. How terrified they are. The attacks stopped when they realized their bombs didn't put a dent in my power, leading to a new tactic with this conference call now.

"I want to assure you all right now," I continue, "that my people and myself have no intentions of going to war. I know this is new for all of us, but we are a people of peace. We may be different, may possess powers you haven't ever imagined outside of superhero movies and books, but we just want to live *freely* and work alongside you toward a greater good."

"Some of your people have already tried to integrate themselves into our countries. What are we supposed to do about that?"

I switch my focus to the projector screen where the leader's voice came from. She's regal looking with the way she sits up straight, her light hair perfectly drawn away from her face that fills the camera. Her eyes are intrigued, maybe even sympathetic.

"Please treat them like you would any other person applying for citizenship. They're just like any other peaceful foreigner visiting your country."

"Foreigner," another leader says. He's a bulbous man who has to be in his late fifties, and is practically glowering at the camera. "That's what you're calling this?"

"What would you have me call it?" I ask. "I was raised in your world, despite being born for another. I understand change is hard, but my people are not here to take anything from you. With our entrance came our world, laid out in perfect harmony next to yours. As it was in the times before the fall. We will be able to help each other in times of need. Your citizens are more than welcome in the New Ather as well. We have resources that can aid in places your world lacks, we have medicine and magic to help heal, and while working together, I feel like we'll bring in a peace the world has never seen before."

Cheers and applause erupt beneath me, and a few of the world leaders nod while others play their hands closer to the vest.

And I understand that. Change will be hard, but nothing worth it is ever easy.

I answer what feels like a million questions, many of which revolve around weapons and war plans, which I have to repeatedly deny. And by the time we're done, I swear I never want to speak to anyone ever again.

"You did great," Draven says as he guides me back into the palace. "You just have to survive one more thing." He turns away from the hallway that will lead us back to our room—and back to my sweats—and heads toward the throne room instead.

"What?" I ask.

He smirks as he pushes open the wide double doors.

"Rainier wants to make it official," he whispers, guiding me deeper into the throne room that was once my father's.

Kazuki is in a fine silver suit as they stand near a mahogany table decorated with a feast fit for royalty. My mother, Ray, Wallace, and Ryder pluck delicacies off the table, grinning and waving at me. Nathan and Anka are there, too, dressed in their finest, and suddenly *this* is more nerve-racking than the millions of strangers I addressed minutes ago.

Draven ushers me past them, aiming for the dais at the head of the room. Rainier stands to the left of his great throne, Wrath sitting stoically on the right. Pagle waddles about the room, her paws tinkling against the stone floor as her ice-crystal fur swishes.

My heart thumps hard with each step we take up to the throne.

"Is this totally necessary?" I ask, eyeing my dad.

He grins. "Your mom wants a picture," he says, motioning for me to take the throne.

"You're joking," I say, laughing despite myself. I glance over my shoulder, and sure enough, my mother has her cell phone out and aimed at me.

These past three weeks have been sort of a reckoning for the two of us. She answered every question I had, regardless of how painful, even down to why she put that bracelet on me all those years ago. The one that subdued my powers. She was trying to hide me from the demons who would try to kill me for my blood, for the power in it. She thought she'd be able to return and help me flee to the Ather before I reached eighteen, but Aphian caught wind and forced her into the Divine Sleep. Hearing all he did to her—did to countless Judges—made me sick to my stomach all over again.

But that's why I'm doing what I'm doing—taking my place in power—so I can help people and learn from them. *All* peoples.

"You already wear the Ather crown, daughter," Rainier says.

"You've made it public, now make it *personal*. In front of your family, claim your birthright."

I swallow hard, eyeing the throne. Draven releases me, moving to step aside. And it feels…*wrong* for him to do that. For my mate to move to the right of me. Our powers are braiding together even as we speak, a delicate practice we've perfected these last weeks. A way to help share the burden of such overwhelming gifts, together. And now that we understand it better, we're bearing the weight together, instead of me alone.

I grin at him, taking back his hand as I tug him toward me.

"What is it, honey badger?" he whispers.

I spin him around, gently nudging him until he sits on that single throne. His gold eyes blaze as he looks up at me, and I plop myself on his lap, sliding an arm behind his neck.

"This okay?" I whisper.

"Whatever you need," he says. "I'm here."

"Good," I say. "We can have you a throne made if you want, but I'm not doing this job without you."

He stifles a laugh. "I rather like the one-throne idea," he says, squeezing my hip.

Rainier growls, then rolls his eyes as he steps down the dais to join my mother.

"Smile," she says.

I shift on Draven's lap to look down at her. She takes way too many pictures, then heads back to the tables of food, chatting with Ray and Kazuki.

Draven runs his fingers along the back of my neck. "Did you think we'd be sitting here all those months ago when I asked you to dance?"

I laugh, shaking my head. "Pretty sure this was the *last* thing I envisioned when you asked me to dance."

He holds me tighter. "Strange world," he says, his lips grazing the shell of my ear.

"And what a world it is," I say, cupping his cheeks in my hands as I lower my mouth to his. "And it's all *ours*."

ACKNOWLEDGMENTS

To my amazing readers, you're always the first I want to thank. I'm blown away by all the love and support you've given this series. I couldn't have done it without you!

Dare, my mate. Thank you for being my inspiration for seriously steamy heroes. Thanks for all the times you've listened to me ramble about plots and plot holes. Thanks for being just as excited as I am for each new release. And finally, thanks for being my favorite snack.

Thanks must be given to my family for supporting this dream of mine, even when I started dreaming about it in the second grade. The encouragement to chase my dreams no matter how hard it is stays with me every single day.

Liz, thank you so much for believing in these characters and helping me shape this awesome new world!

Heather Howland, thank you for stepping in and helping polish this and for loving Pagle Bagel as much as me.

Elizabeth Turner Stokes, I'm forever your fangirl. The art for this series has been so amazing and I'm beyond grateful you brought the world to life!

Also want to give a huge shout out to _lulu_lucky, natasha. reads_, flourishing_fables, and arospaintbrush! The fanart you all have created for the Ember of Night series SLAYS me! You're all fire! Thank you for taking the time to bring my characters to life in such visually stunning ways!

To Hannah Lindsey, Arianne Cruz, Rebecca Paulin, Jessica Turner, Riki Cleveland, Jessica Meig, Heather Riccio, Stacy Abrams, Meredith Johnson, Alex Mathew, Curtis Svehlak, Toni Kerr, Greta Gunselman, Megan Beatie, Stephanie Elliot and all the wonderful people who are at my Entangled home, thank you for all the work behind the scenes! Each one of you has put so much into this series, and it wouldn't be the same without all of your incredible talents! I'm so honored to be part of this awesome family.

To Beth Davey, my amazing agent, thank you for constantly being in my corner and helping me achieve dreams I've had since I was eight! You're simply wonderful.

Molly McAdams, you will always be the coolest half of #MollySquared. Thank you for the phone calls, the vms, and the amazing Loki GIFs that make me smile when I haven't left the writing cave in days. You are wonderful and I love you!

Stoney, you always make me smile even when I'm fully prepared to be grumpy. You somehow find joy in every single situation and I know how lucky I am to be a part of your life. But, I have to say, it is hit or miss with your gift-giving skills. The Tom Hiddleston pillow was fantastic. The noisy chicken you gave my seven-year-old is an absolute disaster. I still love you, though.

Esther. I love you. Then, now, and always.

To the amazing bloggers who constantly work on the behalf of authors and readers alike, you are EVERYTHING. I'm grateful and honored and appreciative of every single one of you who sacrifice time in the name of love for books!

To my new BookTok family, I adore you all! You are the reason authors keep creating and we owe you so much!

And finally, for anyone who relates with Harley's character in more ways than her being a genuinely snarky badass, I want you to know you're in my thoughts. You're not alone. You are worth it. You find your joy and chase the hell out of it.

Thank you again for choosing this book. You are the reason I write!

*Two teens must fight a government that has divided
society into classes living underground.*

JERRI CHISHOLM

In Compound Eleven, the hierarchy of the floors is everything.

My name is Eve Hamilton, and on my floor, we fight.

Which at least is better than the bottom floor, where they toil
away in misery. Only the top floor has any ease in this harsh world;
they rule from their gilded offices.

Because four generations ago, Earth was rendered uninhabitable—
the sun too hot, the land too barren. Those who remained were
forced underground. While not a perfect life down here, I've
learned to survive as a fighter.

Except my latest match is different. Instead of someone from
the circuit, my opponent is a mysterious boy from the top floor.
And the look in his eyes tells me he's different...maybe even kind.

Right before he kicks my ass.

Still, there's something about him—something that says he could
be my salvation...or my undoing. Because I'm no longer content
to just survive in Eleven. Today, I'm ready to fight for more than
my next meal: I'm fighting for my freedom. And this boy may
just be the edge I've been waiting on.

Ready for your next epic adventure?

CROWN OF BONES

A.K. WILDER

In a world on the brink of the next Great Dying, no amount of training can prepare us for what is to come...

A young heir will raise the most powerful phantom in all of Baiseen.

A dangerous High Savant will do anything to control the nine realms.

A mysterious and deadly Mar race will steal children into the sea.

And a handsome guide with far too many secrets will make me fall in love.

My name is Ash. A lowly scribe meant to observe and record. And yet I think I'm destined to surprise us all.

Let's be friends!

𝕏 @EntangledTeen

📷 @EntangledTeen

f @EntangledTeen

📰 bit.ly/TeenNewsletter

entangled teen

an imprint of Entangled Publishing LLC